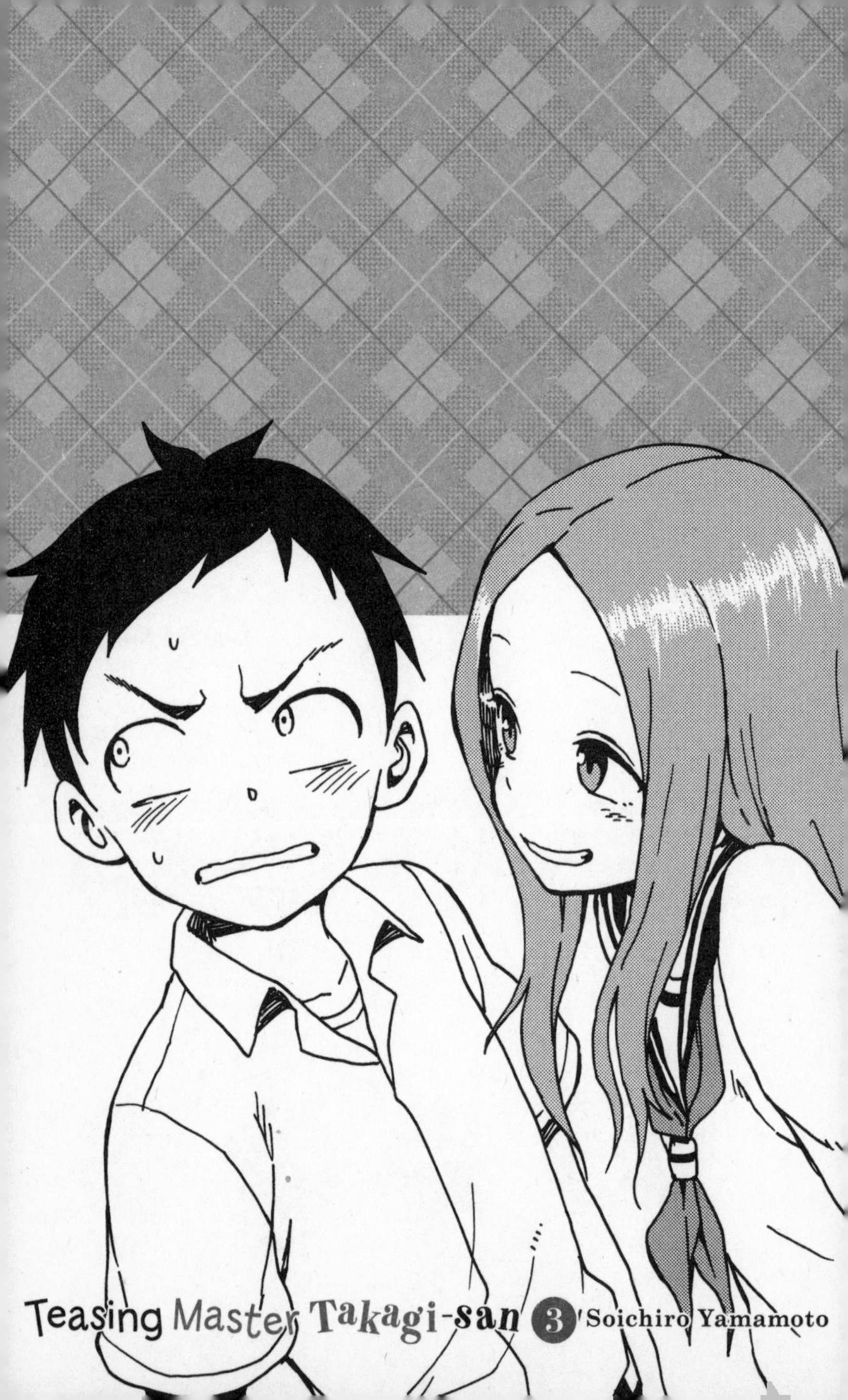

Teasing Master Takagi-san 3 Soichiro Yamamoto

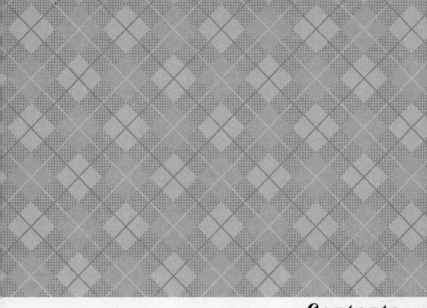

Contents

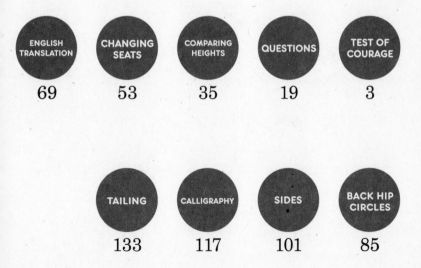

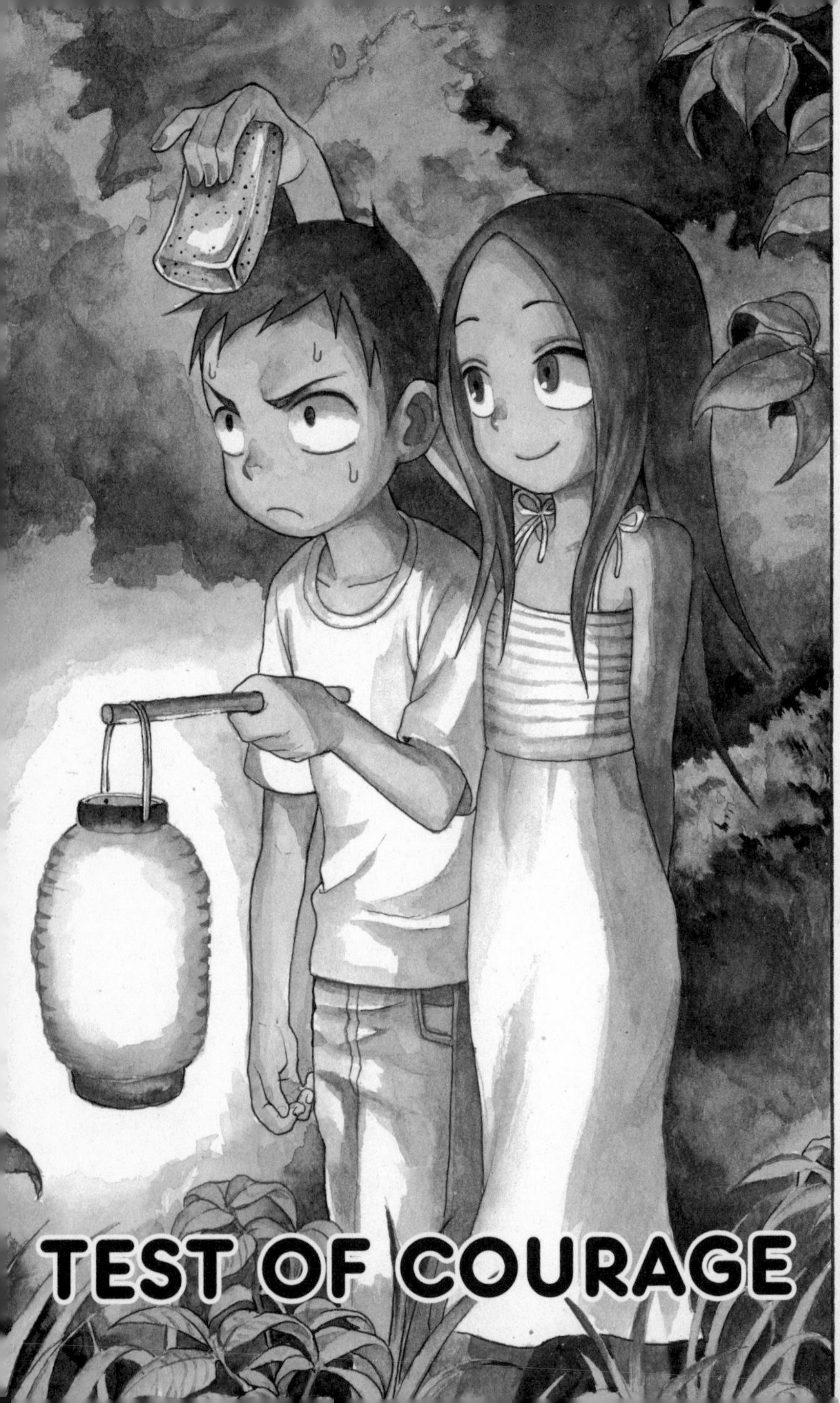
TEST OF COURAGE

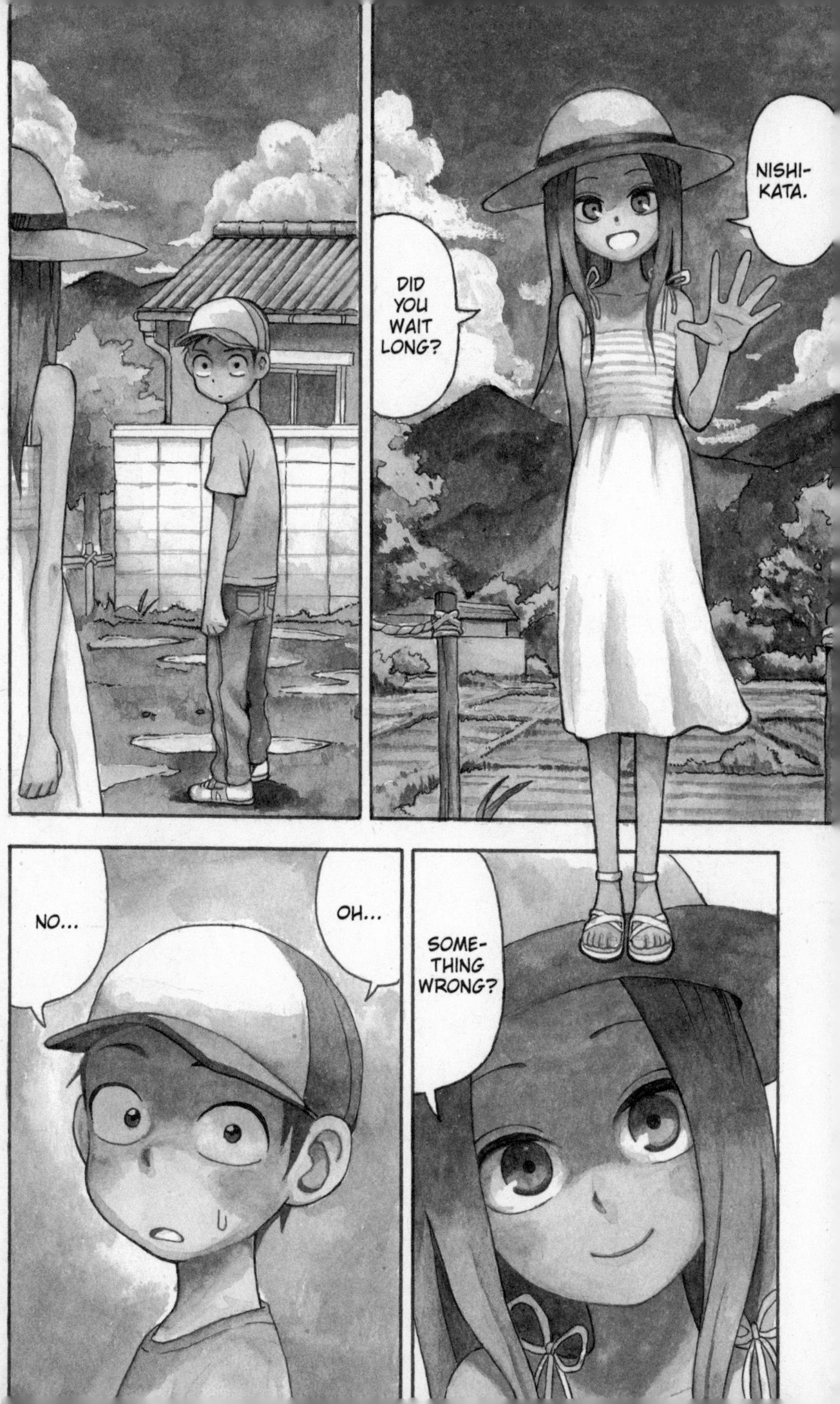
NISHI-KATA.
DID YOU WAIT LONG?
SOME-THING WRONG?
OH...
NO...

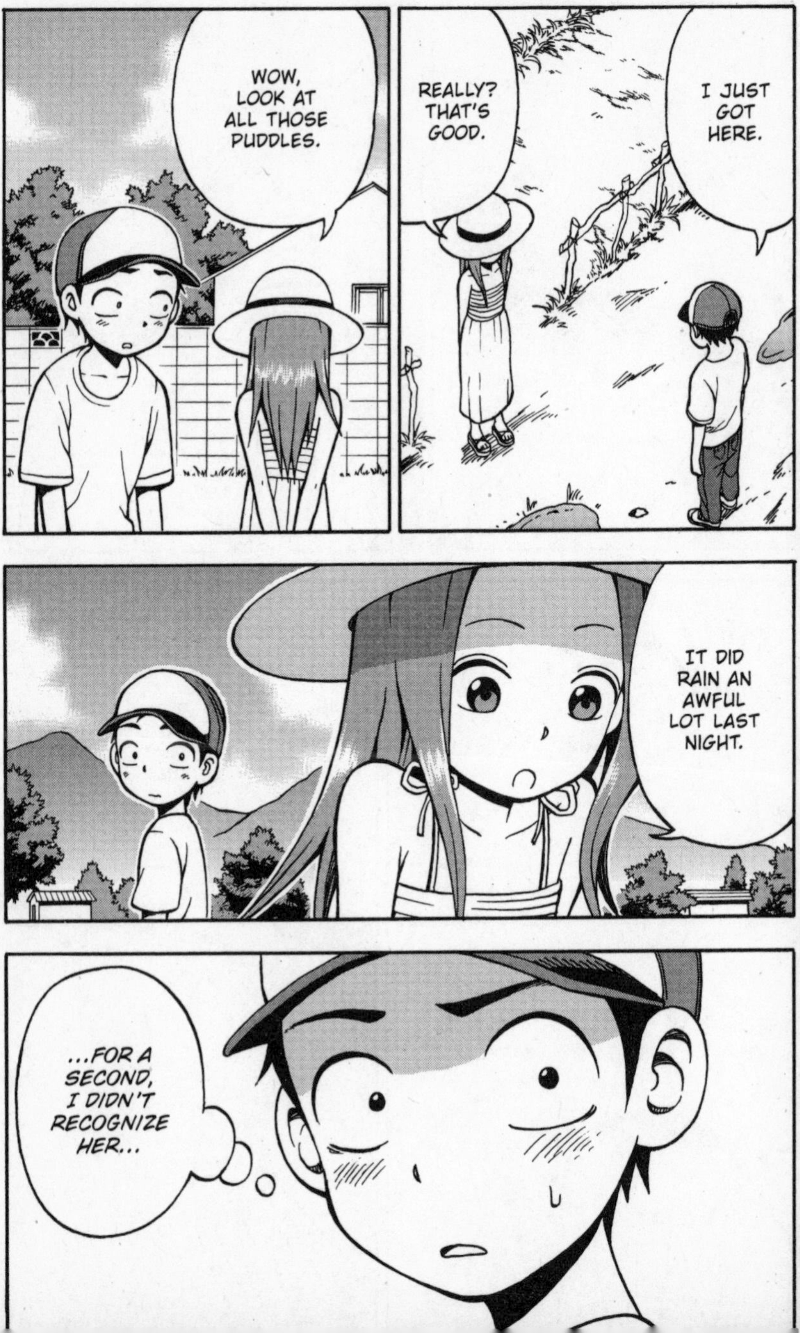
I JUST GOT HERE.
REALLY? THAT'S GOOD.
WOW, LOOK AT ALL THOSE PUDDLES.
IT DID RAIN AN AWFUL LOT LAST NIGHT.
...FOR A SECOND, I DIDN'T RECOGNIZE HER...

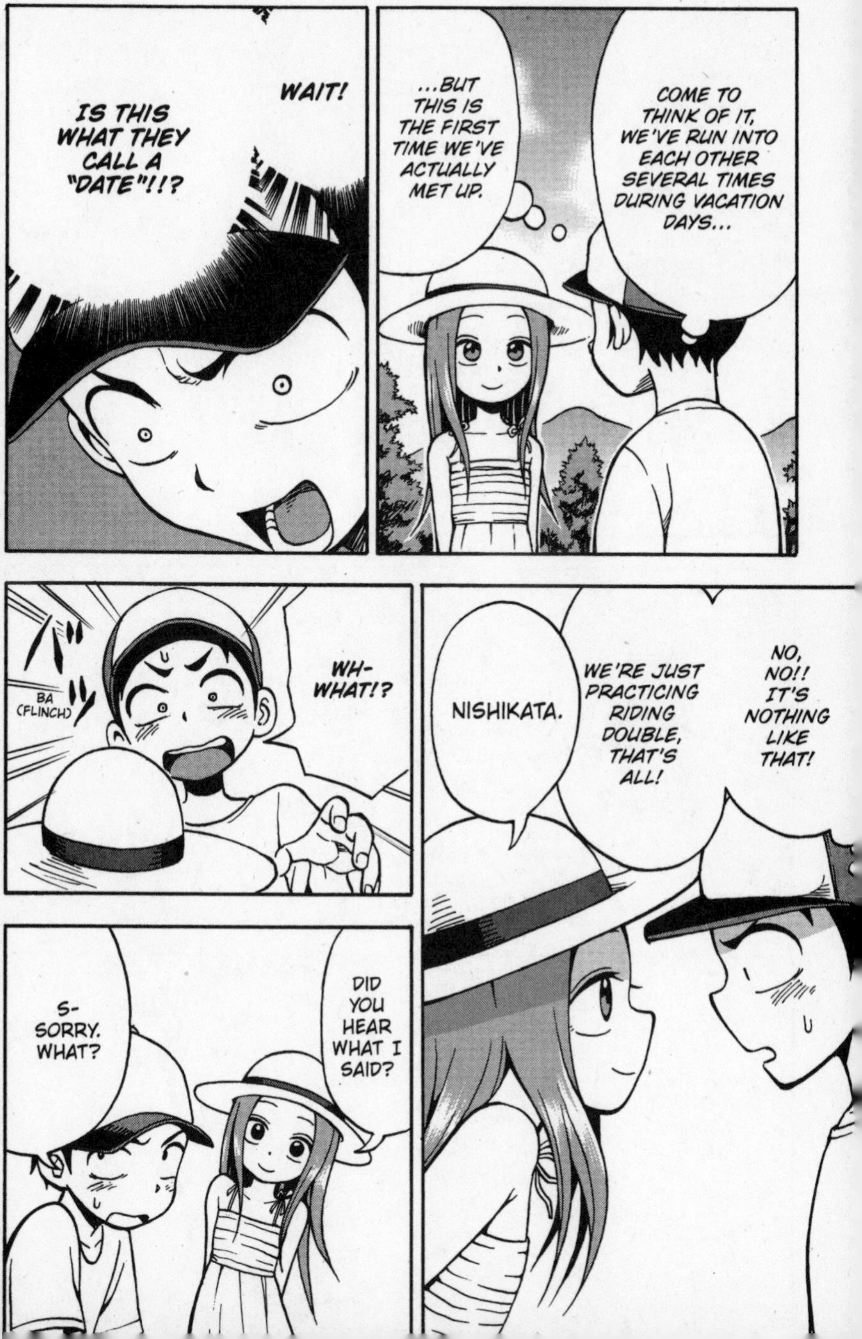
COME TO THINK OF IT, WE'VE RUN INTO EACH OTHER SEVERAL TIMES DURING VACATION DAYS...
...BUT THIS IS THE FIRST TIME WE'VE ACTUALLY MET UP.
WAIT!
IS THIS WHAT THEY CALL A "DATE"!!?
NO, NO!! IT'S NOTHING LIKE THAT!
WE'RE JUST PRACTICING RIDING DOUBLE, THAT'S ALL!
NISHIKATA.
WH- WHAT!?
BA (FLINCH)
DID YOU HEAR WHAT I SAID?
S- SORRY. WHAT?

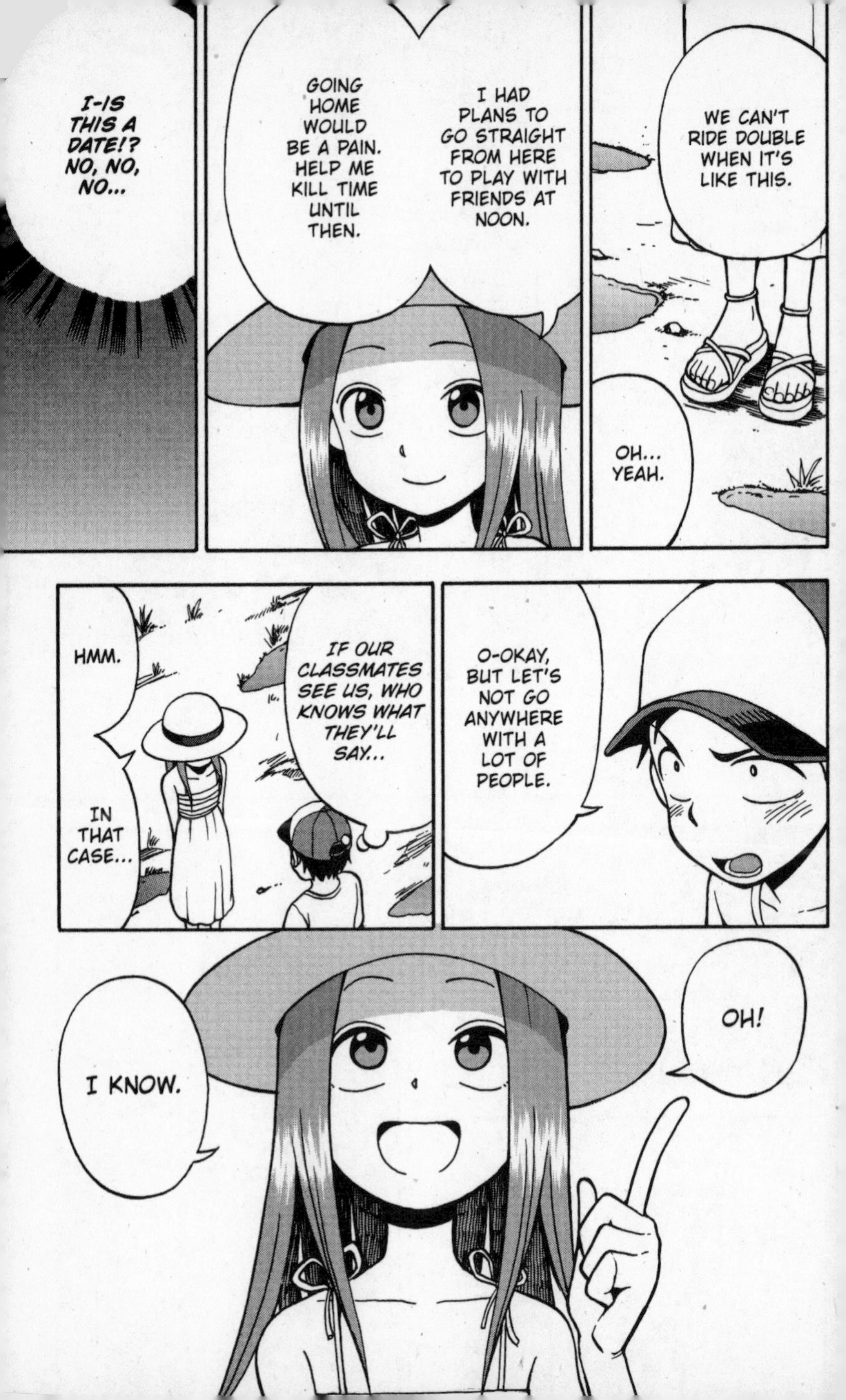
WE CAN'T RIDE DOUBLE WHEN IT'S LIKE THIS.
OH... YEAH.
I HAD PLANS TO GO STRAIGHT FROM HERE TO PLAY WITH FRIENDS AT NOON.
GOING HOME WOULD BE A PAIN. HELP ME KILL TIME UNTIL THEN.
I-IS THIS A DATE!? NO, NO, NO...
O-OKAY, BUT LET'S NOT GO ANYWHERE WITH A LOT OF PEOPLE.
IF OUR CLASSMATES SEE US, WHO KNOWS WHAT THEY'LL SAY...
HMM.
IN THAT CASE...
OH!
I KNOW.

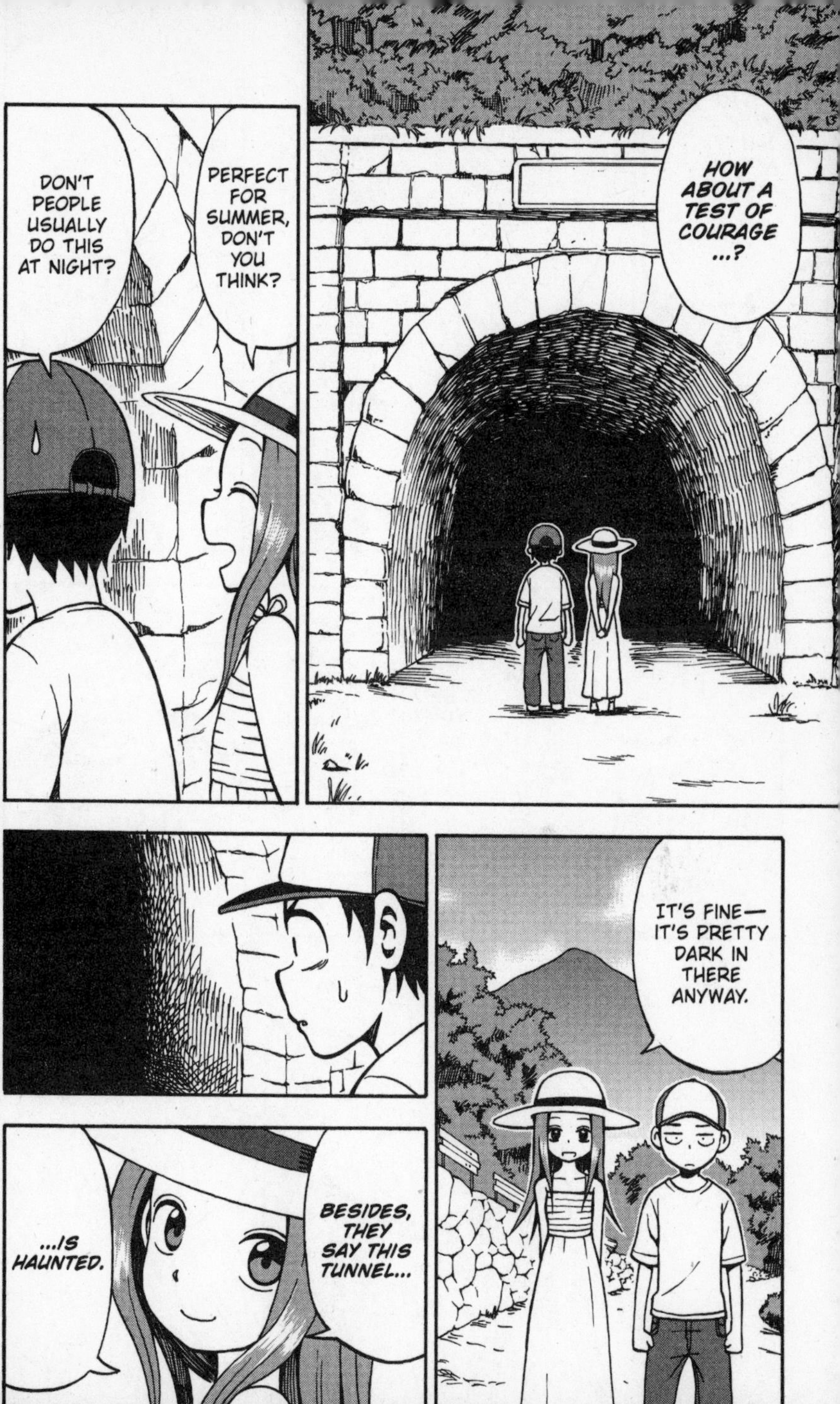
HOW ABOUT A TEST OF COURAGE ...?
PERFECT FOR SUMMER, DON'T YOU THINK?
DON'T PEOPLE USUALLY DO THIS AT NIGHT?
IT'S FINE— IT'S PRETTY DARK IN THERE ANYWAY.
BESIDES, THEY SAY THIS TUNNEL...
...IS HAUNTED.

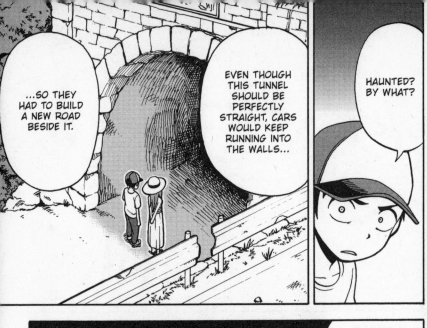

HAUNTED? BY WHAT?
EVEN THOUGH THIS TUNNEL SHOULD BE PERFECTLY STRAIGHT, CARS WOULD KEEP RUNNING INTO THE WALLS...
...SO THEY HAD TO BUILD A NEW ROAD BESIDE IT.
EVER SINCE THEN, IT APPEARS EVERY NIGHT—
A GHOST STARVED FOR BLOOD AFTER LOSING ITS PREY...
YOU'RE NOT GOING IN?
......

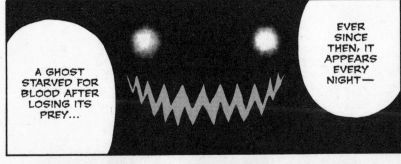

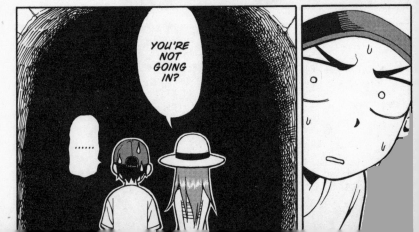

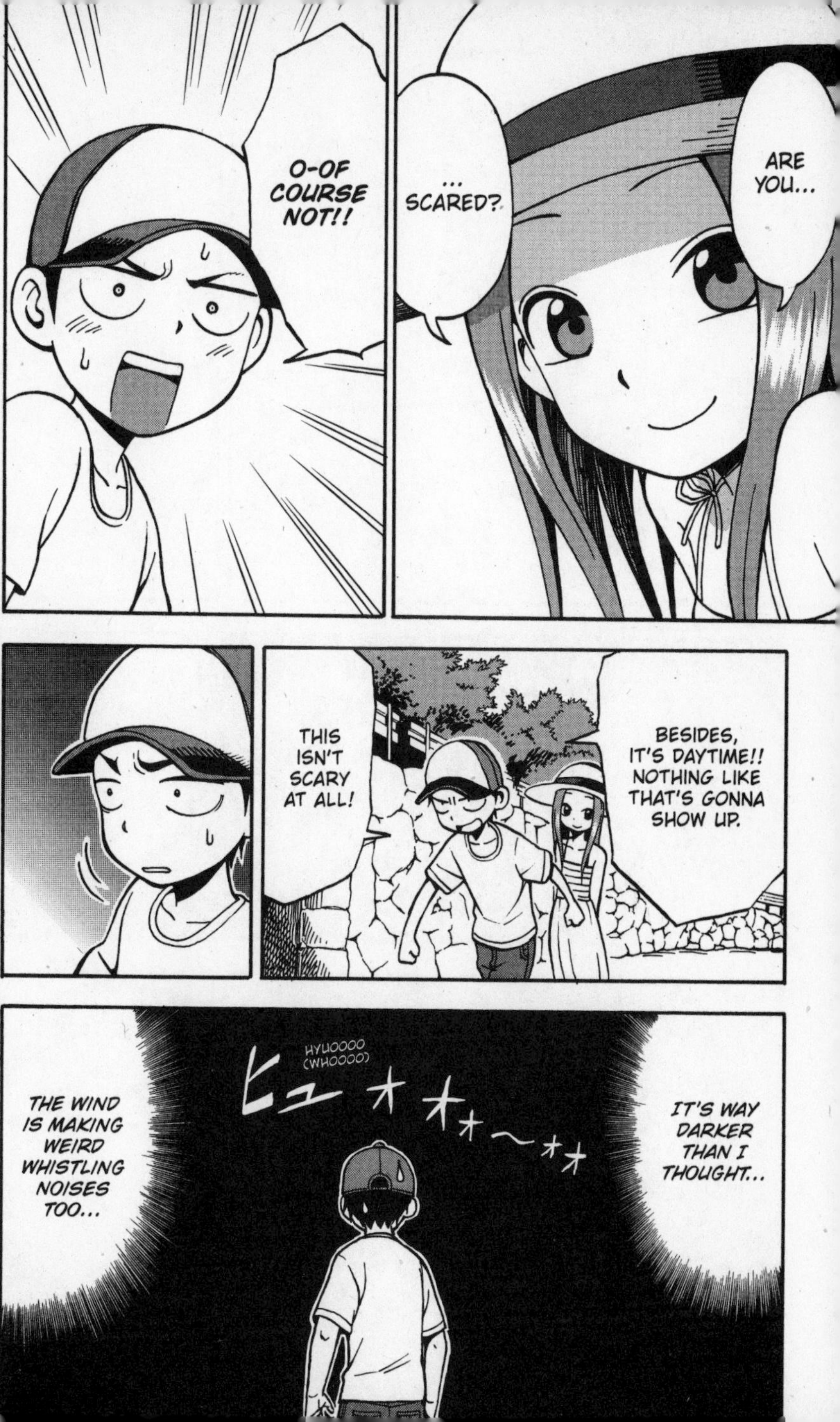

ARE YOU...
...SCARED?
O-OF COURSE NOT!!
BESIDES, IT'S DAYTIME!! NOTHING LIKE THAT'S GONNA SHOW UP.
THIS ISN'T SCARY AT ALL!
IT'S WAY DARKER THAN I THOUGHT...
ヒュオオォ～オオ
HYUOOOO (WHOOOO)
THE WIND IS MAKING WEIRD WHISTLING NOISES TOO...

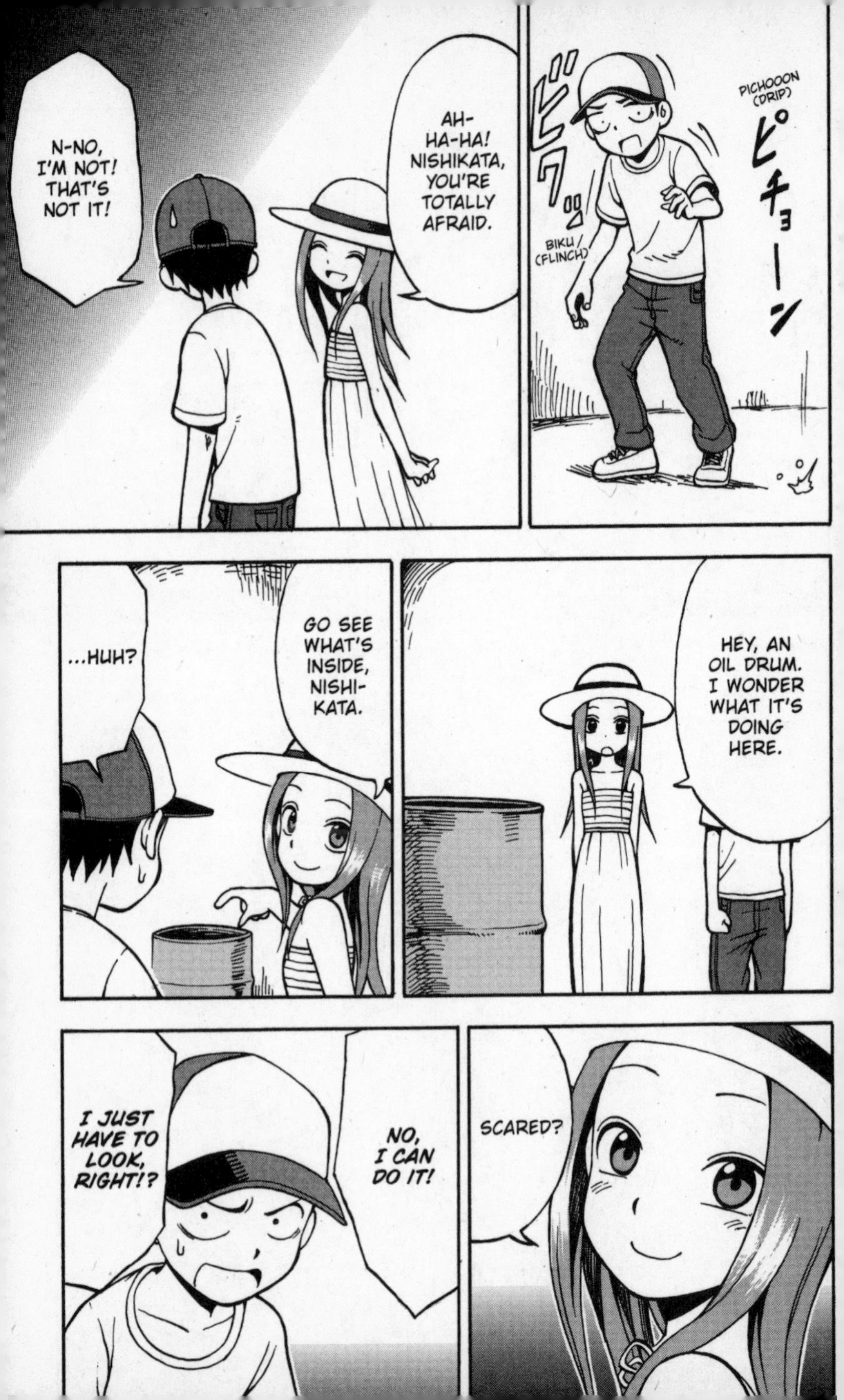
PICHOOON (DRIP)
ピチョーン
ビクッ
BIKU (FLINCH)
AH-HA-HA! NISHIKATA, YOU'RE TOTALLY AFRAID.
N-NO, I'M NOT! THAT'S NOT IT!
HEY, AN OIL DRUM. I WONDER WHAT IT'S DOING HERE.
GO SEE WHAT'S INSIDE, NISHIKATA.
...HUH?
SCARED?
NO, I CAN DO IT!
I JUST HAVE TO LOOK, RIGHT!?

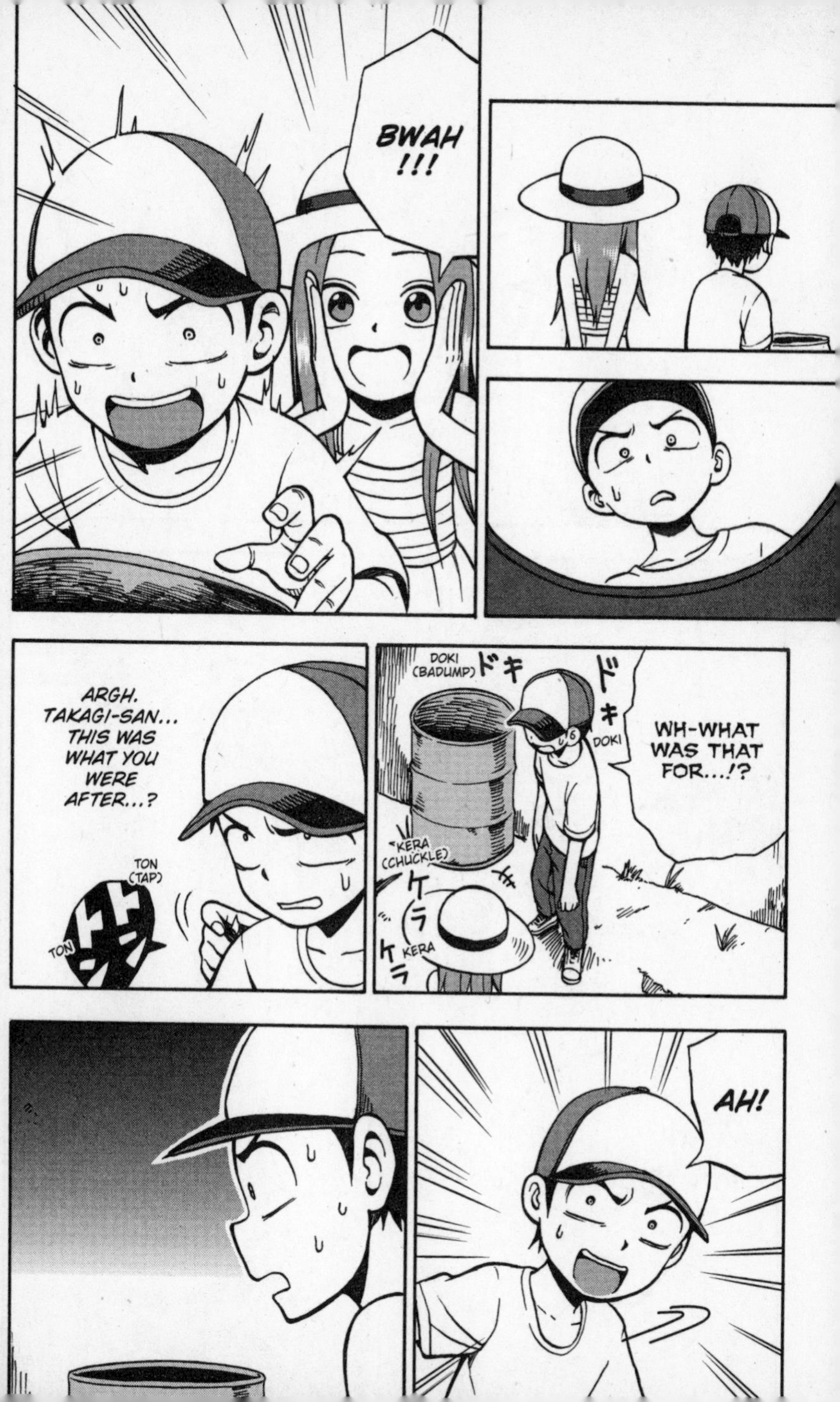
BWAH!!!
DOKI (BADUMP) ドキ
ドキ DOKI
WH-WHAT WAS THAT FOR...!?
KERA (CHUCKLE) ケラ
ケラ KERA
ARGH. TAKAGI-SAN... THIS WAS WHAT YOU WERE AFTER...?
TON (TAP)
TON
AH!

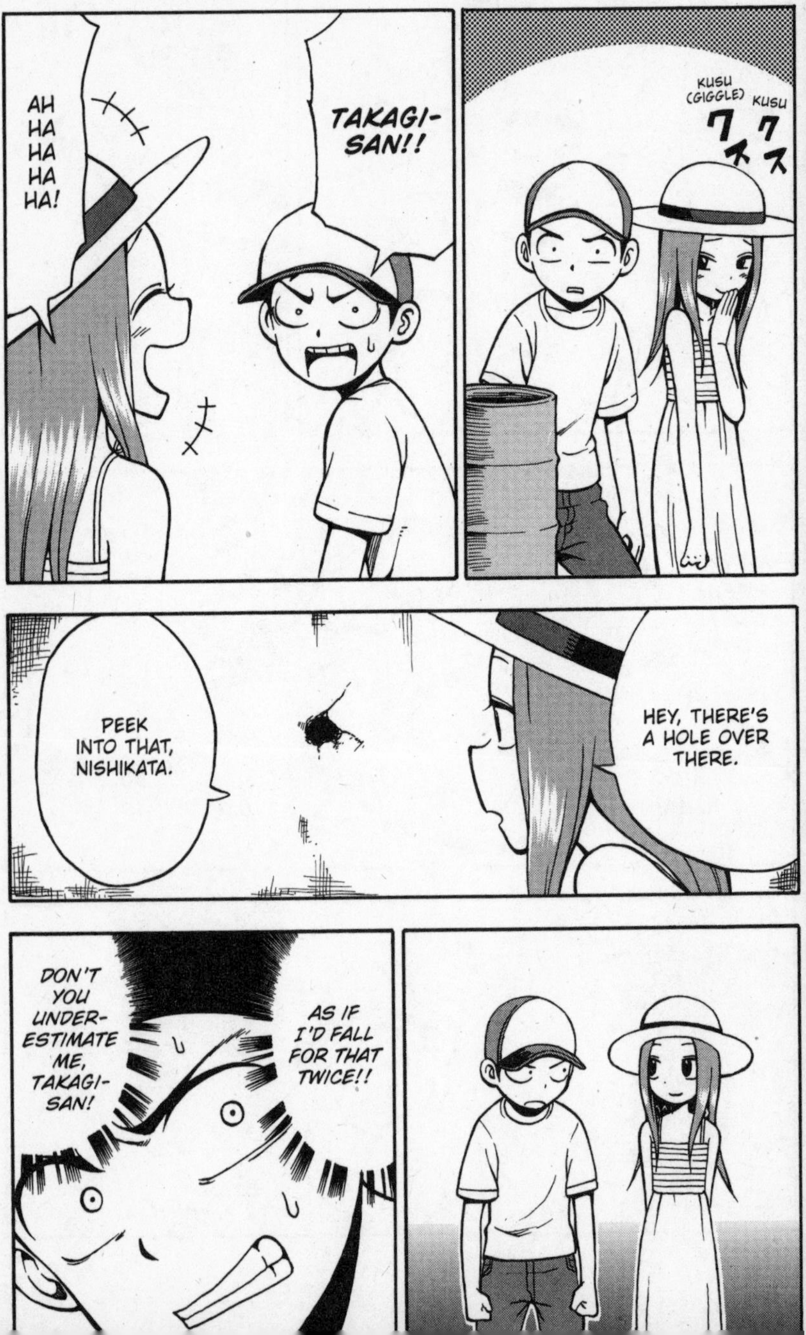
KUSU (GIGGLE) KUSU
クス クス
TAKAGI-SAN!!
AH HA HA HA HA!
HEY, THERE'S A HOLE OVER THERE.
PEEK INTO THAT, NISHIKATA.
AS IF I'D FALL FOR THAT TWICE!!
DON'T YOU UNDER-ESTIMATE ME, TAKAGI-SAN!

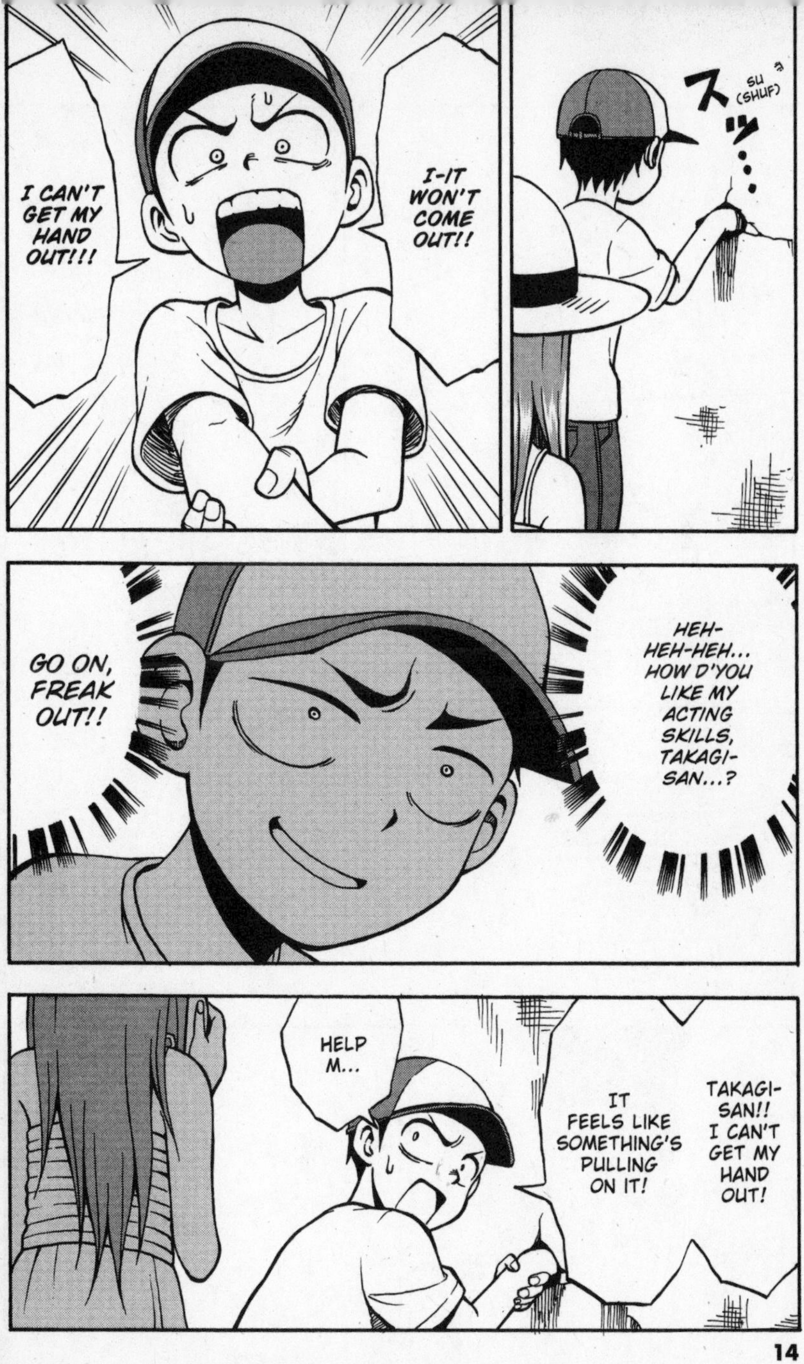
スッ…
SU (SHUF)
I-IT WON'T COME OUT!!
I CAN'T GET MY HAND OUT!!!
HEH-HEH-HEH... HOW D'YOU LIKE MY ACTING SKILLS, TAKAGI-SAN...?
GO ON, FREAK OUT!!
TAKAGI-SAN!! I CAN'T GET MY HAND OUT!
IT FEELS LIKE SOMETHING'S PULLING ON IT!
HELP M...

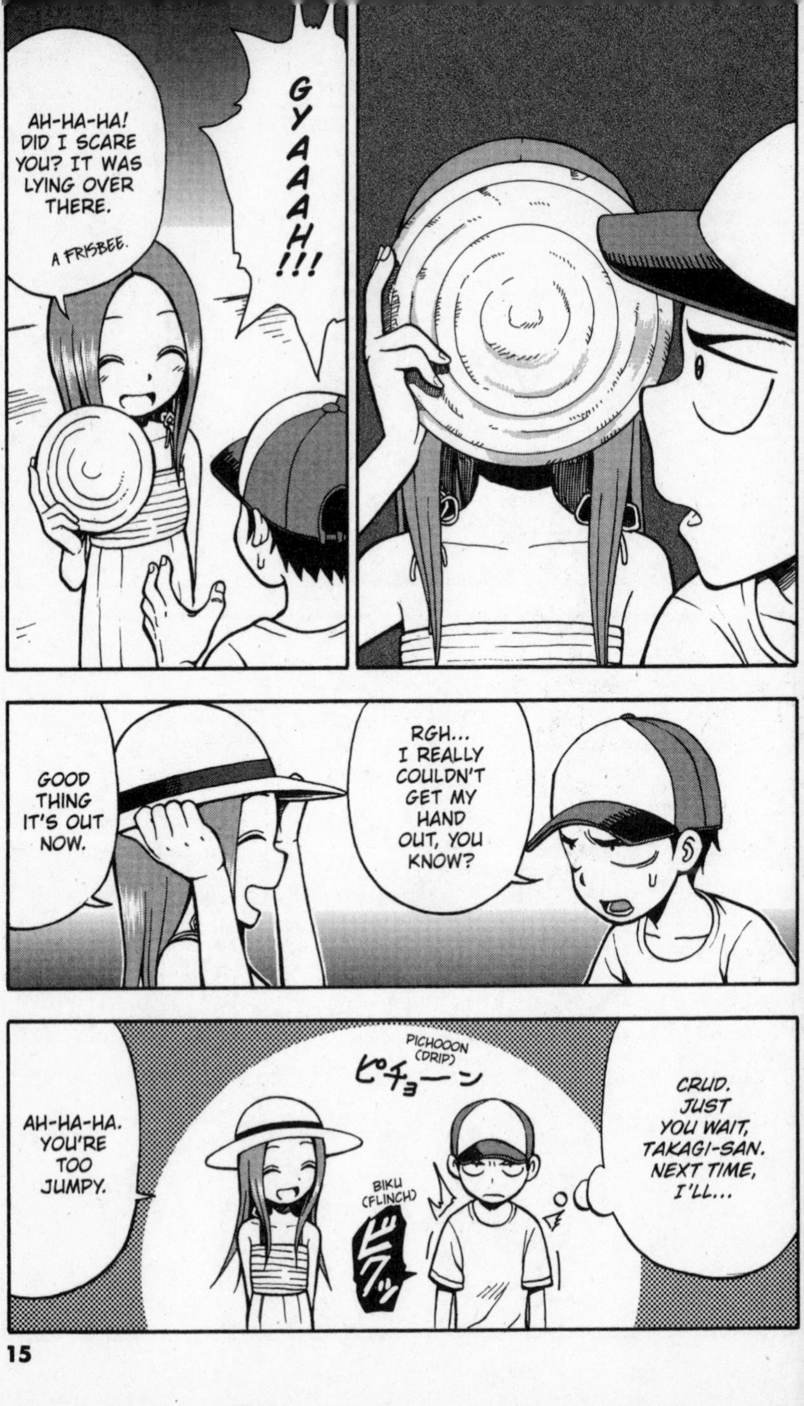
GYAAAAH!!!
AH-HA-HA! DID I SCARE YOU? IT WAS LYING OVER THERE.
A FRISBEE.
RGH... I REALLY COULDN'T GET MY HAND OUT, YOU KNOW?
GOOD THING IT'S OUT NOW.
CRUD. JUST YOU WAIT, TAKAGI-SAN. NEXT TIME, I'LL...
PICHOOON (DRIP)
ピチョーン
BIKU (FLINCH)
AH-HA-HA. YOU'RE TOO JUMPY.

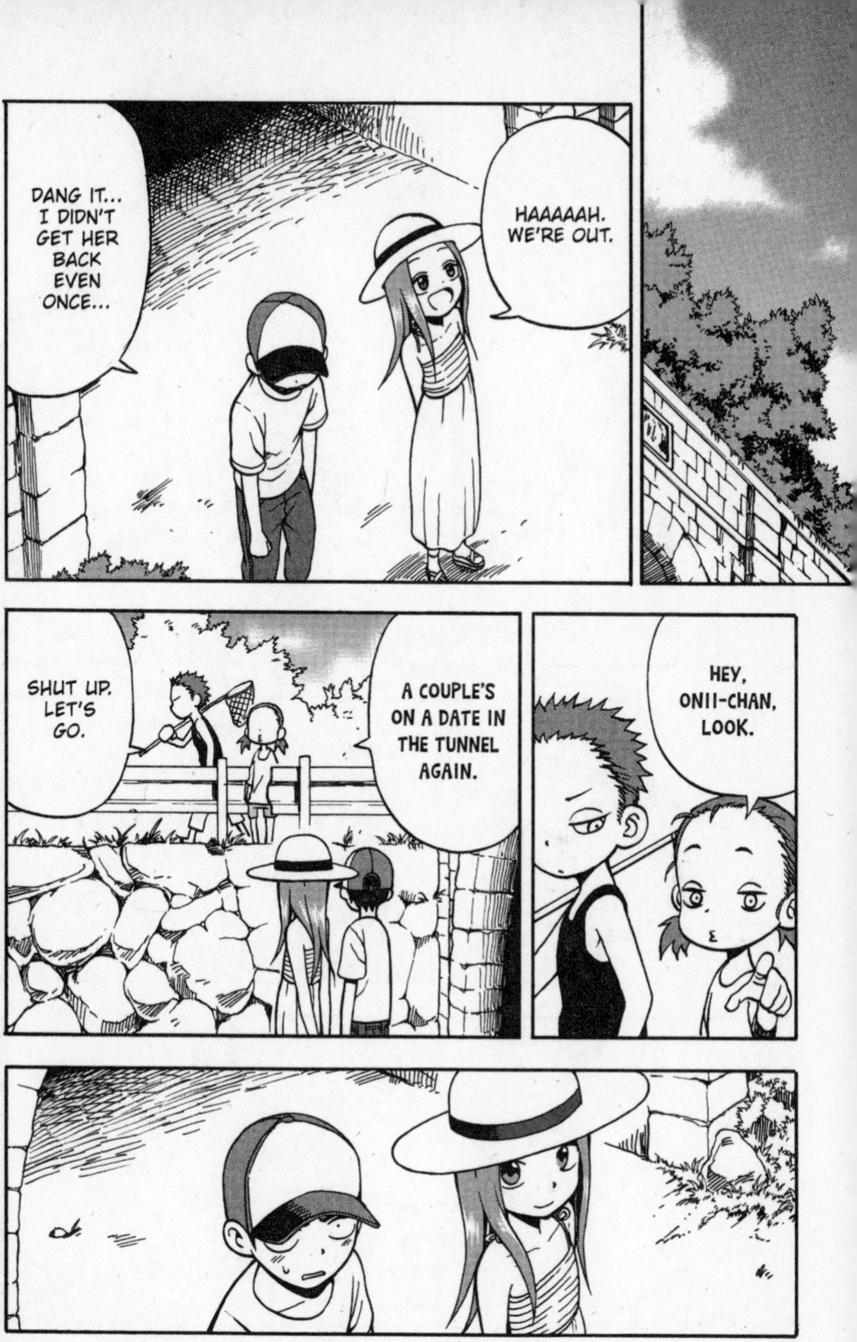
HAAAAAH. WE'RE OUT.
DANG IT... I DIDN'T GET HER BACK EVEN ONCE...
HEY, ONII-CHAN, LOOK.
A COUPLE'S ON A DATE IN THE TUNNEL AGAIN.
SHUT UP. LET'S GO.

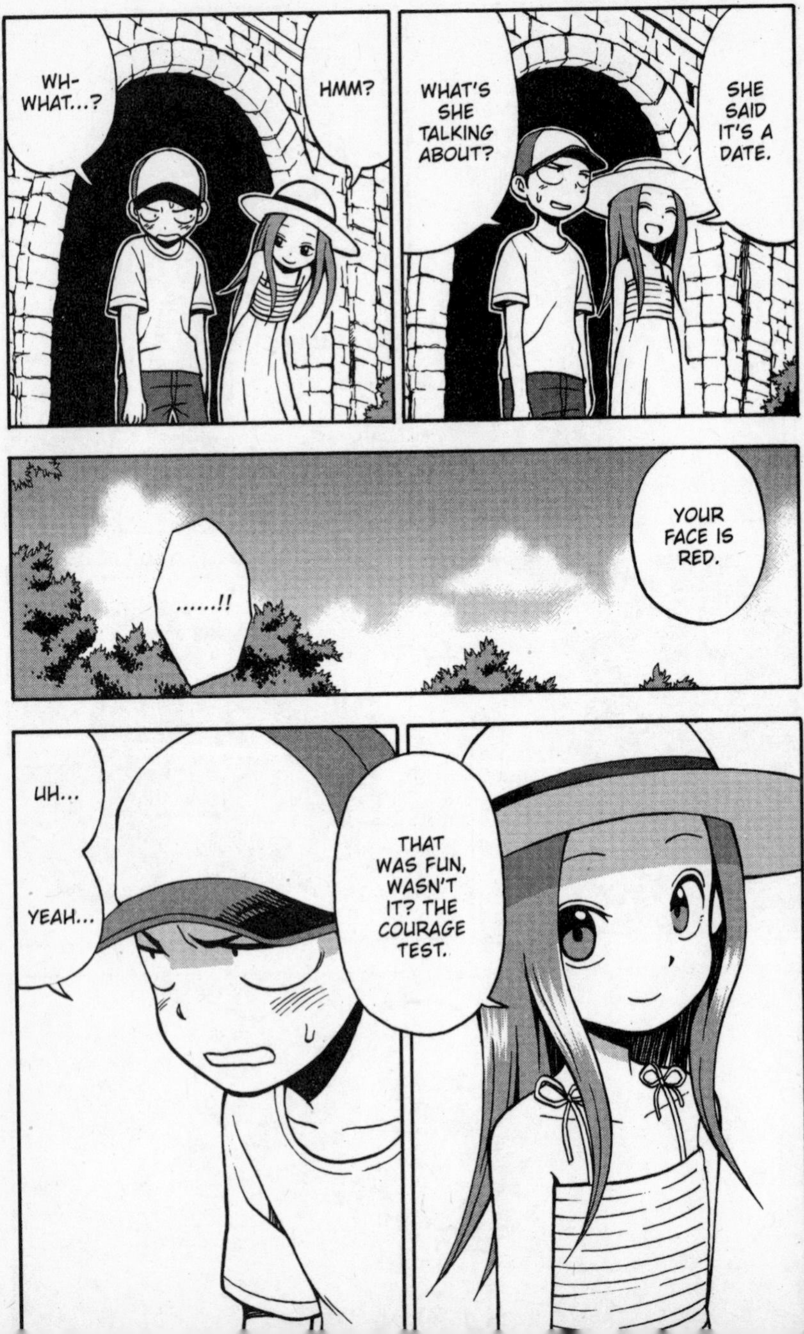
SHE SAID IT'S A DATE.
WHAT'S SHE TALKING ABOUT?
HMM?
WH-WHAT...?
YOUR FACE IS RED.
......!!
THAT WAS FUN, WASN'T IT? THE COURAGE TEST.
UH... YEAH...

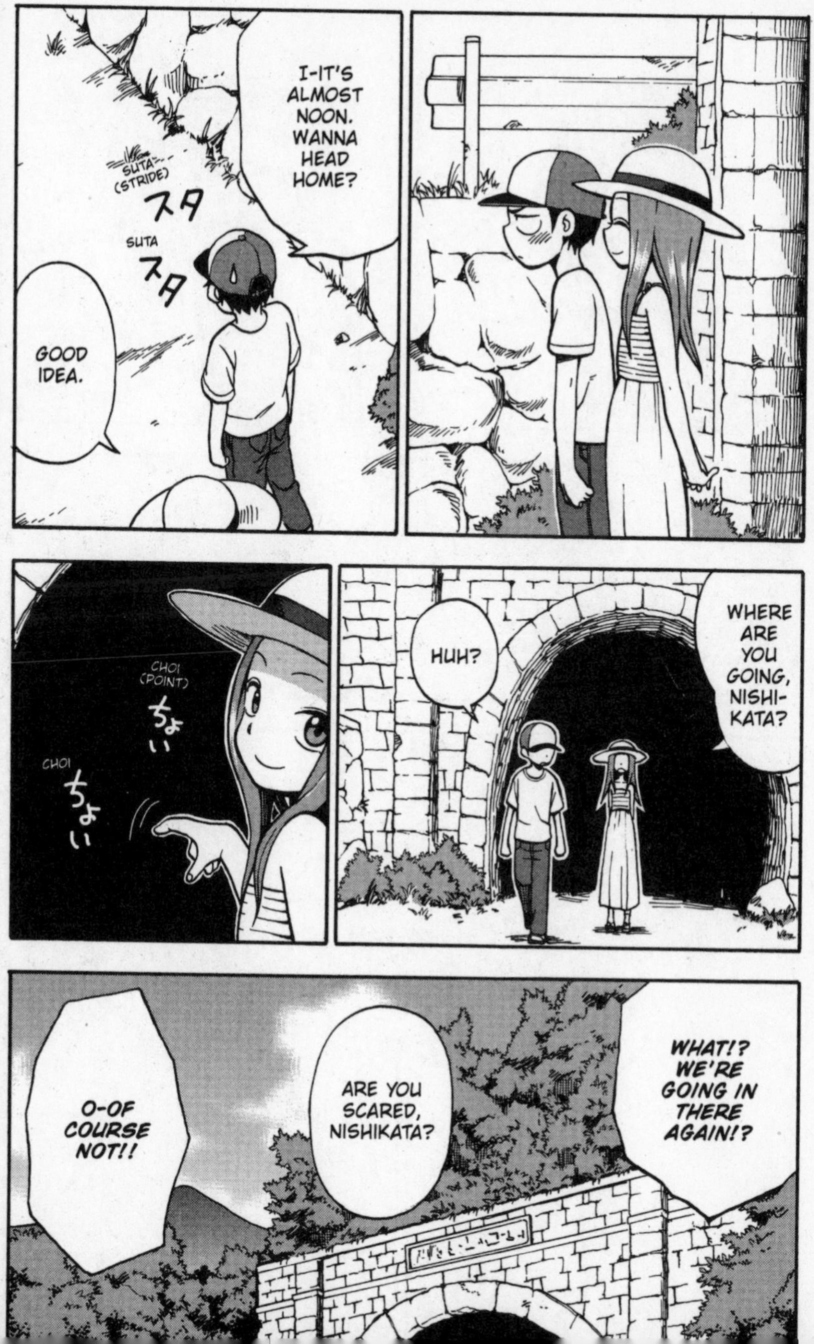
I-IT'S ALMOST NOON. WANNA HEAD HOME?
SUTA (STRIDE)
スタ
SUTA
スタ
GOOD IDEA.
WHERE ARE YOU GOING, NISHIKATA?
HUH?
CHOI (POINT)
ちょい
CHOI
ちょい
WHAT!? WE'RE GOING IN THERE AGAIN!?
ARE YOU SCARED, NISHIKATA?
O-OF COURSE NOT!!

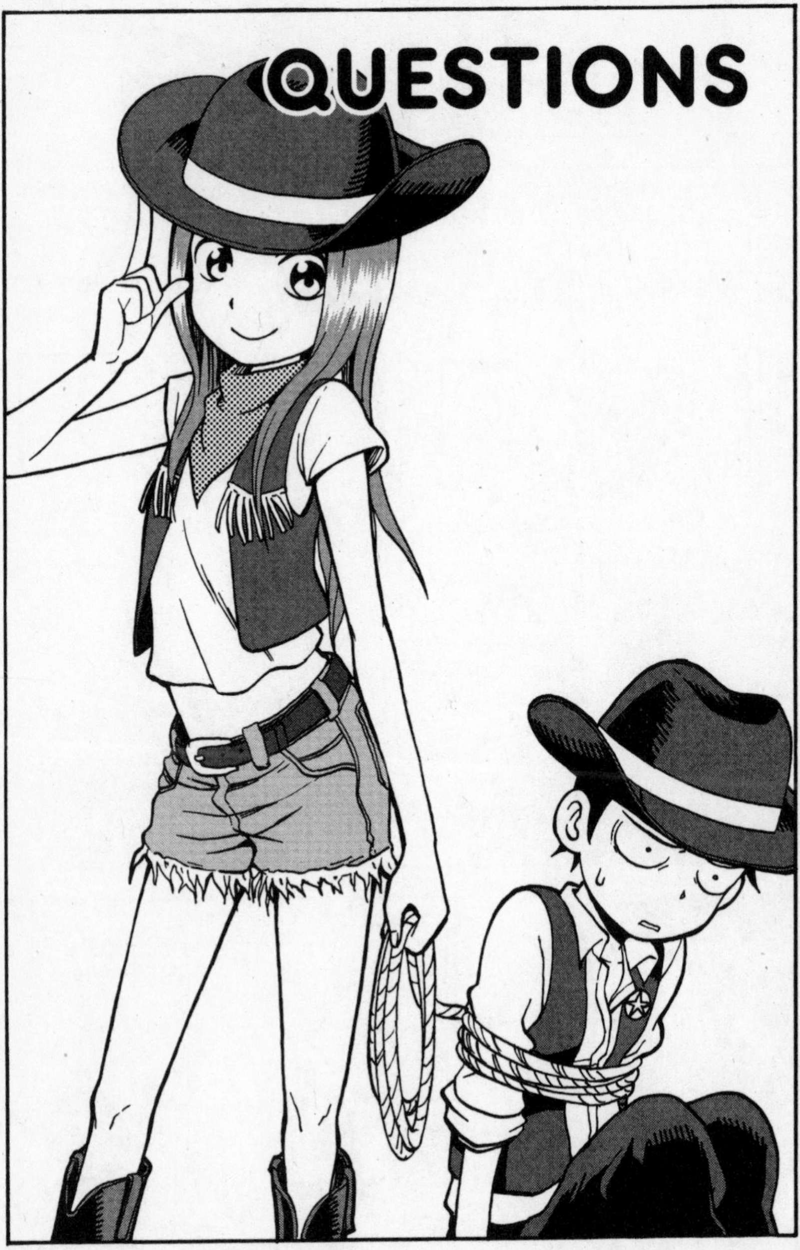
QUESTIONS

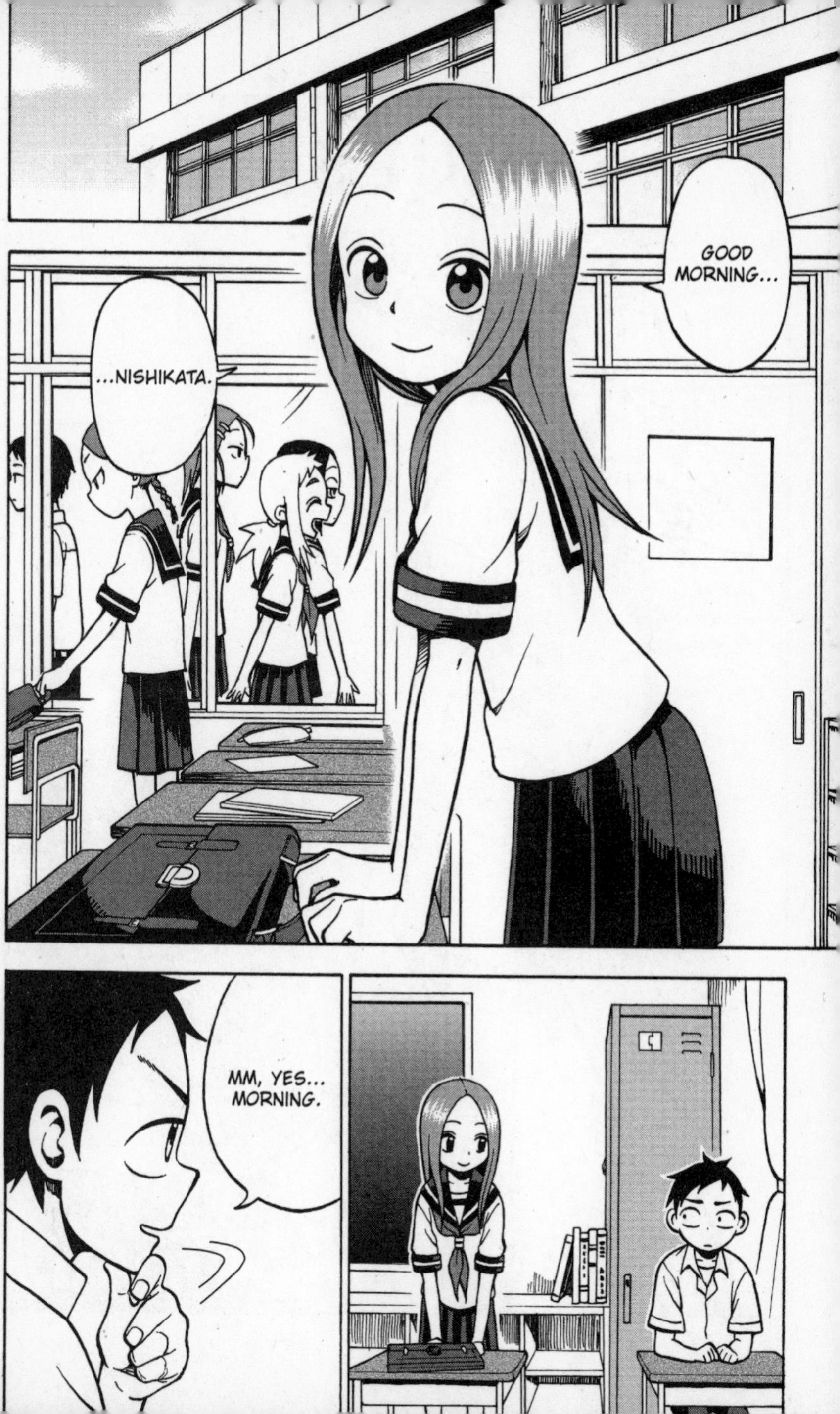
GOOD MORNING...
...NISHIKATA.
MM, YES... MORNING.

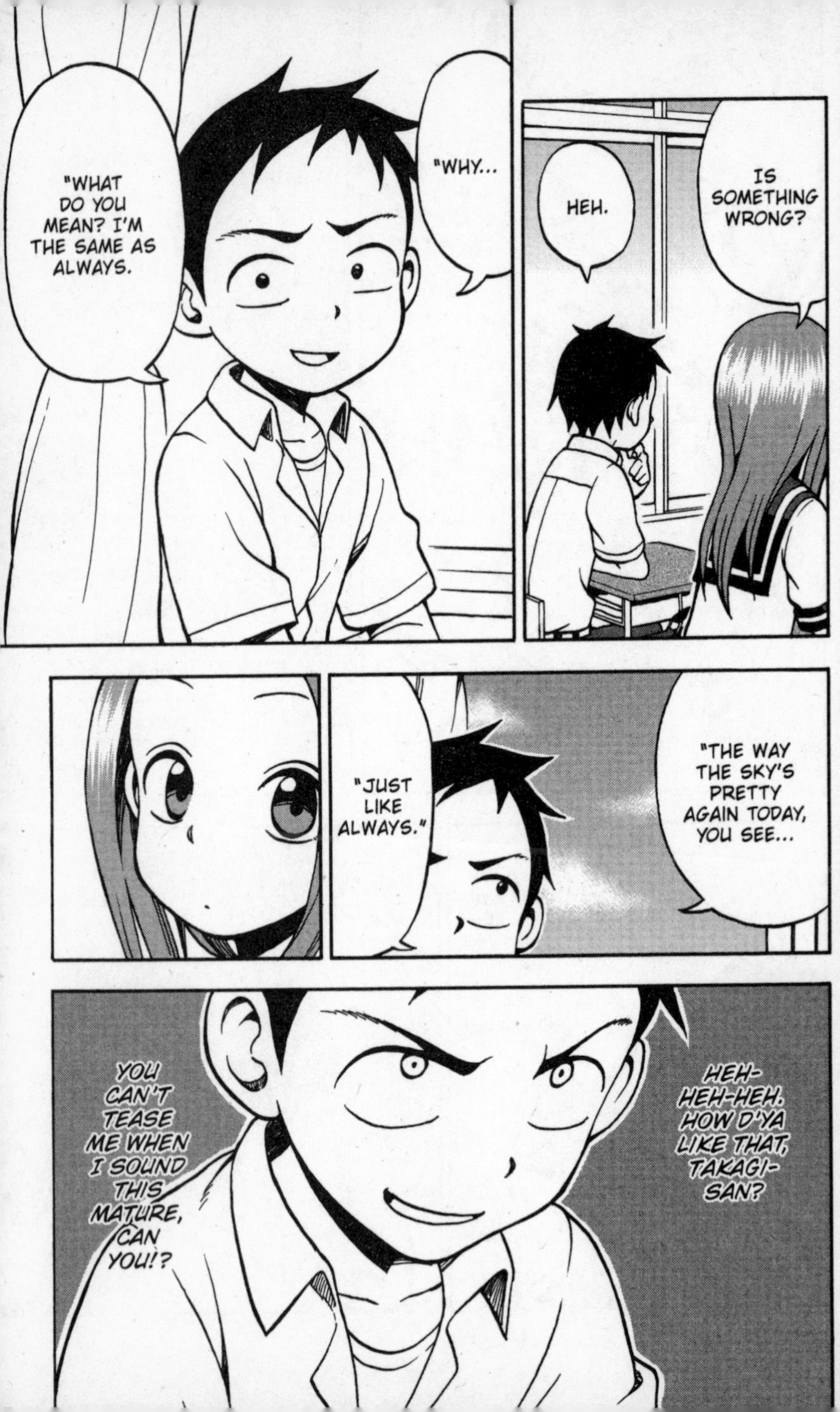
IS SOMETHING WRONG?
HEH.
"WHY...
"WHAT DO YOU MEAN? I'M THE SAME AS ALWAYS.
"THE WAY THE SKY'S PRETTY AGAIN TODAY, YOU SEE...
"JUST LIKE ALWAYS."
HEH-HEH-HEH. HOW D'YA LIKE THAT, TAKAGI-SAN?
YOU CAN'T TEASE ME WHEN I SOUND THIS MATURE, CAN YOU!?

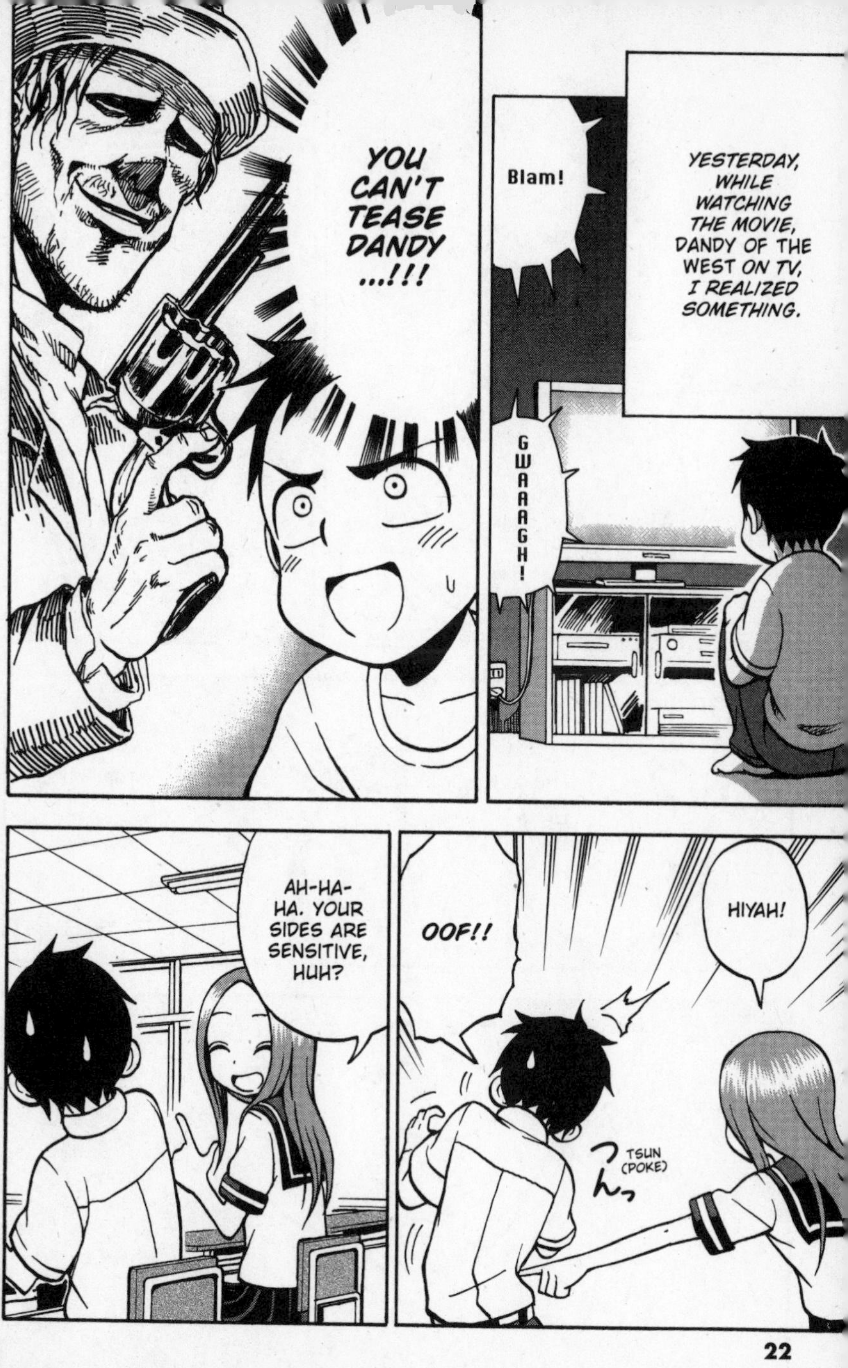
YESTERDAY, WHILE WATCHING THE MOVIE, DANDY OF THE WEST ON TV, I REALIZED SOMETHING.
Blam!
GWAAAGH!
YOU CAN'T TEASE DANDY ...!!!
HIYAH!
TSUN (POKE)
OOF!!
AH-HA-HA. YOUR SIDES ARE SENSITIVE, HUH?

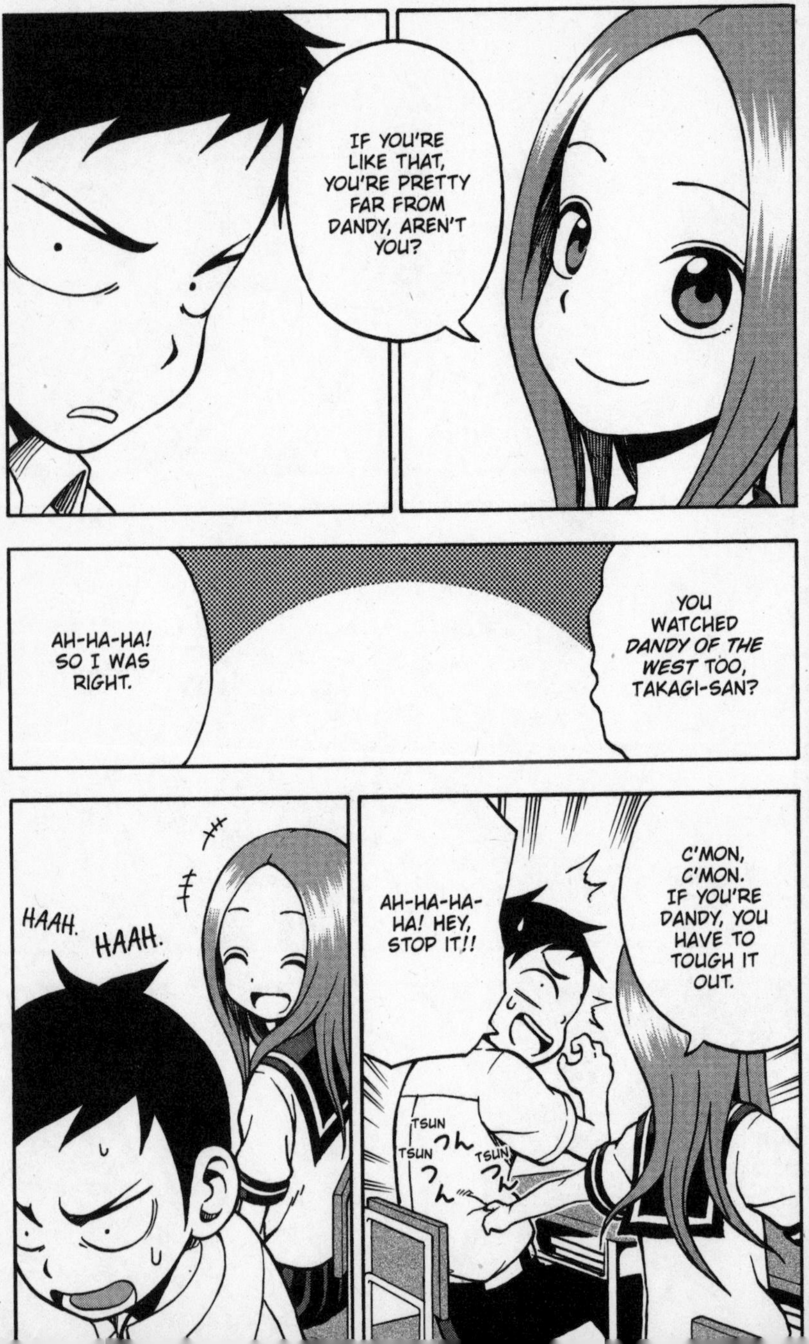
IF YOU'RE LIKE THAT, YOU'RE PRETTY FAR FROM DANDY, AREN'T YOU?
YOU WATCHED DANDY OF THE WEST TOO, TAKAGI-SAN?
AH-HA-HA! SO I WAS RIGHT.
C'MON, C'MON. IF YOU'RE DANDY, YOU HAVE TO TOUGH IT OUT.
AH-HA-HA-HA! HEY, STOP IT!!
TSUN
TSUN
TSUN
HAAH.
HAAH.

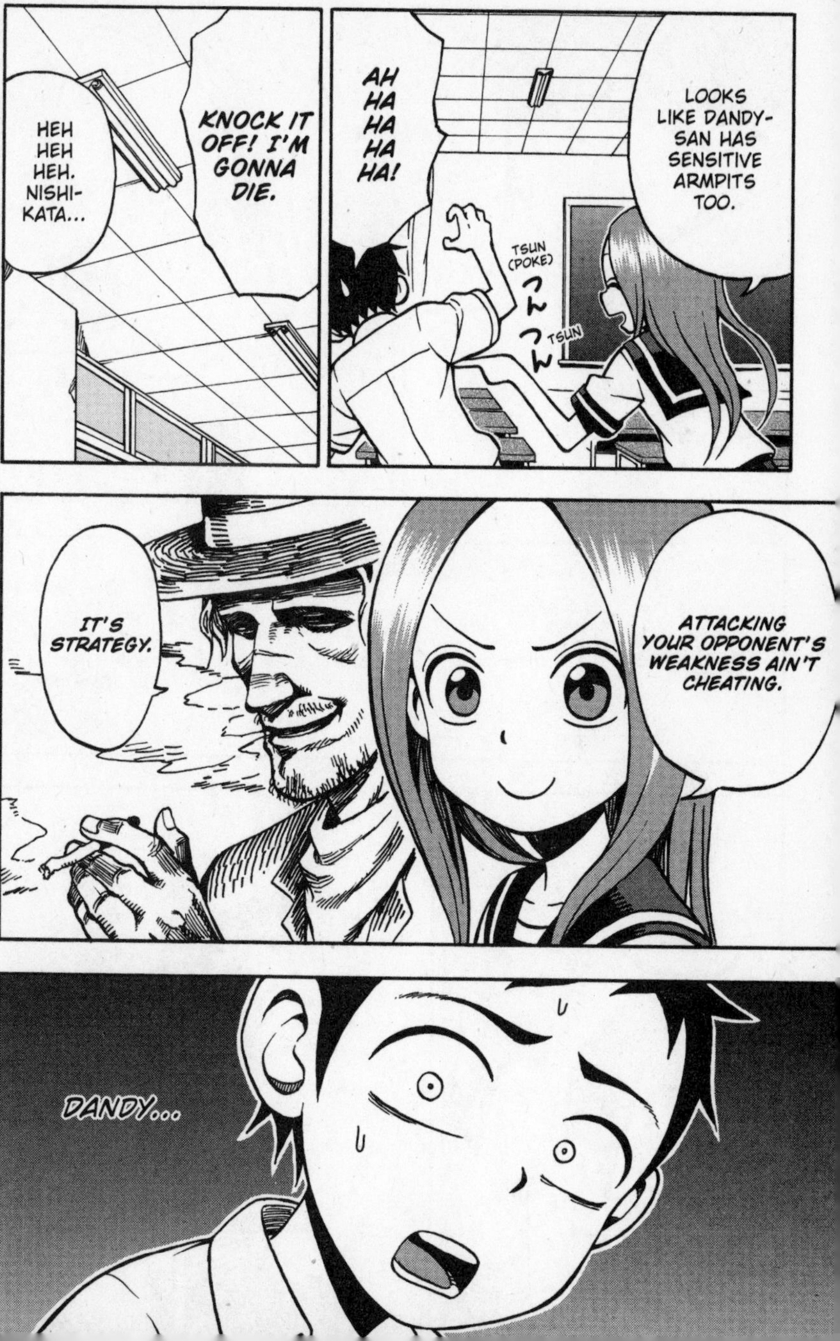
LOOKS LIKE DANDY-SAN HAS SENSITIVE ARMPITS TOO.
AH HA HA HA HA!
TSUN (POKE)
つんつん
TSUN
KNOCK IT OFF! I'M GONNA DIE.
HEH HEH HEH. NISHIKATA...
ATTACKING YOUR OPPONENT'S WEAKNESS AIN'T CHEATING.
IT'S STRATEGY.
DANDY...

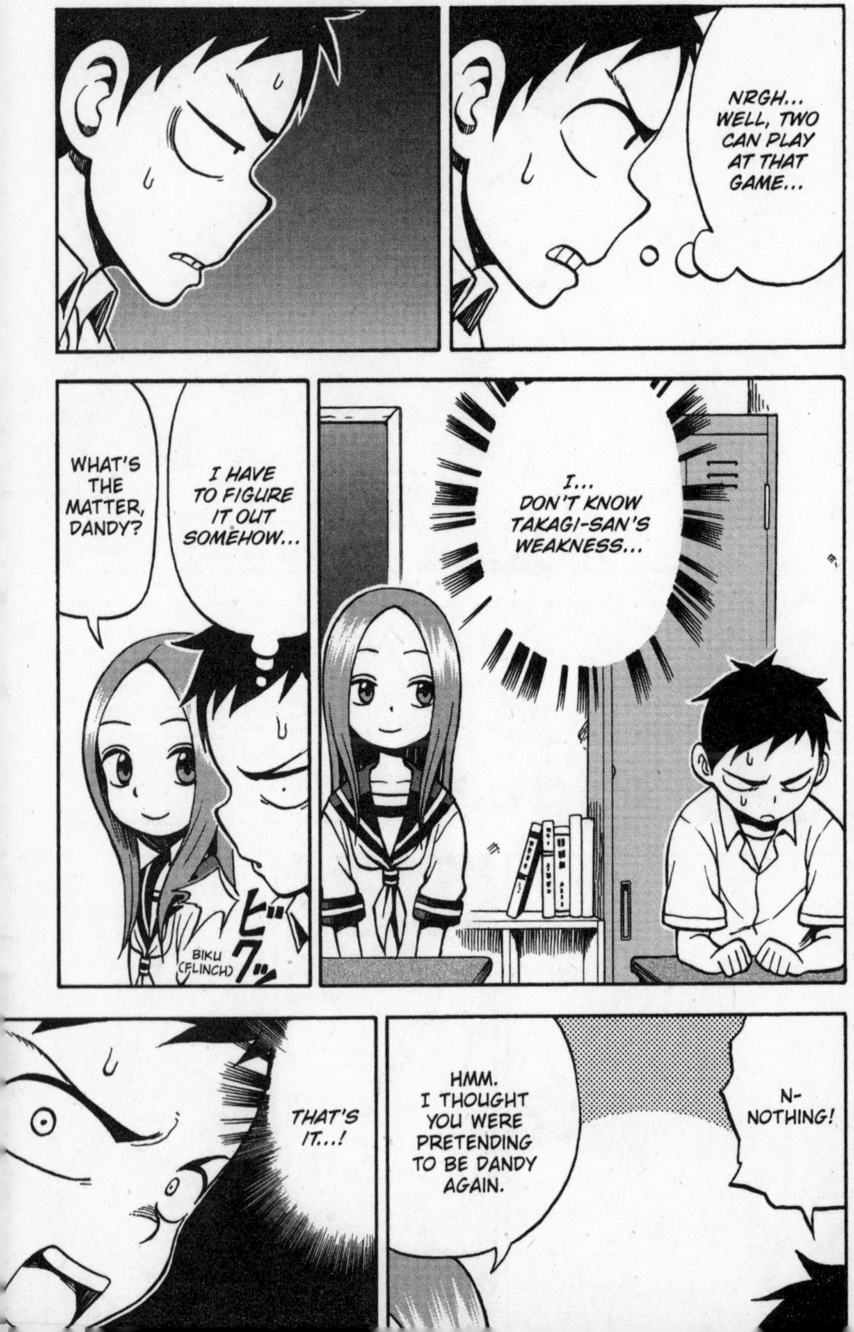
NRGH... WELL, TWO CAN PLAY AT THAT GAME...
I... DON'T KNOW TAKAGI-SAN'S WEAKNESS...
I HAVE TO FIGURE IT OUT SOMEHOW...
WHAT'S THE MATTER, DANDY?
BIKU (FLINCH)
N-NOTHING!
HMM. I THOUGHT YOU WERE PRETENDING TO BE DANDY AGAIN.
THAT'S IT...!

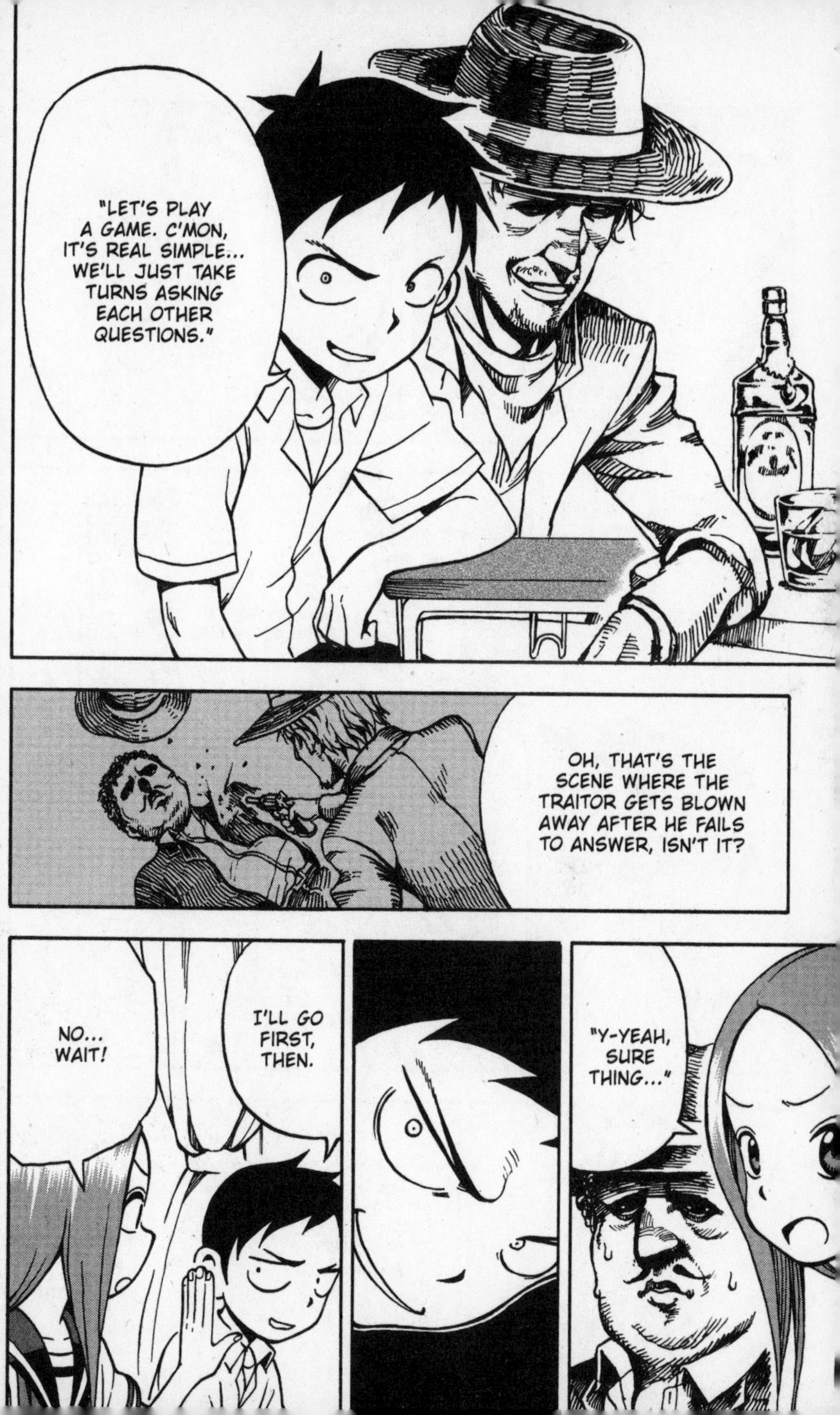
"LET'S PLAY A GAME. C'MON, IT'S REAL SIMPLE... WE'LL JUST TAKE TURNS ASKING EACH OTHER QUESTIONS."
OH, THAT'S THE SCENE WHERE THE TRAITOR GETS BLOWN AWAY AFTER HE FAILS TO ANSWER, ISN'T IT?
"Y-YEAH, SURE THING..."
I'LL GO FIRST, THEN.
NO... WAIT!

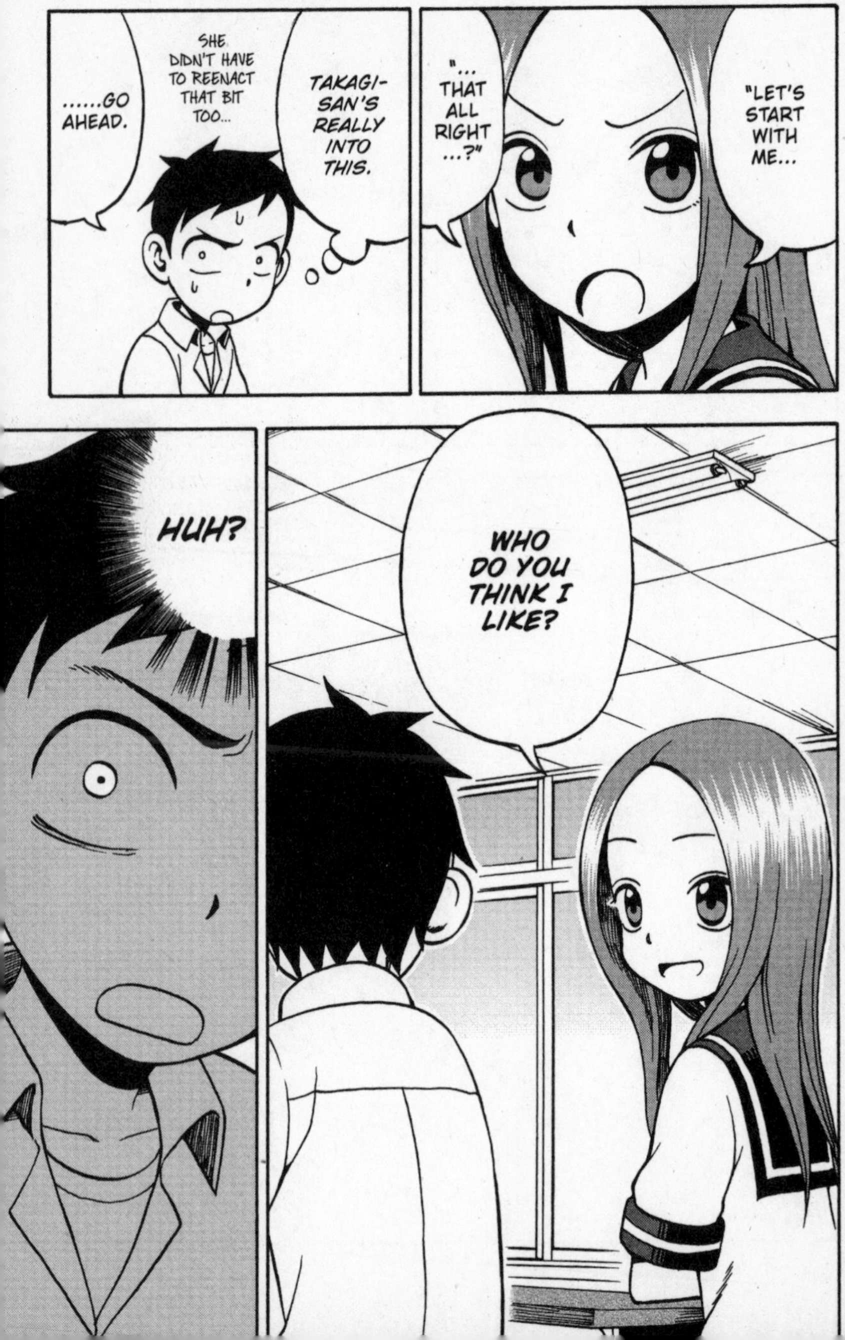
"LET'S START WITH ME...
"... THAT ALL RIGHT ...?"
TAKAGI-SAN'S REALLY INTO THIS.
SHE DIDN'T HAVE TO REENACT THAT BIT TOO...
......GO AHEAD.
WHO DO YOU THINK I LIKE?
HUH?

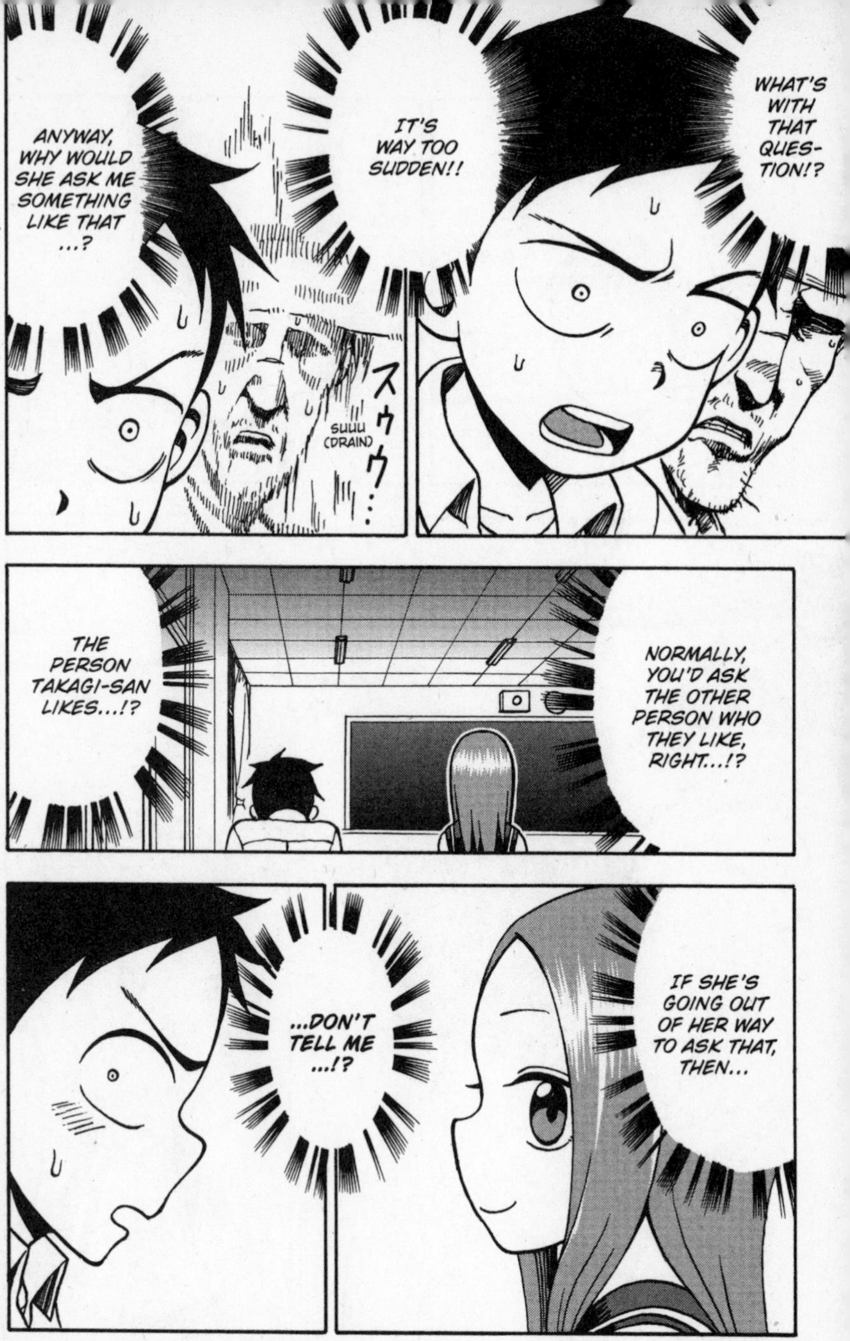
WHAT'S WITH THAT QUES-TION!?
IT'S WAY TOO SUDDEN!!
ANYWAY, WHY WOULD SHE ASK ME SOMETHING LIKE THAT ...?
スゥウ…
SUUU (DRAIN)
NORMALLY, YOU'D ASK THE OTHER PERSON WHO THEY LIKE, RIGHT...!?
THE PERSON TAKAGI-SAN LIKES...!?
IF SHE'S GOING OUT OF HER WAY TO ASK THAT, THEN...
...DON'T TELL ME ...!?

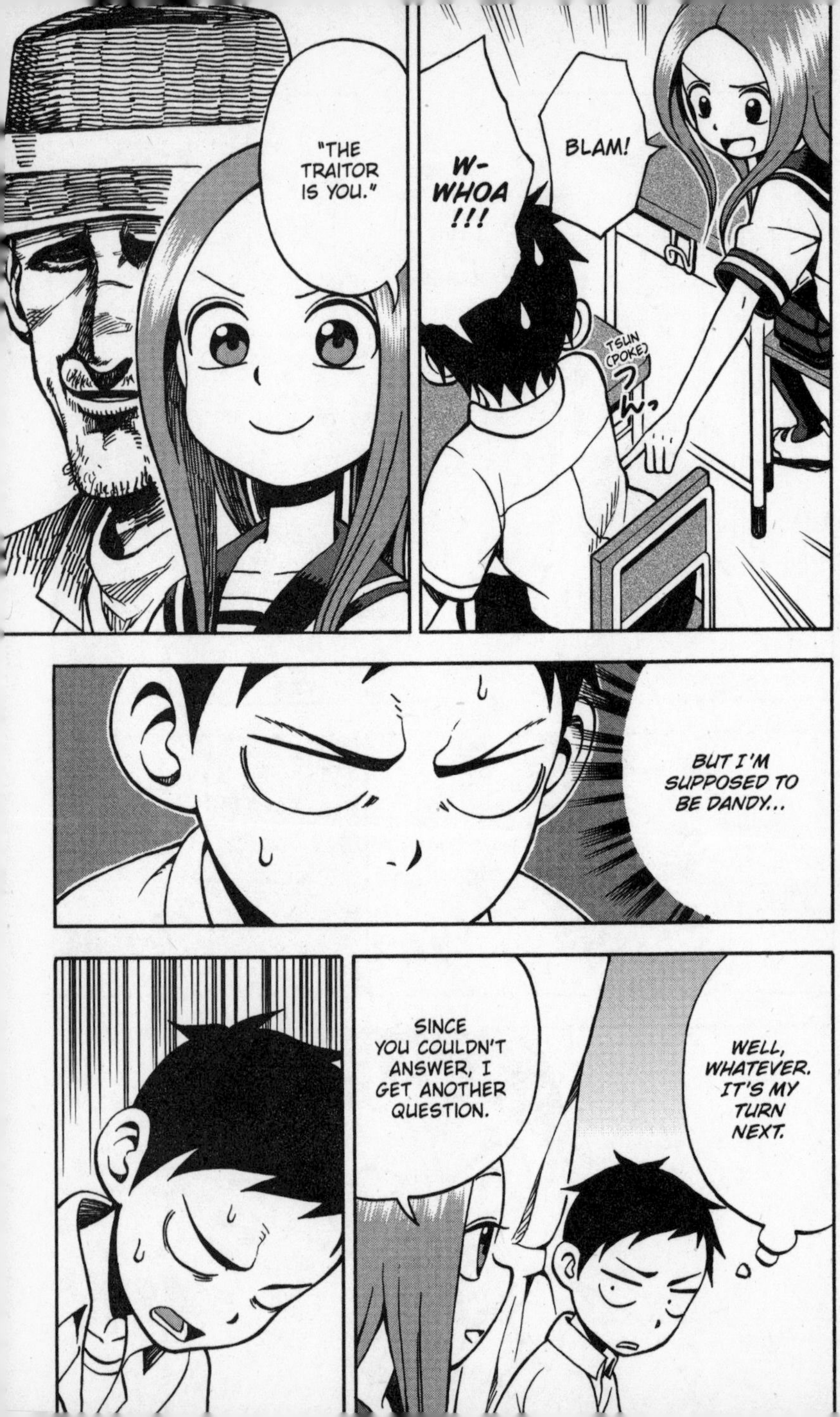
BLAM!
W-WHOA!!!
TSUN (POKE)
"THE TRAITOR IS YOU."
BUT I'M SUPPOSED TO BE DANDY...
WELL, WHATEVER. IT'S MY TURN NEXT.
SINCE YOU COULDN'T ANSWER, I GET ANOTHER QUESTION.

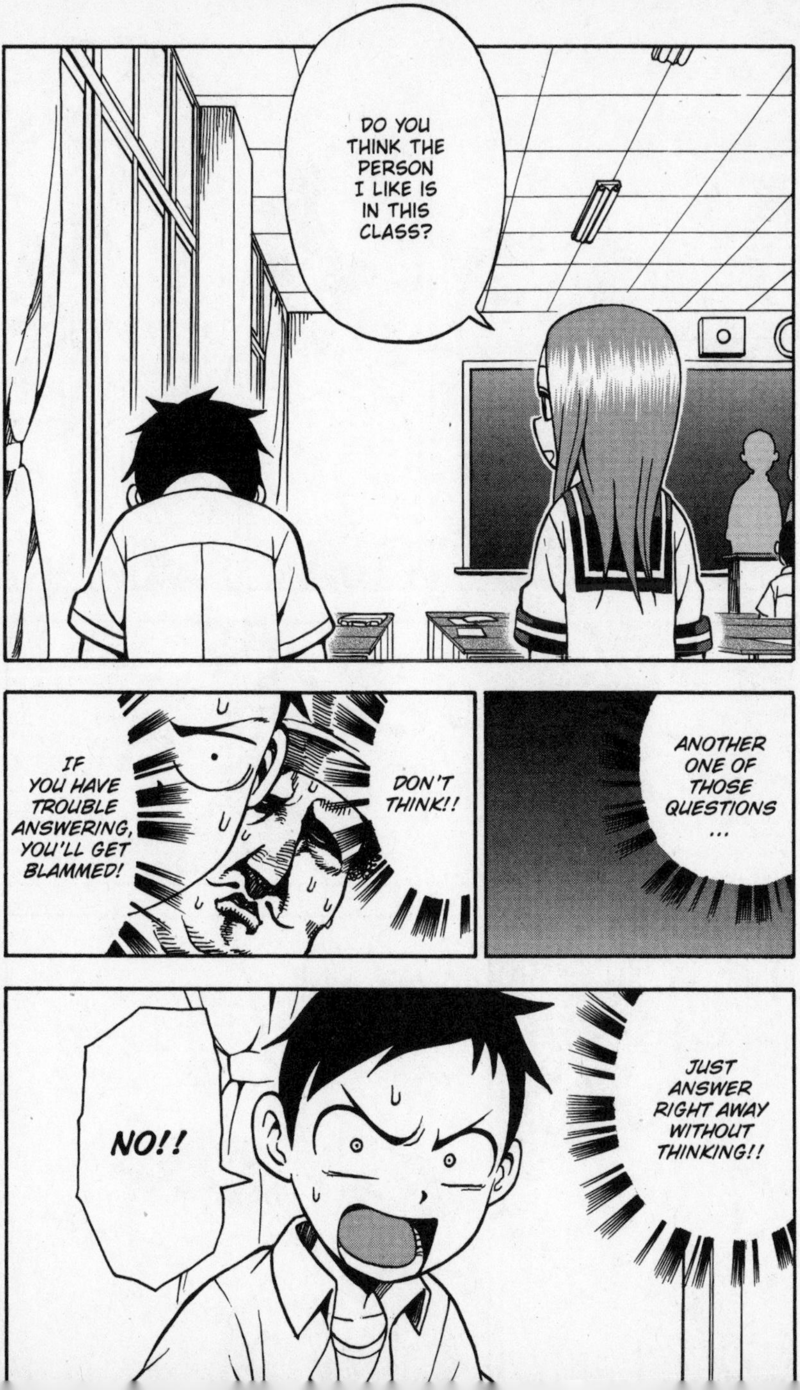
DO YOU THINK THE PERSON I LIKE IS IN THIS CLASS?
ANOTHER ONE OF THOSE QUESTIONS ...
DON'T THINK!!
IF YOU HAVE TROUBLE ANSWERING, YOU'LL GET BLAMMED!
JUST ANSWER RIGHT AWAY WITHOUT THINKING!!
NO!!

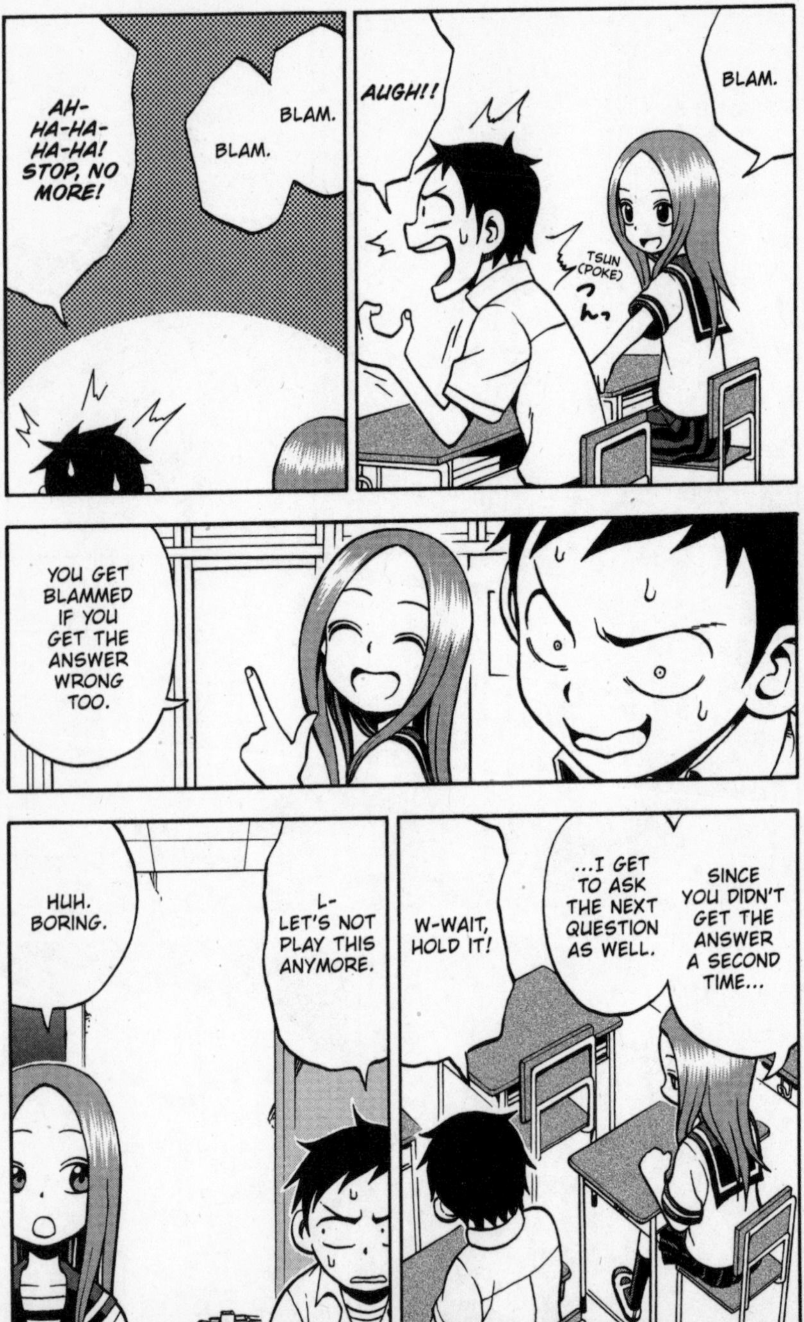
BLAM.
AUGH!!
TSUN (POKE)
BLAM.
BLAM.
AH-HA-HA-HA! STOP, NO MORE!
YOU GET BLAMMED IF YOU GET THE ANSWER WRONG TOO.
SINCE YOU DIDN'T GET THE ANSWER A SECOND TIME...
...I GET TO ASK THE NEXT QUESTION AS WELL.
W-WAIT, HOLD IT!
L-LET'S NOT PLAY THIS ANYMORE.
HUH. BORING.

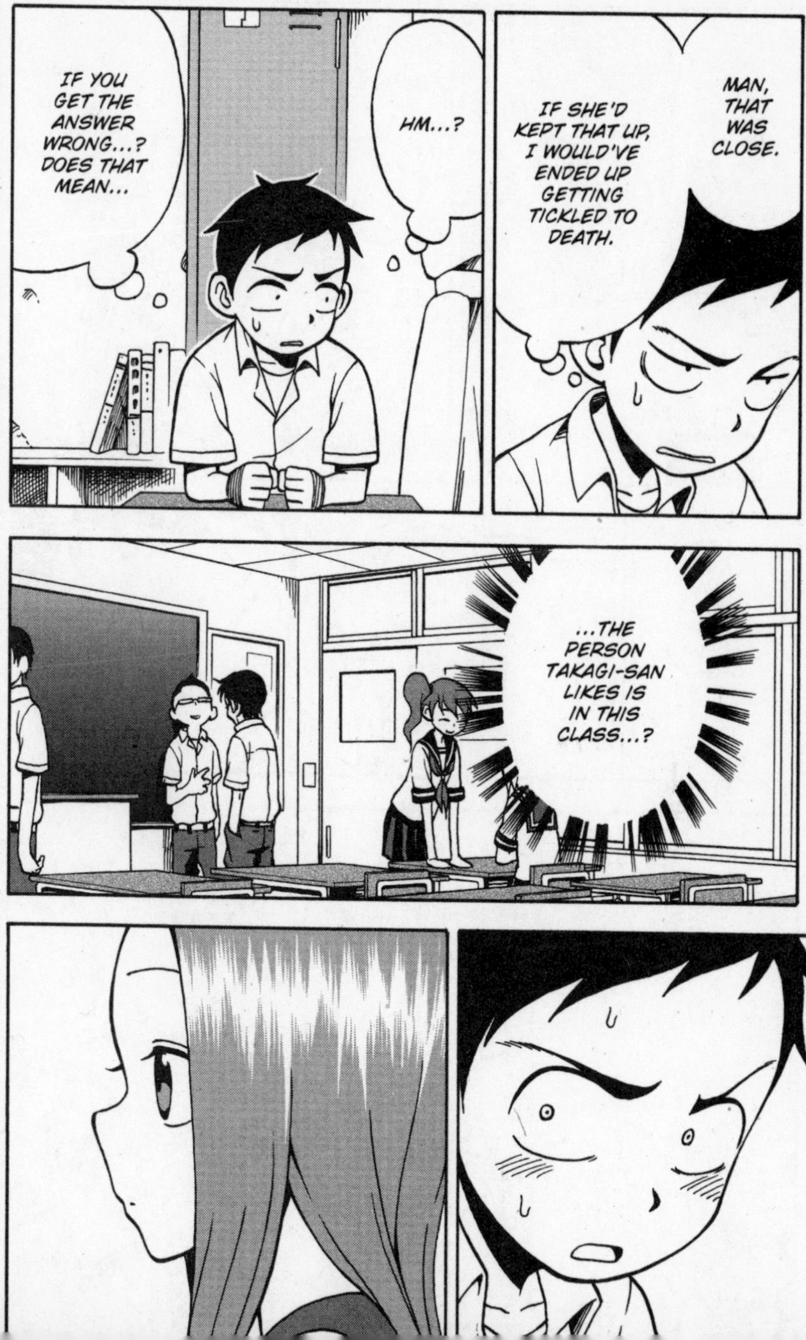
MAN, THAT WAS CLOSE.
IF SHE'D KEPT THAT UP, I WOULD'VE ENDED UP GETTING TICKLED TO DEATH.
HM...?
IF YOU GET THE ANSWER WRONG...? DOES THAT MEAN...
...THE PERSON TAKAGI-SAN LIKES IS IN THIS CLASS...?

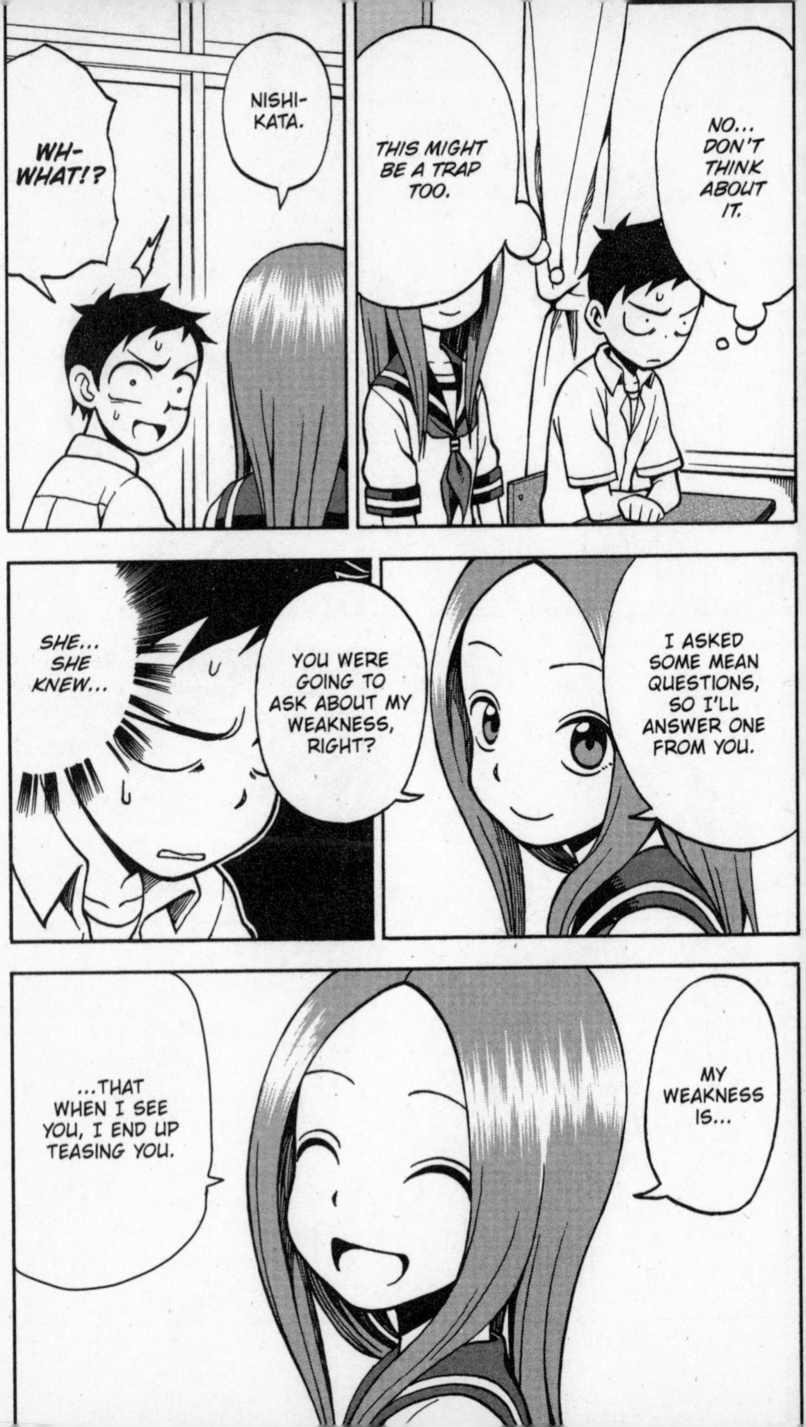
NO... DON'T THINK ABOUT IT.
THIS MIGHT BE A TRAP TOO.
NISHI-KATA.
WH-WHAT!?
I ASKED SOME MEAN QUESTIONS, SO I'LL ANSWER ONE FROM YOU.
YOU WERE GOING TO ASK ABOUT MY WEAKNESS, RIGHT?
SHE... SHE KNEW...
MY WEAKNESS IS...
...THAT WHEN I SEE YOU, I END UP TEASING YOU.

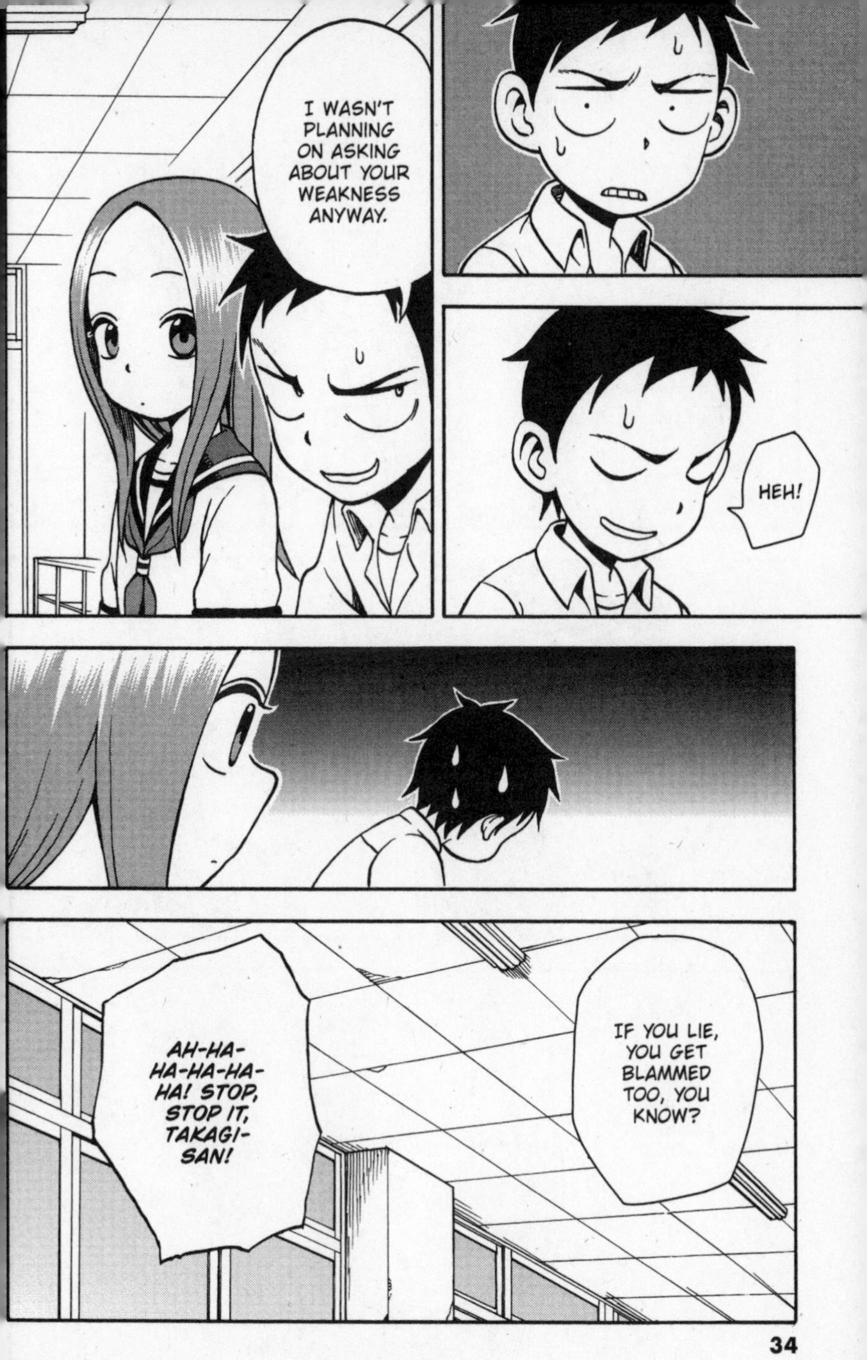
HEH!
I WASN'T PLANNING ON ASKING ABOUT YOUR WEAKNESS ANYWAY.
IF YOU LIE, YOU GET BLAMMED TOO, YOU KNOW?
AH-HA-HA-HA-HA-HA! STOP, STOP IT, TAKAGI-SAN!

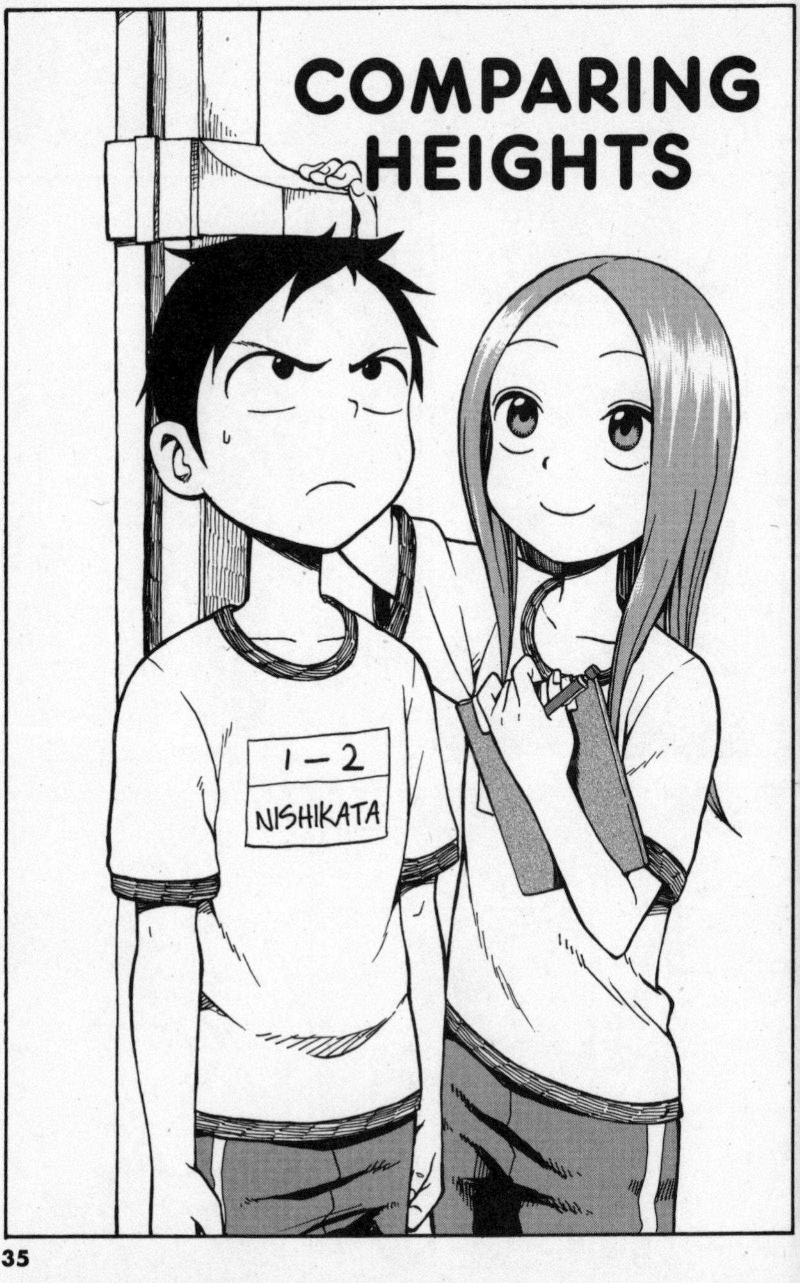
COMPARING HEIGHTS
1-2
NISHIKATA

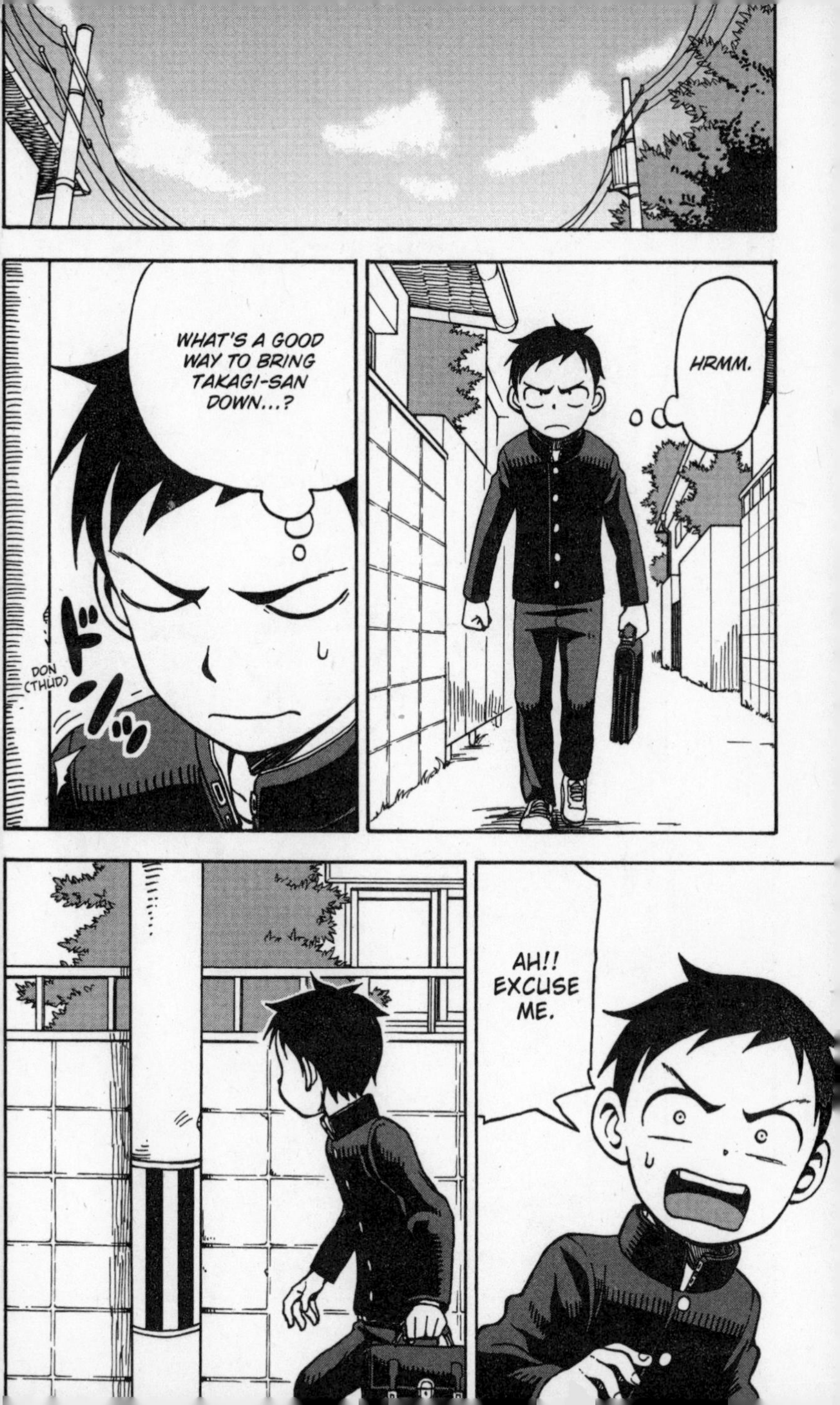
HRMM.
WHAT'S A GOOD WAY TO BRING TAKAGI-SAN DOWN...?
DON (THUD)
AH!! EXCUSE ME.

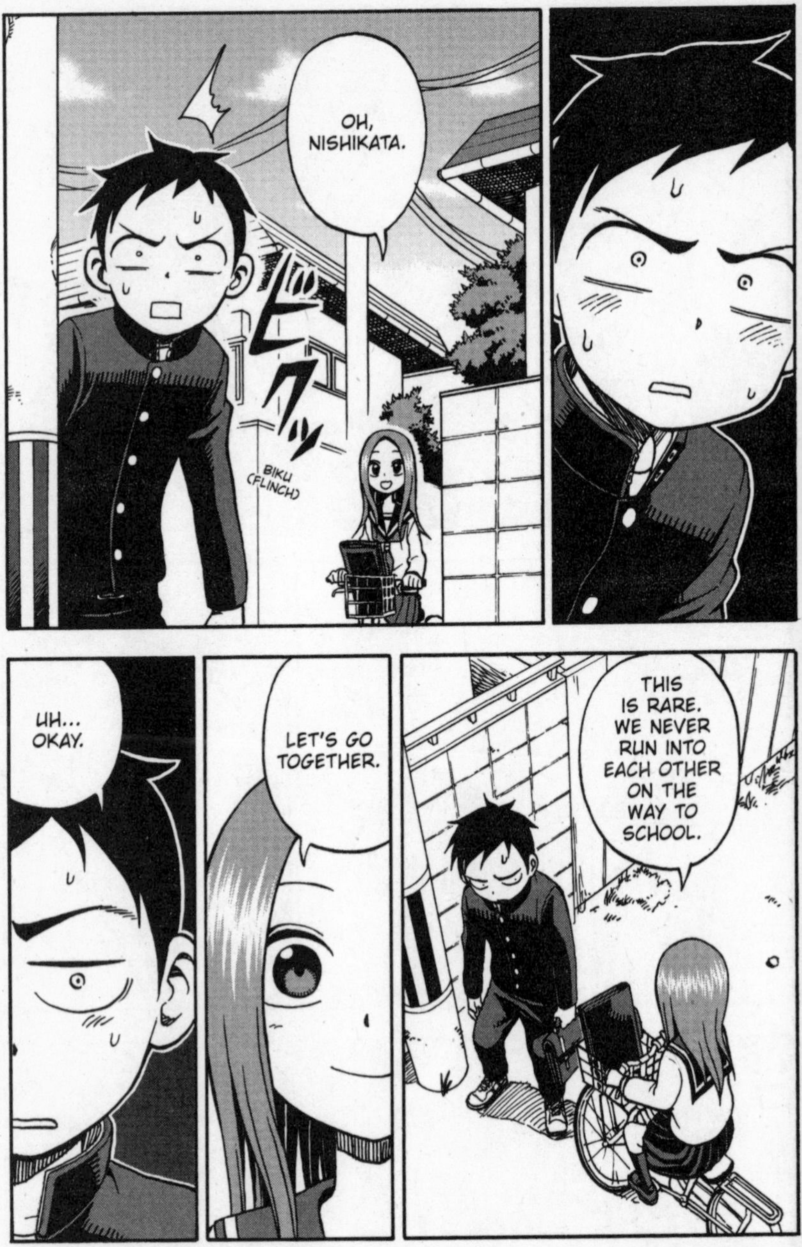
OH, NISHIKATA.
BIKU (FLINCH)
THIS IS RARE. WE NEVER RUN INTO EACH OTHER ON THE WAY TO SCHOOL.
LET'S GO TOGETHER.
UH... OKAY.

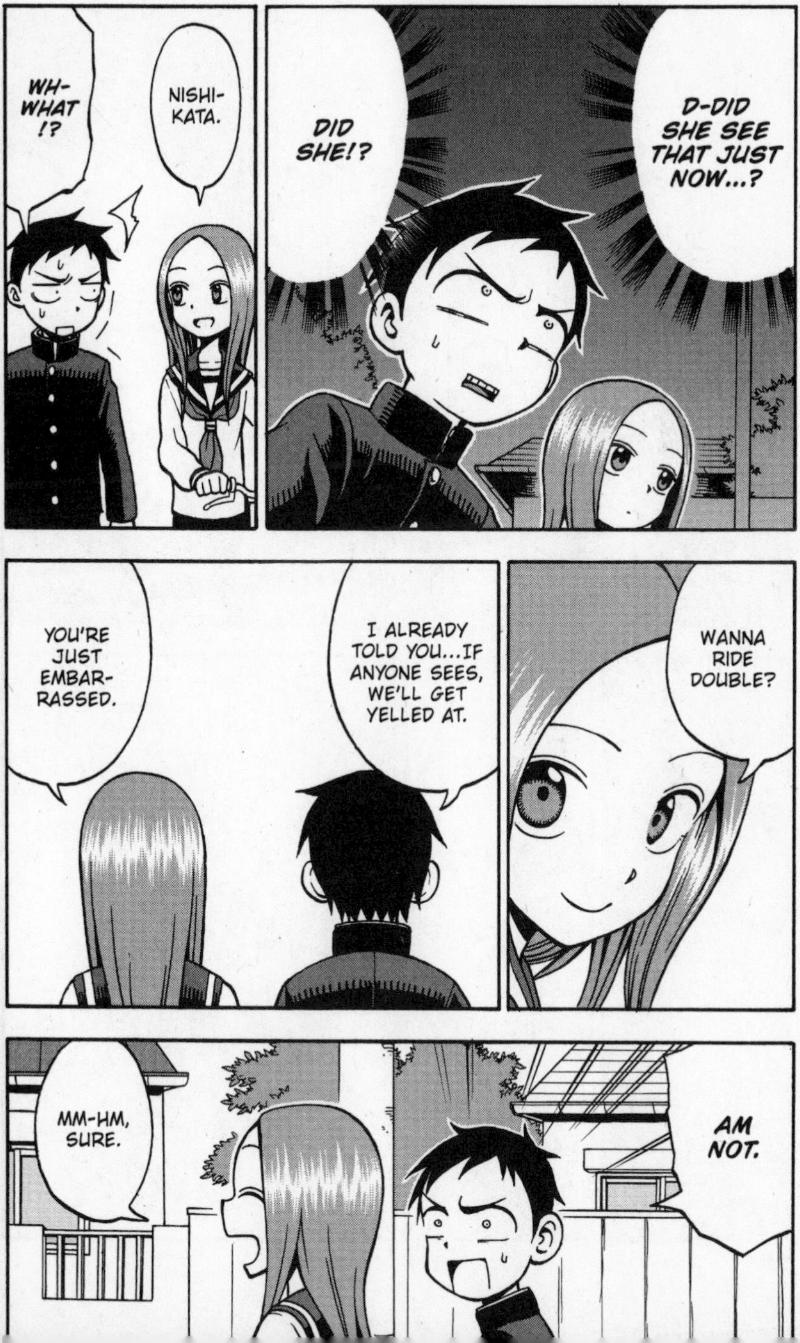
D-DID SHE SEE THAT JUST NOW...?
DID SHE!?
NISHI-KATA.
WH-WHAT!?
WANNA RIDE DOUBLE?
I ALREADY TOLD YOU...IF ANYONE SEES, WE'LL GET YELLED AT.
YOU'RE JUST EMBARRASSED.
AM NOT.
MM-HM, SURE.

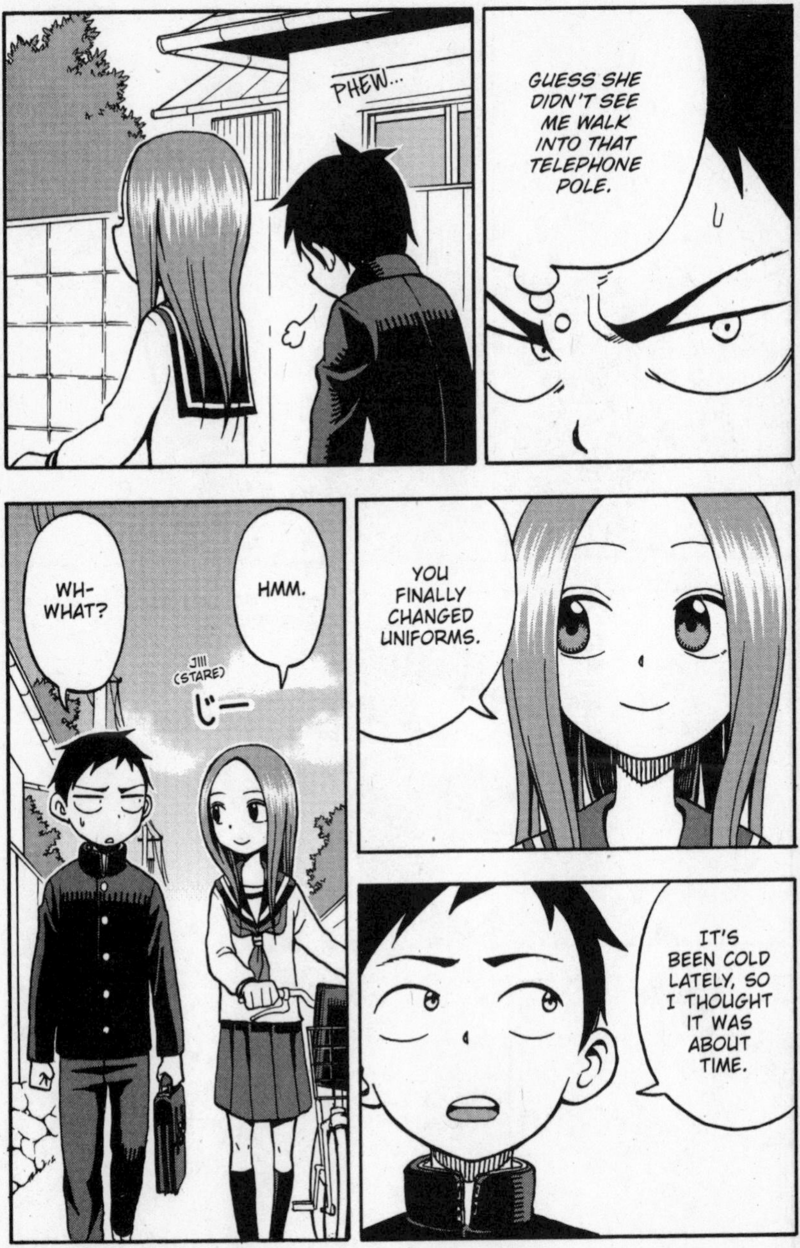
GUESS SHE DIDN'T SEE ME WALK INTO THAT TELEPHONE POLE.
PHEW...
YOU FINALLY CHANGED UNIFORMS.
IT'S BEEN COLD LATELY, SO I THOUGHT IT WAS ABOUT TIME.
HMM.
JIII (STARE)
じー
WH-WHAT?

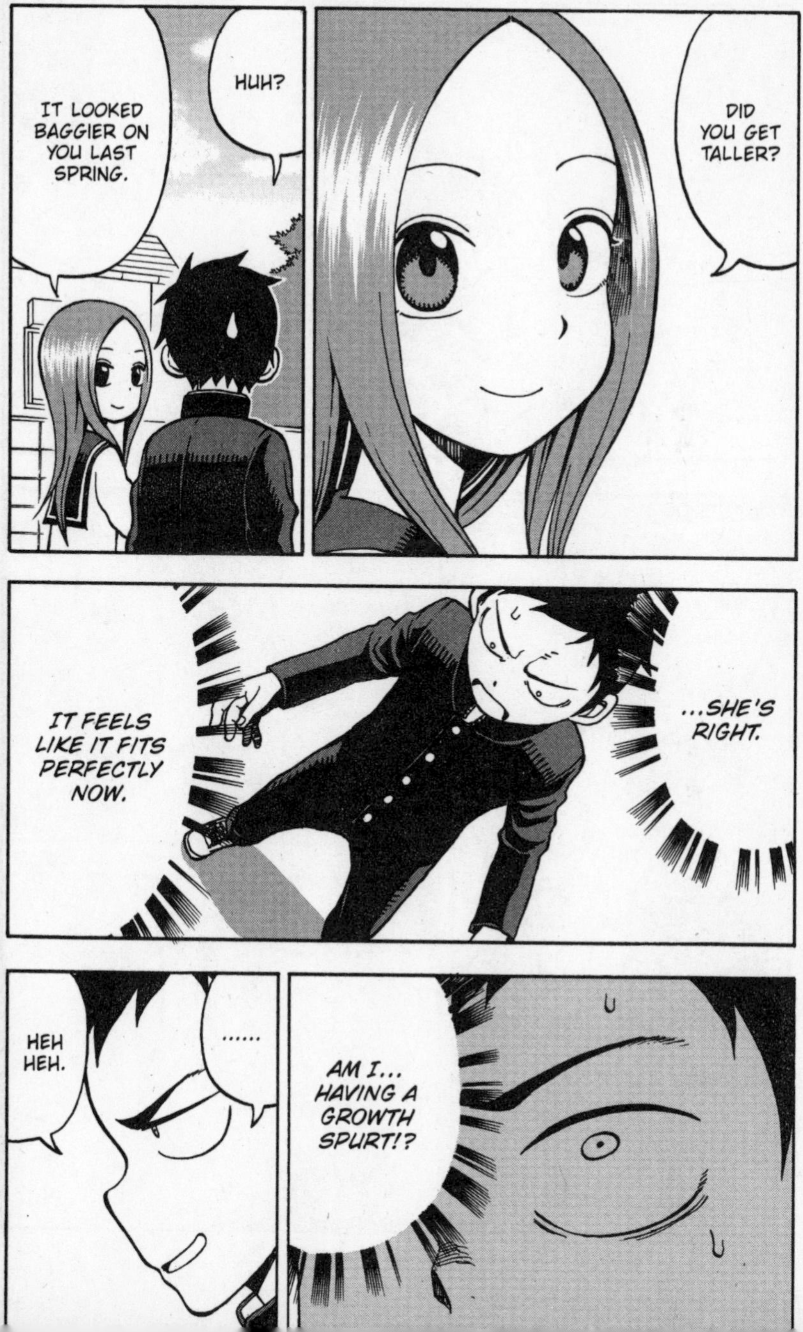
DID YOU GET TALLER?
HUH?
IT LOOKED BAGGIER ON YOU LAST SPRING.
...SHE'S RIGHT.
IT FEELS LIKE IT FITS PERFECTLY NOW.
AM I... HAVING A GROWTH SPURT!?
......
HEH HEH.

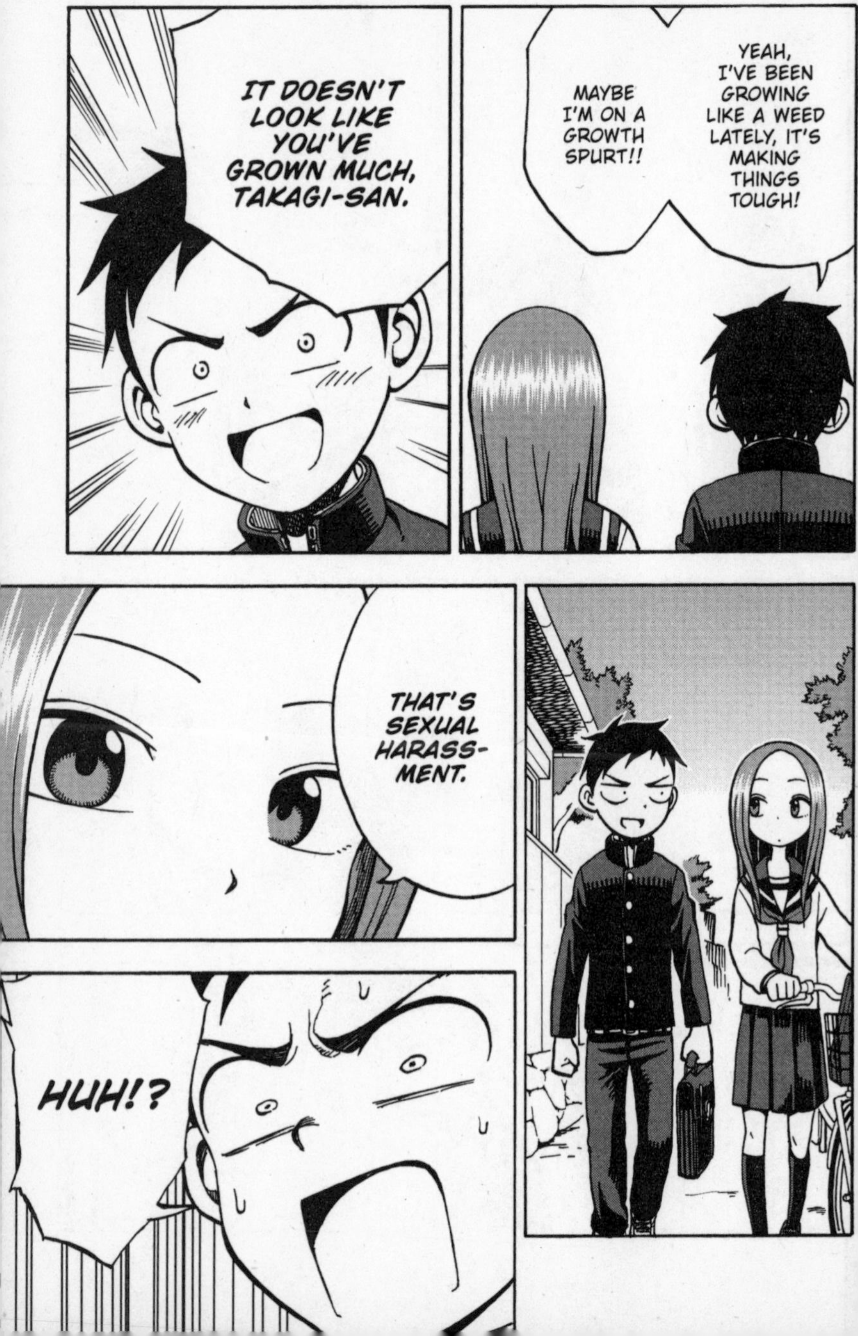
YEAH, I'VE BEEN GROWING LIKE A WEED LATELY, IT'S MAKING THINGS TOUGH!
MAYBE I'M ON A GROWTH SPURT!!
IT DOESN'T LOOK LIKE YOU'VE GROWN MUCH, TAKAGI-SAN.
THAT'S SEXUAL HARASS-MENT.
HUH!?

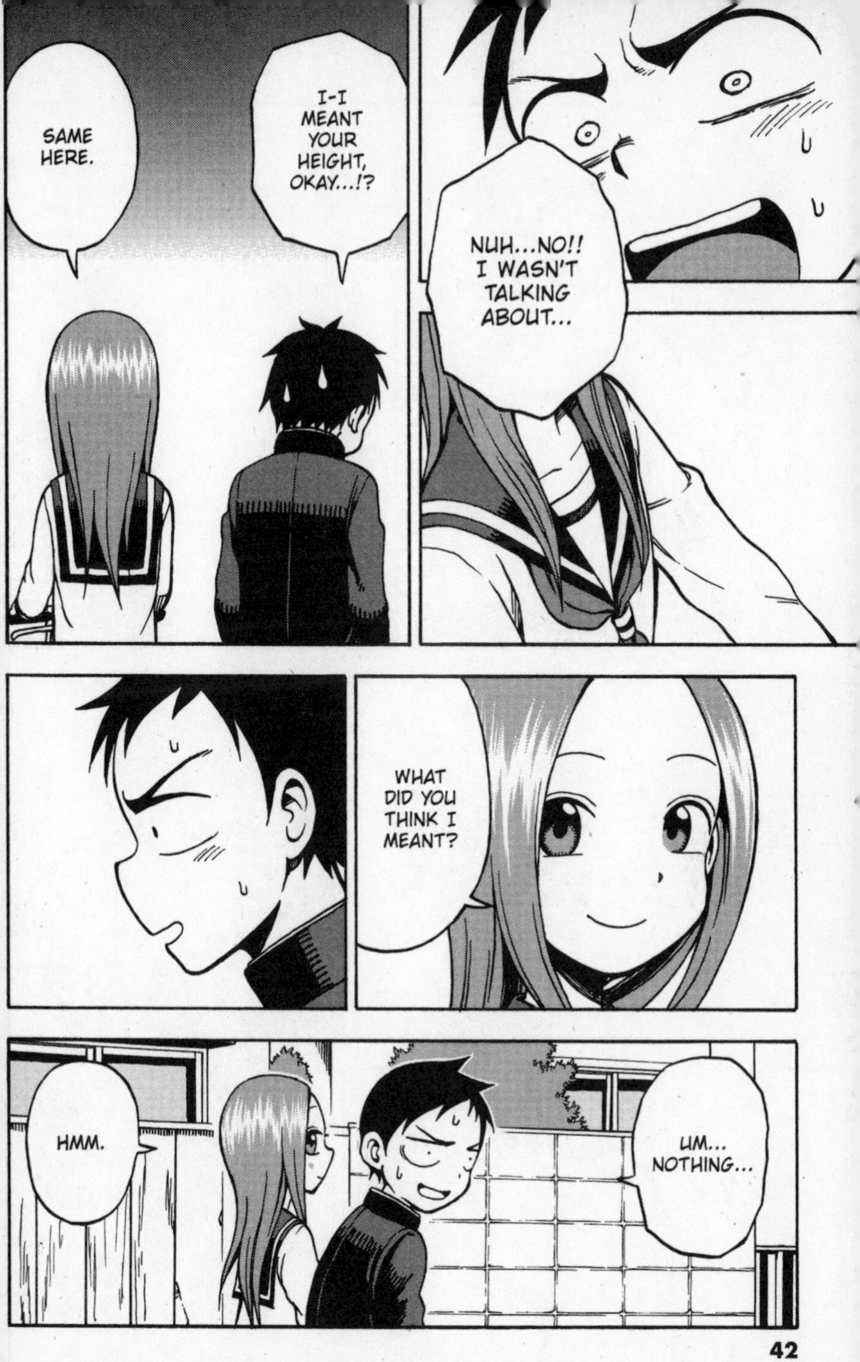
NUH...NO!! I WASN'T TALKING ABOUT...
I-I MEANT YOUR HEIGHT, OKAY...!?
SAME HERE.
WHAT DID YOU THINK I MEANT?
UM... NOTHING...
HMM.

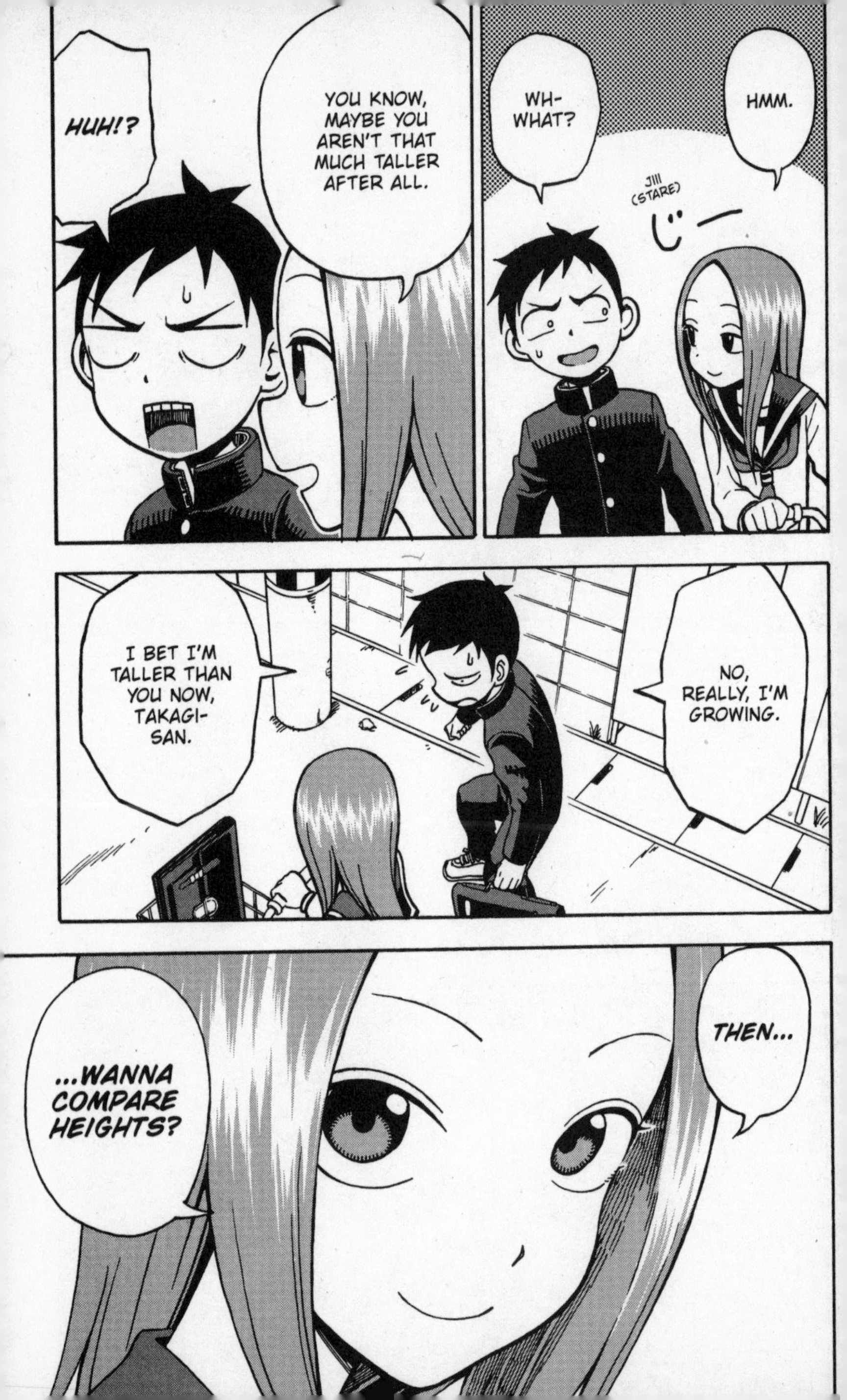
HMM.
JIII (STARE)
じー
WH-WHAT?
YOU KNOW, MAYBE YOU AREN'T THAT MUCH TALLER AFTER ALL.
HUH!?
NO, REALLY, I'M GROWING.
I BET I'M TALLER THAN YOU NOW, TAKAGI-SAN.
THEN...
...WANNA COMPARE HEIGHTS?

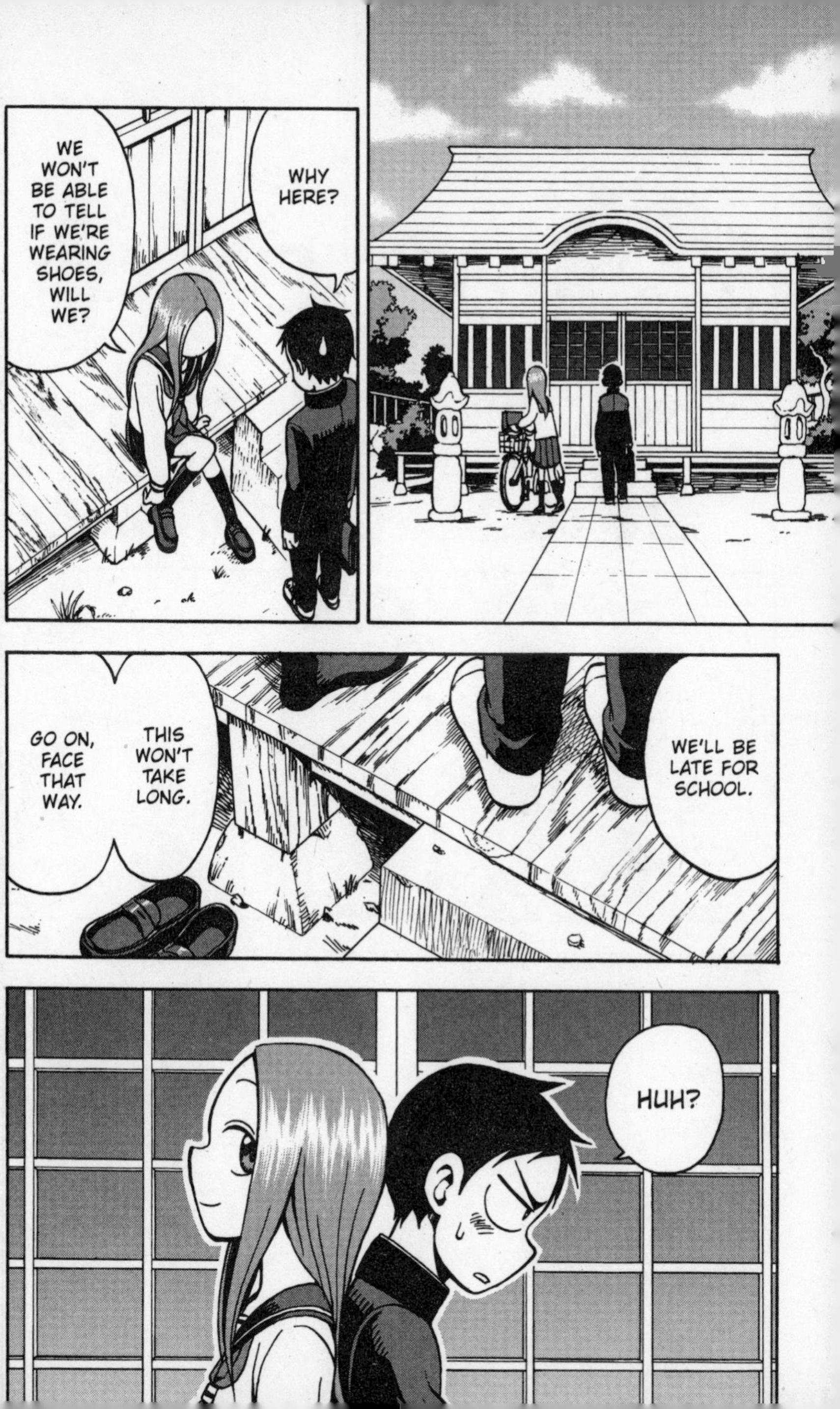
WHY HERE?
WE WON'T BE ABLE TO TELL IF WE'RE WEARING SHOES, WILL WE?
WE'LL BE LATE FOR SCHOOL.
THIS WON'T TAKE LONG.
GO ON, FACE THAT WAY.
HUH?

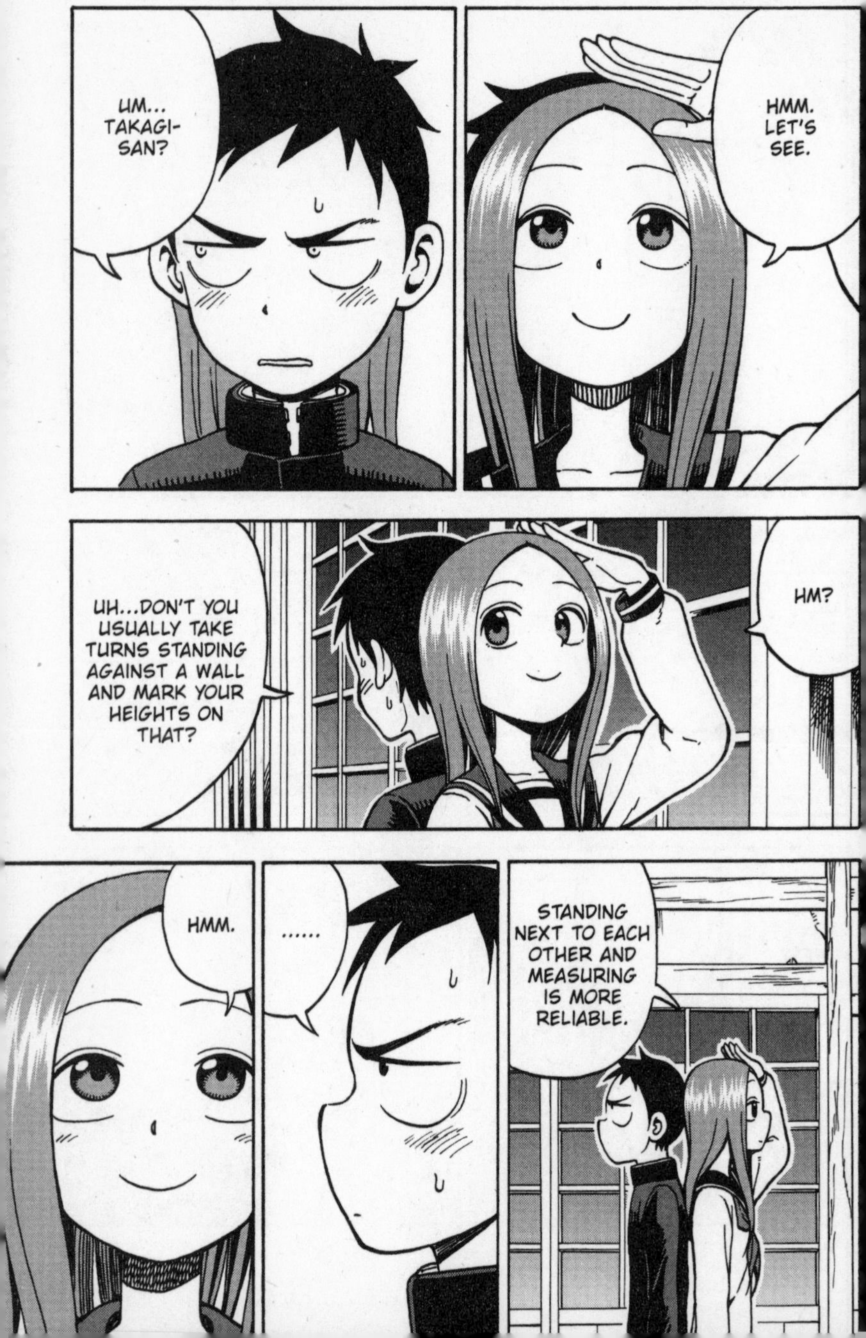
HMM. LET'S SEE.
UM... TAKAGI-SAN?
HM?
UH...DON'T YOU USUALLY TAKE TURNS STANDING AGAINST A WALL AND MARK YOUR HEIGHTS ON THAT?
STANDING NEXT TO EACH OTHER AND MEASURING IS MORE RELIABLE.
......
HMM.

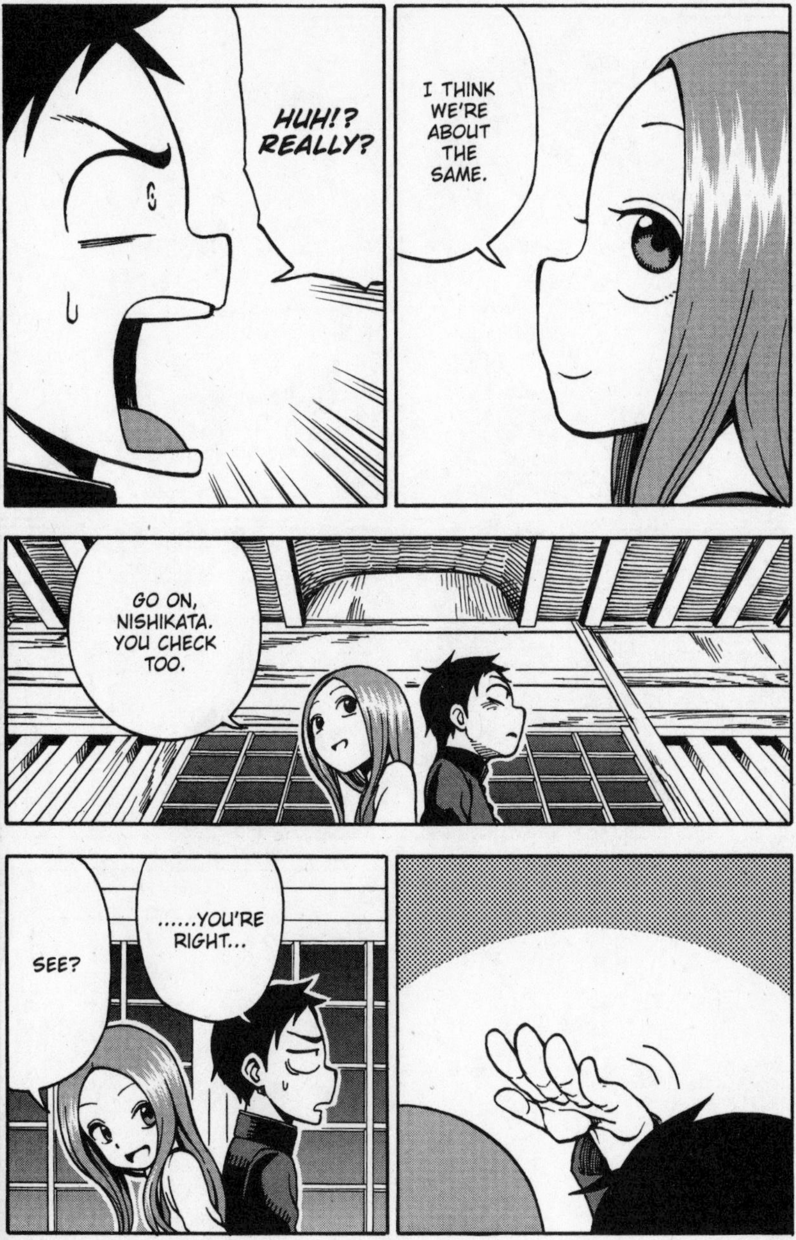
I THINK WE'RE ABOUT THE SAME.
HUH!? REALLY?
GO ON, NISHIKATA. YOU CHECK TOO.
......YOU'RE RIGHT...
SEE?

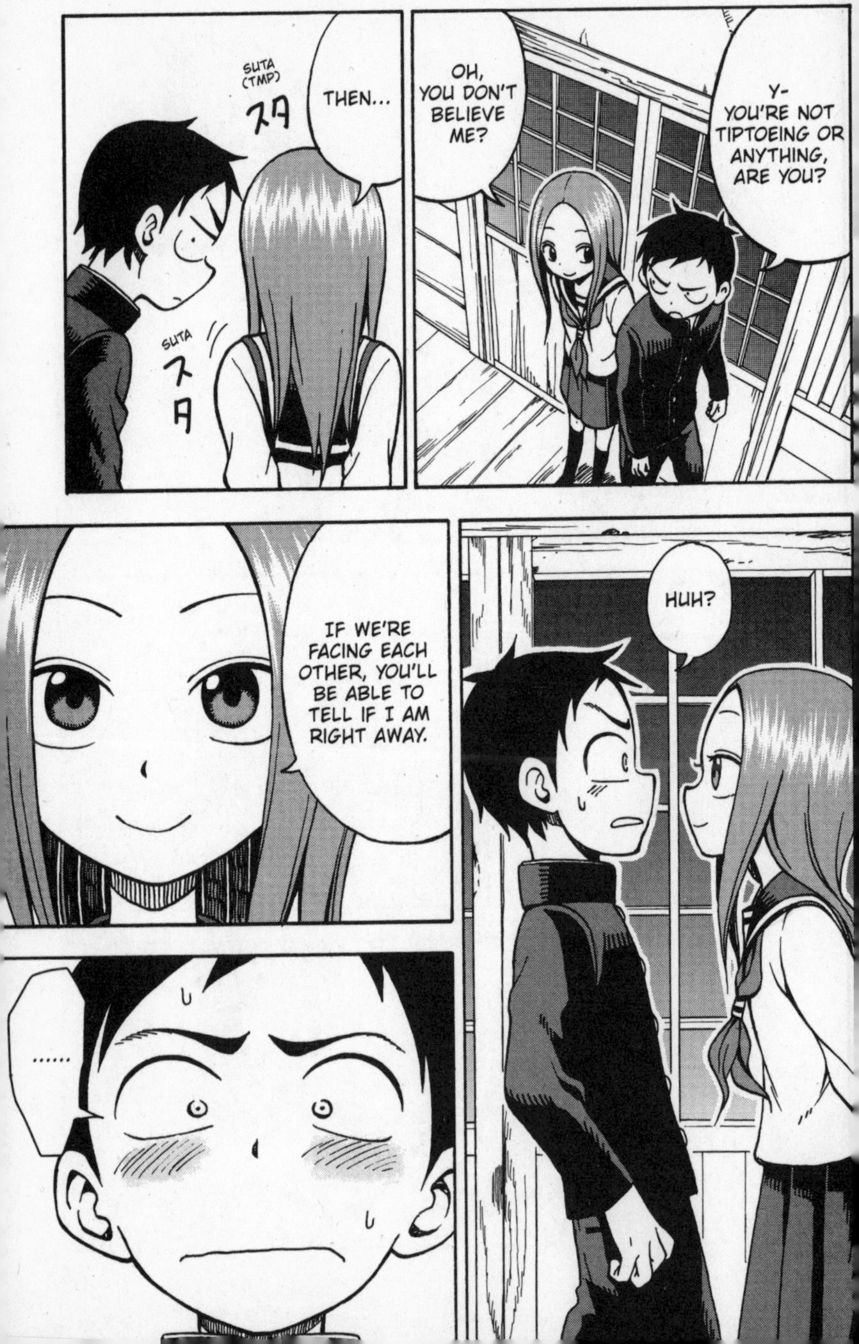
Y- YOU'RE NOT TIPTOEING OR ANYTHING, ARE YOU?
OH, YOU DON'T BELIEVE ME?
THEN...
SUTA (TMP)
スタ
SUTA
スタ
HUH?
IF WE'RE FACING EACH OTHER, YOU'LL BE ABLE TO TELL IF I AM RIGHT AWAY.
......

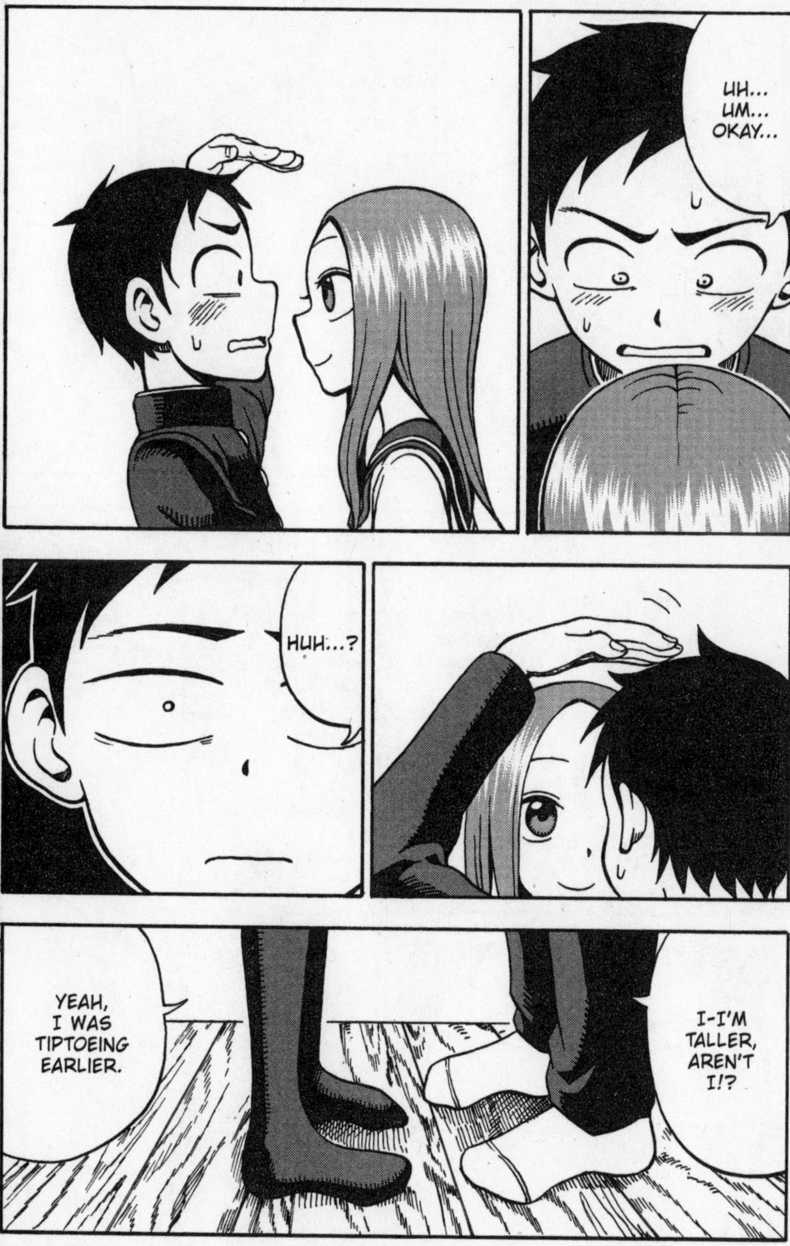
UH... UM... OKAY...
HUH...?
I-I'M TALLER, AREN'T I!?
YEAH, I WAS TIPTOEING EARLIER.

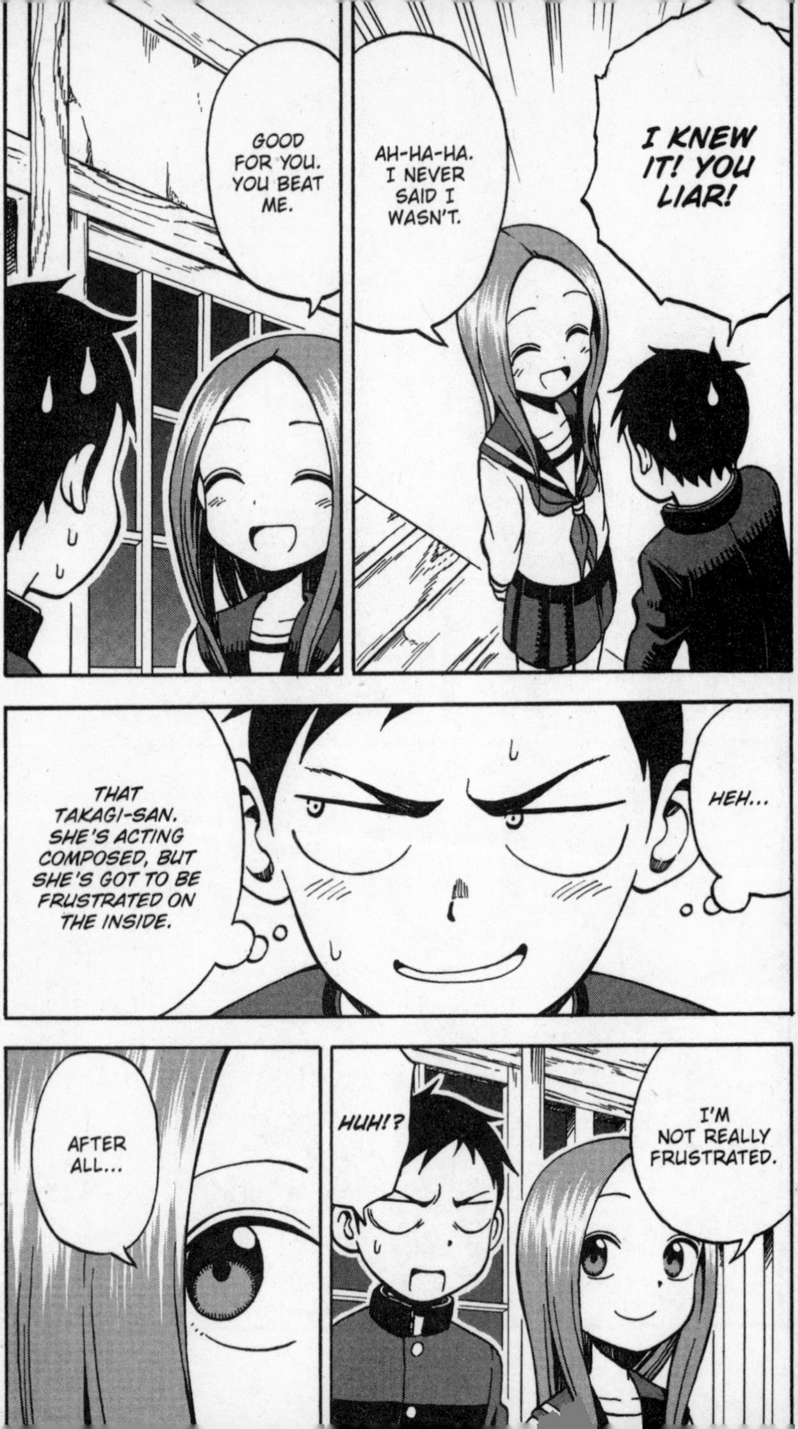

I KNEW IT! YOU LIAR!
AH-HA-HA. I NEVER SAID I WASN'T.
GOOD FOR YOU. YOU BEAT ME.
HEH...
THAT TAKAGI-SAN. SHE'S ACTING COMPOSED, BUT SHE'S GOT TO BE FRUSTRATED ON THE INSIDE.
I'M NOT REALLY FRUSTRATED.
HUH!?
AFTER ALL...

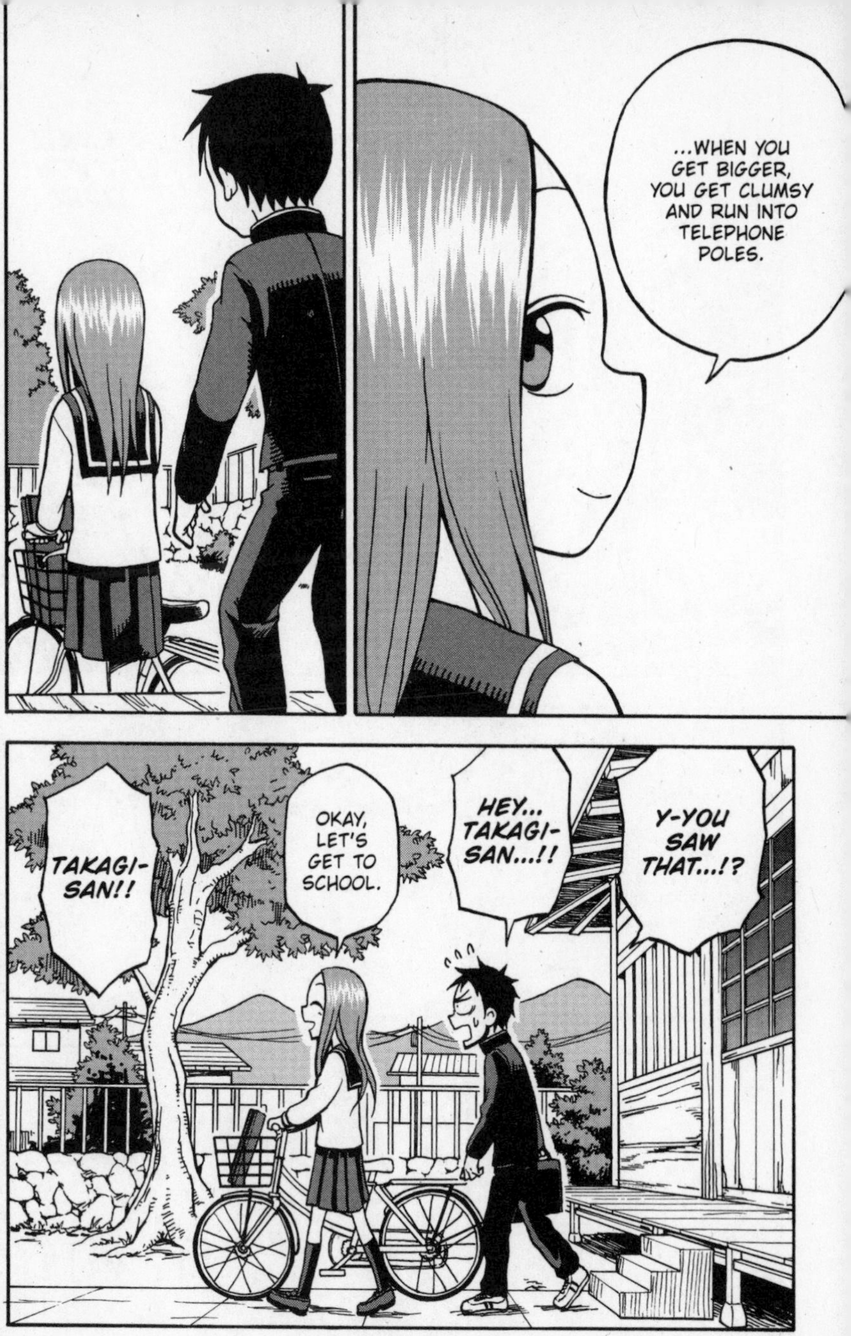
...WHEN YOU GET BIGGER, YOU GET CLUMSY AND RUN INTO TELEPHONE POLES.
Y-YOU SAW THAT...!?
HEY... TAKAGI-SAN...!!
OKAY, LET'S GET TO SCHOOL.
TAKAGI-SAN!!

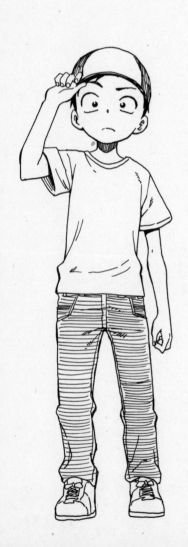

Teasing Master
Takagi-san

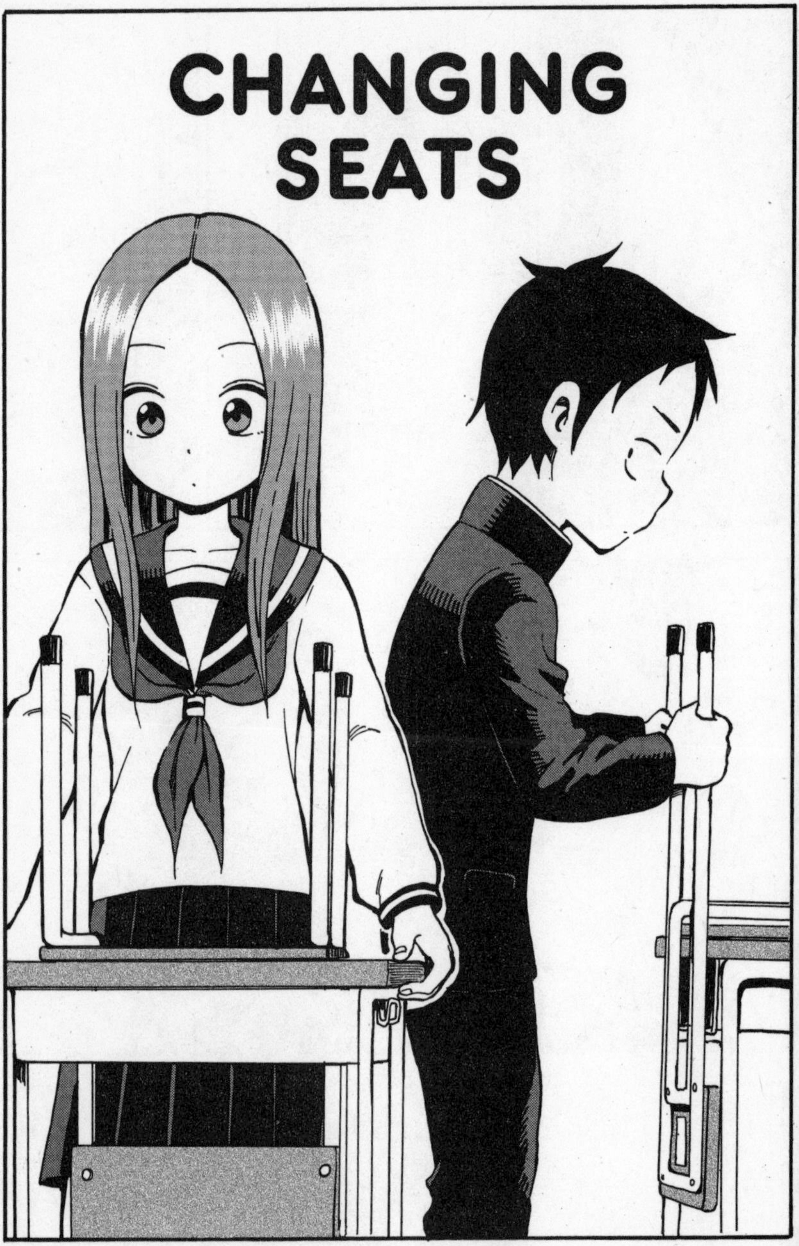
CHANGING
SEATS

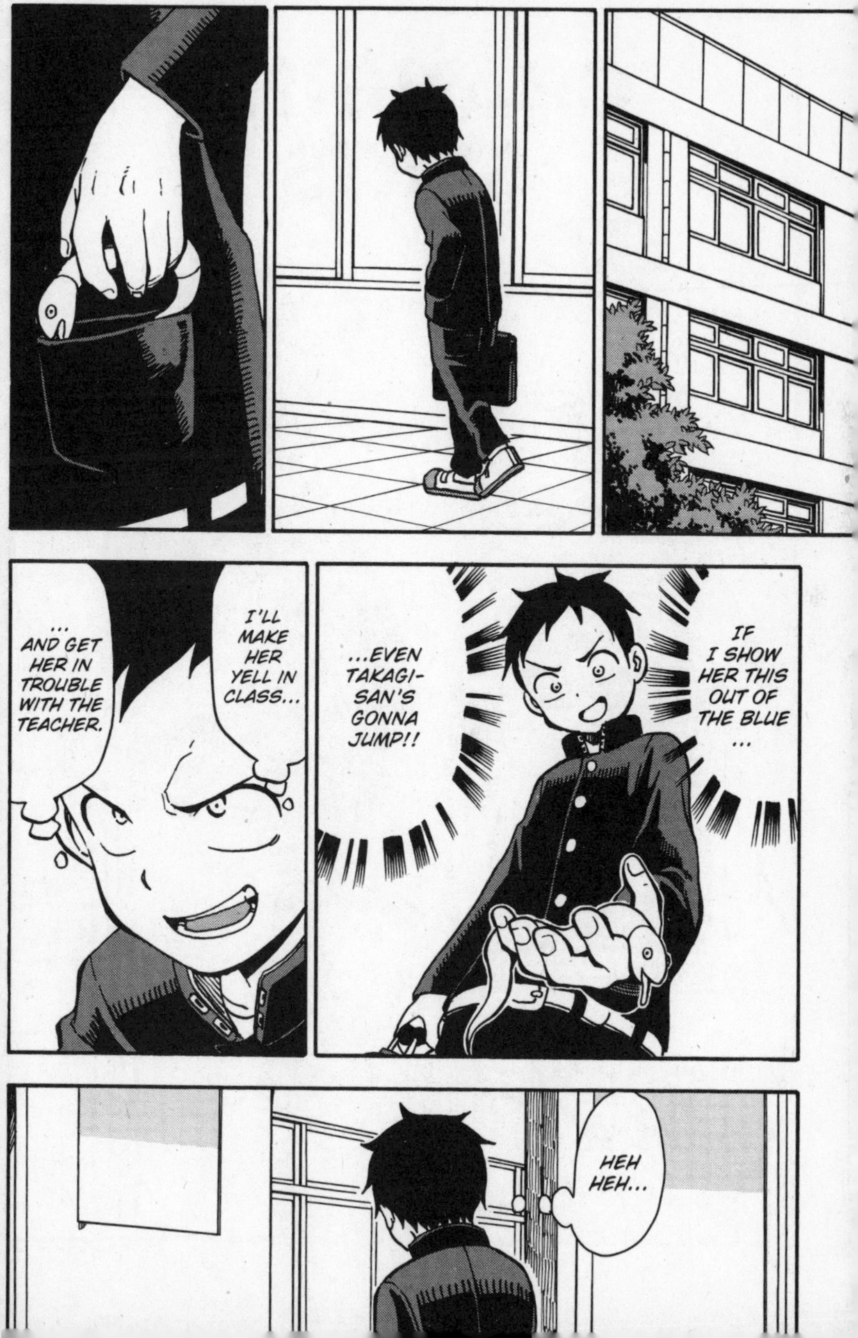
IF I SHOW HER THIS OUT OF THE BLUE...
...EVEN TAKAGI-SAN'S GONNA JUMP!!
I'LL MAKE HER YELL IN CLASS...
...AND GET HER IN TROUBLE WITH THE TEACHER.
HEH HEH...

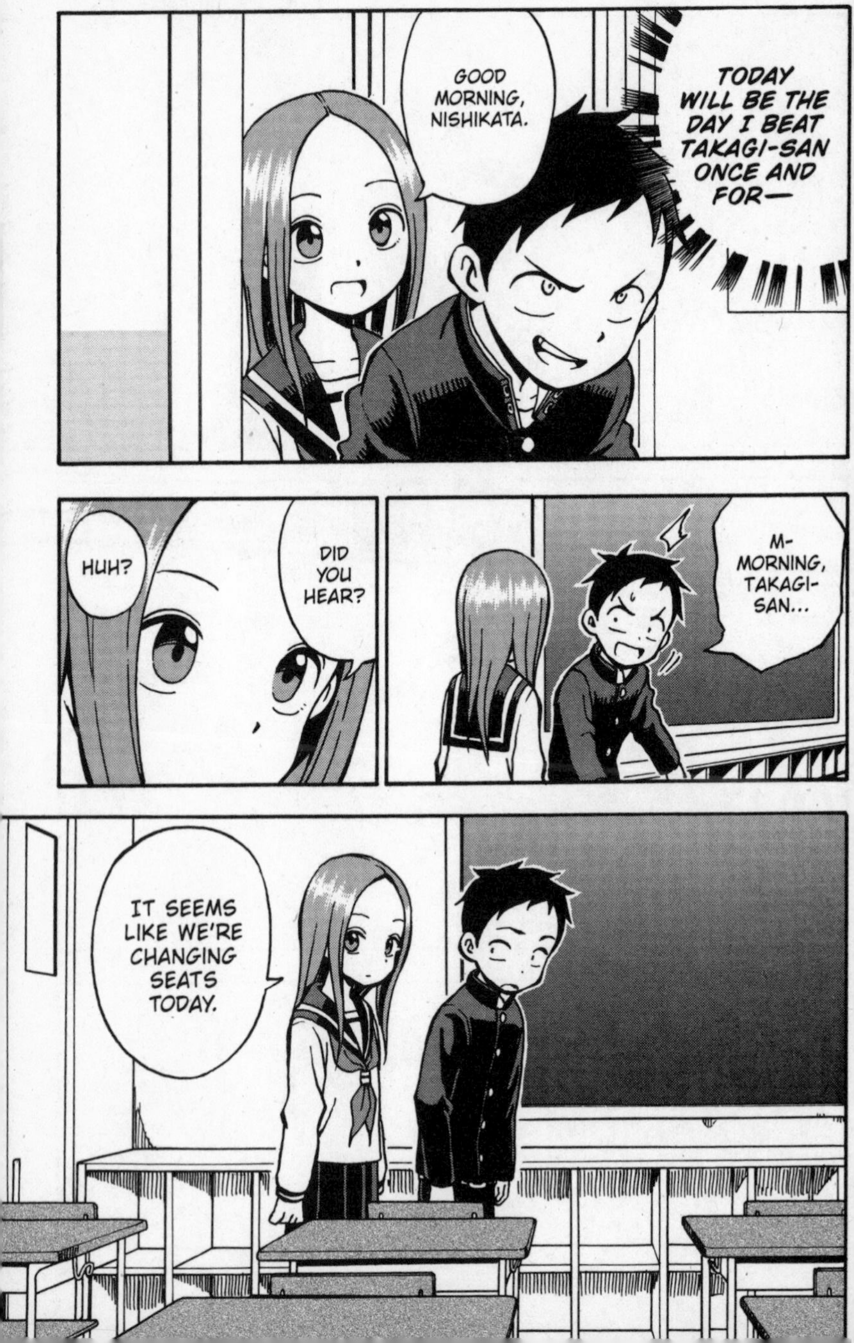
TODAY WILL BE THE DAY I BEAT TAKAGI-SAN ONCE AND FOR—
GOOD MORNING, NISHIKATA.
M-MORNING, TAKAGI-SAN...
DID YOU HEAR?
HUH?
IT SEEMS LIKE WE'RE CHANGING SEATS TODAY.

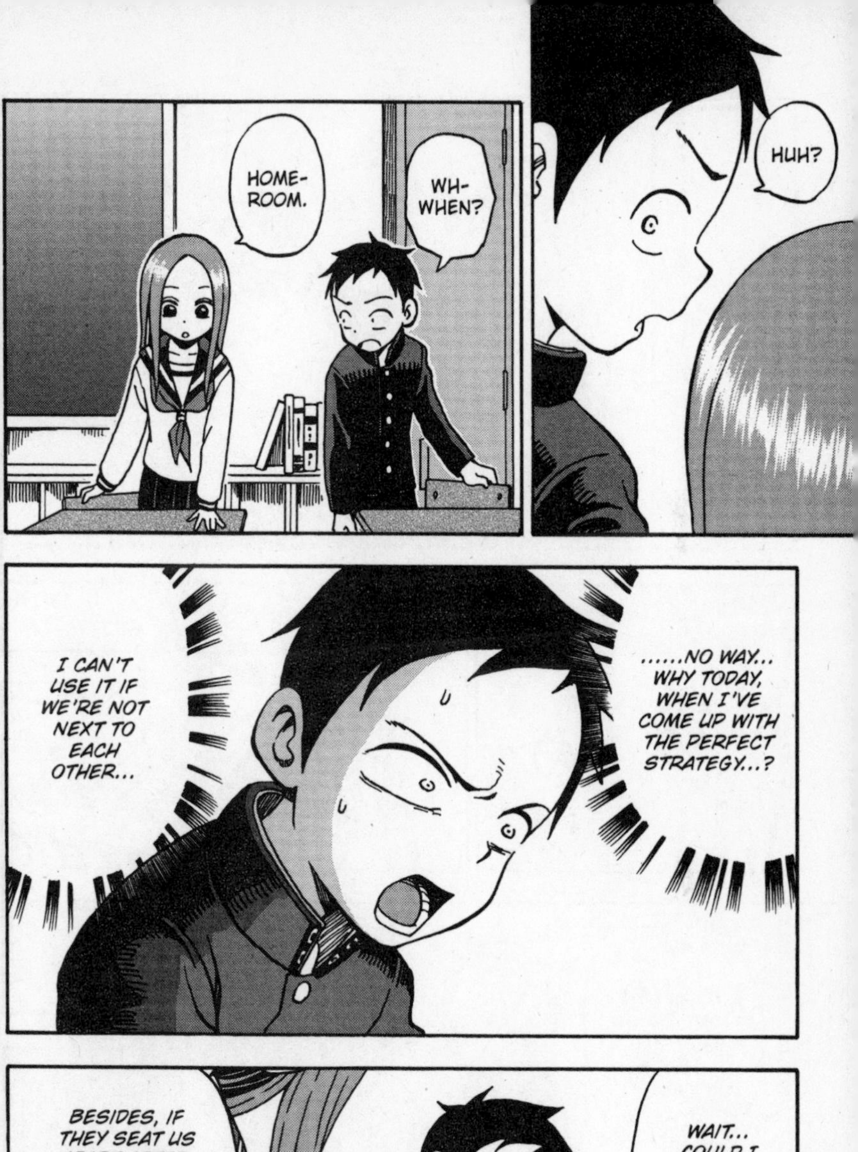

HUH?
WH- WHEN?
HOME- ROOM.
......NO WAY... WHY TODAY, WHEN I'VE COME UP WITH THE PERFECT STRATEGY...?
I CAN'T USE IT IF WE'RE NOT NEXT TO EACH OTHER...
WAIT... COULD I JUST DO IT DURING HOME- ROOM...?
BESIDES, IF THEY SEAT US APART AFTER, I'LL WIN WITHOUT GIVING TAKAGI-SAN A CHANCE TO GET ME BACK, AND SHE'LL GET ALL FRUSTRATED...

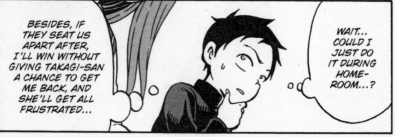

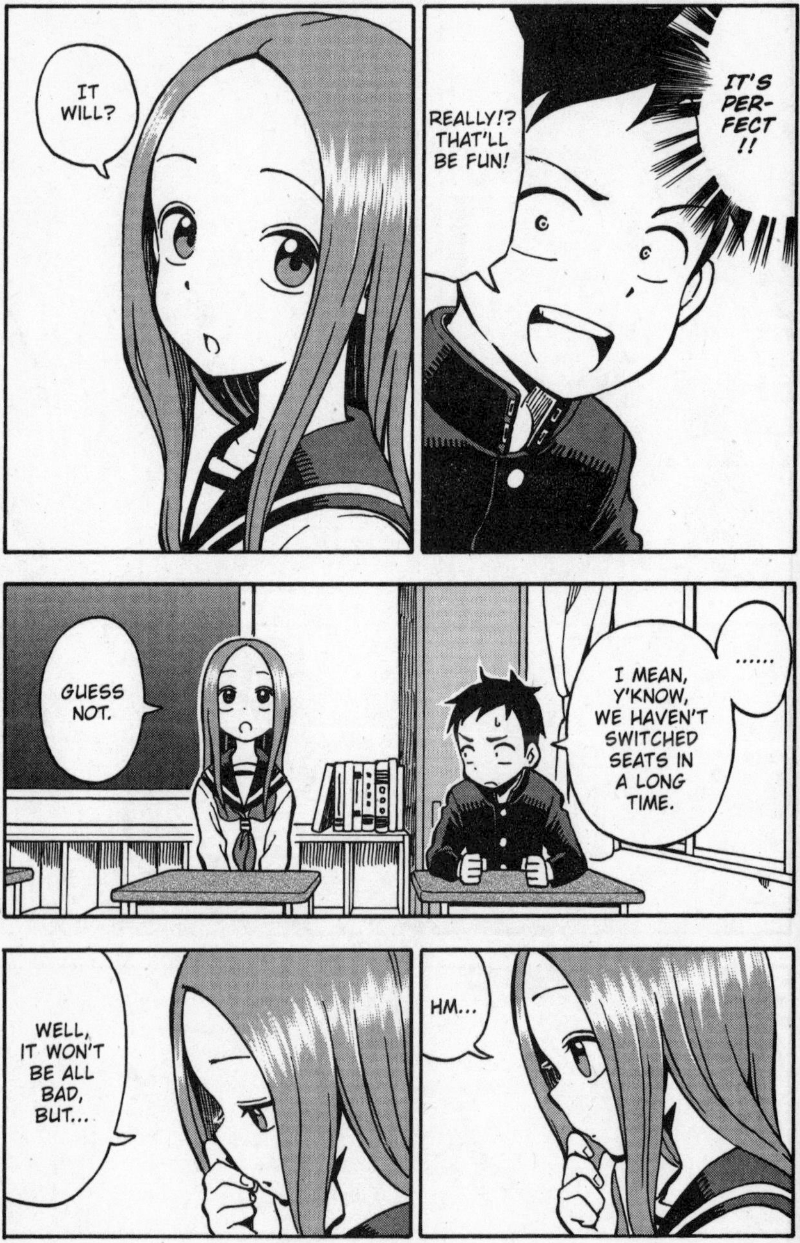
IT'S PER-FECT!!
REALLY!? THAT'LL BE FUN!
IT WILL?
......
I MEAN, Y'KNOW, WE HAVEN'T SWITCHED SEATS IN A LONG TIME.
GUESS NOT.
HM...
WELL, IT WON'T BE ALL BAD, BUT...

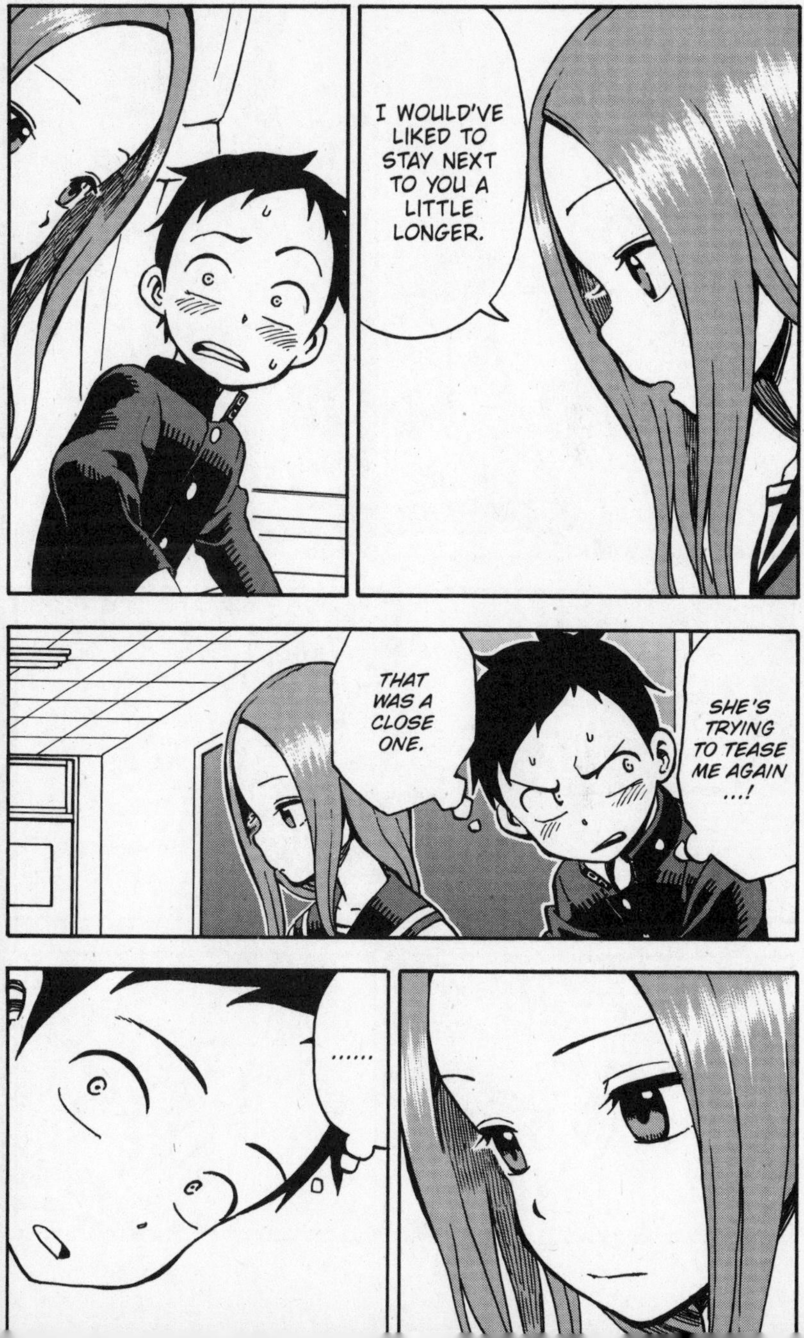
I WOULD'VE LIKED TO STAY NEXT TO YOU A LITTLE LONGER.
SHE'S TRYING TO TEASE ME AGAIN ...!
THAT WAS A CLOSE ONE.
......

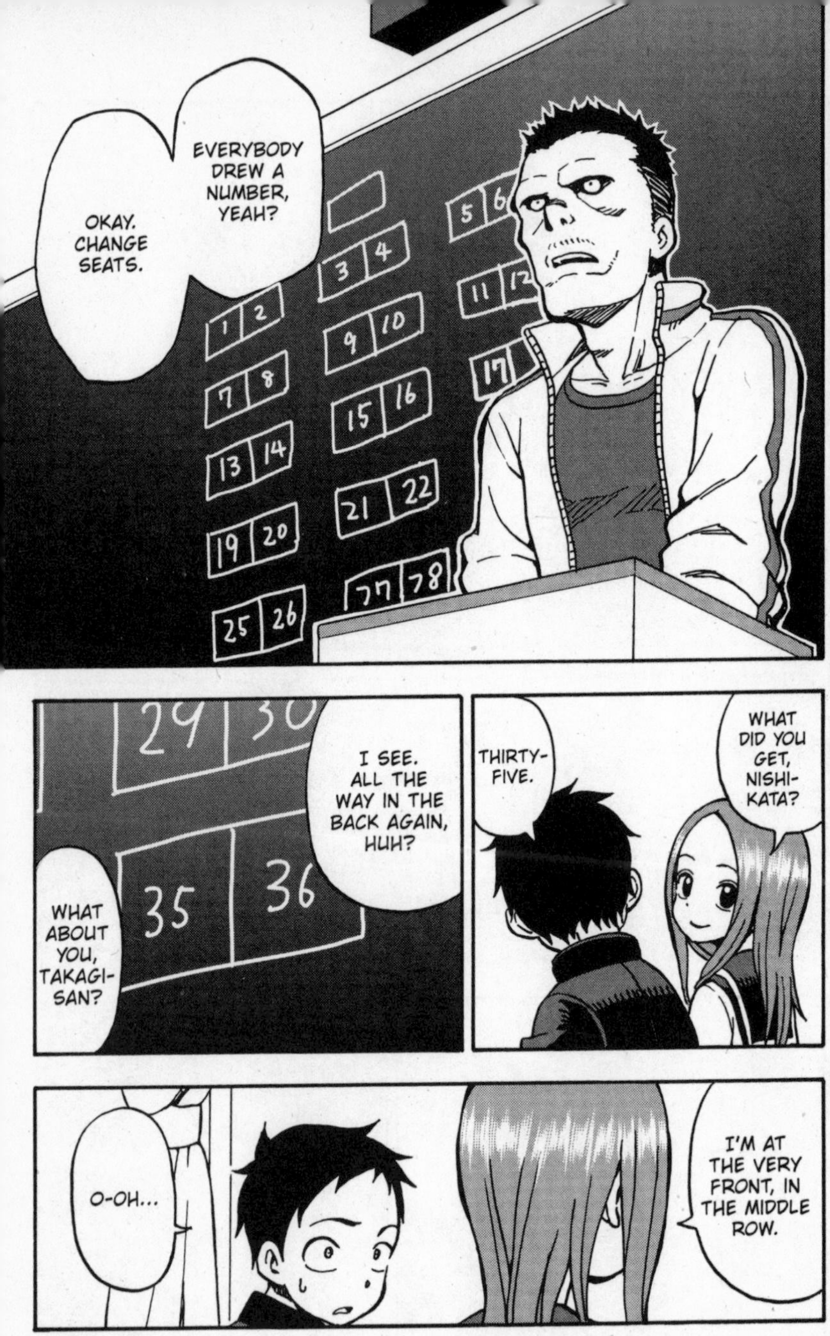
EVERYBODY DREW A NUMBER, YEAH?
OKAY. CHANGE SEATS.
WHAT DID YOU GET, NISHI-KATA?
THIRTY-FIVE.
I SEE. ALL THE WAY IN THE BACK AGAIN, HUH?
WHAT ABOUT YOU, TAKAGI-SAN?
I'M AT THE VERY FRONT, IN THE MIDDLE ROW.
O-OH...

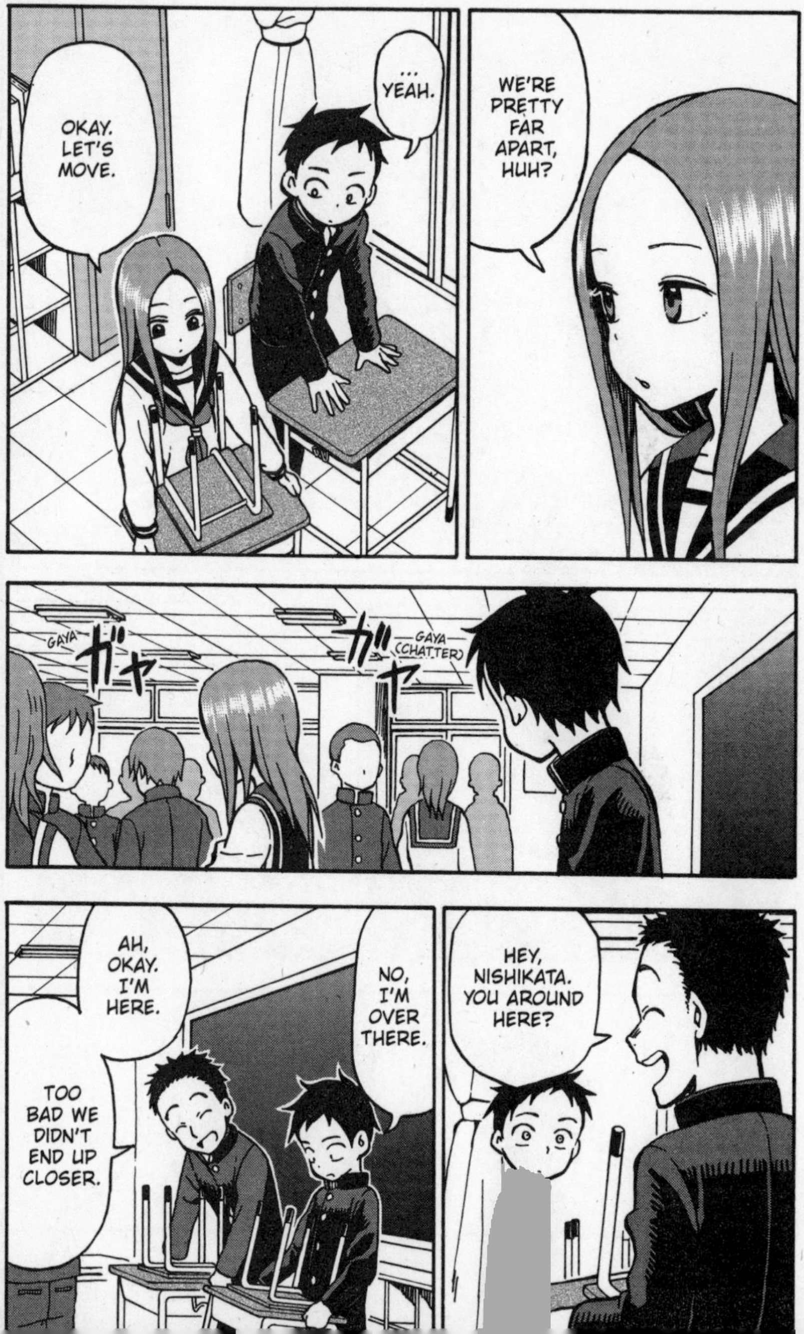
WE'RE PRETTY FAR APART, HUH?
... YEAH.
OKAY. LET'S MOVE.
GAYA (CHATTER)
GAYA
HEY, NISHIKATA. YOU AROUND HERE?
NO, I'M OVER THERE.
AH, OKAY. I'M HERE.
TOO BAD WE DIDN'T END UP CLOSER.

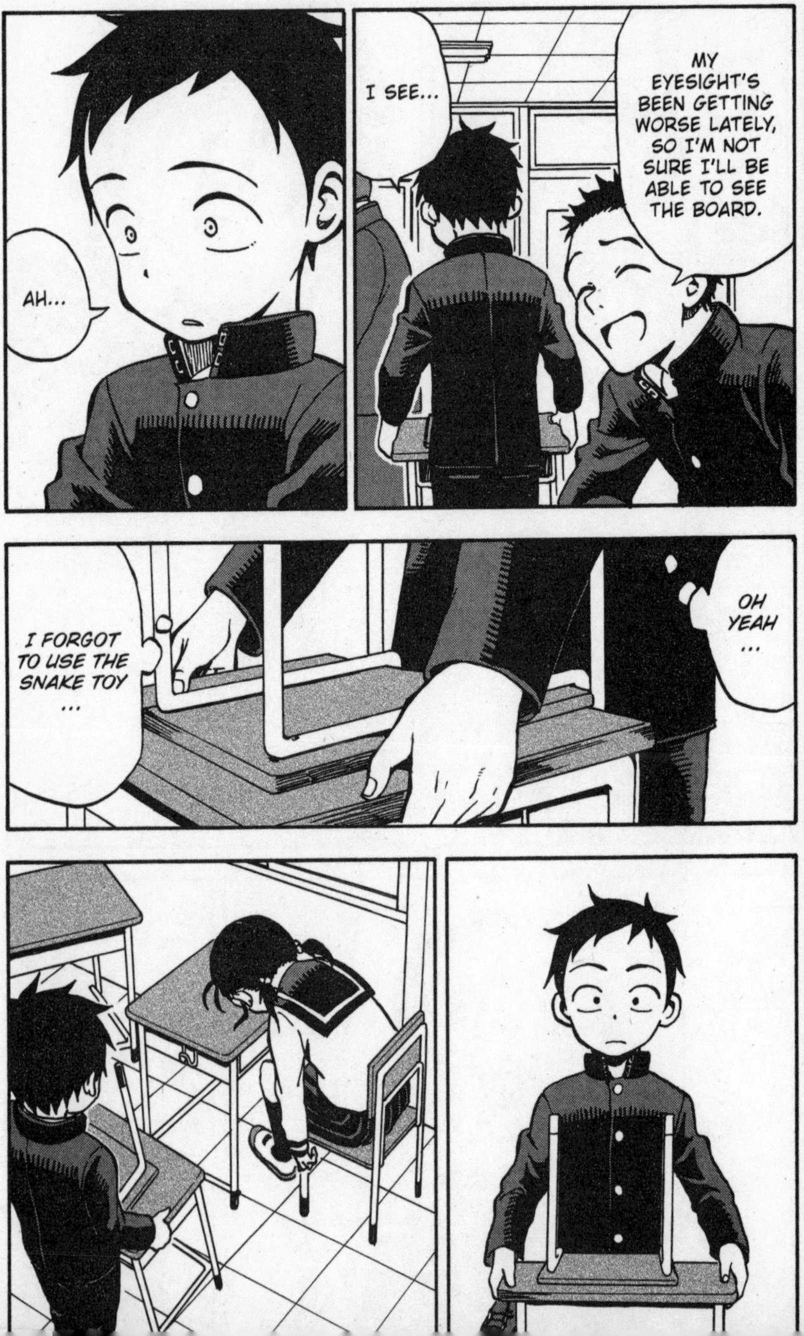
MY EYESIGHT'S BEEN GETTING WORSE LATELY, SO I'M NOT SURE I'LL BE ABLE TO SEE THE BOARD.
I SEE...
AH...
OH YEAH ...
I FORGOT TO USE THE SNAKE TOY ...

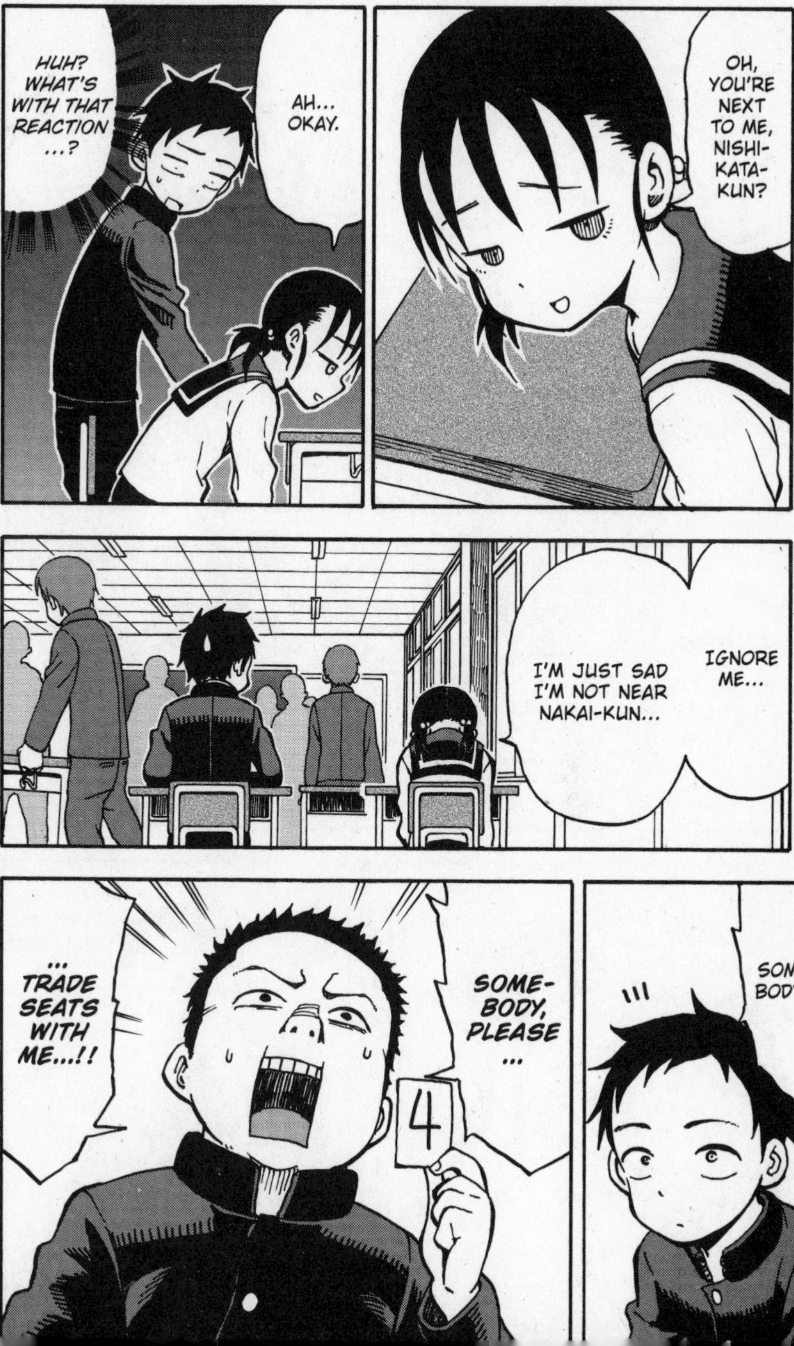
OH, YOU'RE NEXT TO ME, NISHI-KATA-KUN?
AH... OKAY.
HUH? WHAT'S WITH THAT REACTION ...?
IGNORE ME...
I'M JUST SAD I'M NOT NEAR NAKAI-KUN...
SOME-BODY...
SOME-BODY, PLEASE ...
4
... TRADE SEATS WITH ME...!!

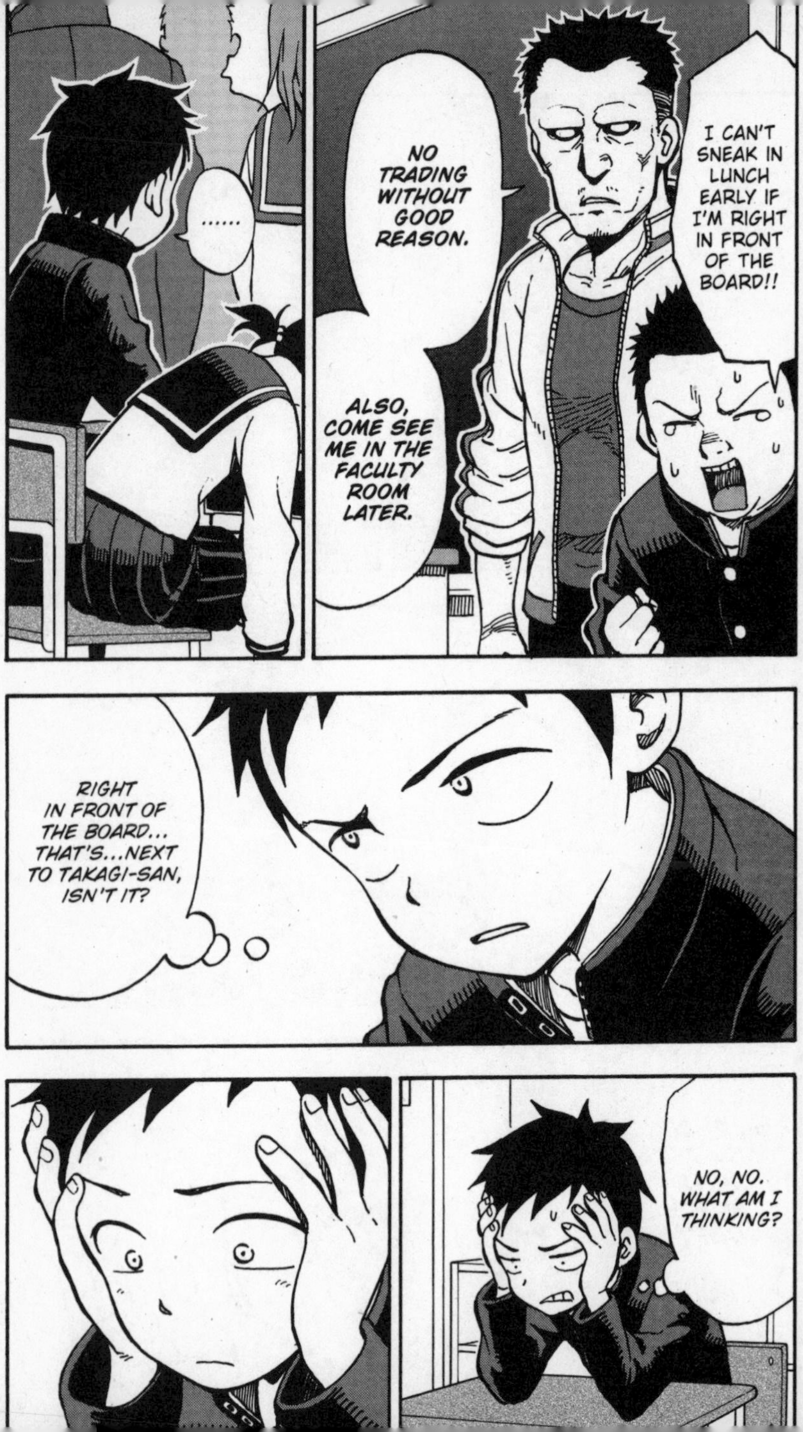
I CAN'T SNEAK IN LUNCH EARLY IF I'M RIGHT IN FRONT OF THE BOARD!!
NO TRADING WITHOUT GOOD REASON.
ALSO, COME SEE ME IN THE FACULTY ROOM LATER.
......
RIGHT IN FRONT OF THE BOARD... THAT'S...NEXT TO TAKAGI-SAN, ISN'T IT?
NO, NO. WHAT AM I THINKING?

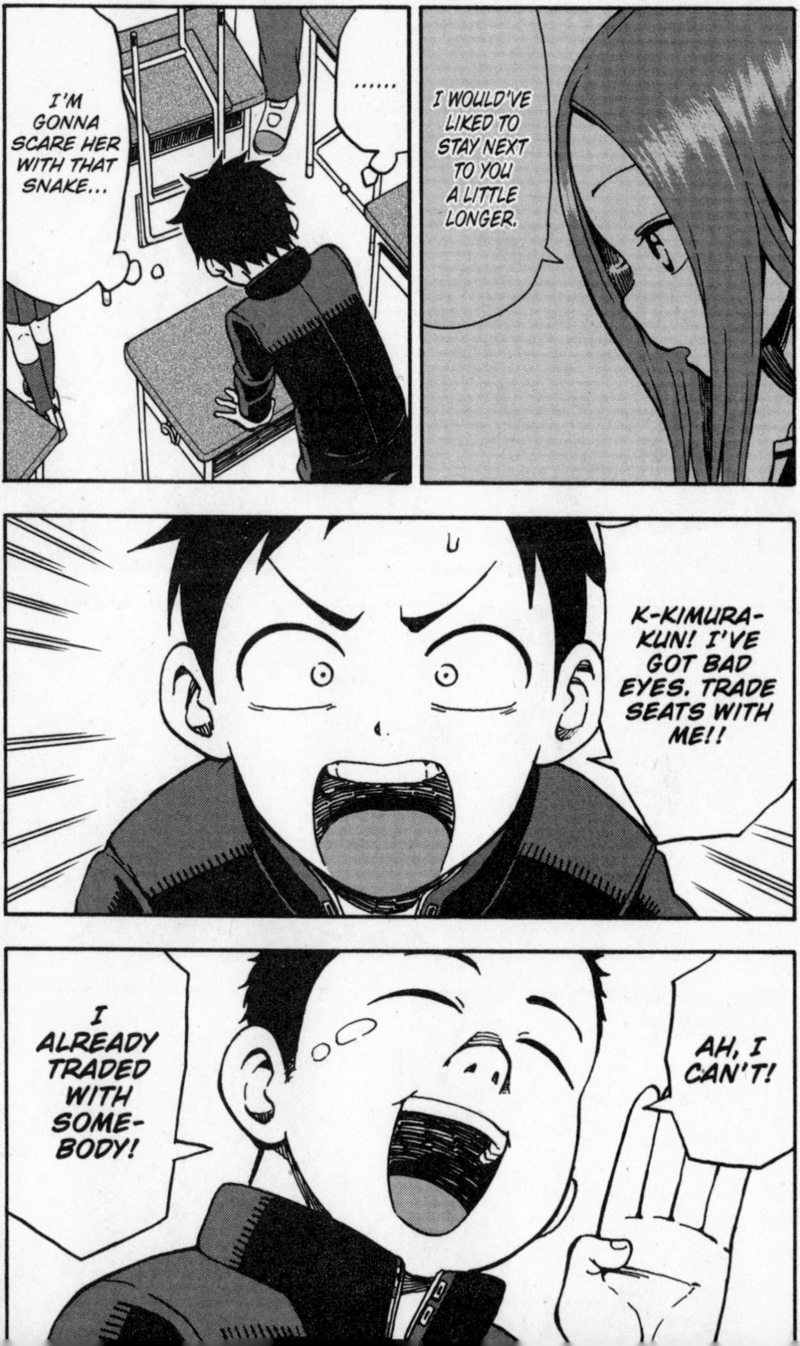
I WOULD'VE LIKED TO STAY NEXT TO YOU A LITTLE LONGER.
......
I'M GONNA SCARE HER WITH THAT SNAKE...
K-KIMURA-KUN! I'VE GOT BAD EYES. TRADE SEATS WITH ME!!
AH, I CAN'T!
I ALREADY TRADED WITH SOME-BODY!

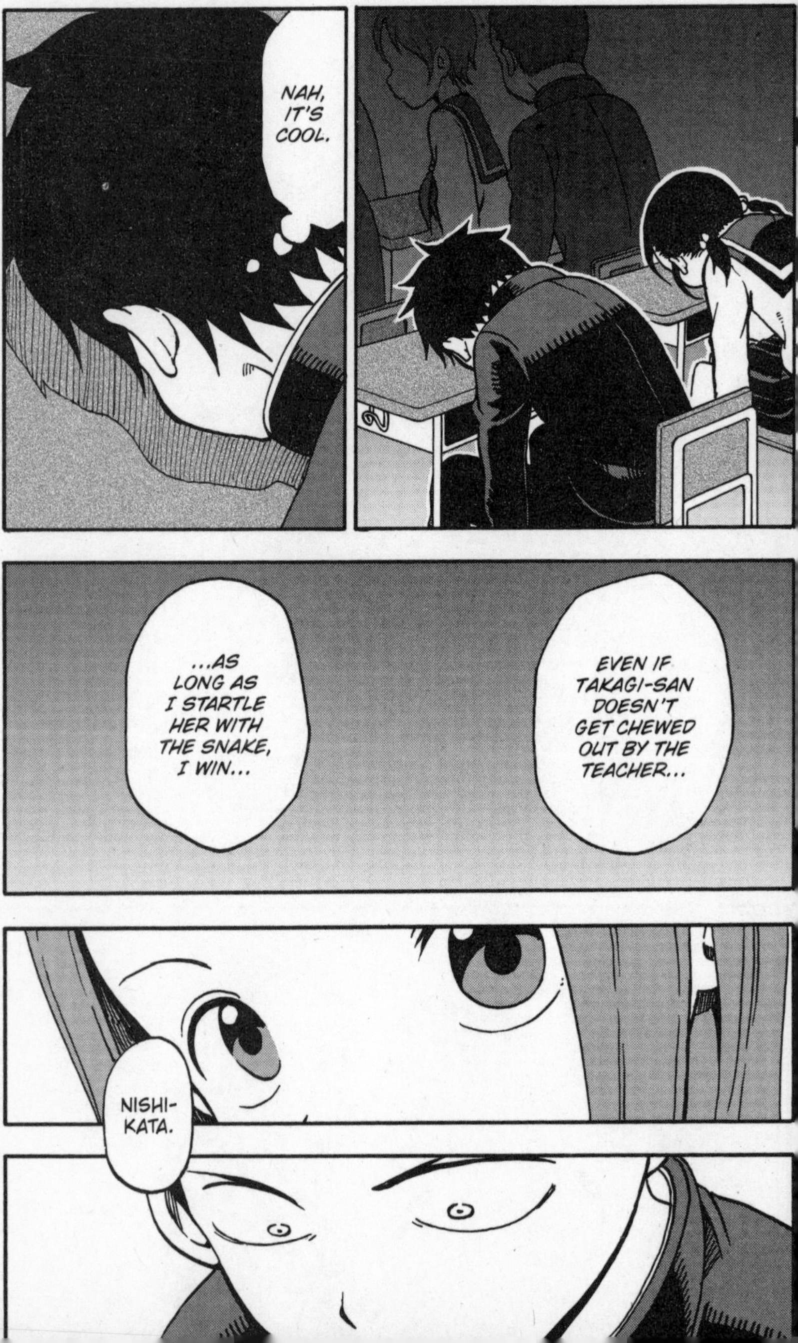
NAH, IT'S COOL.
EVEN IF TAKAGI-SAN DOESN'T GET CHEWED OUT BY THE TEACHER...
...AS LONG AS I STARTLE HER WITH THE SNAKE, I WIN...
NISHI-KATA.

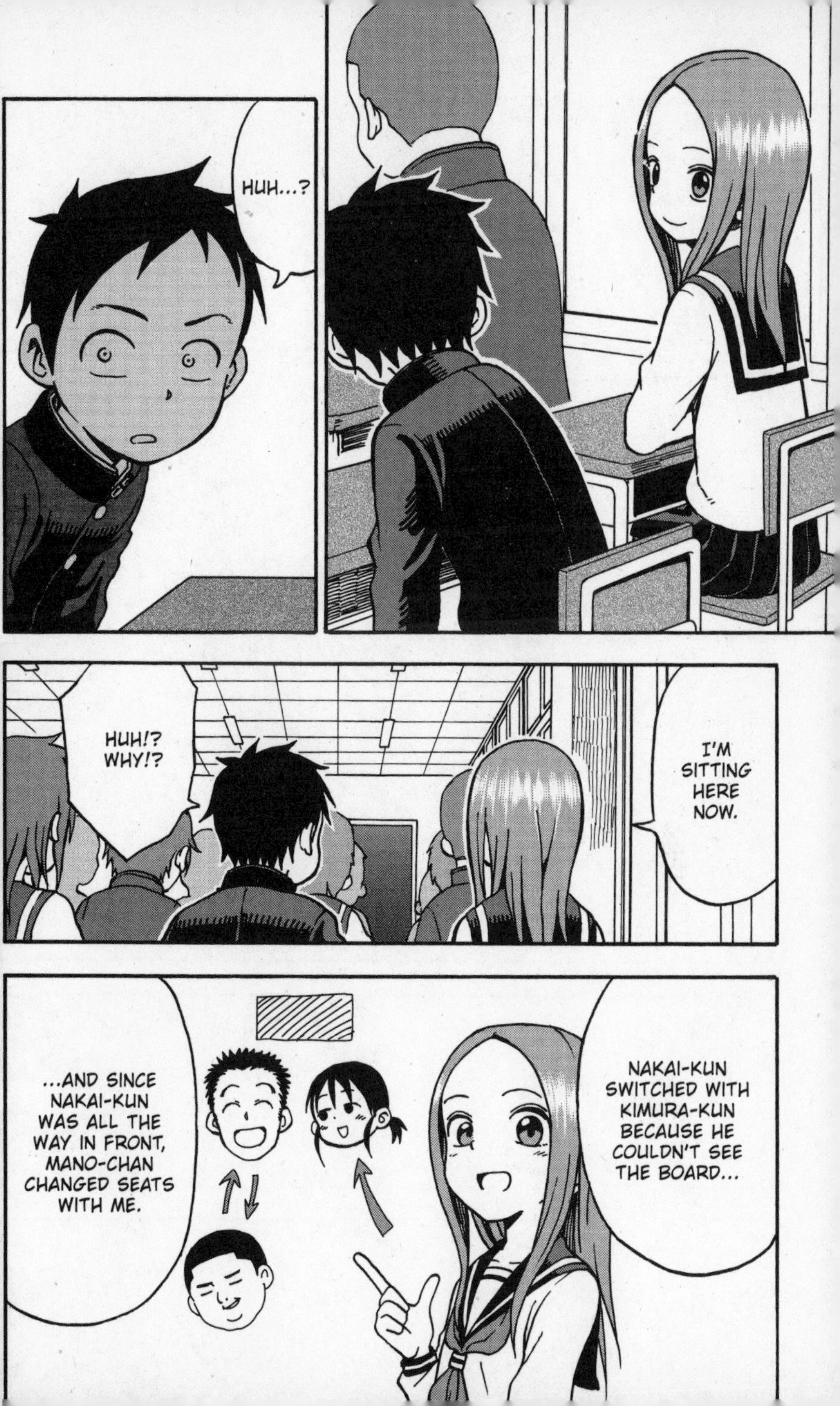
HUH...?
I'M SITTING HERE NOW.
HUH!? WHY!?
NAKAI-KUN SWITCHED WITH KIMURA-KUN BECAUSE HE COULDN'T SEE THE BOARD...
...AND SINCE NAKAI-KUN WAS ALL THE WAY IN FRONT, MANO-CHAN CHANGED SEATS WITH ME.

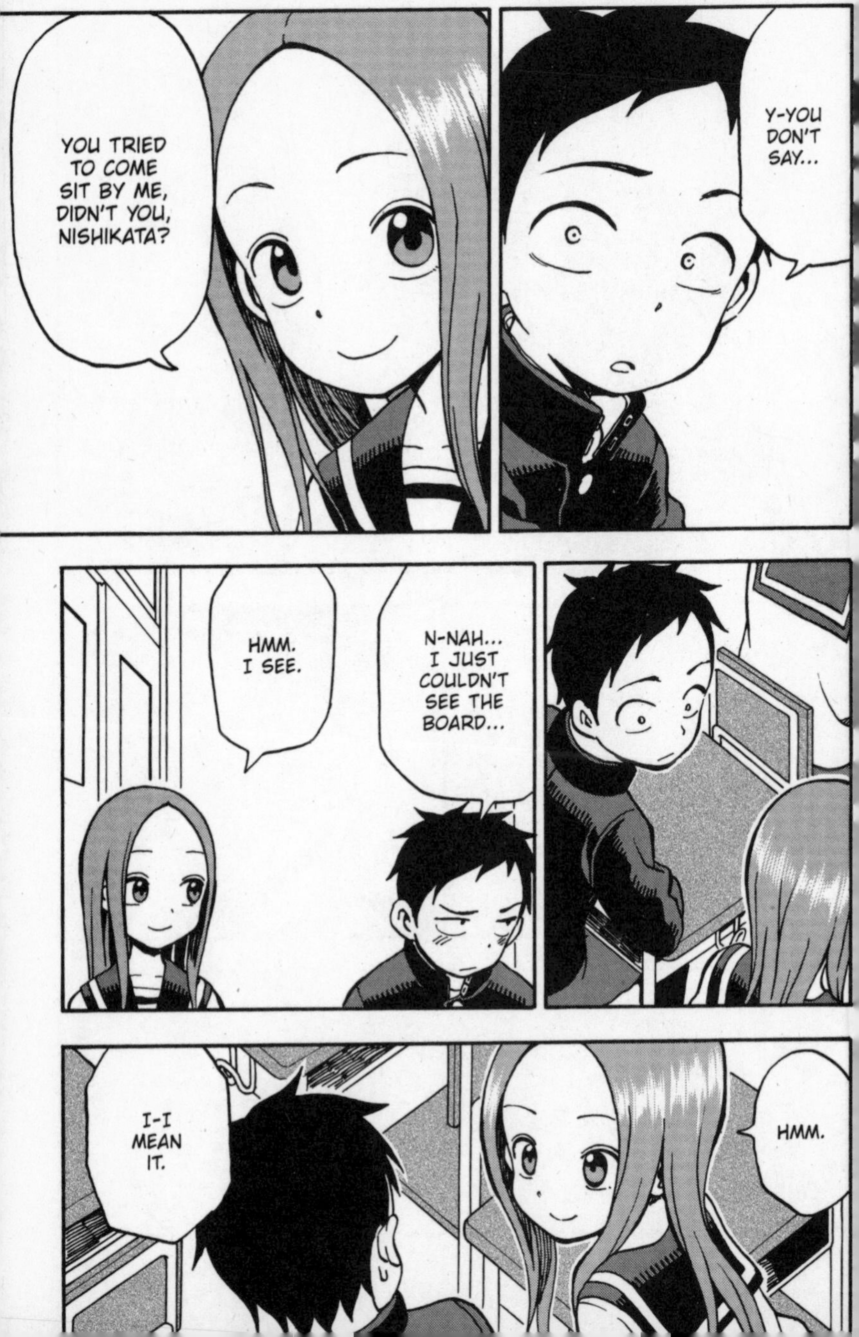
Y-YOU DON'T SAY...
YOU TRIED TO COME SIT BY ME, DIDN'T YOU, NISHIKATA?
N-NAH... I JUST COULDN'T SEE THE BOARD...
HMM. I SEE.
HMM.
I-I MEAN IT.

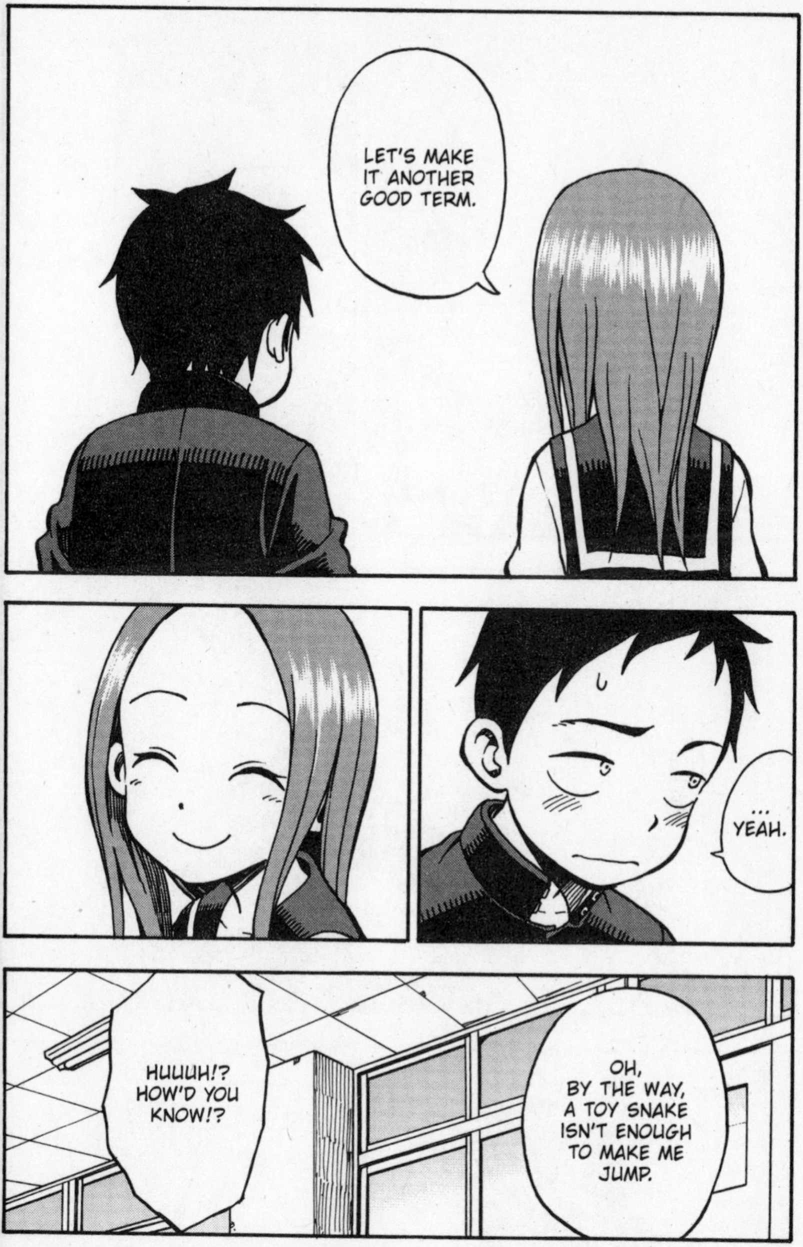
LET'S MAKE IT ANOTHER GOOD TERM.
... YEAH.
OH, BY THE WAY, A TOY SNAKE ISN'T ENOUGH TO MAKE ME JUMP.
HUUUH!? HOW'D YOU KNOW!?

ENGLISH TRANSLATION

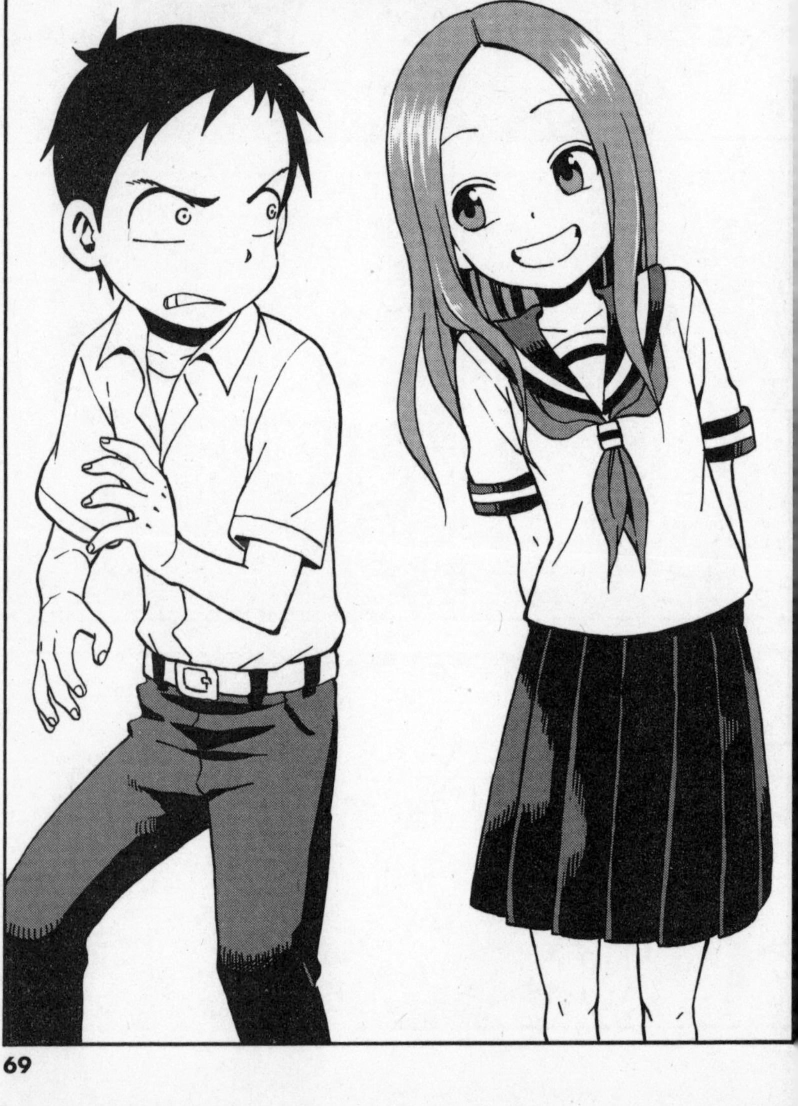

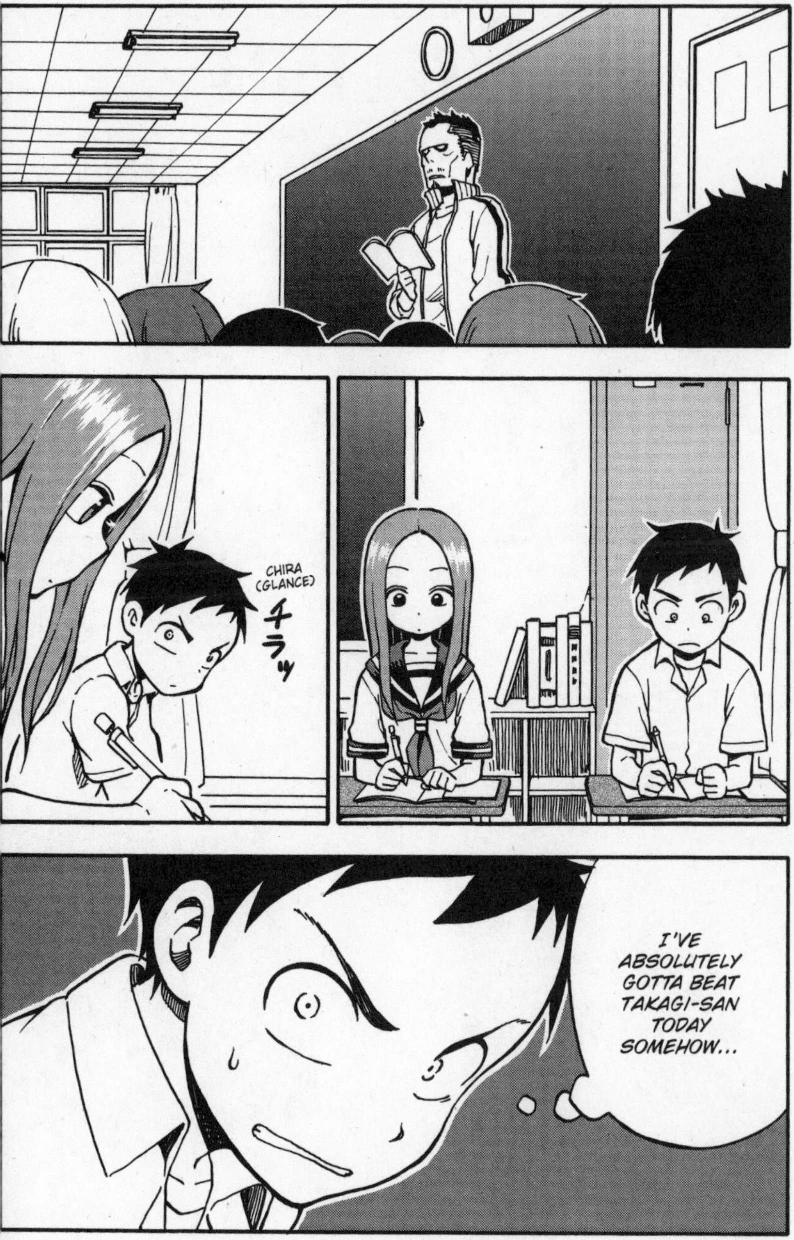
CHIRA (GLANCE)
チラッ
I'VE ABSOLUTELY GOTTA BEAT TAKAGI-SAN TODAY SOMEHOW...

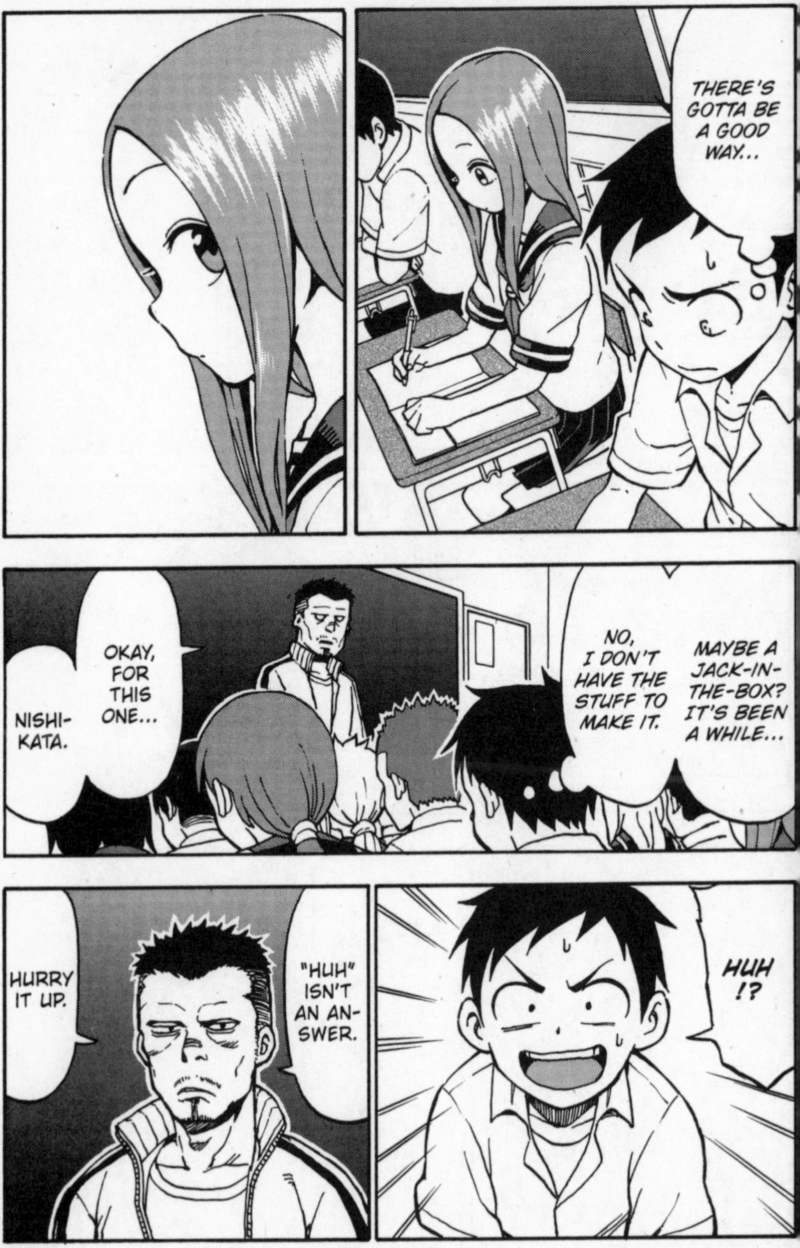
THERE'S GOTTA BE A GOOD WAY...
MAYBE A JACK-IN-THE-BOX? IT'S BEEN A WHILE...
NO, I DON'T HAVE THE STUFF TO MAKE IT.
OKAY, FOR THIS ONE...
NISHI-KATA.
HUH!?
"HUH" ISN'T AN AN-SWER.
HURRY IT UP.

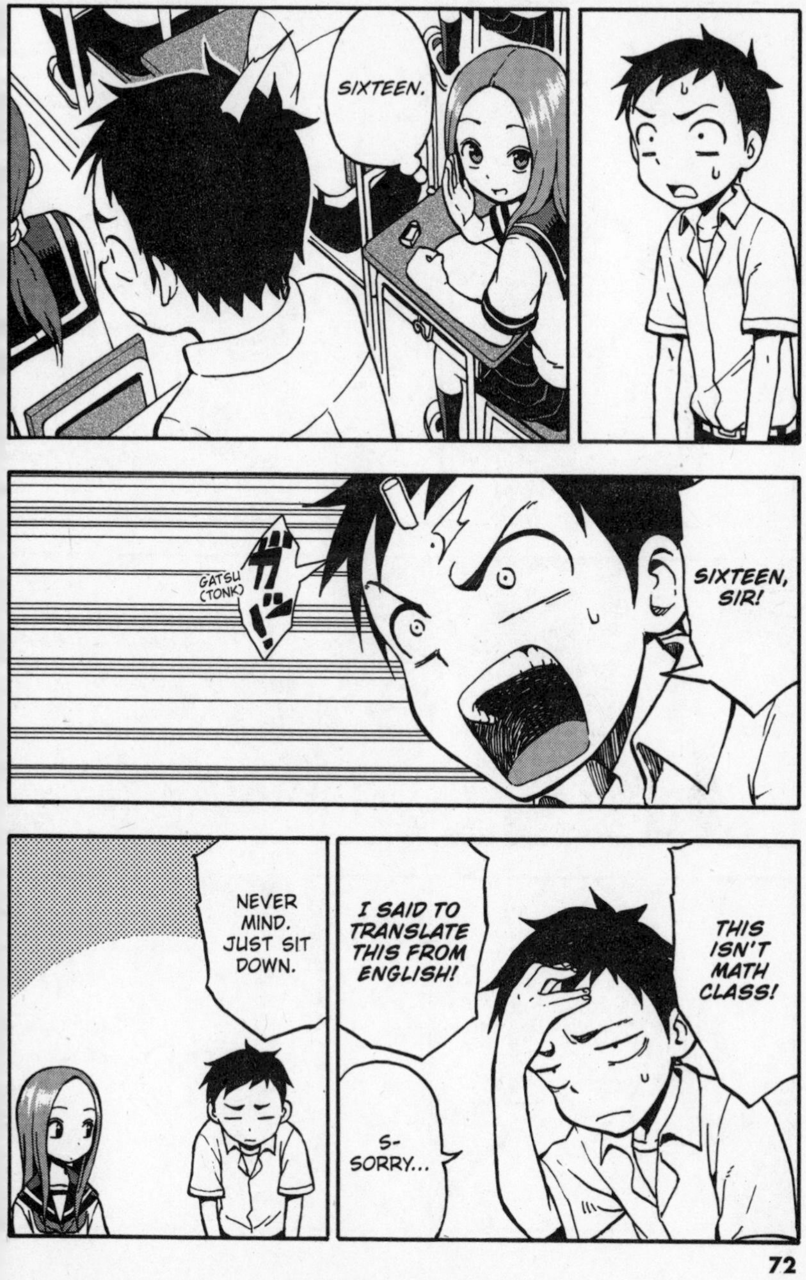
SIXTEEN.
SIXTEEN, SIR!
GATSU (TONK)
THIS ISN'T MATH CLASS!
I SAID TO TRANSLATE THIS FROM ENGLISH!
S- SORRY...
NEVER MIND. JUST SIT DOWN.

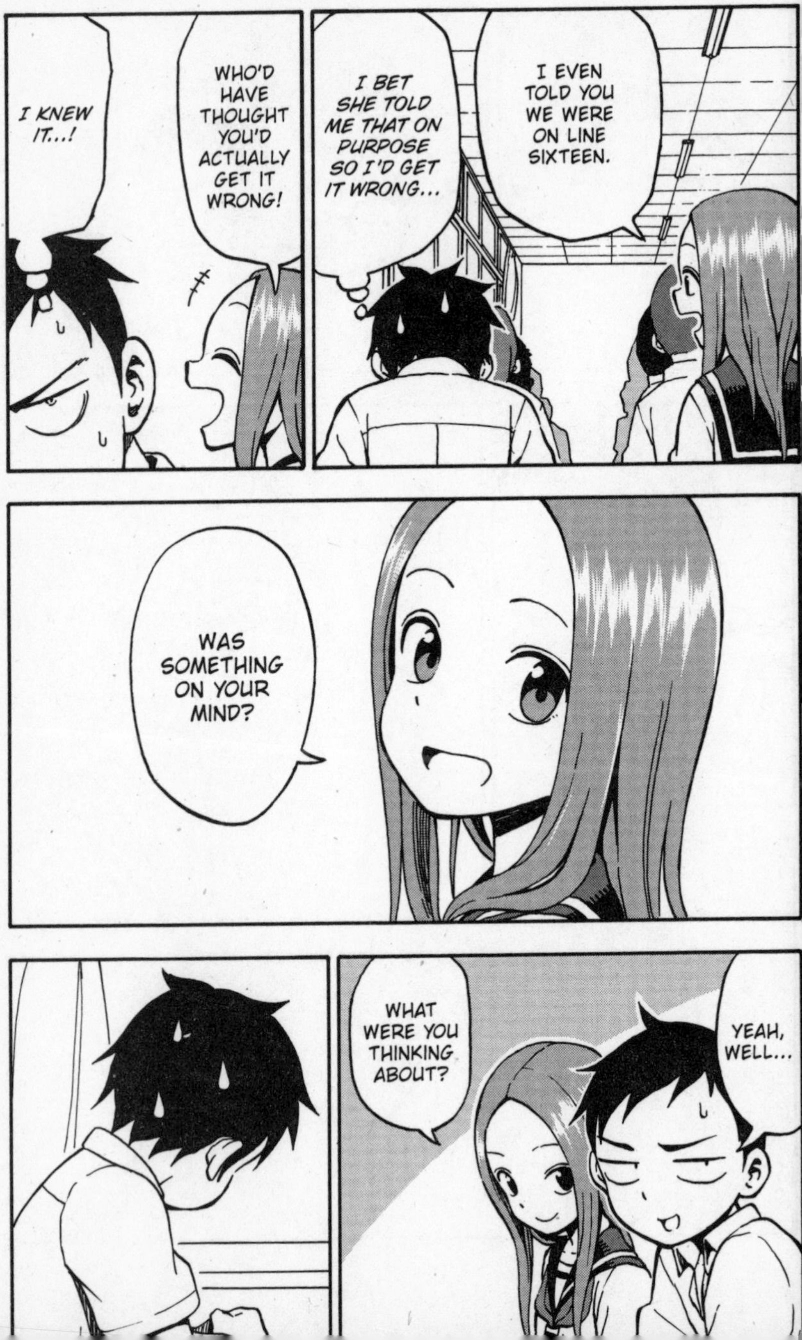
I EVEN TOLD YOU WE WERE ON LINE SIXTEEN.
I BET SHE TOLD ME THAT ON PURPOSE SO I'D GET IT WRONG...
WHO'D HAVE THOUGHT YOU'D ACTUALLY GET IT WRONG!
I KNEW IT...!
WAS SOMETHING ON YOUR MIND?
YEAH, WELL...
WHAT WERE YOU THINKING ABOUT?

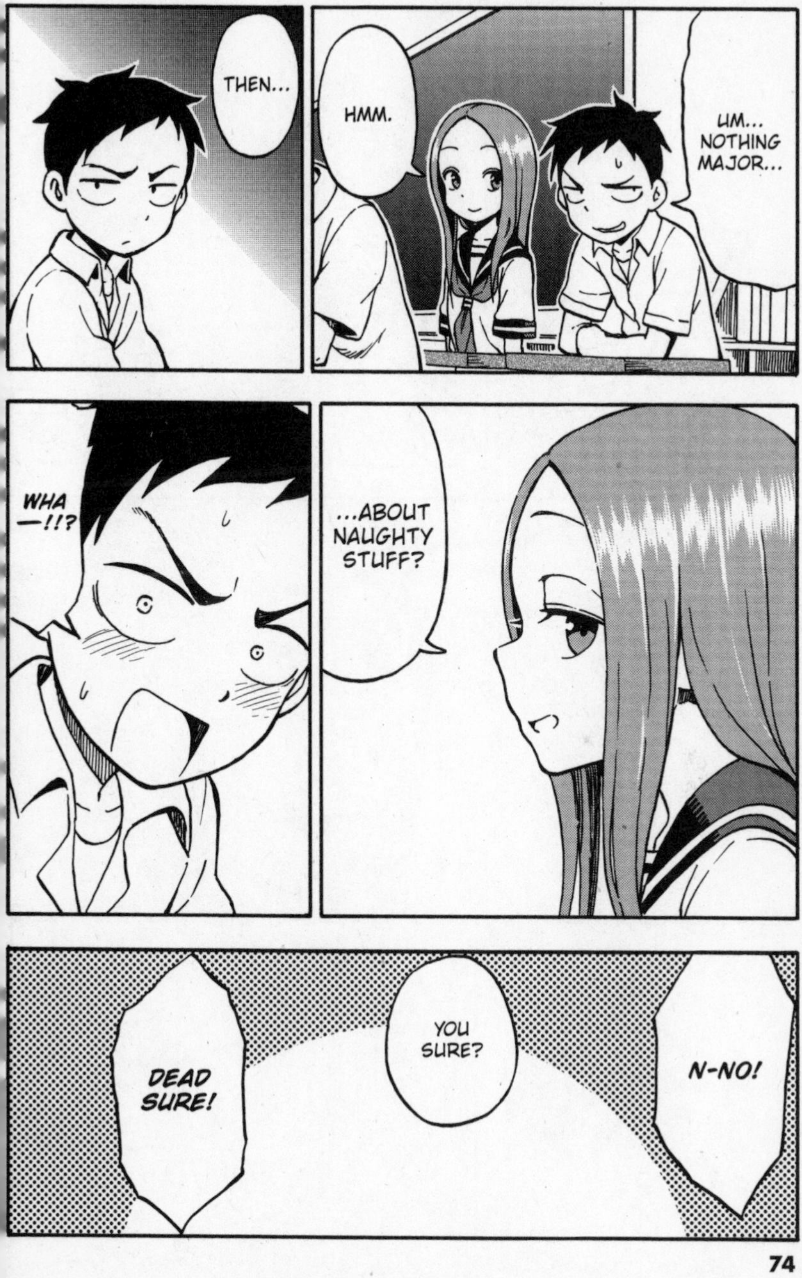
UM... NOTHING MAJOR...
HMM.
THEN...
...ABOUT NAUGHTY STUFF?
WHA—!!?
N-NO!
YOU SURE?
DEAD SURE!

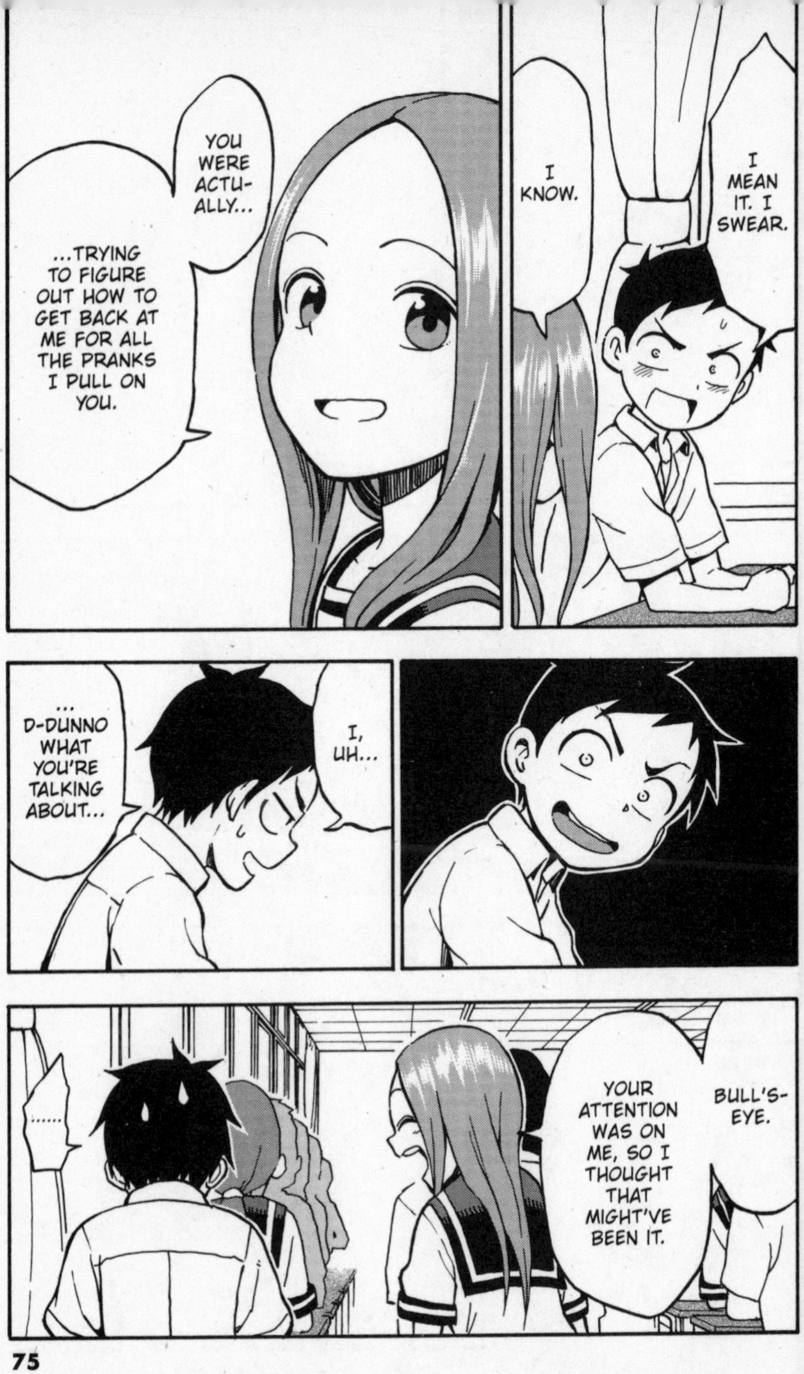
I MEAN IT. I SWEAR.
I KNOW.
YOU WERE ACTU-ALLY...
...TRYING TO FIGURE OUT HOW TO GET BACK AT ME FOR ALL THE PRANKS I PULL ON YOU.
I, UH...
...D-DUNNO WHAT YOU'RE TALKING ABOUT...
BULL'S-EYE.
YOUR ATTENTION WAS ON ME, SO I THOUGHT THAT MIGHT'VE BEEN IT.
......

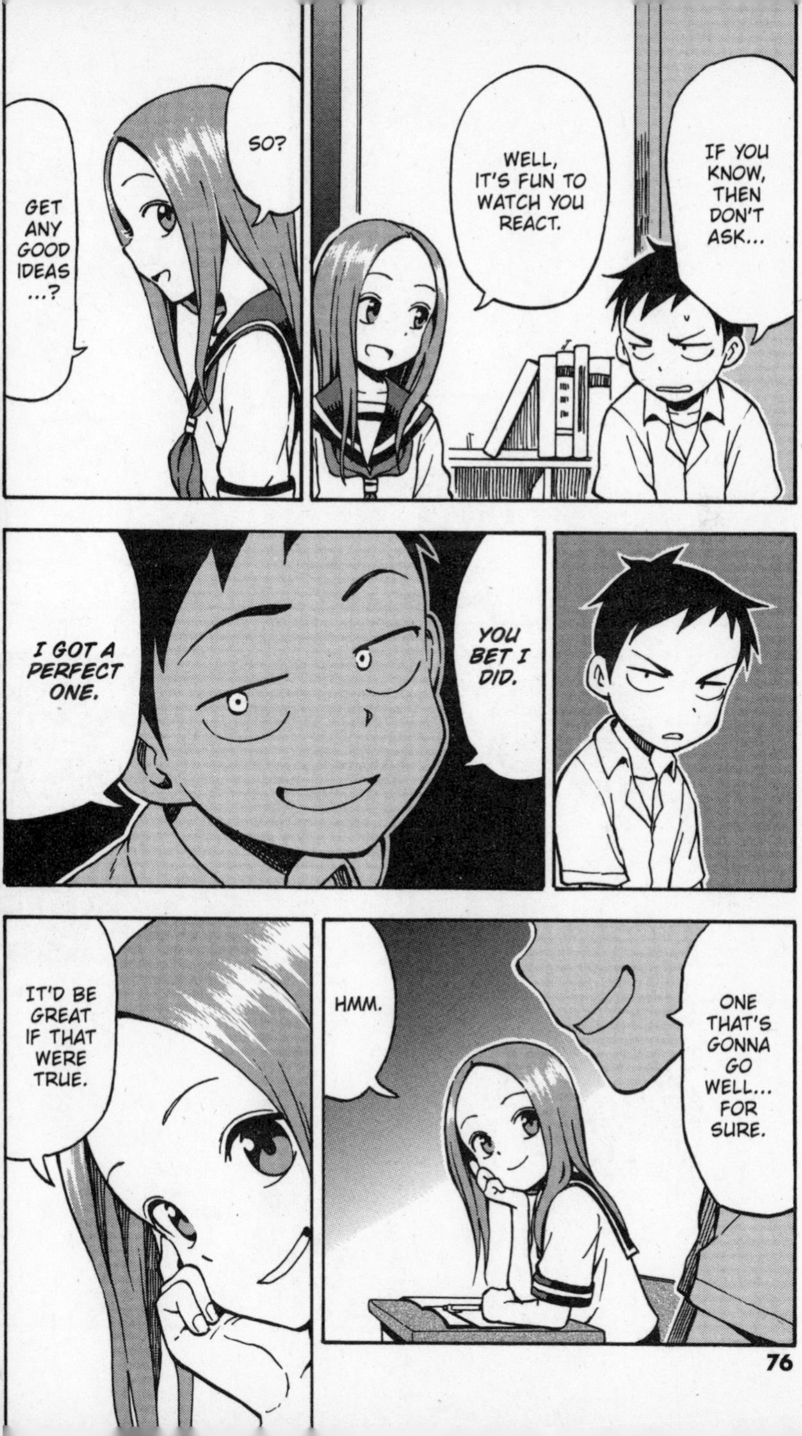
IF YOU KNOW, THEN DON'T ASK...
WELL, IT'S FUN TO WATCH YOU REACT.
SO?
GET ANY GOOD IDEAS ...?
YOU BET I DID.
I GOT A PERFECT ONE.
ONE THAT'S GONNA GO WELL... FOR SURE.
HMM.
IT'D BE GREAT IF THAT WERE TRUE.

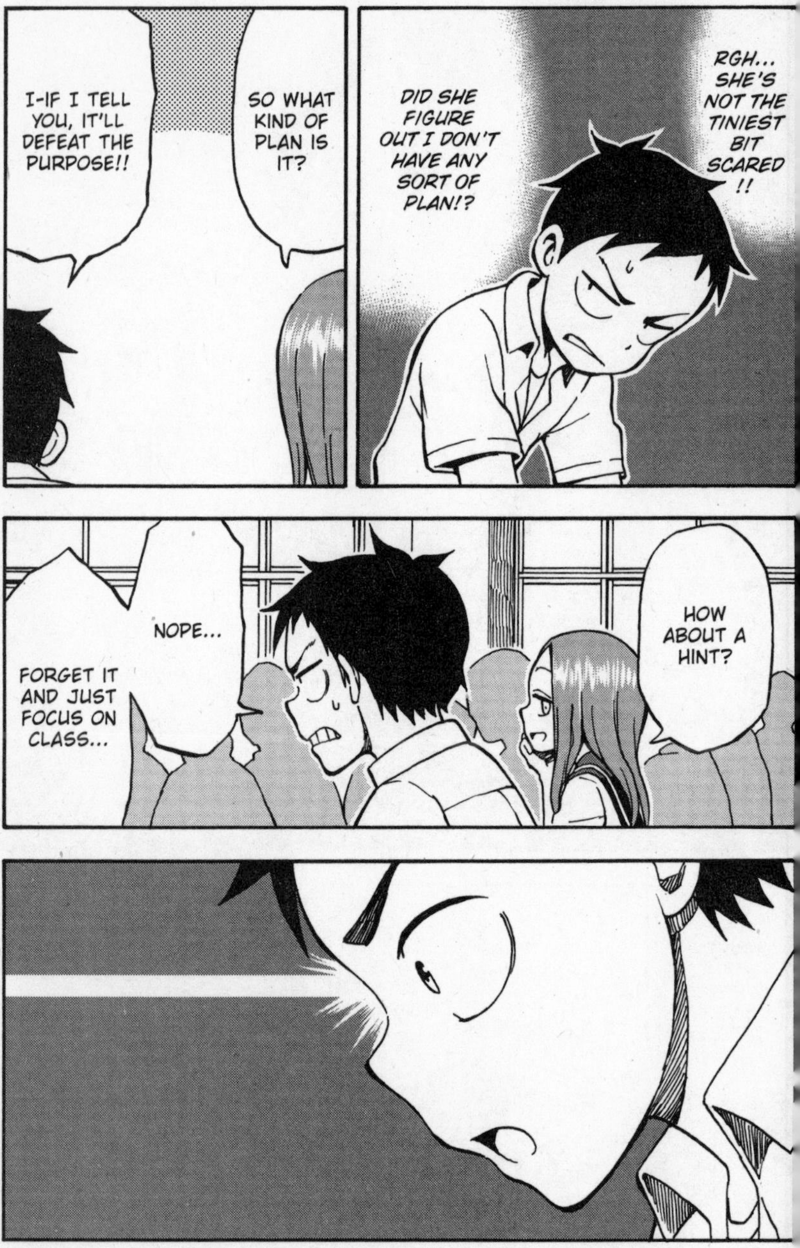
RGH... SHE'S NOT THE TINIEST BIT SCARED!!
DID SHE FIGURE OUT I DON'T HAVE ANY SORT OF PLAN!?
SO WHAT KIND OF PLAN IS IT?
I-IF I TELL YOU, IT'LL DEFEAT THE PURPOSE!!
HOW ABOUT A HINT?
NOPE...
FORGET IT AND JUST FOCUS ON CLASS...

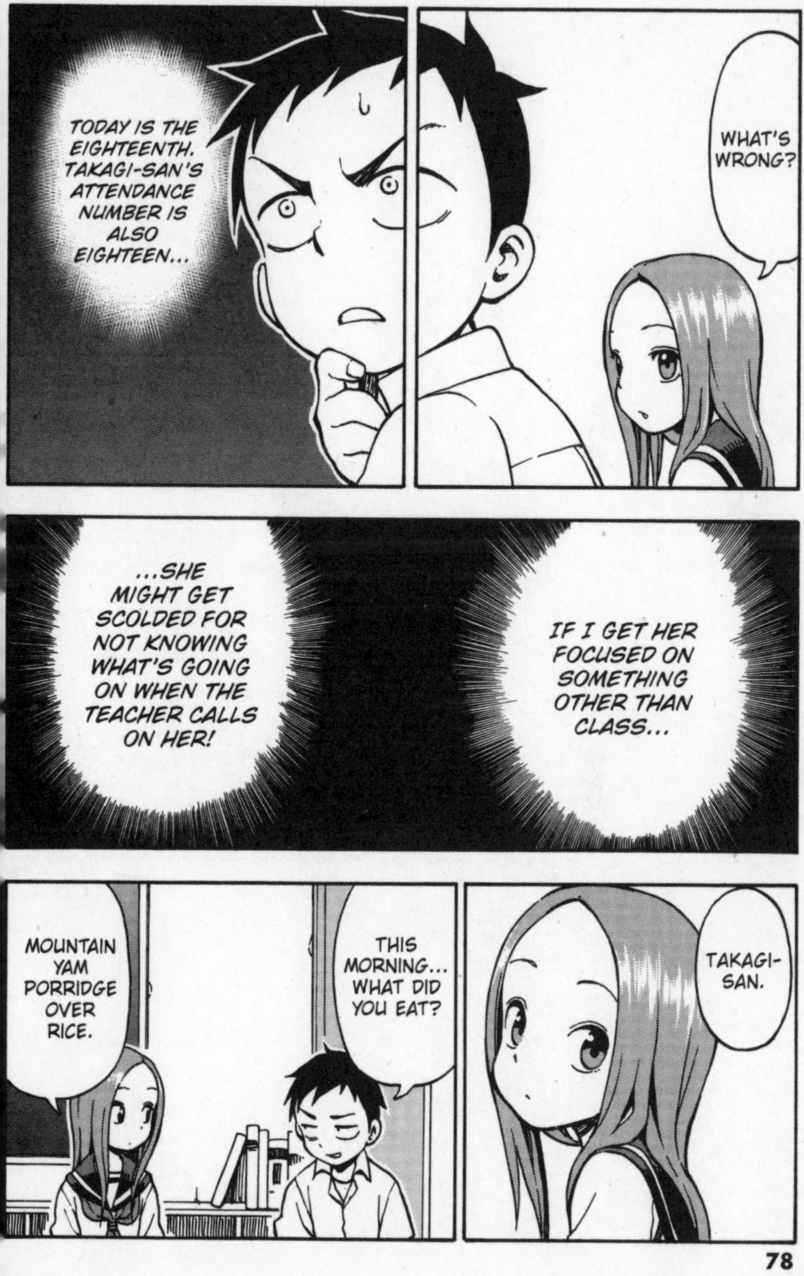
WHAT'S WRONG?
TODAY IS THE EIGHTEENTH. TAKAGI-SAN'S ATTENDANCE NUMBER IS ALSO EIGHTEEN...
IF I GET HER FOCUSED ON SOMETHING OTHER THAN CLASS...
...SHE MIGHT GET SCOLDED FOR NOT KNOWING WHAT'S GOING ON WHEN THE TEACHER CALLS ON HER!
TAKAGI-SAN.
THIS MORNING... WHAT DID YOU EAT?
MOUNTAIN YAM PORRIDGE OVER RICE.

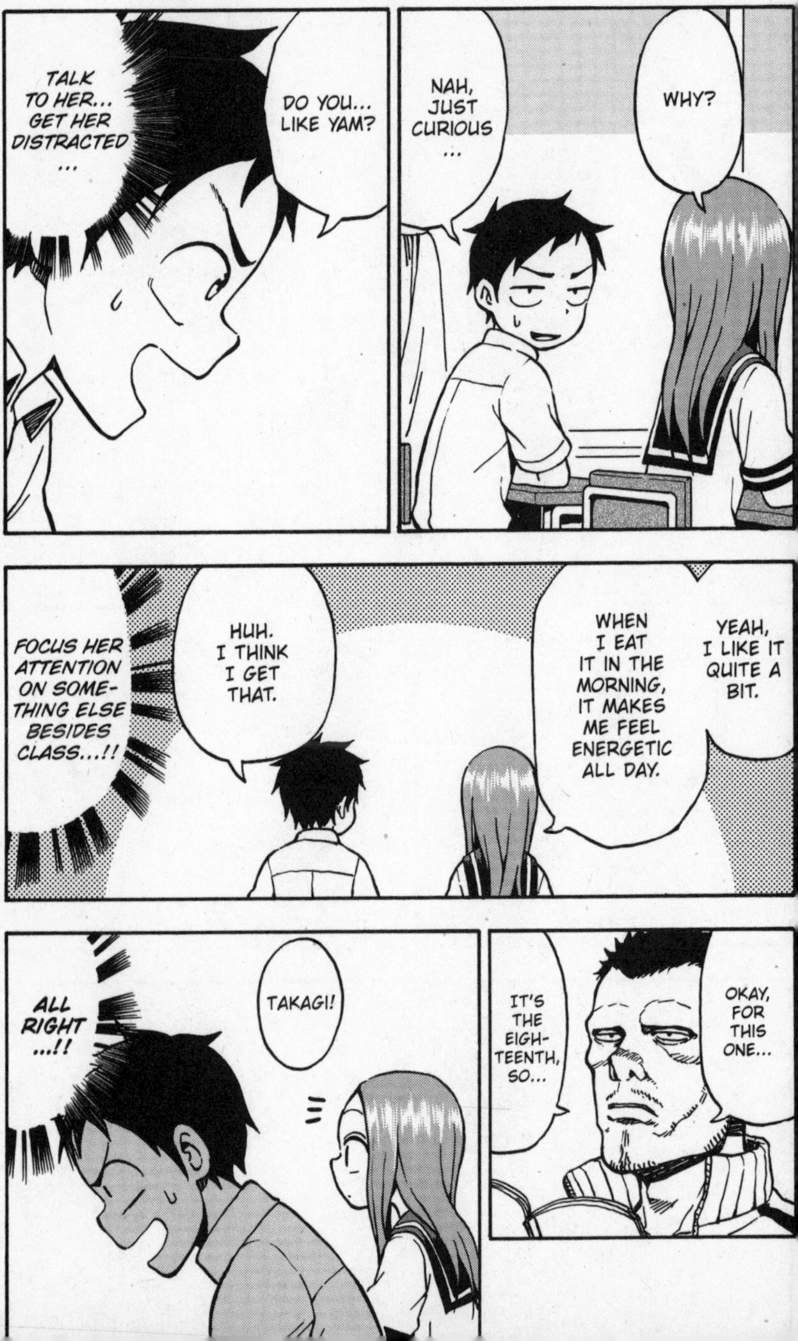

WHY?
NAH, JUST CURIOUS ...
DO YOU... LIKE YAM?
TALK TO HER... GET HER DISTRACTED ...
YEAH, I LIKE IT QUITE A BIT.
WHEN I EAT IT IN THE MORNING, IT MAKES ME FEEL ENERGETIC ALL DAY.
HUH. I THINK I GET THAT.
FOCUS HER ATTENTION ON SOME-THING ELSE BESIDES CLASS...!!
OKAY, FOR THIS ONE...
IT'S THE EIGH-TEENTH, SO...
TAKAGI!
ALL RIGHT ...!!

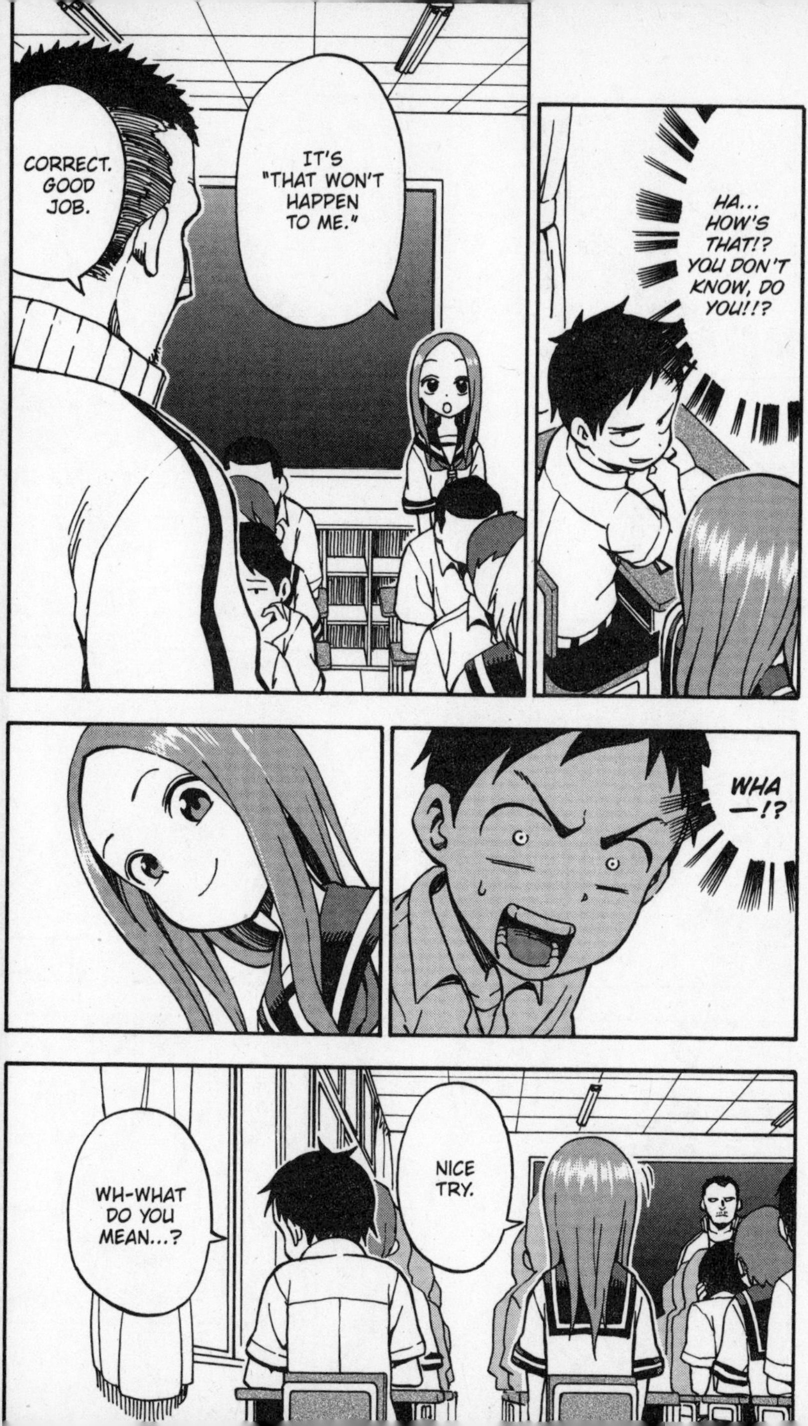
HA... HOW'S THAT!? YOU DON'T KNOW, DO YOU!!?
IT'S "THAT WON'T HAPPEN TO ME."
CORRECT. GOOD JOB.
WHA—!?
NICE TRY.
WH-WHAT DO YOU MEAN...?

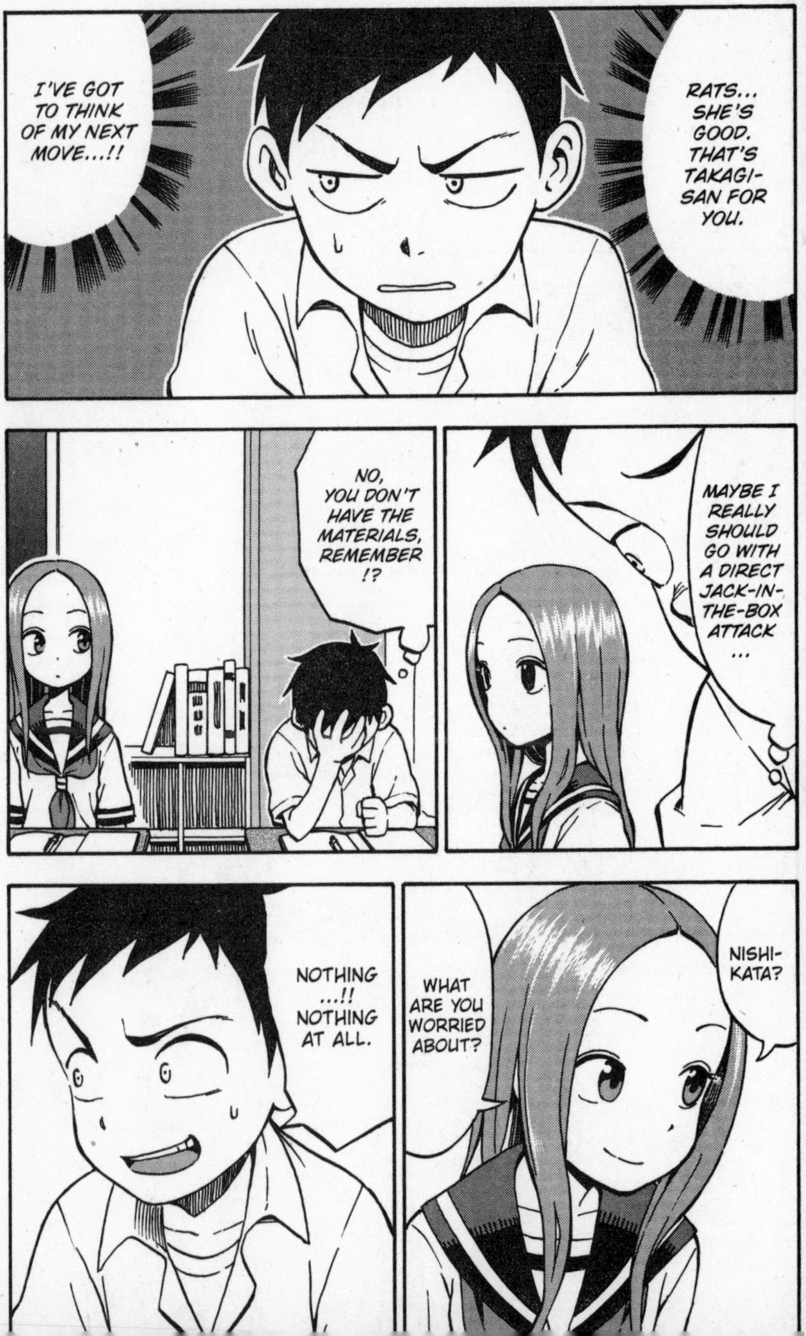
RATS... SHE'S GOOD. THAT'S TAKAGI-SAN FOR YOU.
I'VE GOT TO THINK OF MY NEXT MOVE...!!
MAYBE I REALLY SHOULD GO WITH A DIRECT JACK-IN-THE-BOX ATTACK ...
NO, YOU DON'T HAVE THE MATERIALS, REMEMBER !?
NISHI-KATA?
WHAT ARE YOU WORRIED ABOUT?
NOTHING ...!! NOTHING AT ALL.

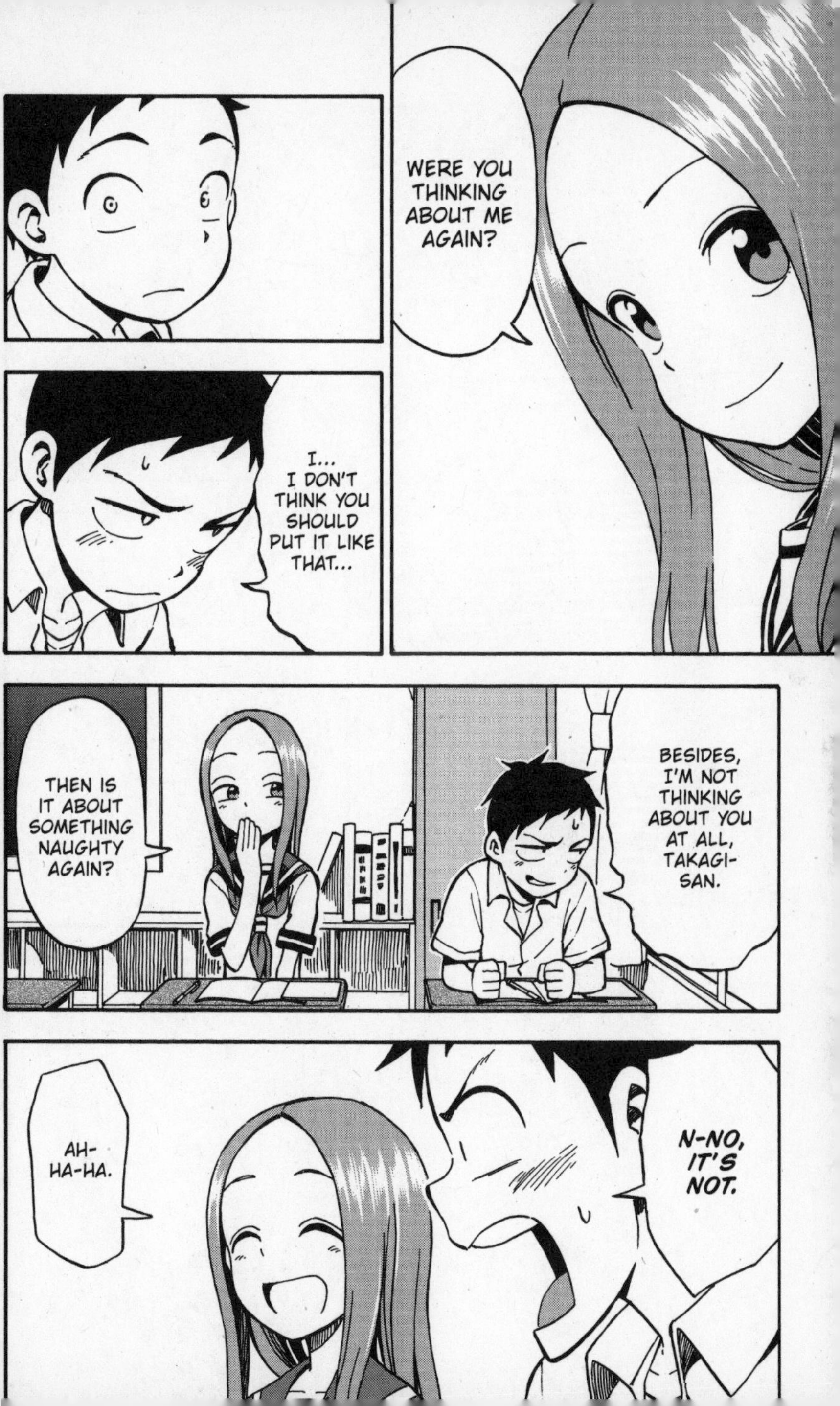
WERE YOU THINKING ABOUT ME AGAIN?
I... I DON'T THINK YOU SHOULD PUT IT LIKE THAT...
BESIDES, I'M NOT THINKING ABOUT YOU AT ALL, TAKAGI-SAN.
THEN IS IT ABOUT SOMETHING NAUGHTY AGAIN?
N-NO, IT'S NOT.
AH-HA-HA.

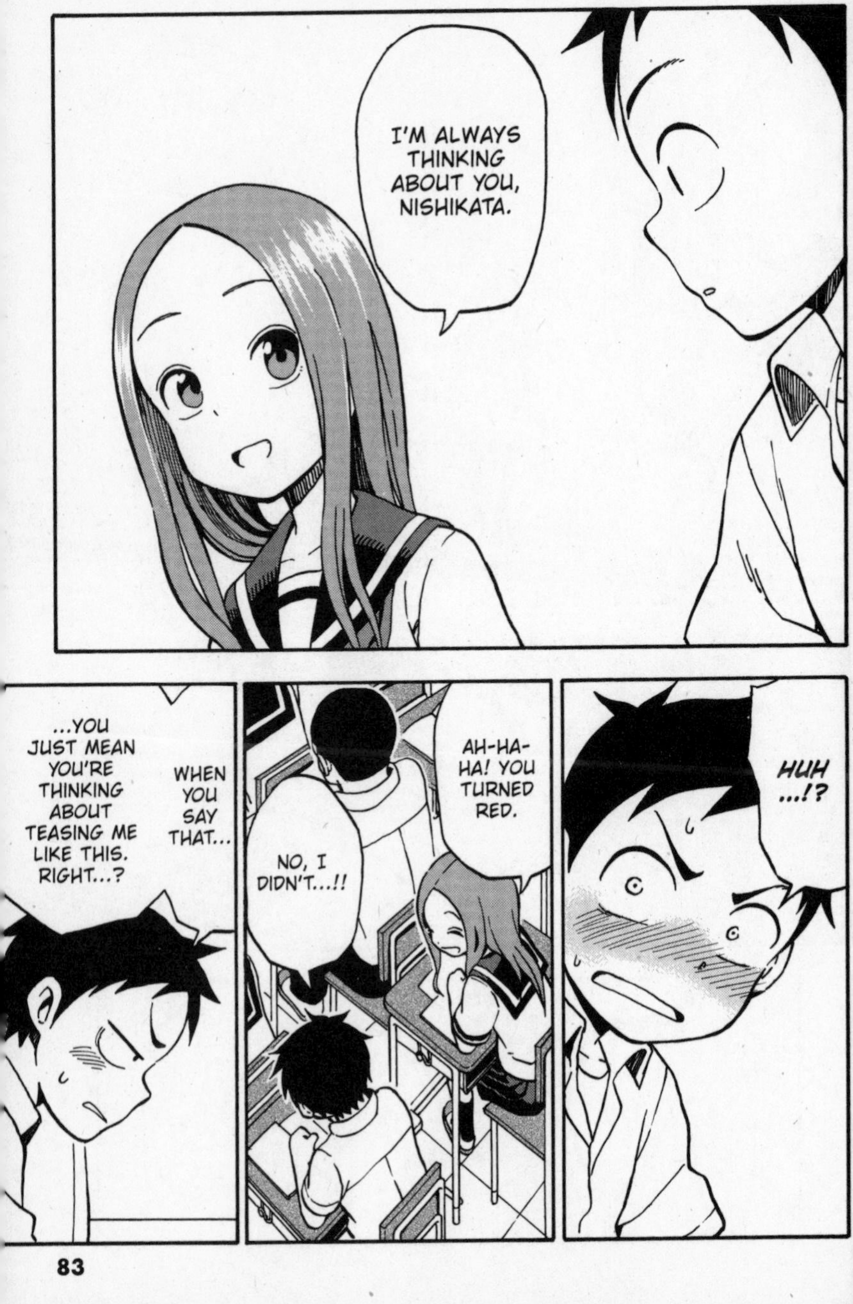
I'M ALWAYS THINKING ABOUT YOU, NISHIKATA.
HUH ...!?
AH-HA-HA! YOU TURNED RED.
NO, I DIDN'T...!!
WHEN YOU SAY THAT...
...YOU JUST MEAN YOU'RE THINKING ABOUT TEASING ME LIKE THIS. RIGHT...?

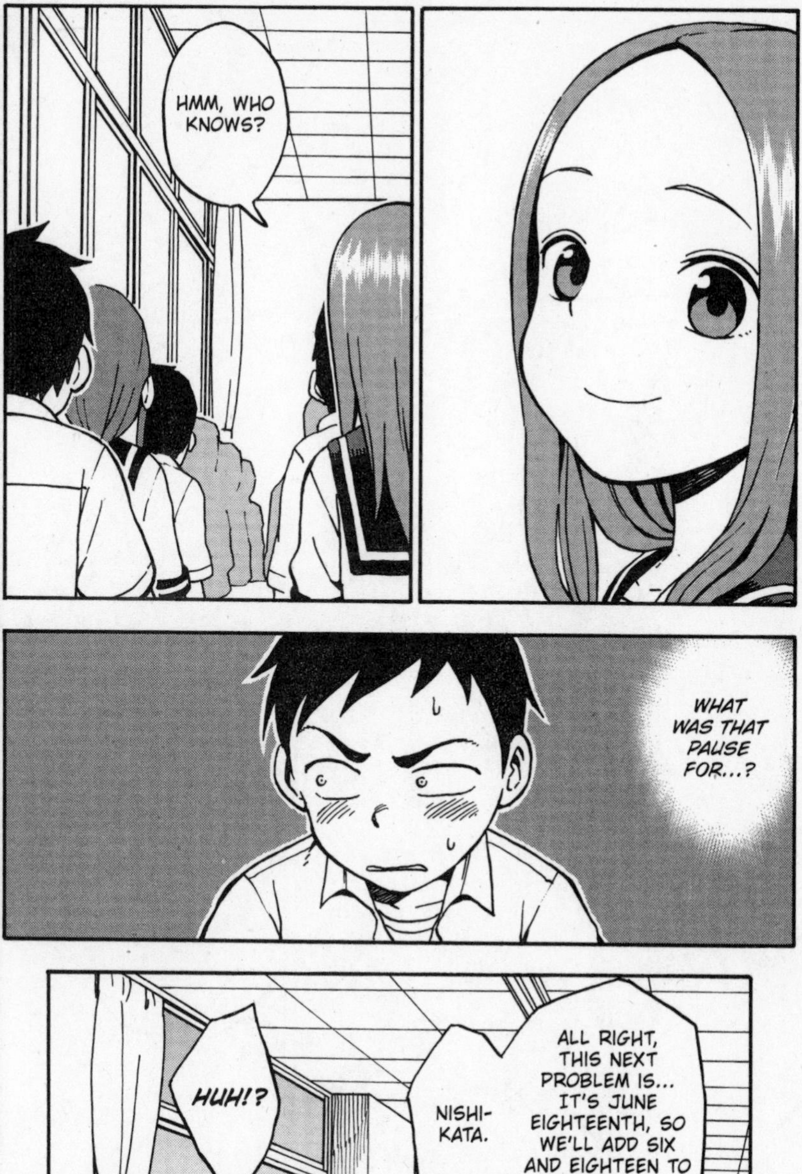
HMM, WHO KNOWS?
WHAT WAS THAT PAUSE FOR...?
ALL RIGHT, THIS NEXT PROBLEM IS... IT'S JUNE EIGHTEENTH, SO WE'LL ADD SIX AND EIGHTEEN TO GET TWENTY-FOUR...
NISHI-KATA.
HUH!?

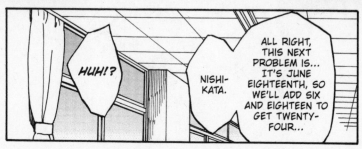

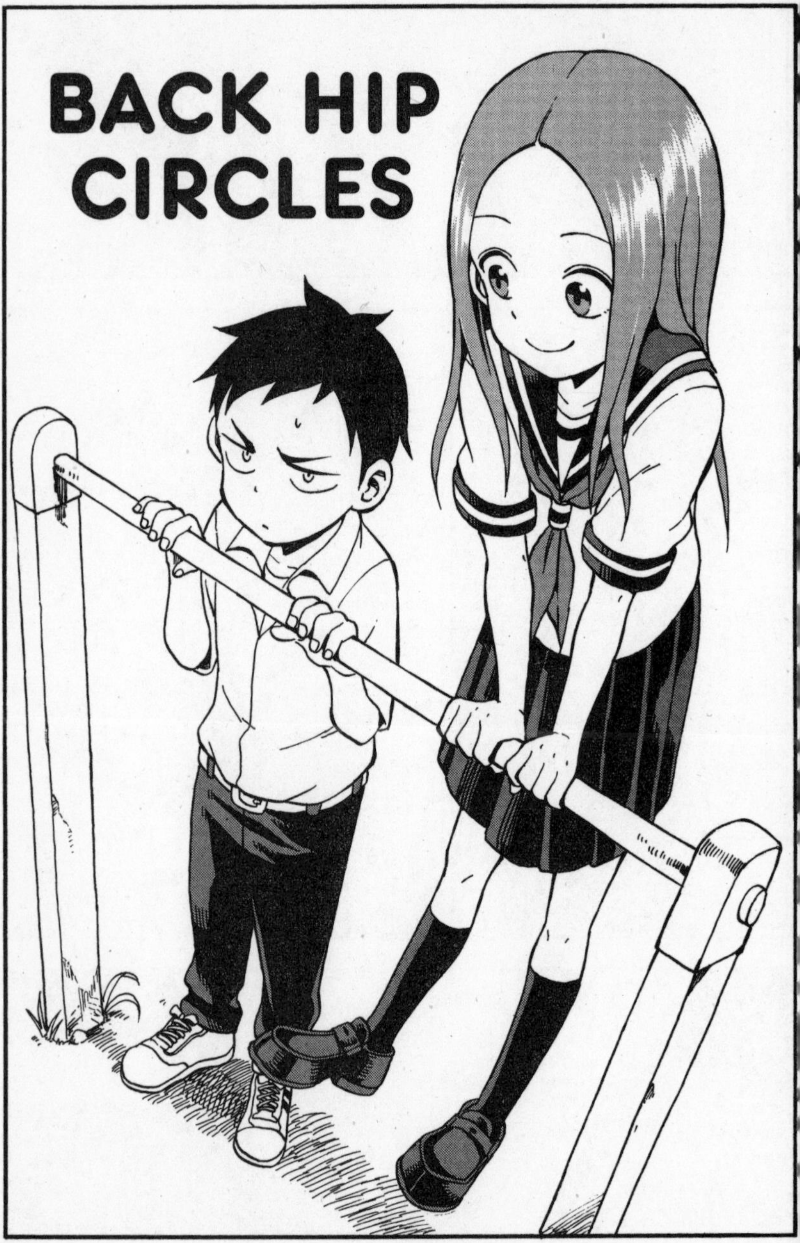
BACK HIP
CIRCLES

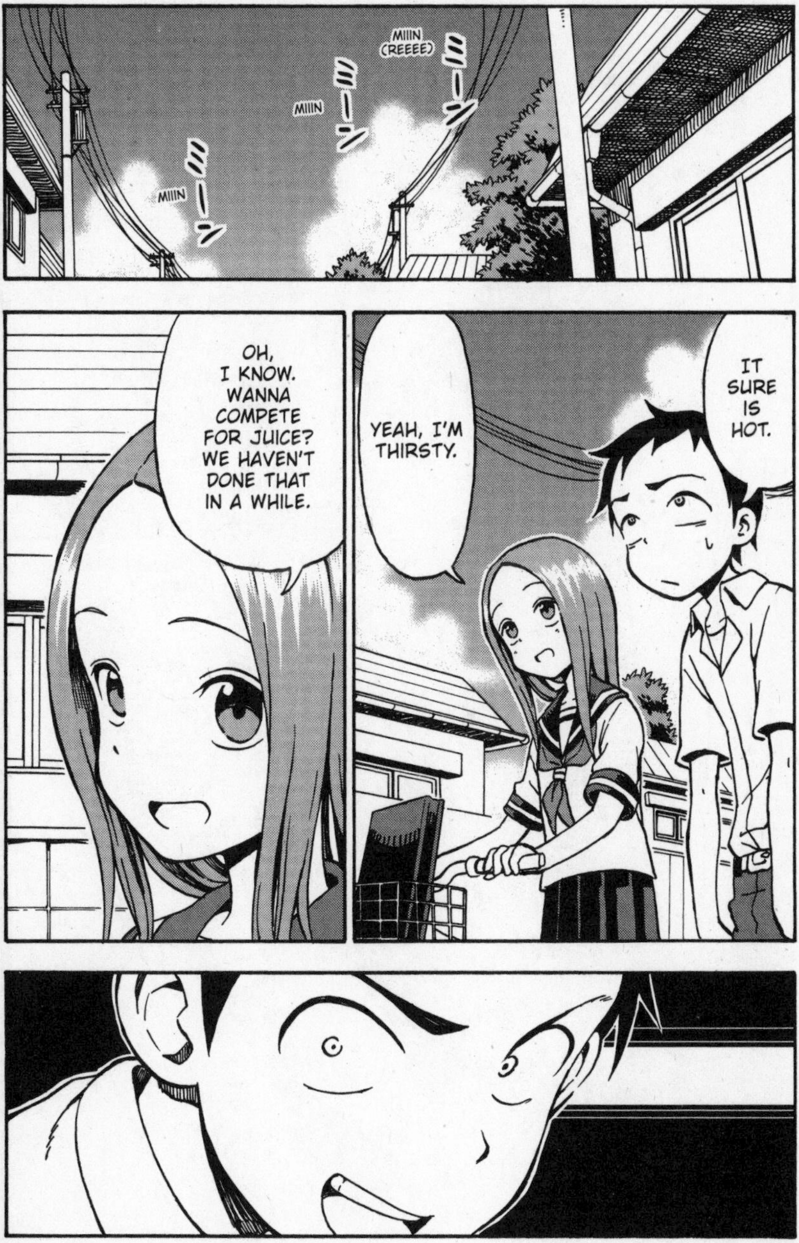
MIIN (REEEE)
MIIN
MIIN
IT SURE IS HOT.
YEAH, I'M THIRSTY.
OH, I KNOW. WANNA COMPETE FOR JUICE? WE HAVEN'T DONE THAT IN A WHILE.

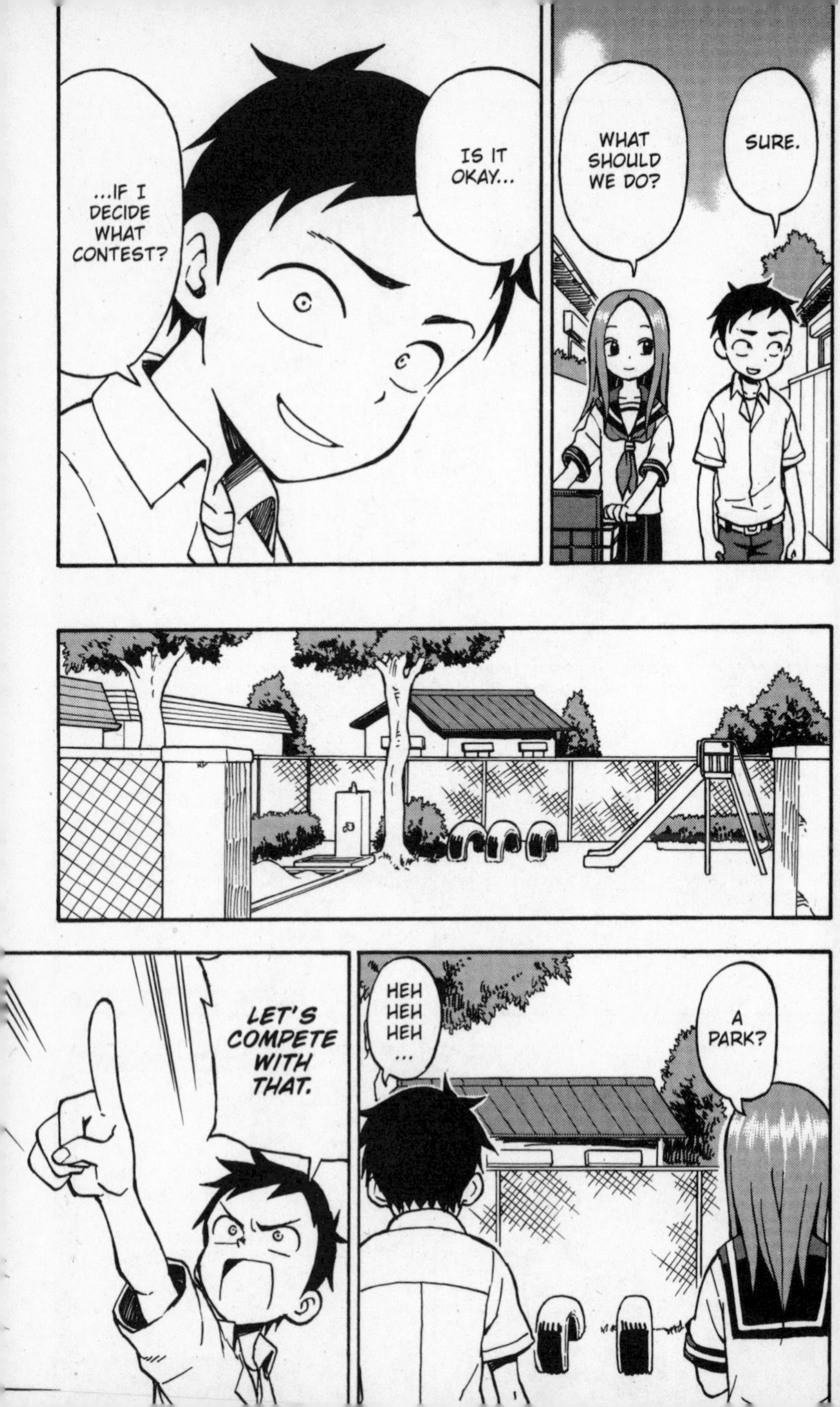
SURE.
WHAT SHOULD WE DO?
IS IT OKAY...
...IF I DECIDE WHAT CONTEST?
A PARK?
HEH HEH HEH...
LET'S COMPETE WITH THAT.

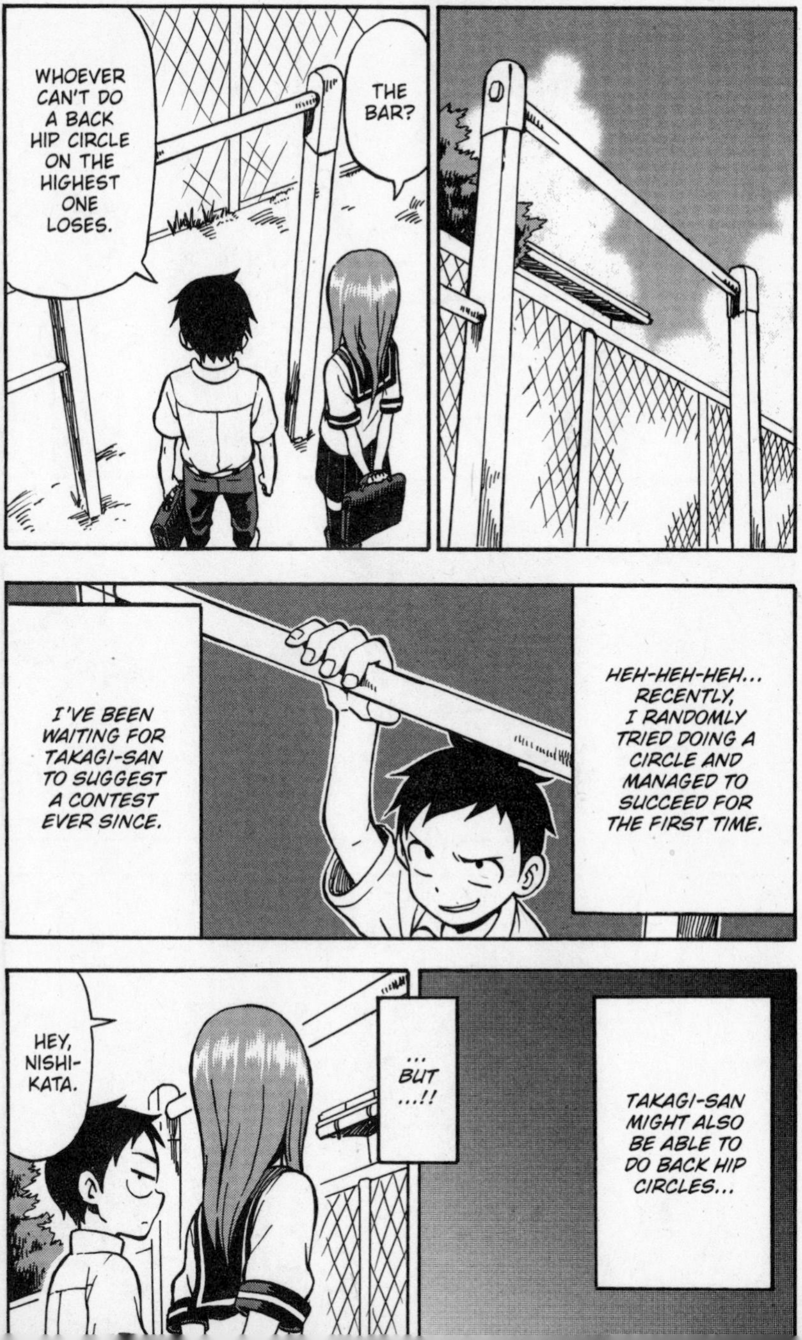
THE BAR?
WHOEVER CAN'T DO A BACK HIP CIRCLE ON THE HIGHEST ONE LOSES.
HEH-HEH-HEH... RECENTLY, I RANDOMLY TRIED DOING A CIRCLE AND MANAGED TO SUCCEED FOR THE FIRST TIME.
I'VE BEEN WAITING FOR TAKAGI-SAN TO SUGGEST A CONTEST EVER SINCE.
TAKAGI-SAN MIGHT ALSO BE ABLE TO DO BACK HIP CIRCLES...
...BUT ...!!
HEY, NISHI-KATA.

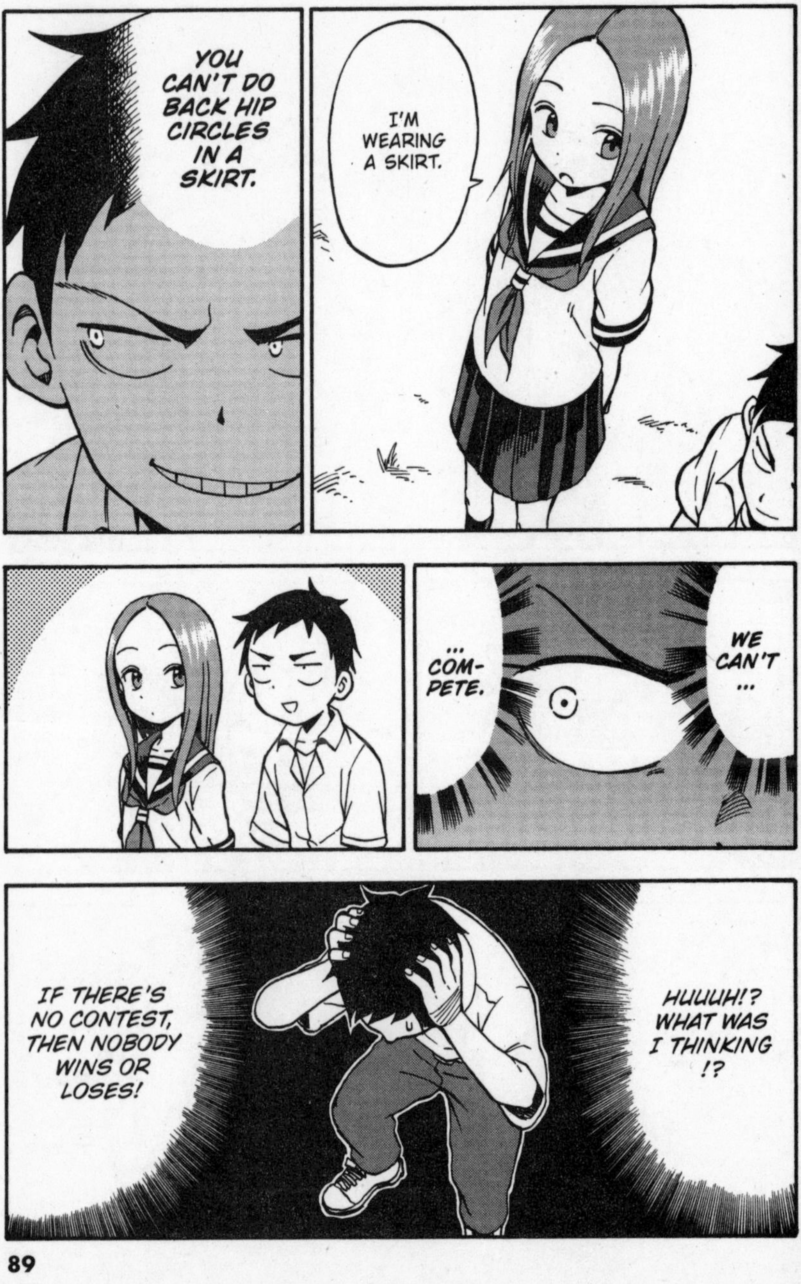
I'M WEARING A SKIRT.
YOU CAN'T DO BACK HIP CIRCLES IN A SKIRT.
WE CAN'T ...
... COMPETE.
HUUUH!? WHAT WAS I THINKING !?
IF THERE'S NO CONTEST, THEN NOBODY WINS OR LOSES!

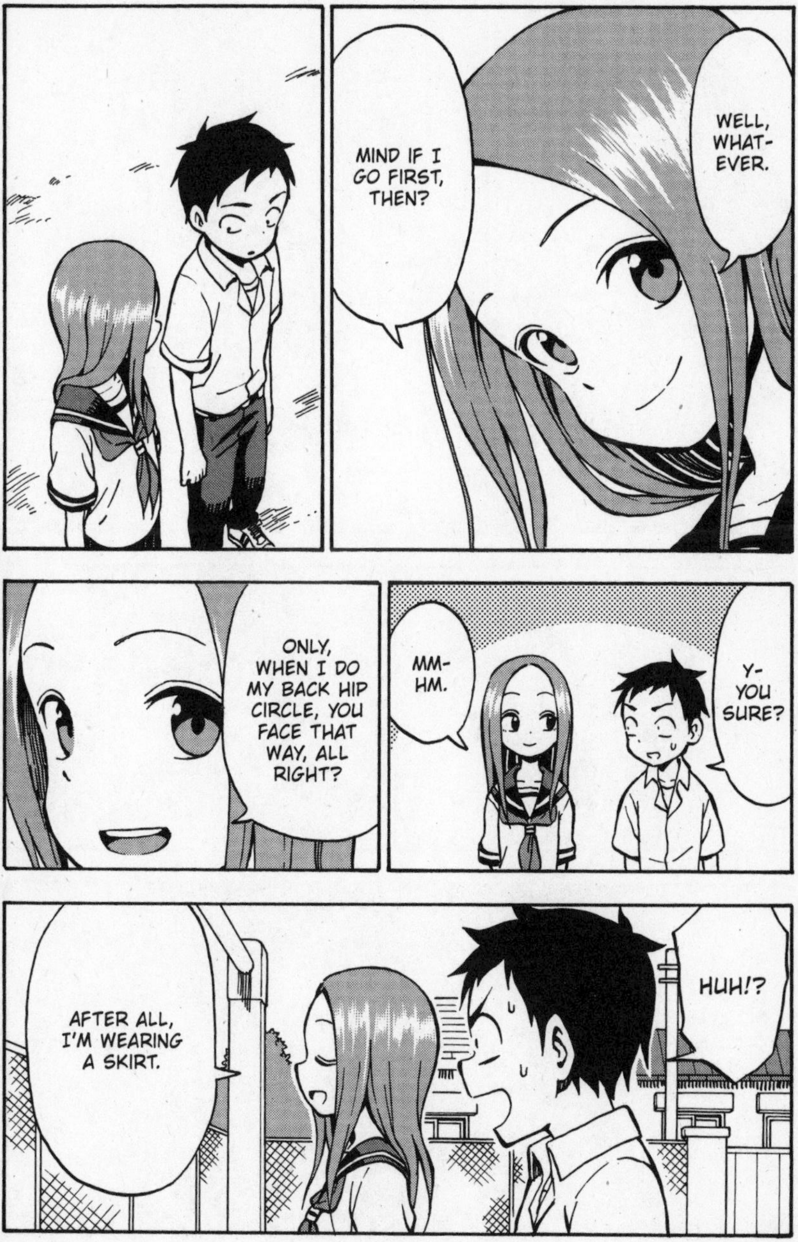
WELL, WHAT-EVER.
MIND IF I GO FIRST, THEN?
Y- YOU SURE?
MM-HM.
ONLY, WHEN I DO MY BACK HIP CIRCLE, YOU FACE THAT WAY, ALL RIGHT?
HUH!?
AFTER ALL, I'M WEARING A SKIRT.

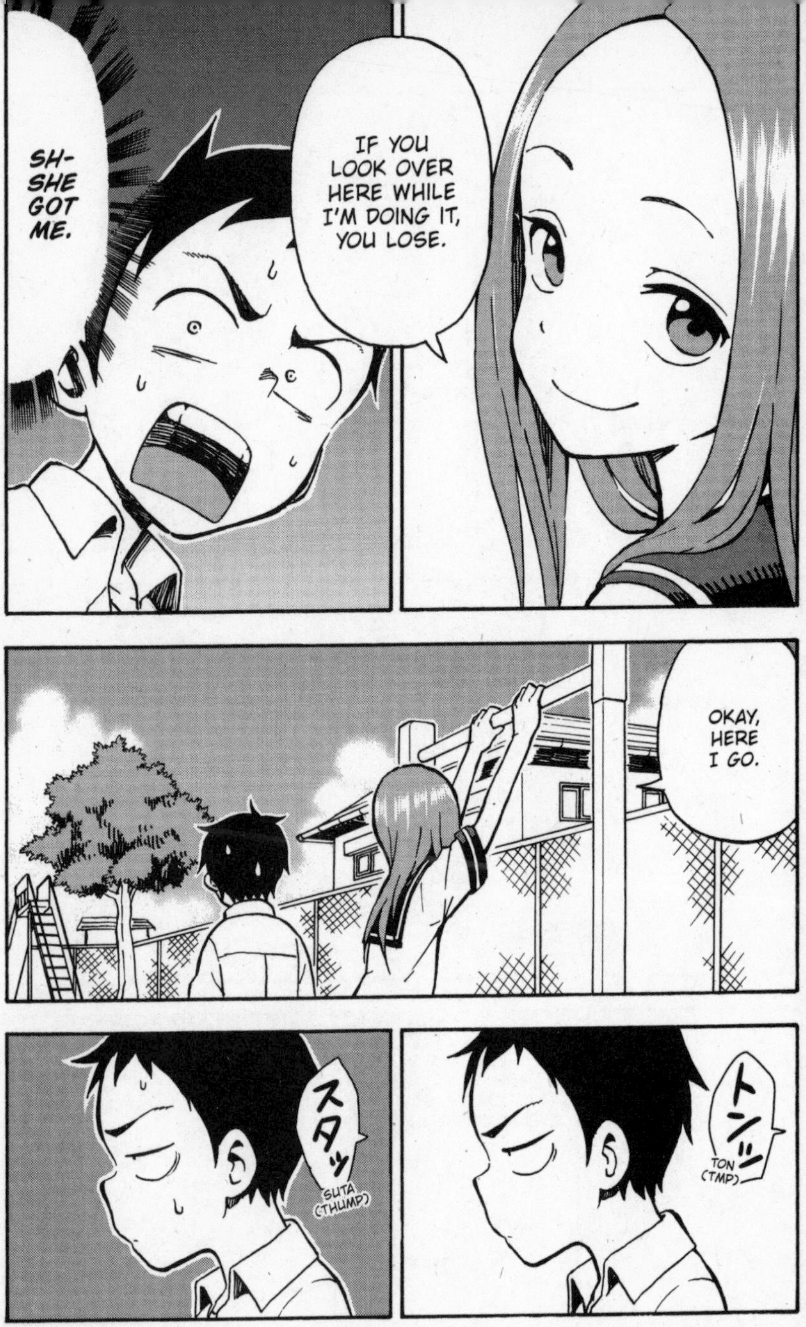
IF YOU LOOK OVER HERE WHILE I'M DOING IT, YOU LOSE.
SH-SHE GOT ME.
OKAY, HERE I GO.
トンッ
TON (TMP)
スタッ
SUTA (THUMP)

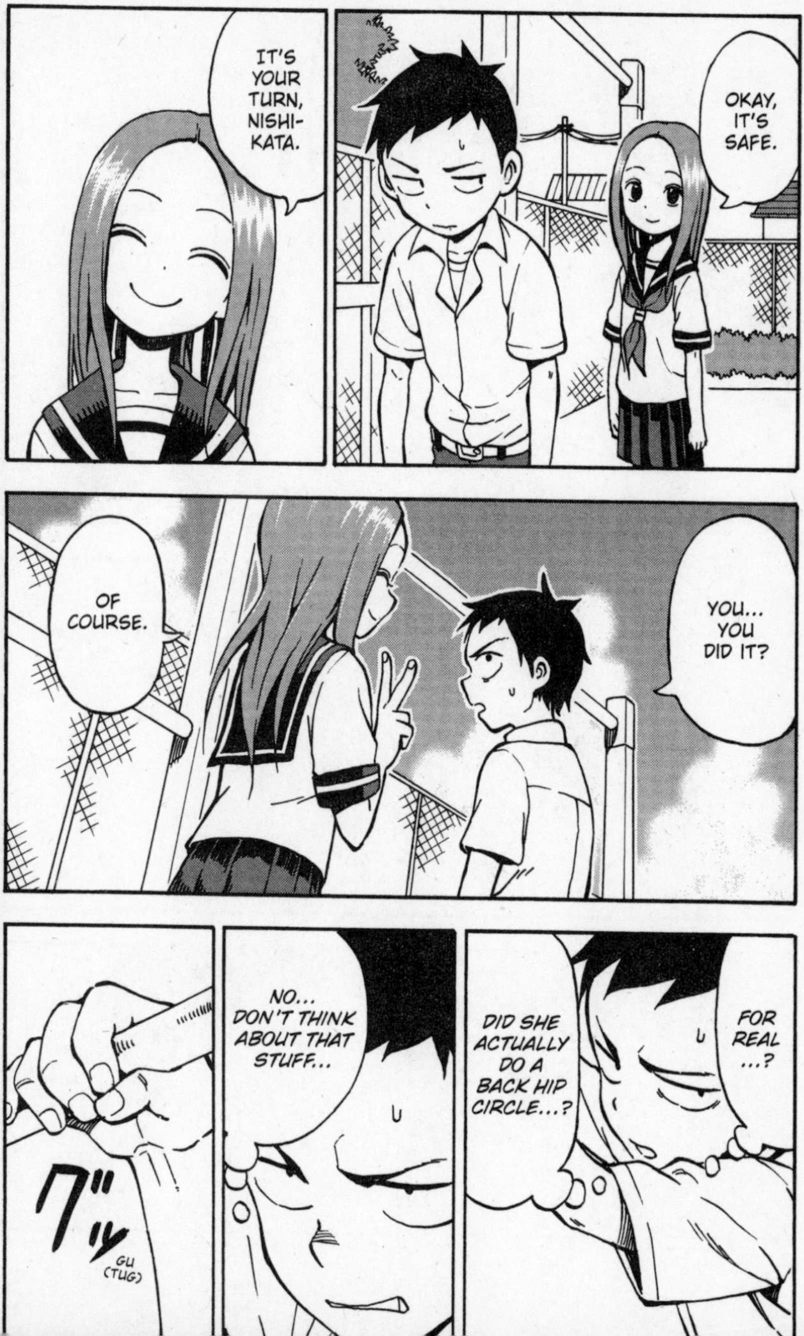
OKAY, IT'S SAFE.
IT'S YOUR TURN, NISHI-KATA.
YOU... YOU DID IT?
OF COURSE.
FOR REAL ...?
DID SHE ACTUALLY DO A BACK HIP CIRCLE...?
NO... DON'T THINK ABOUT THAT STUFF...
グッ
GU (TUG)

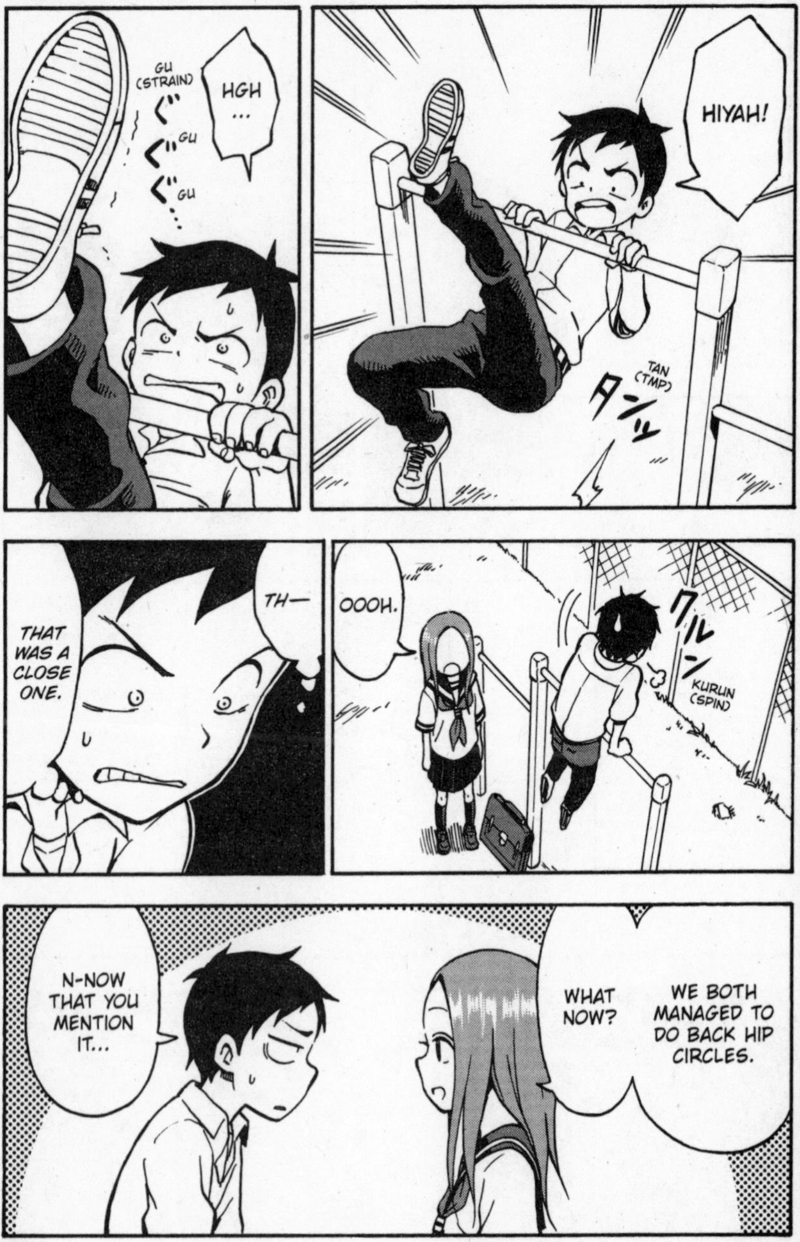
HIYAH!
TAN (TMP)
タンッ
HGH...
GU (STRAIN)
ぐ
ぐ GU
ぐ GU
OOOH.
クルン
KURUN (SPIN)
TH—
THAT WAS A CLOSE ONE.
WE BOTH MANAGED TO DO BACK HIP CIRCLES.
WHAT NOW?
N-NOW THAT YOU MENTION IT...

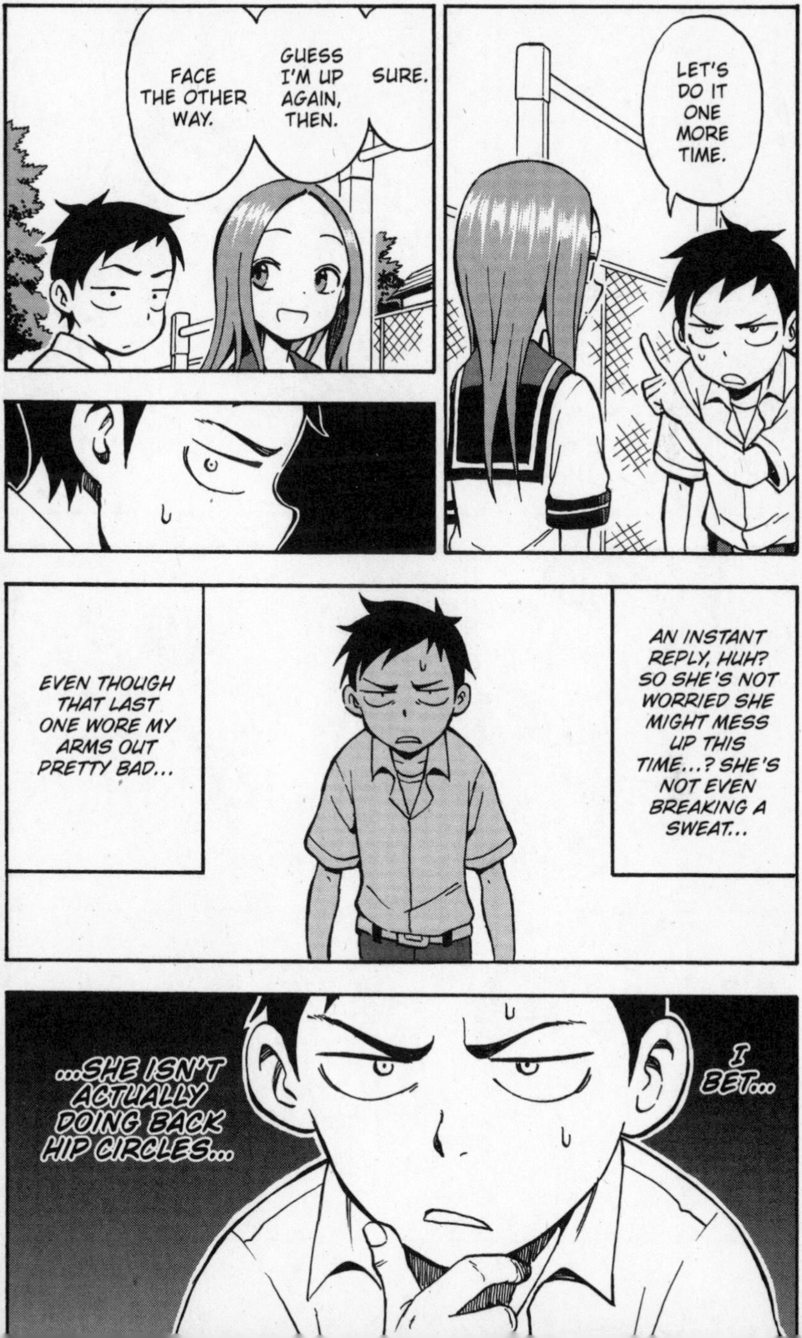
LET'S DO IT ONE MORE TIME.
SURE.
GUESS I'M UP AGAIN, THEN.
FACE THE OTHER WAY.
AN INSTANT REPLY, HUH? SO SHE'S NOT WORRIED SHE MIGHT MESS UP THIS TIME...? SHE'S NOT EVEN BREAKING A SWEAT...
EVEN THOUGH THAT LAST ONE WORE MY ARMS OUT PRETTY BAD...
I BET...
...SHE ISN'T ACTUALLY DOING BACK HIP CIRCLES...

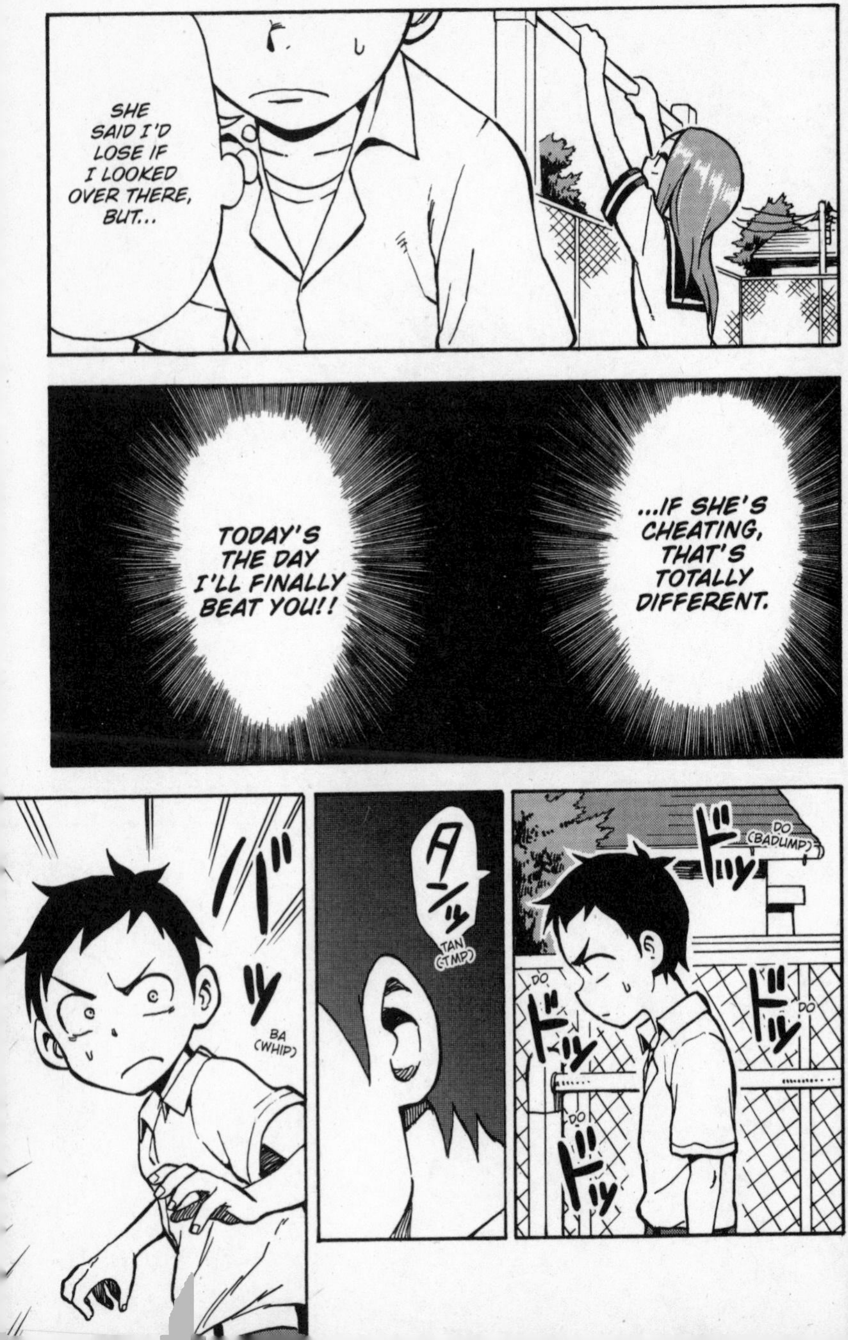
SHE SAID I'D LOSE IF I LOOKED OVER THERE, BUT...
...IF SHE'S CHEATING, THAT'S TOTALLY DIFFERENT.
TODAY'S THE DAY I'LL FINALLY BEAT YOU!!
DO (BADUMP)
DO
DO
DO
TAN (TMP)
BA (WHIP)

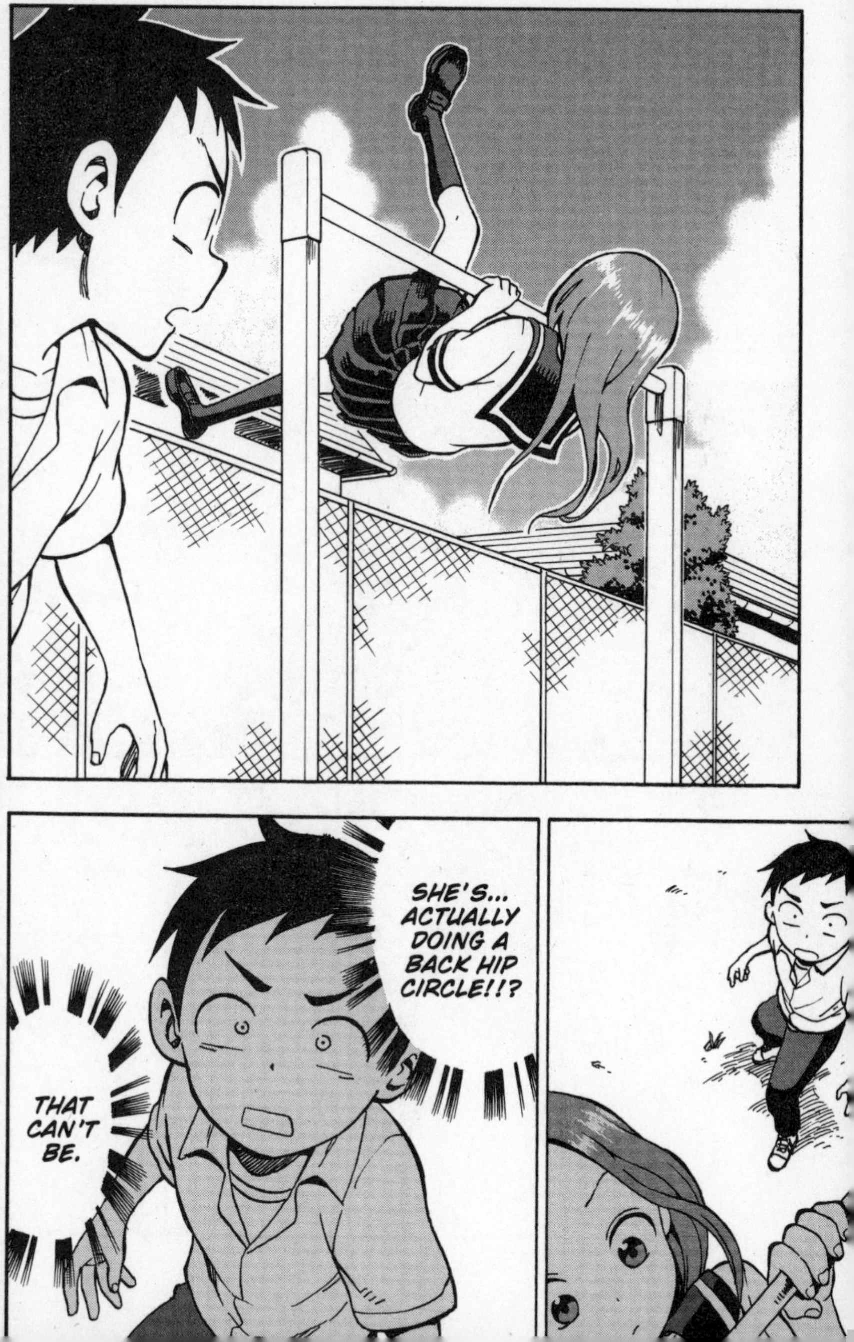
SHE'S... ACTUALLY DOING A BACK HIP CIRCLE!!?
THAT CAN'T BE.

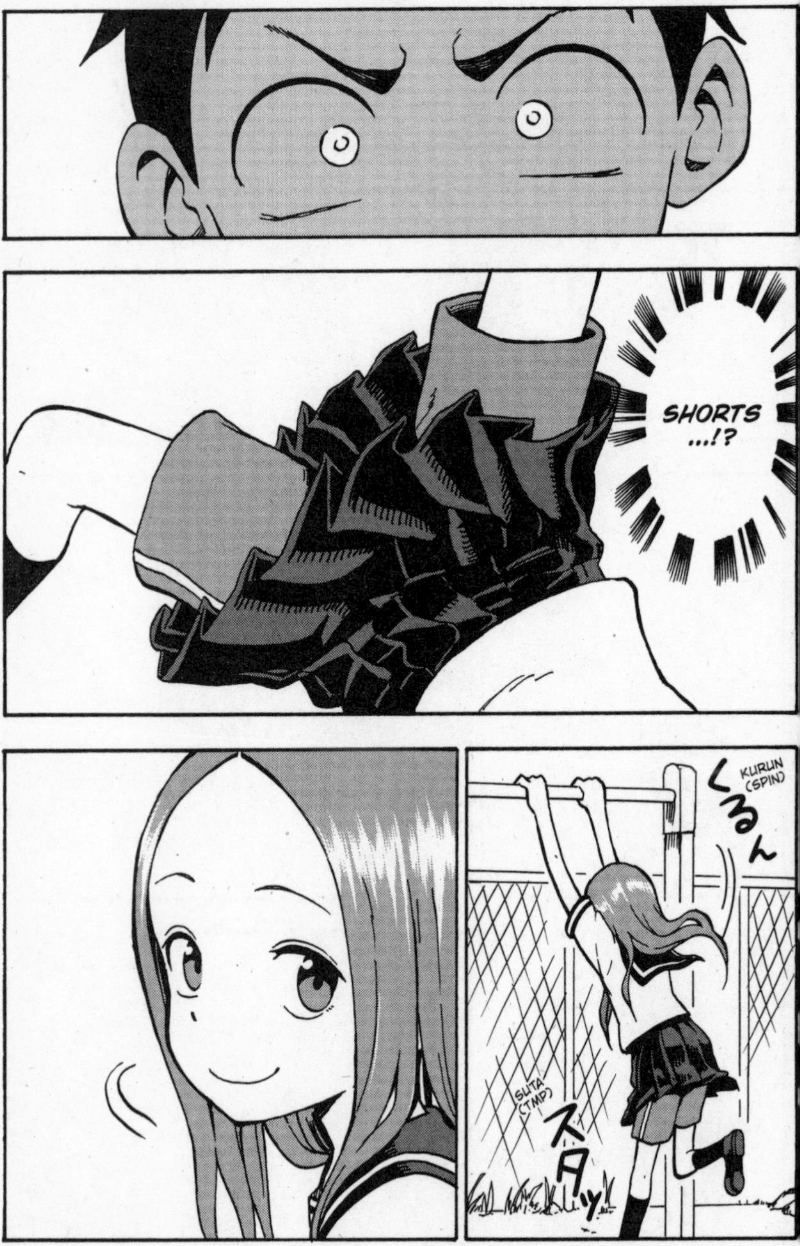
SHORTS ...!?
KURUN (SPIN)
くるん
SUTA (TMP)
スタッ

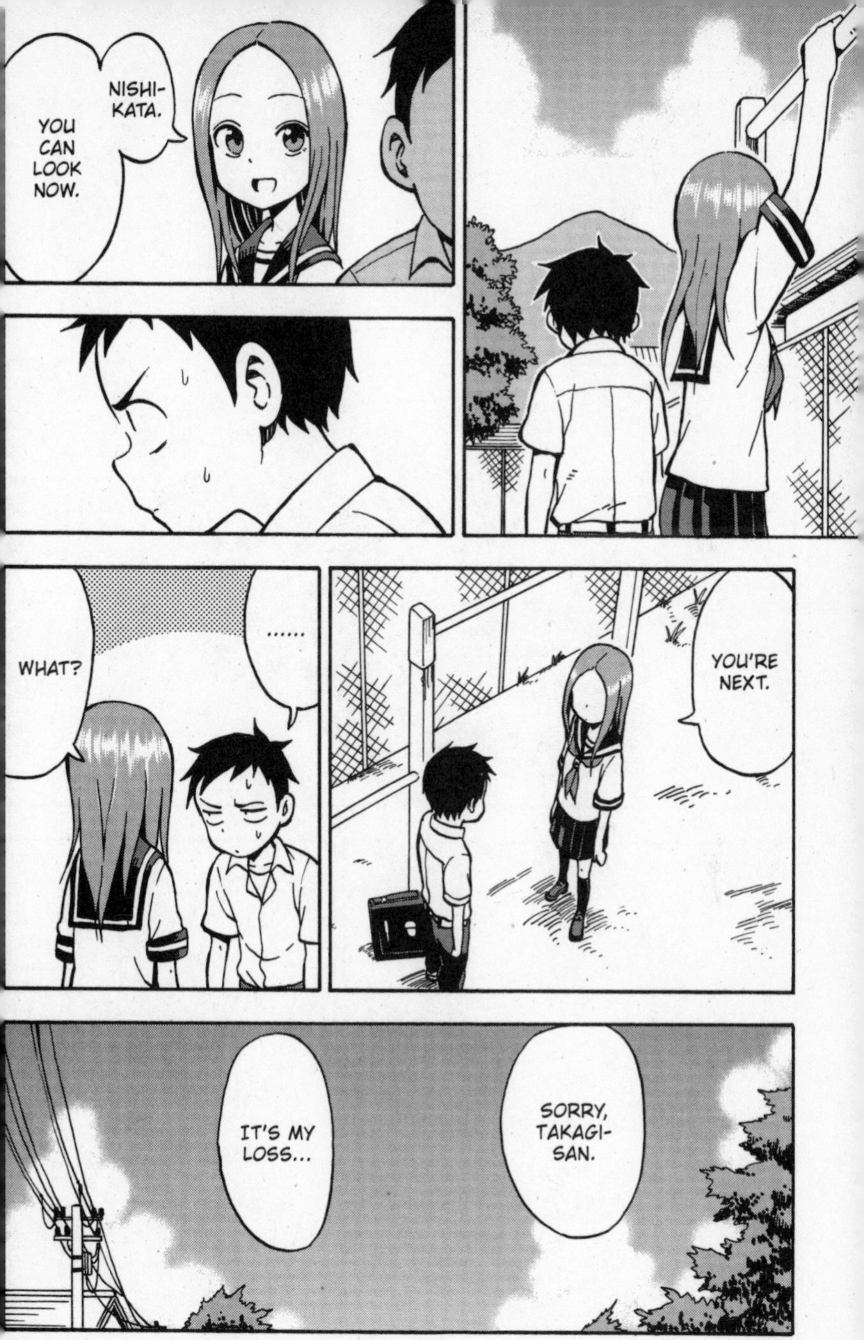
NISHI-KATA.
YOU CAN LOOK NOW.
YOU'RE NEXT.
......
WHAT?
SORRY, TAKAGI-SAN.
IT'S MY LOSS...

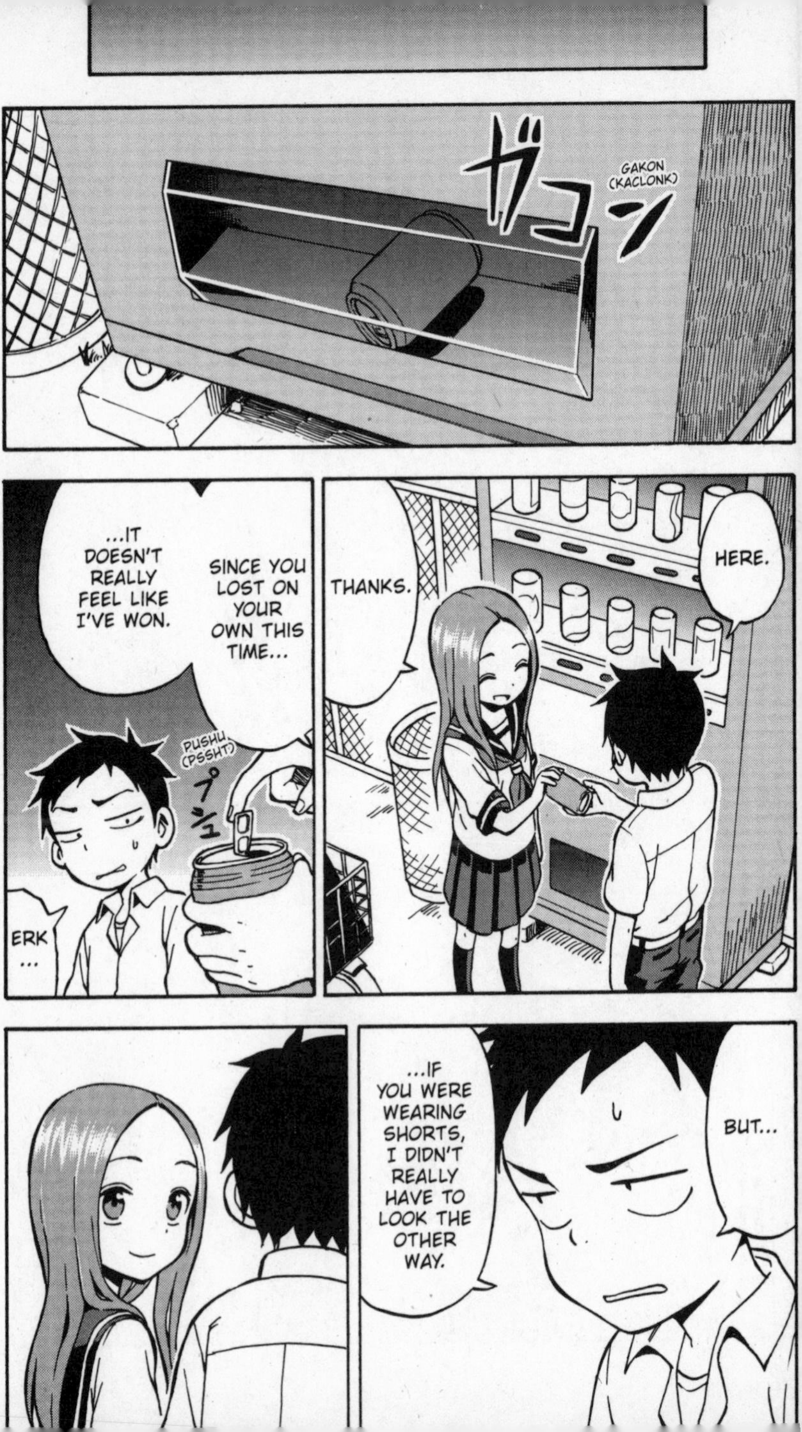
GAKON (KACLONK)
ガコン
HERE.
THANKS.
SINCE YOU LOST ON YOUR OWN THIS TIME...
...IT DOESN'T REALLY FEEL LIKE I'VE WON.
PUSHU (PSSHT)
プシュ
ERK ...
BUT...
...IF YOU WERE WEARING SHORTS, I DIDN'T REALLY HAVE TO LOOK THE OTHER WAY.

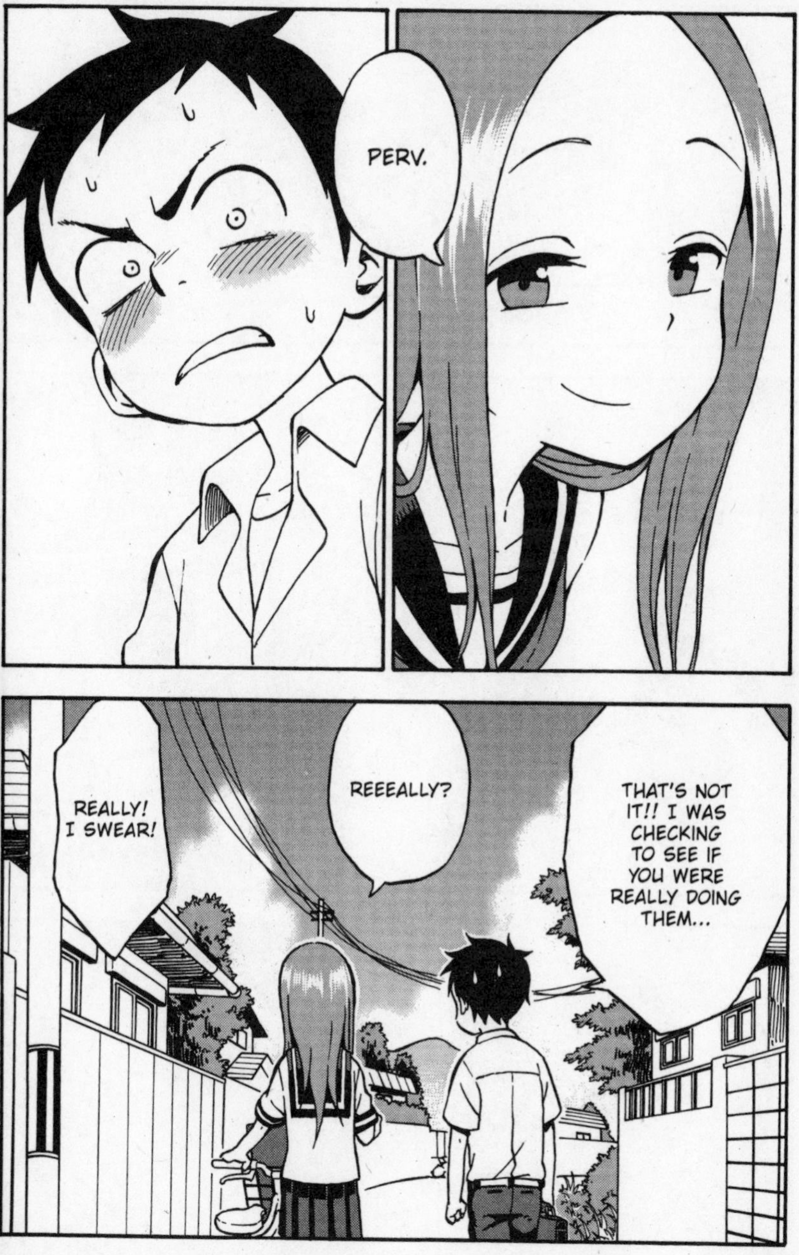
PERV.
THAT'S NOT IT!! I WAS CHECKING TO SEE IF YOU WERE REALLY DOING THEM...
REEEALLY?
REALLY! I SWEAR!

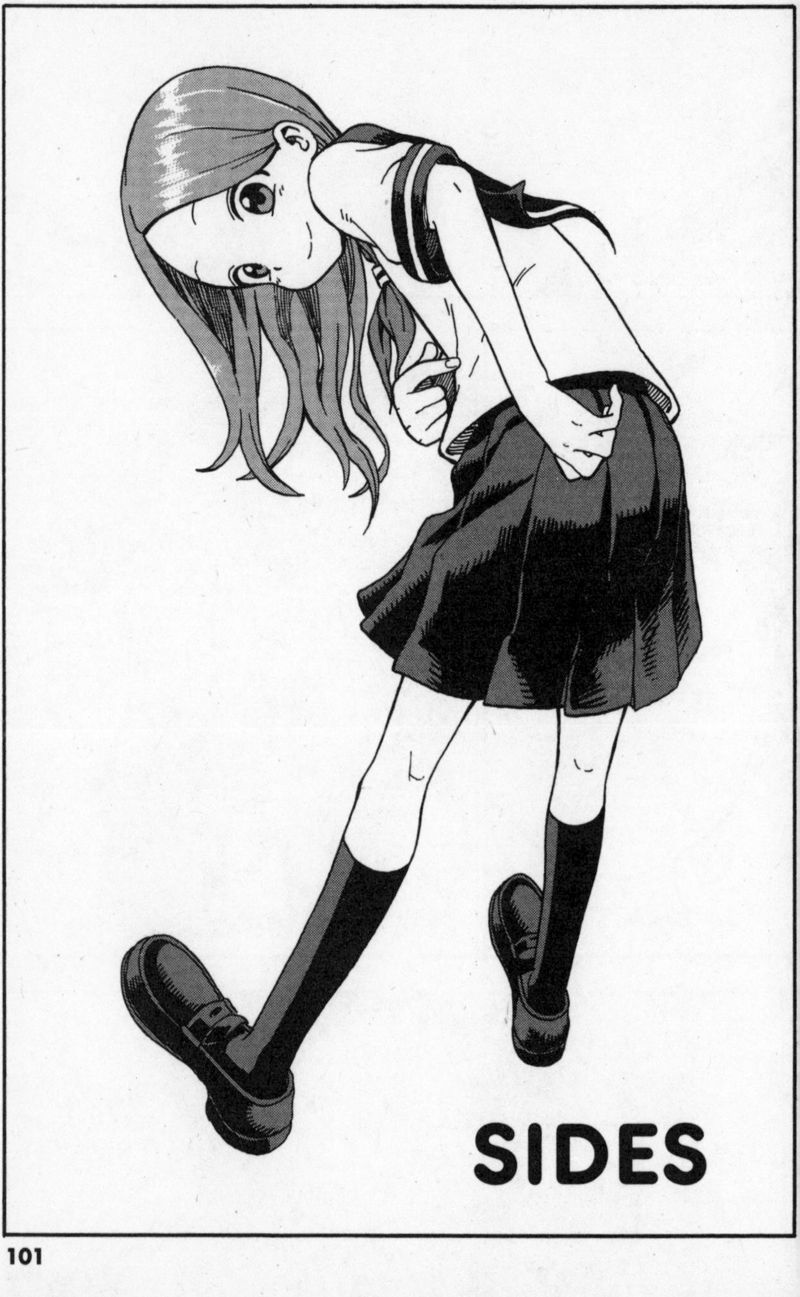
SIDES

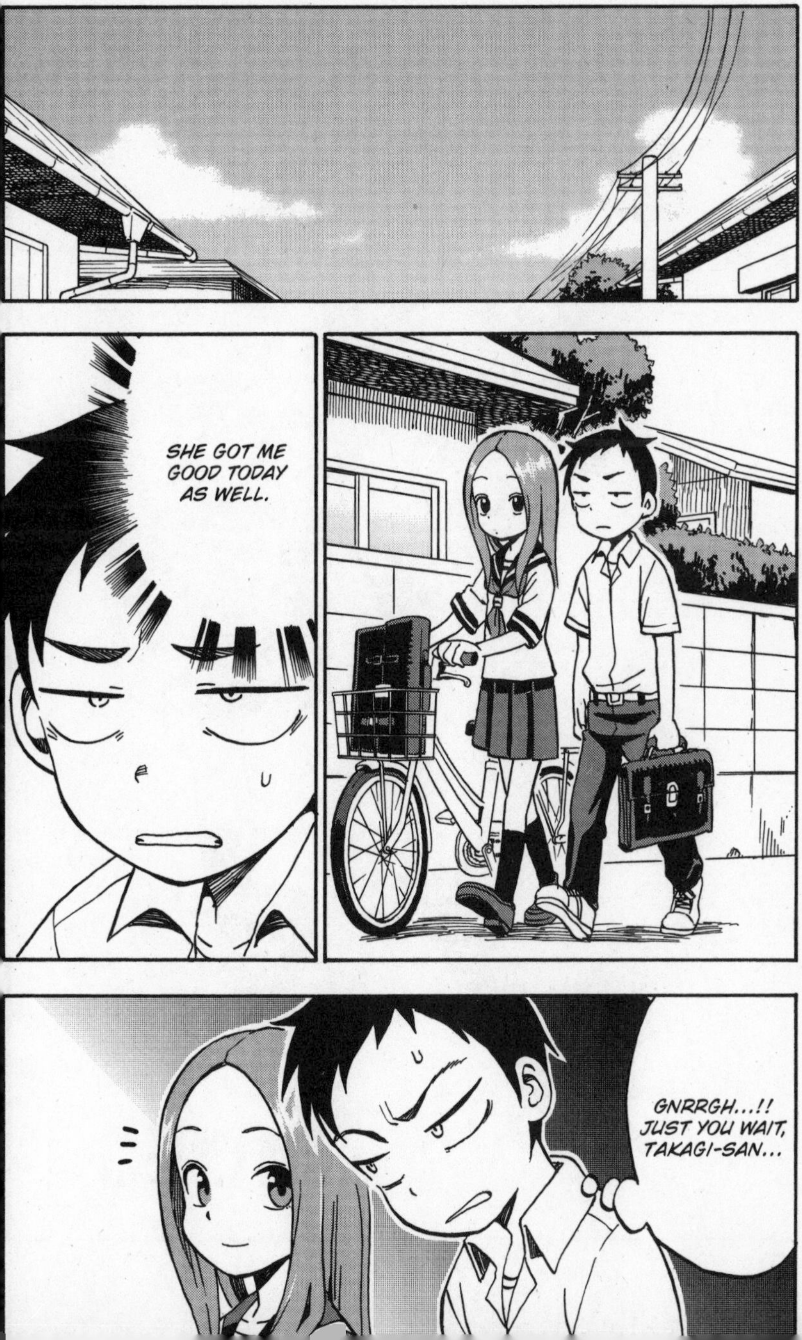
SHE GOT ME GOOD TODAY AS WELL.
GNRRGH...!! JUST YOU WAIT, TAKAGI-SAN...

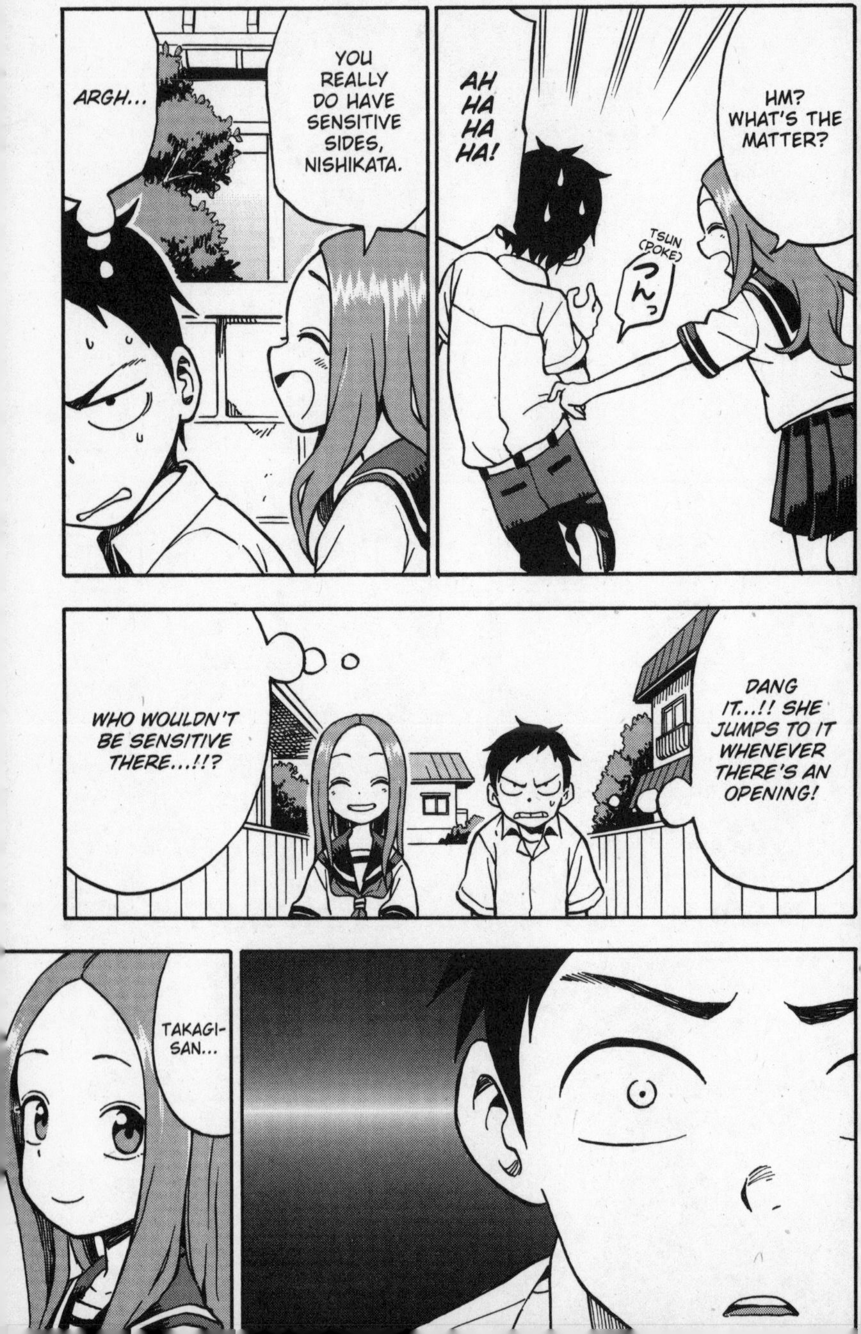
HM? WHAT'S THE MATTER?
TSUN (POKE)
つんっ
AH HA HA HA!
YOU REALLY DO HAVE SENSITIVE SIDES, NISHIKATA.
ARGH...
DANG IT...!! SHE JUMPS TO IT WHENEVER THERE'S AN OPENING!
WHO WOULDN'T BE SENSITIVE THERE...!!?
TAKAGI-SAN...

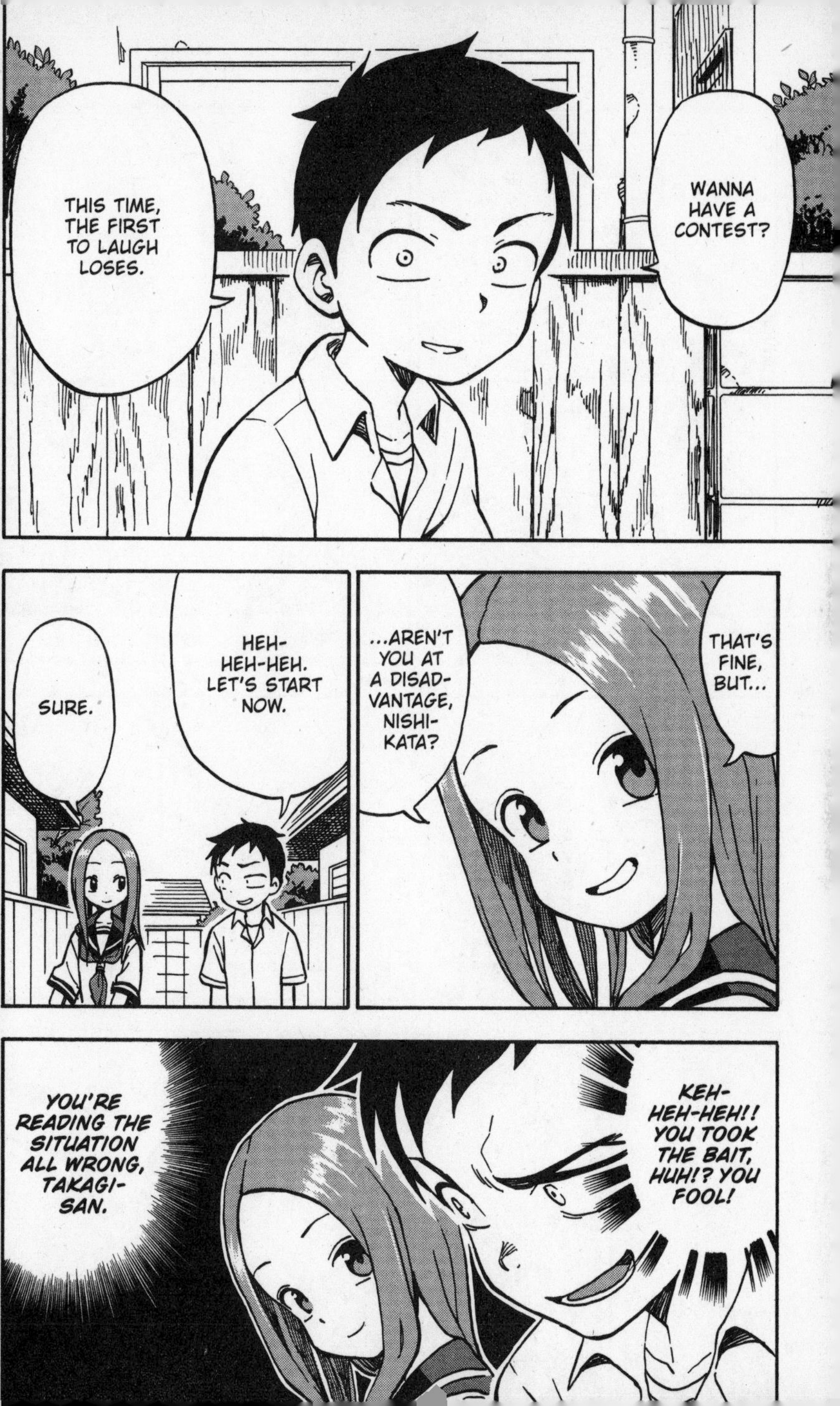
WANNA HAVE A CONTEST?
THIS TIME, THE FIRST TO LAUGH LOSES.
THAT'S FINE, BUT...
...AREN'T YOU AT A DISADVANTAGE, NISHIKATA?
HEH-HEH-HEH. LET'S START NOW.
SURE.
KEH-HEH-HEH!! YOU TOOK THE BAIT, HUH!? YOU FOOL!
YOU'RE READING THE SITUATION ALL WRONG, TAKAGI-SAN.

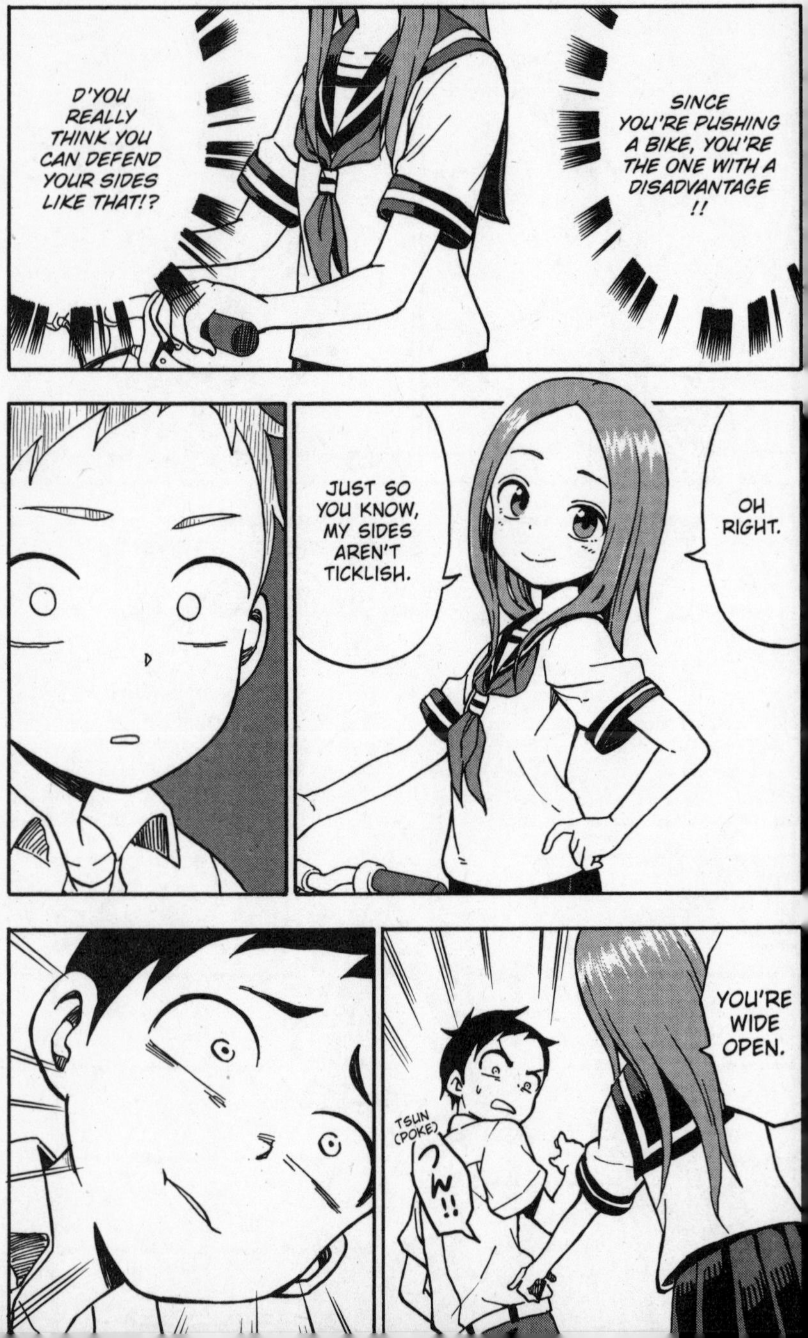
SINCE YOU'RE PUSHING A BIKE, YOU'RE THE ONE WITH A DISADVANTAGE !!
D'YOU REALLY THINK YOU CAN DEFEND YOUR SIDES LIKE THAT!?
OH RIGHT.
JUST SO YOU KNOW, MY SIDES AREN'T TICKLISH.
YOU'RE WIDE OPEN.
TSUN (POKE)

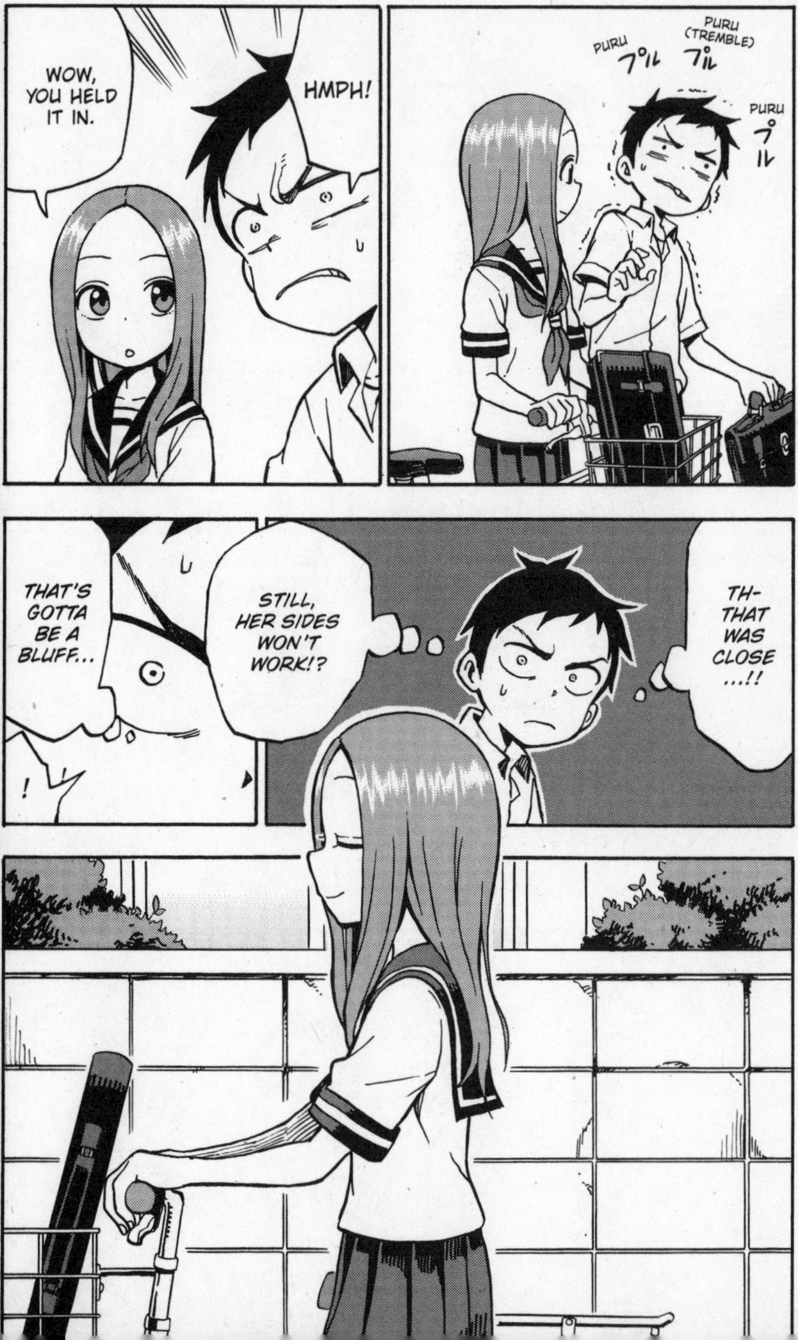
PURU (TREMBLE) プル
PURU プル
PURU プル
HMPH!
WOW, YOU HELD IT IN.
TH-THAT WAS CLOSE ...!!
STILL, HER SIDES WON'T WORK!?
THAT'S GOTTA BE A BLUFF...
!

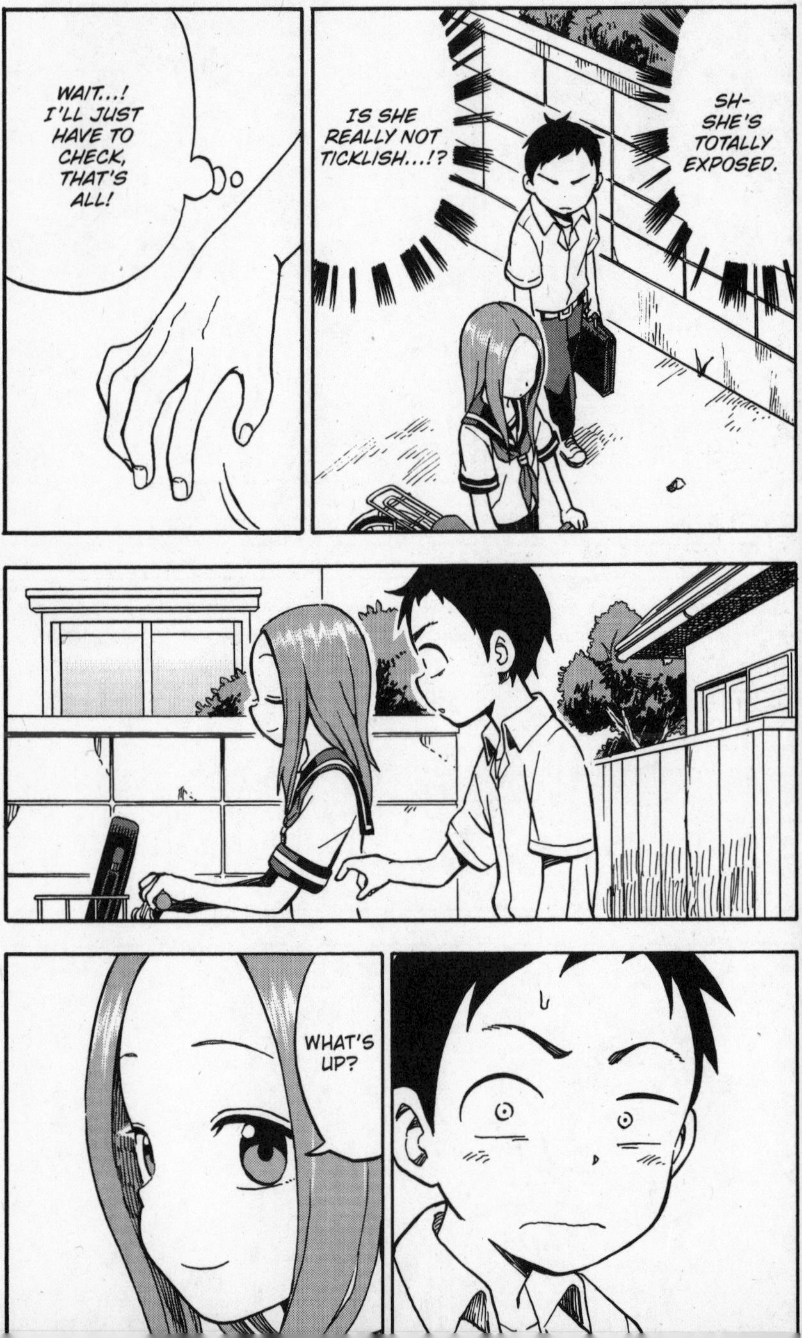
SH- SHE'S TOTALLY EXPOSED.
IS SHE REALLY NOT TICKLISH...!?
WAIT...! I'LL JUST HAVE TO CHECK, THAT'S ALL!
WHAT'S UP?

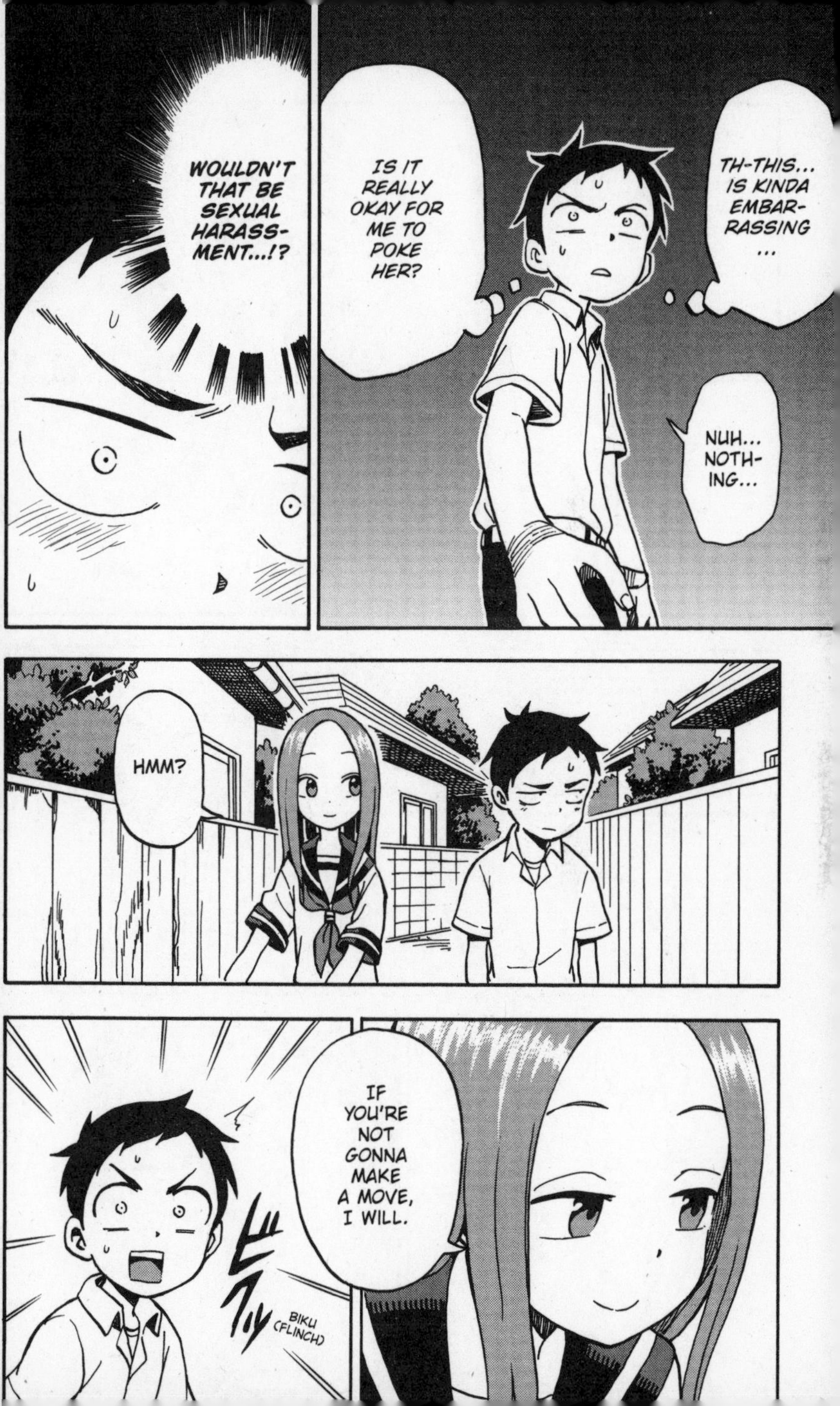
TH-THIS... IS KINDA EMBARRASSING...
IS IT REALLY OKAY FOR ME TO POKE HER?
NUH... NOTHING...
WOULDN'T THAT BE SEXUAL HARASSMENT...!?
HMM?
IF YOU'RE NOT GONNA MAKE A MOVE, I WILL.
BIKU (FLINCH)

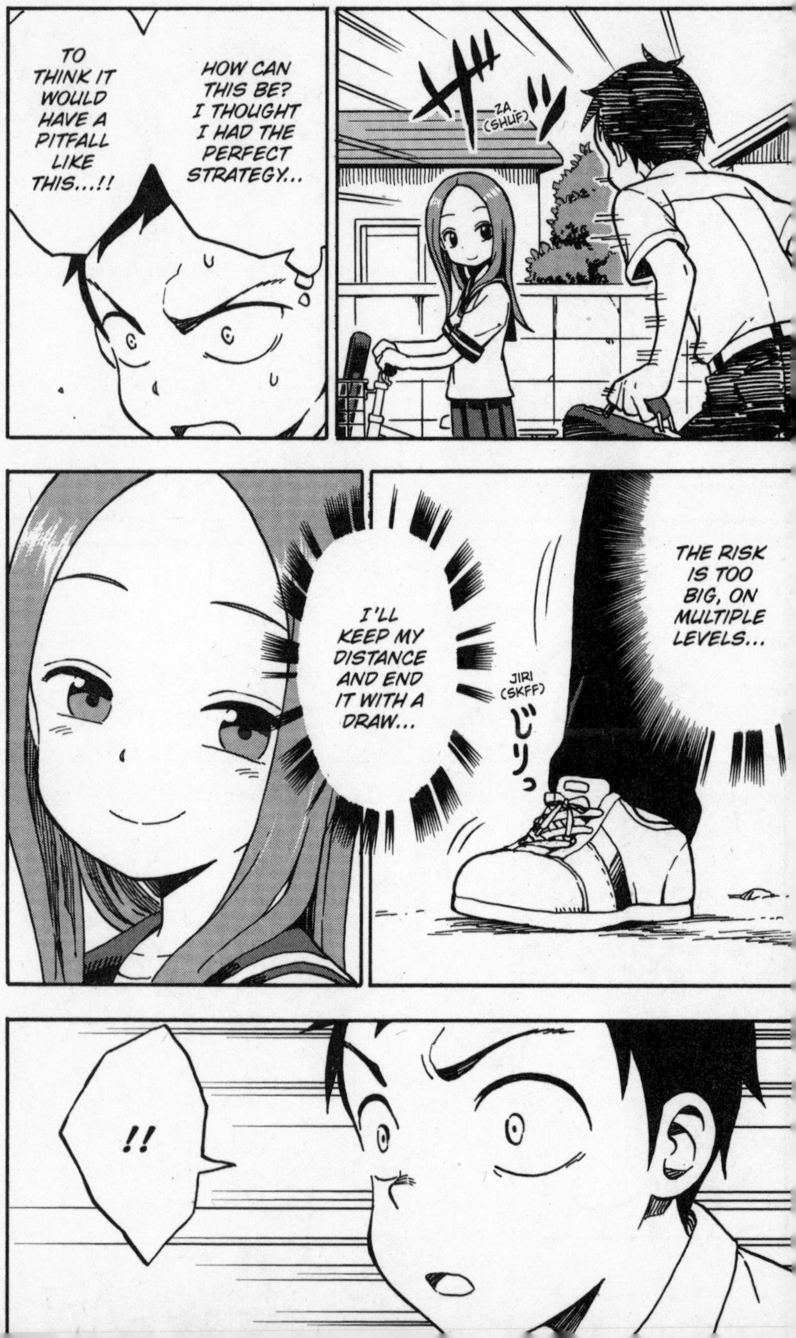
ZA (SHUF)
HOW CAN THIS BE? I THOUGHT I HAD THE PERFECT STRATEGY...
TO THINK IT WOULD HAVE A PITFALL LIKE THIS...!!
THE RISK IS TOO BIG, ON MULTIPLE LEVELS...
JIRI (SKFF)
じりっ
I'LL KEEP MY DISTANCE AND END IT WITH A DRAW...
!!

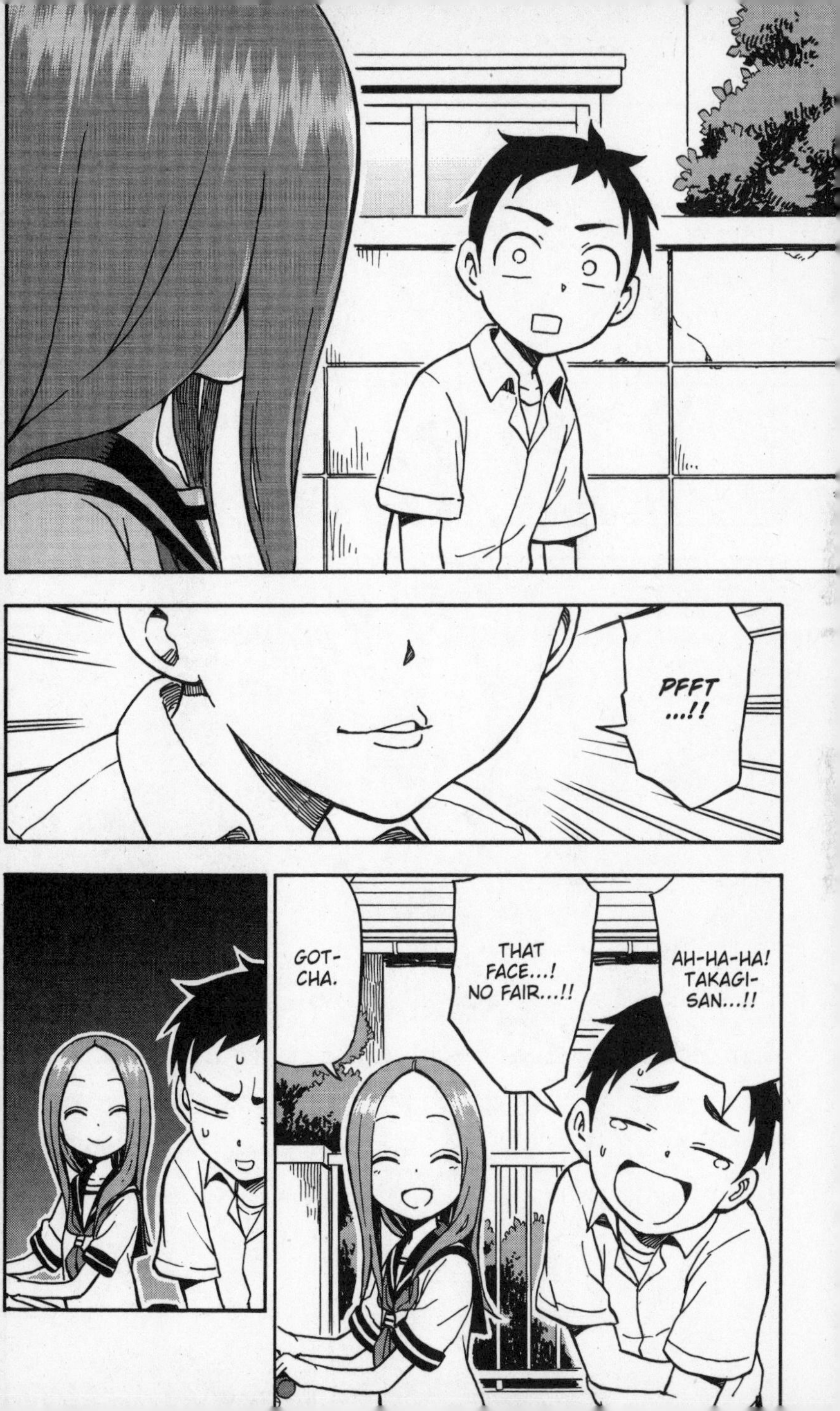
...
PFFT ...!!
AH-HA-HA! TAKAGI-SAN...!!
THAT FACE...! NO FAIR...!!
GOT-CHA.

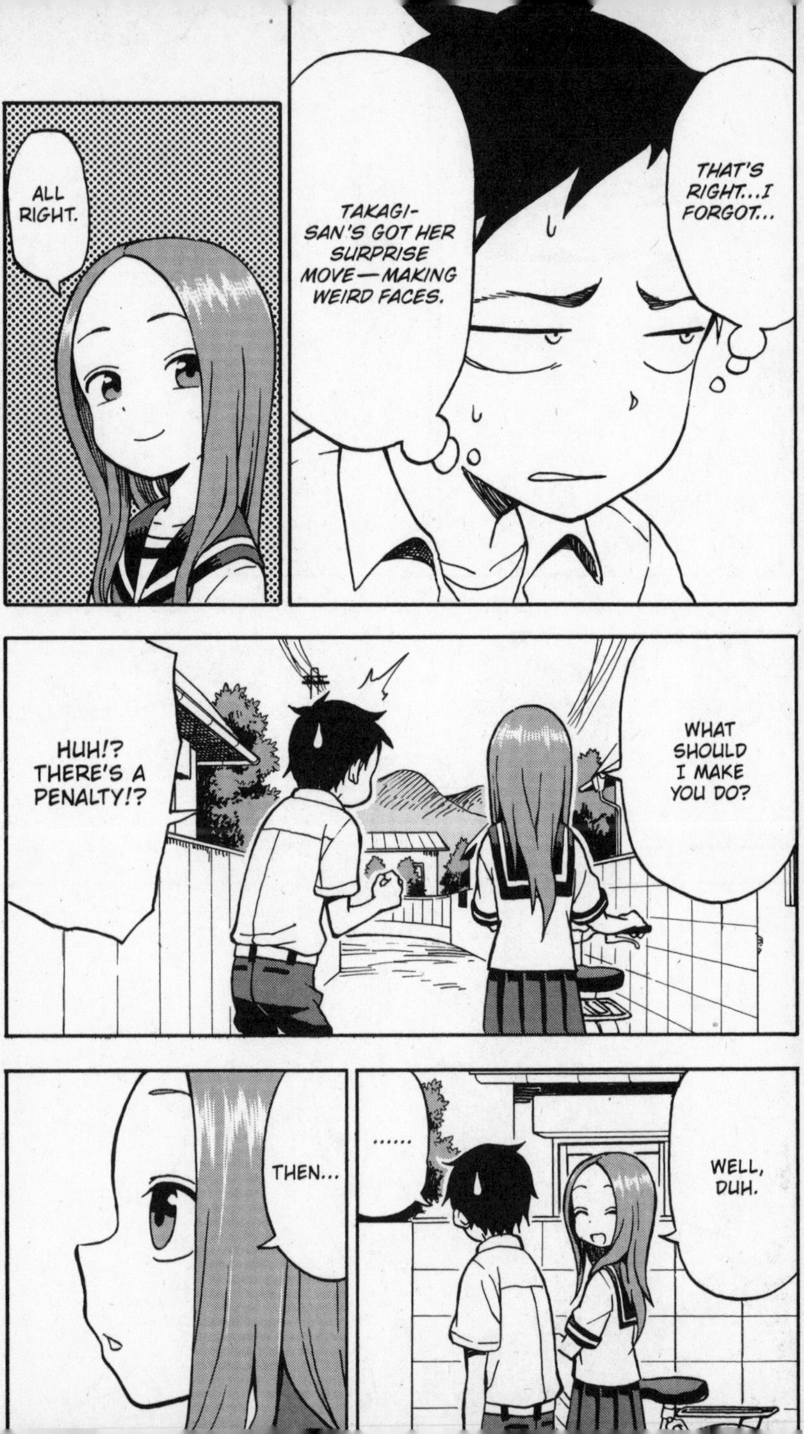
THAT'S RIGHT...I FORGOT...
TAKAGI-SAN'S GOT HER SURPRISE MOVE—MAKING WEIRD FACES.
ALL RIGHT.
WHAT SHOULD I MAKE YOU DO?
HUH!? THERE'S A PENALTY!?
WELL, DUH.
......
THEN...

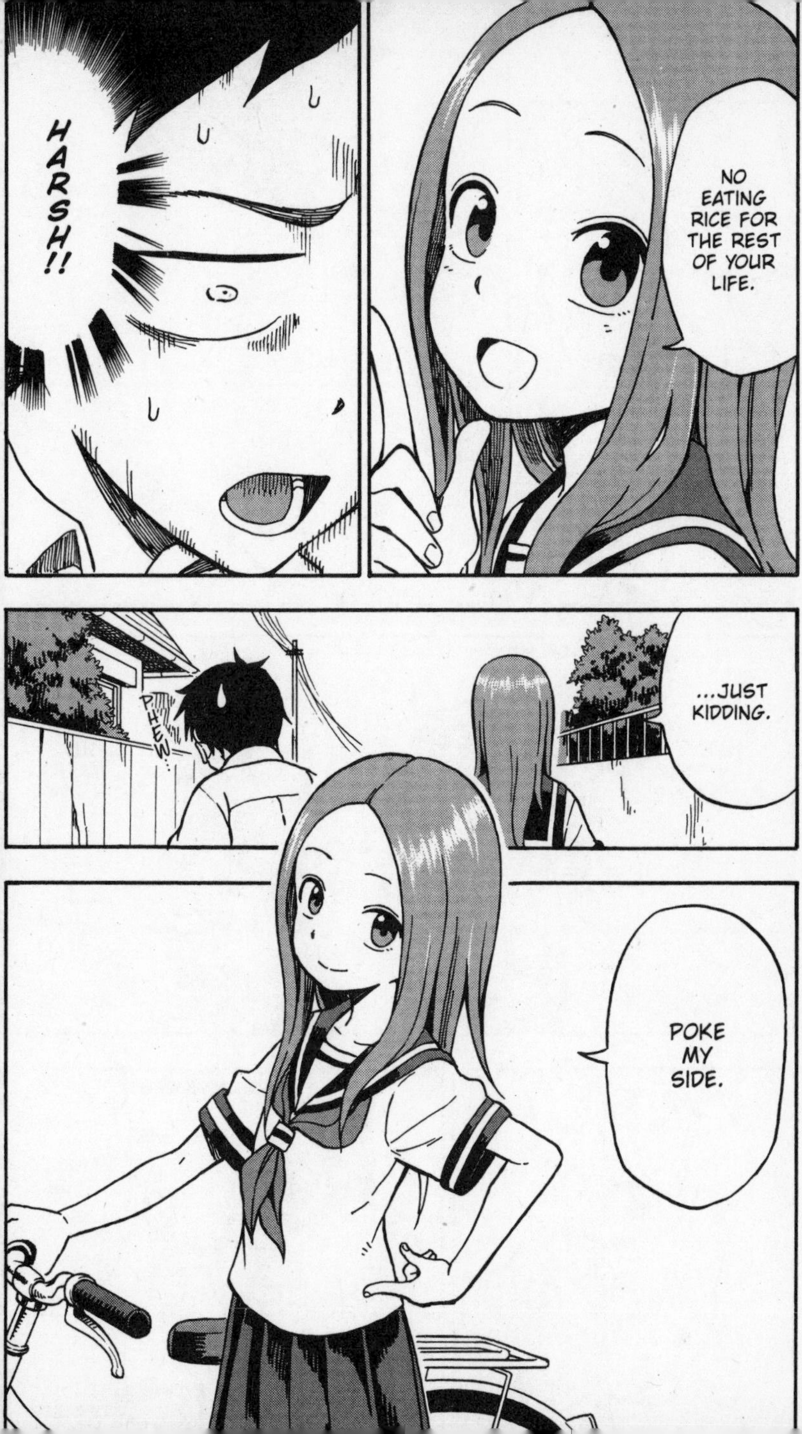
NO EATING RICE FOR THE REST OF YOUR LIFE.
HARSH!!
...JUST KIDDING.
PHEW...
POKE MY SIDE.

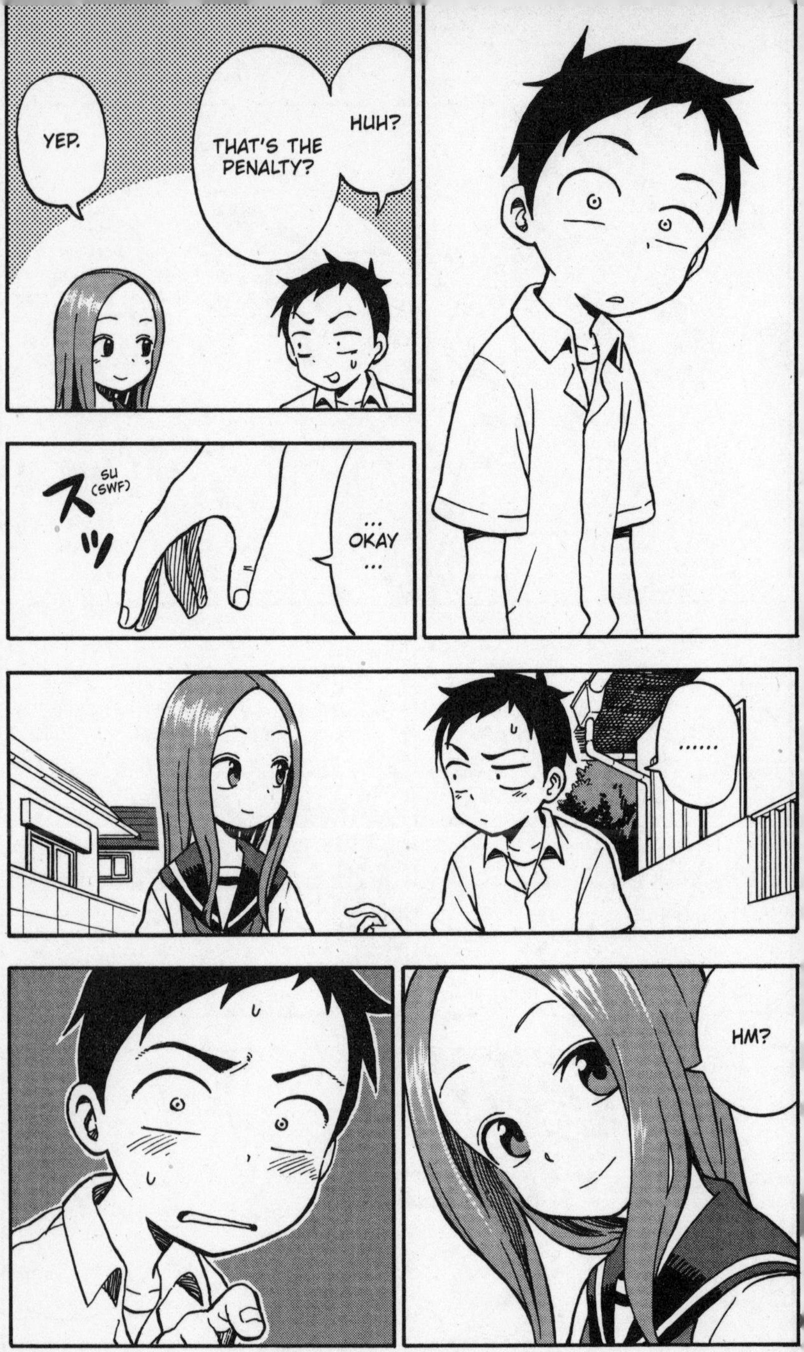
HUH?
THAT'S THE PENALTY?
YEP.
... OKAY ...
SU (SWF)
......
HM?

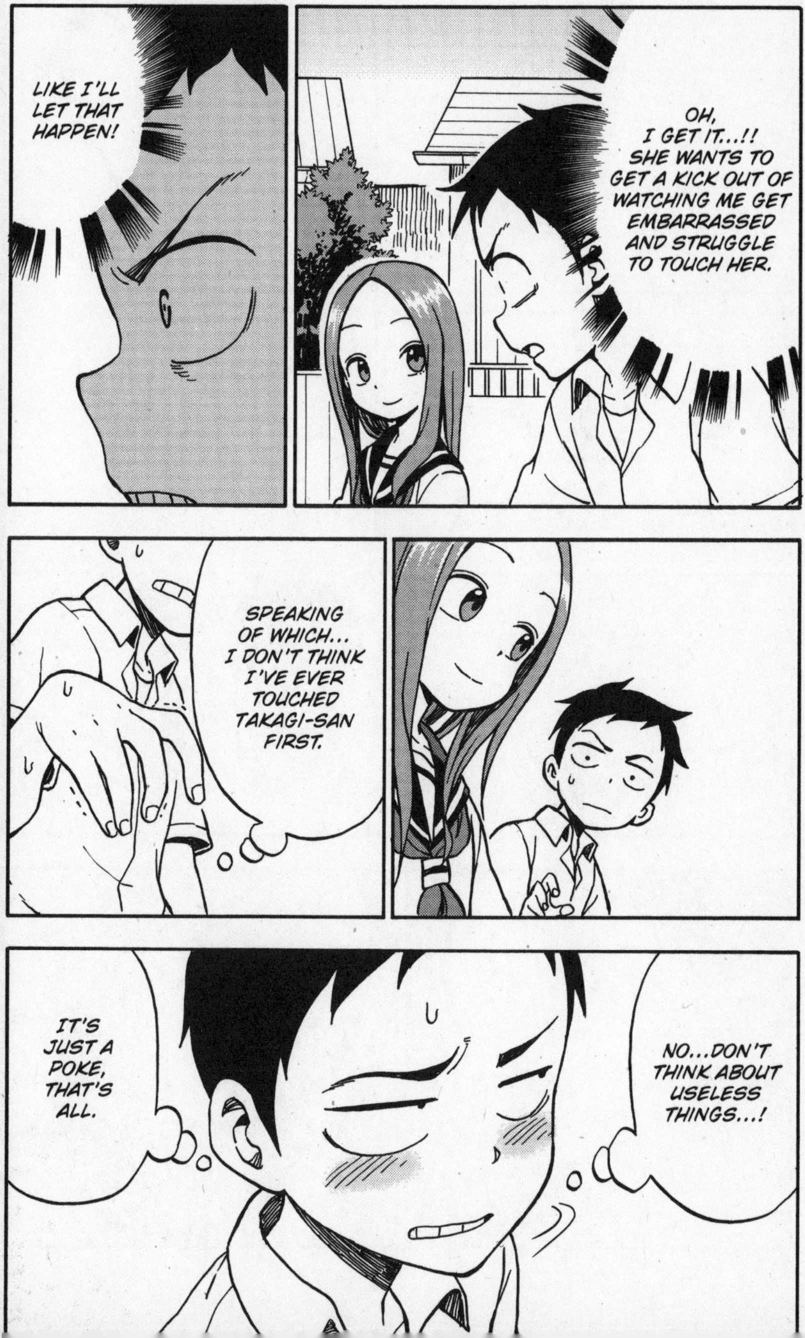
OH, I GET IT...!! SHE WANTS TO GET A KICK OUT OF WATCHING ME GET EMBARRASSED AND STRUGGLE TO TOUCH HER.
LIKE I'LL LET THAT HAPPEN!
SPEAKING OF WHICH... I DON'T THINK I'VE EVER TOUCHED TAKAGI-SAN FIRST.
NO...DON'T THINK ABOUT USELESS THINGS...!
IT'S JUST A POKE, THAT'S ALL.

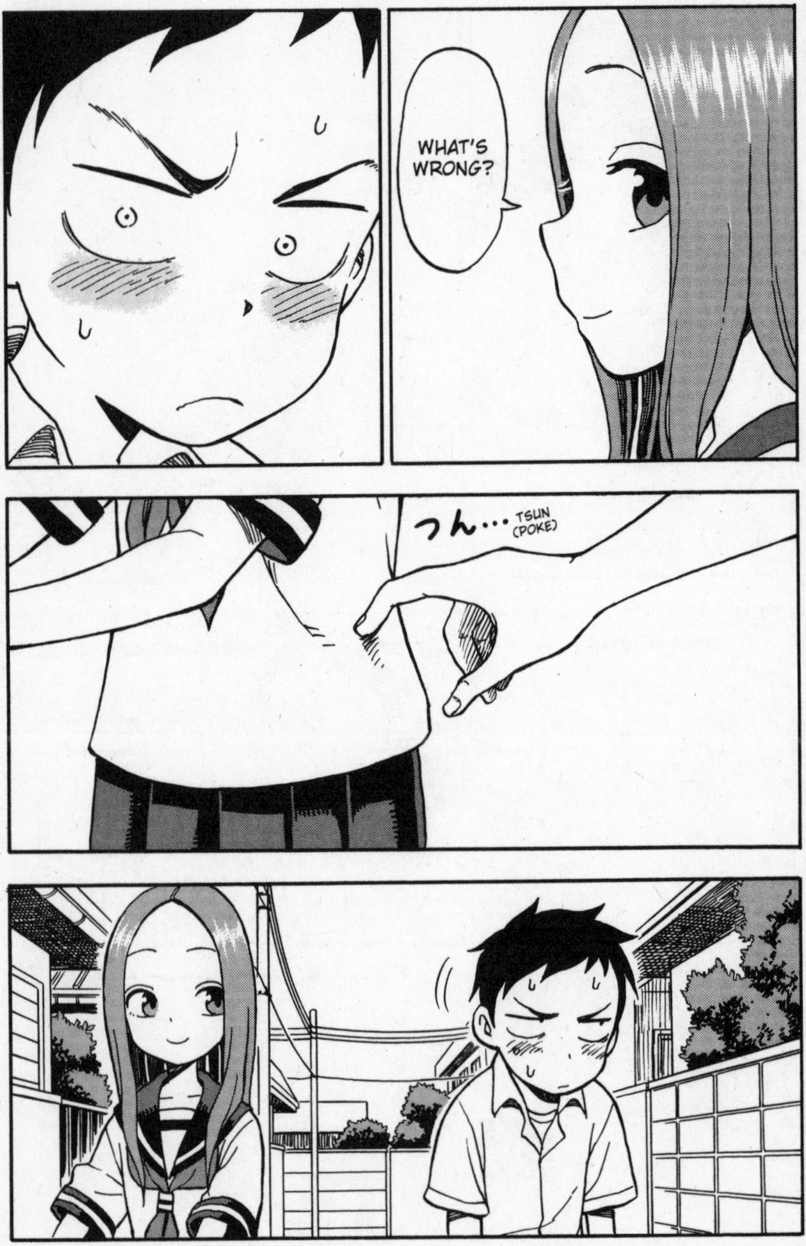
WHAT'S WRONG?
つん… TSUN (POKE)

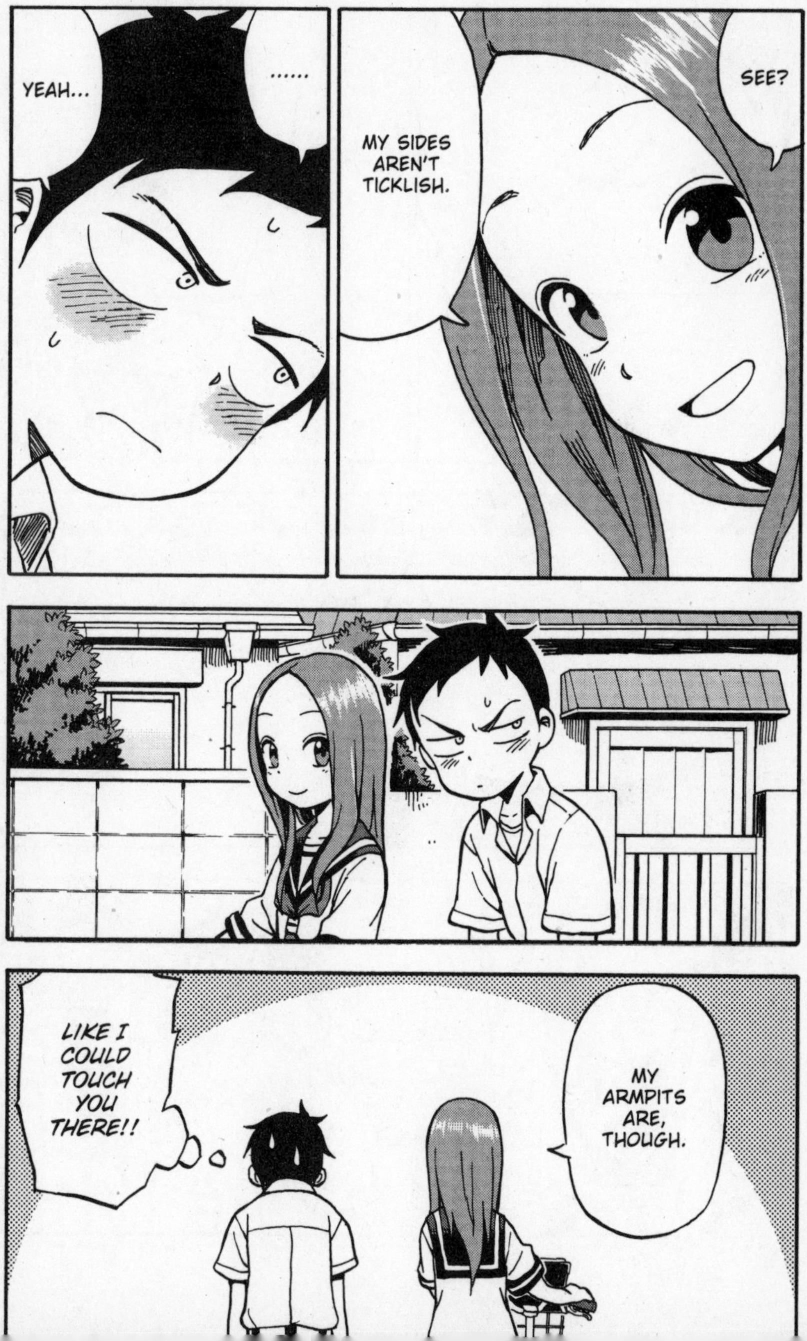
SEE?
MY SIDES AREN'T TICKLISH.
......
YEAH...
..
MY ARMPITS ARE, THOUGH.
LIKE I COULD TOUCH YOU THERE!!

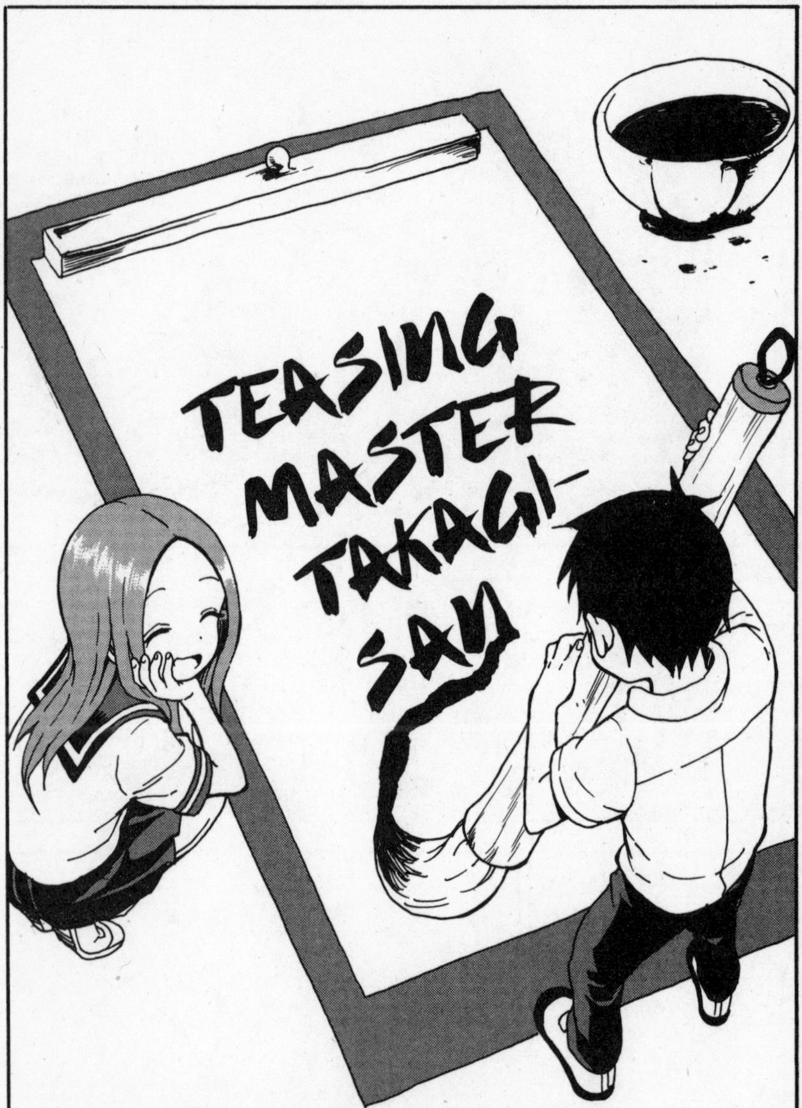
TEASING MASTER TAKAGI-SAN

CALLIGRAPHY

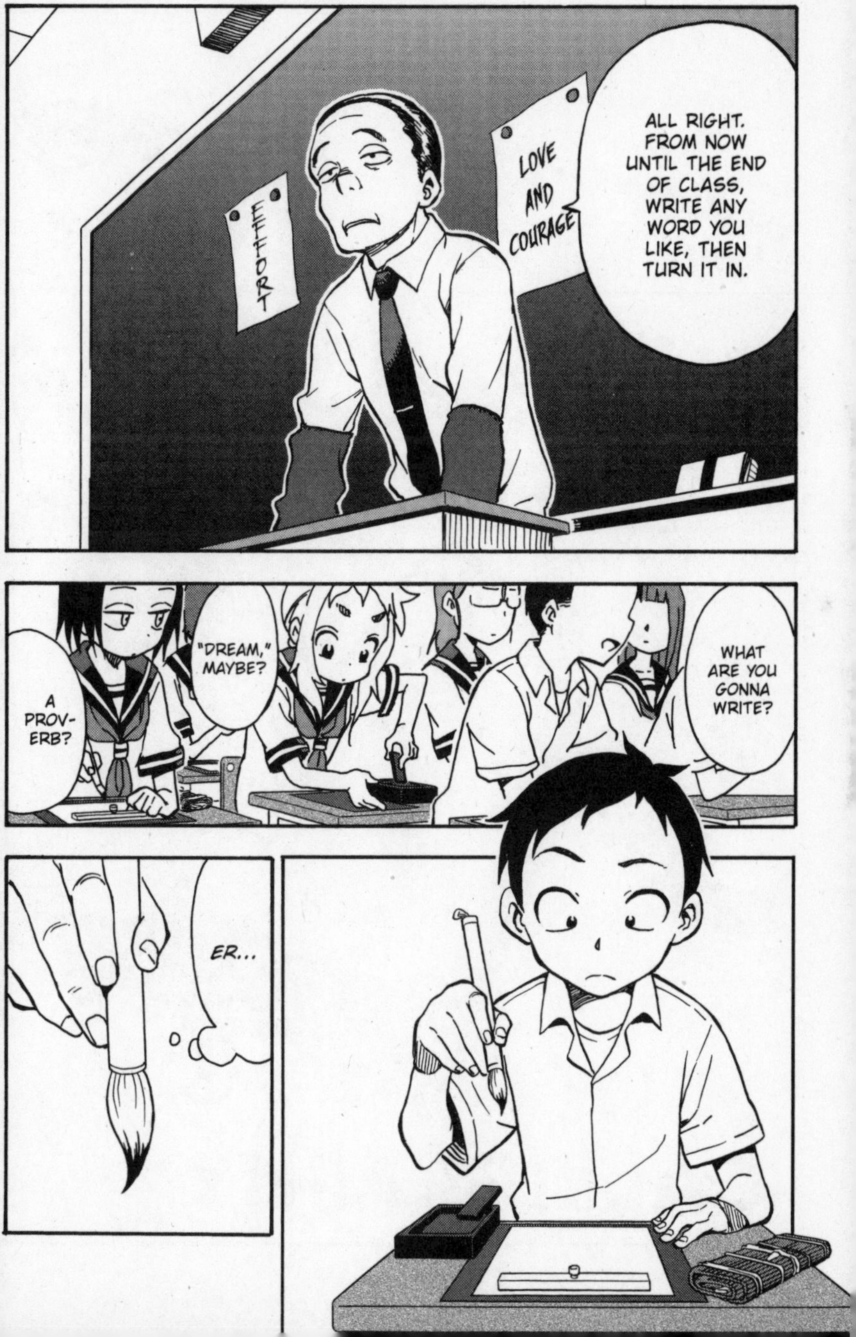
ALL RIGHT. FROM NOW UNTIL THE END OF CLASS, WRITE ANY WORD YOU LIKE, THEN TURN IT IN.
LOVE AND COURAGE
EFFORT
WHAT ARE YOU GONNA WRITE?
"DREAM," MAYBE?
A PROV-ERB?
ER...

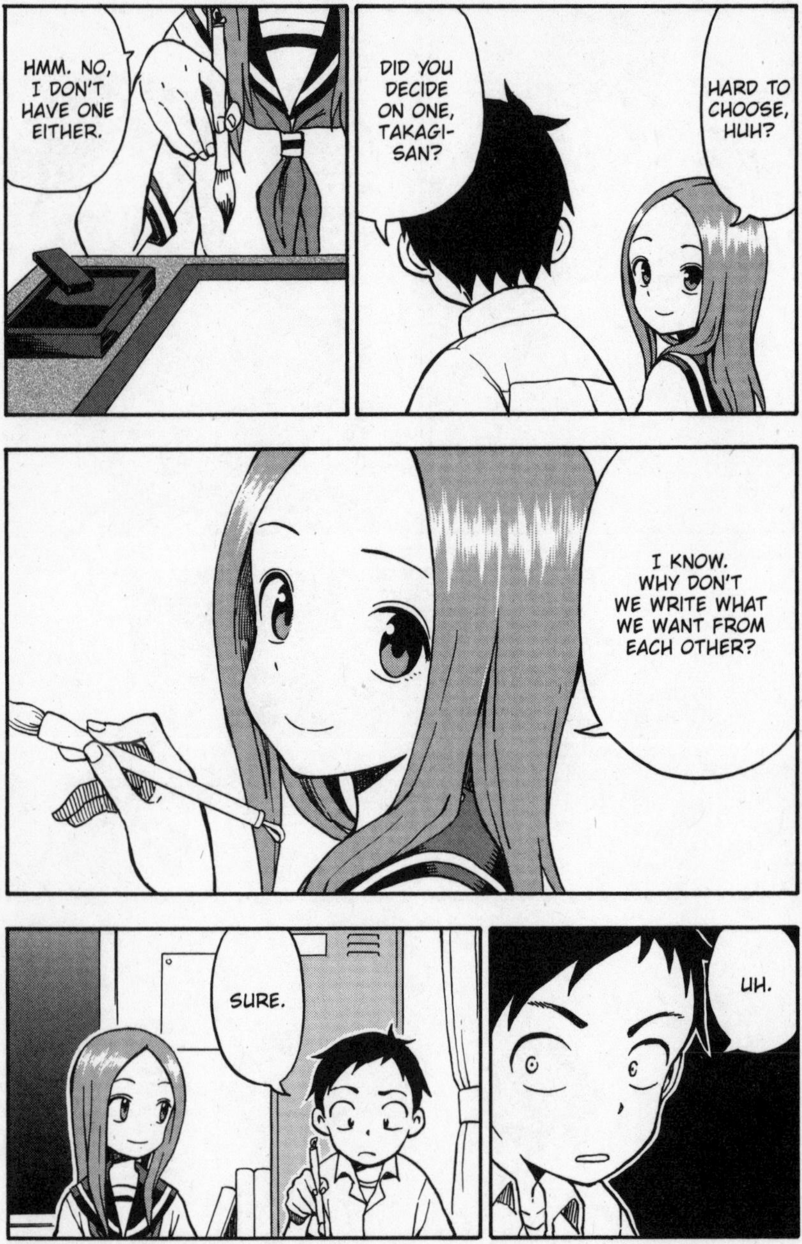
HARD TO CHOOSE, HUH?
DID YOU DECIDE ON ONE, TAKAGI-SAN?
HMM. NO, I DON'T HAVE ONE EITHER.
I KNOW. WHY DON'T WE WRITE WHAT WE WANT FROM EACH OTHER?
UH.
SURE.

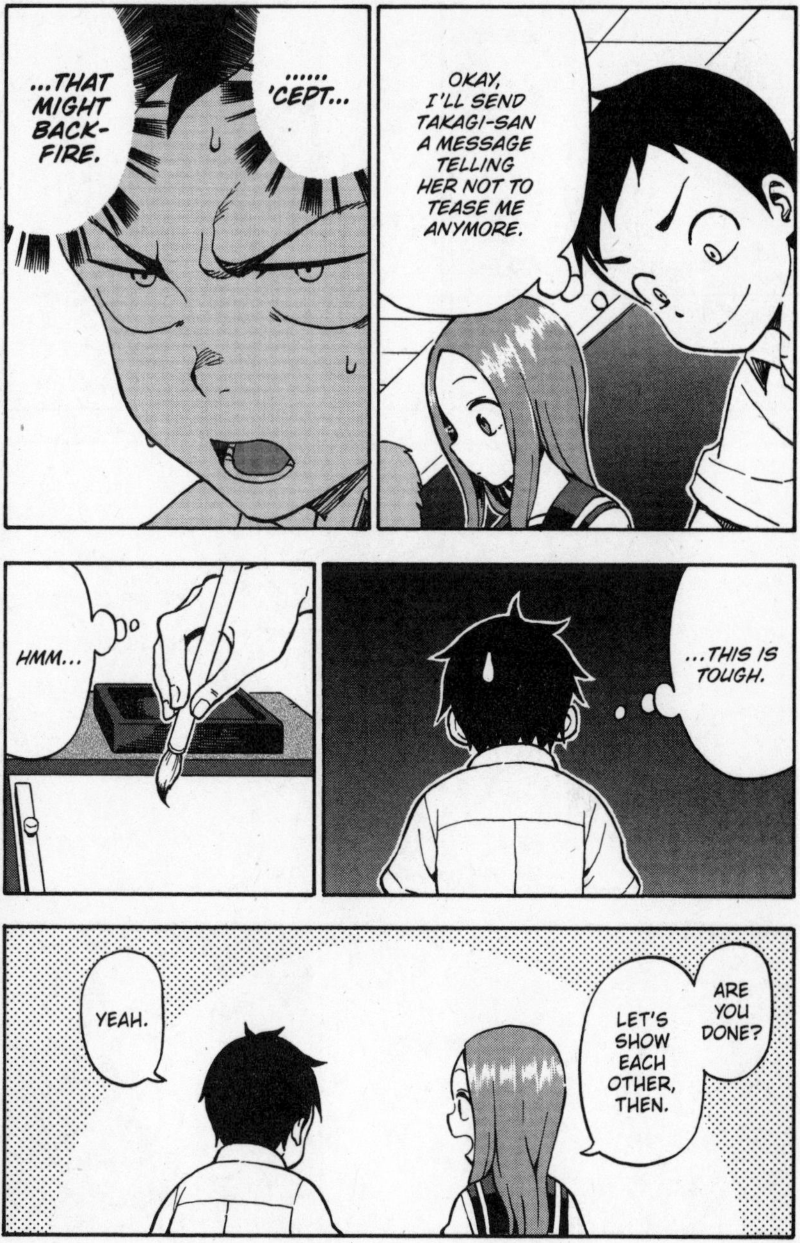
OKAY, I'LL SEND TAKAGI-SAN A MESSAGE TELLING HER NOT TO TEASE ME ANYMORE.
......'CEPT...
...THAT MIGHT BACK-FIRE.
...THIS IS TOUGH.
HMM...
ARE YOU DONE?
LET'S SHOW EACH OTHER, THEN.
YEAH.

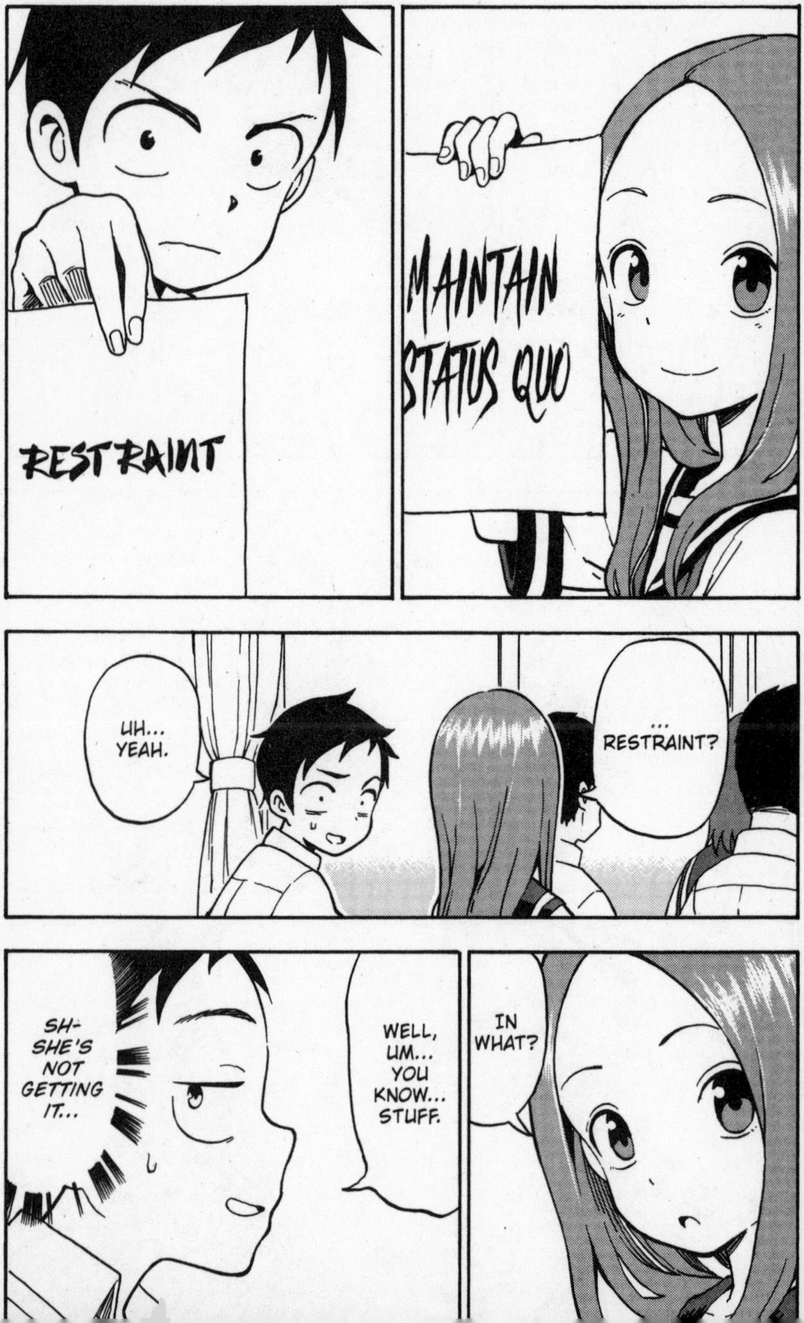
MAINTAIN STATUS QUO
RESTRAINT
...RESTRAINT?
UH... YEAH.
IN WHAT?
WELL, UM... YOU KNOW... STUFF.
SH-SHE'S NOT GETTING IT...

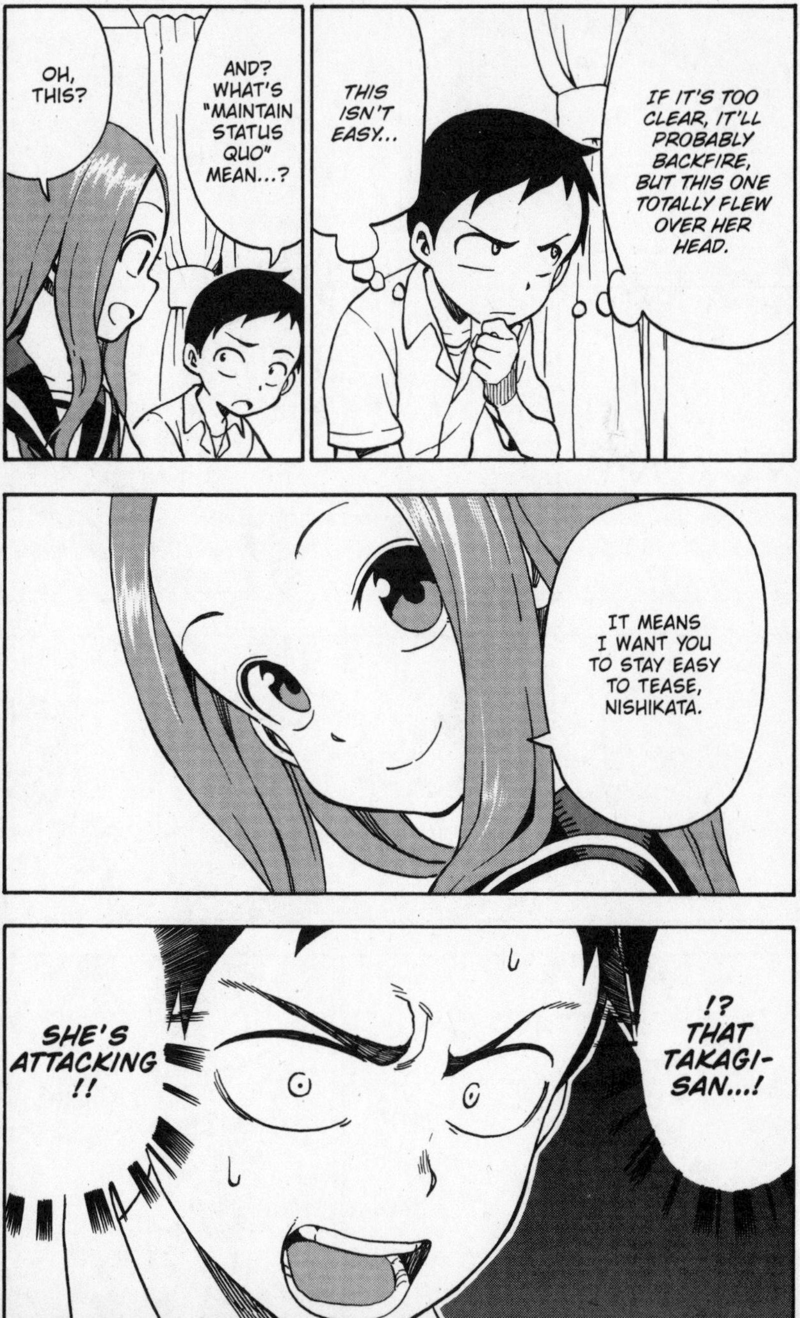
IF IT'S TOO CLEAR, IT'LL PROBABLY BACKFIRE, BUT THIS ONE TOTALLY FLEW OVER HER HEAD.
THIS ISN'T EASY...
AND? WHAT'S "MAINTAIN STATUS QUO" MEAN...?
OH, THIS?
IT MEANS I WANT YOU TO STAY EASY TO TEASE, NISHIKATA.
!? THAT TAKAGI-SAN...!
SHE'S ATTACKING!!

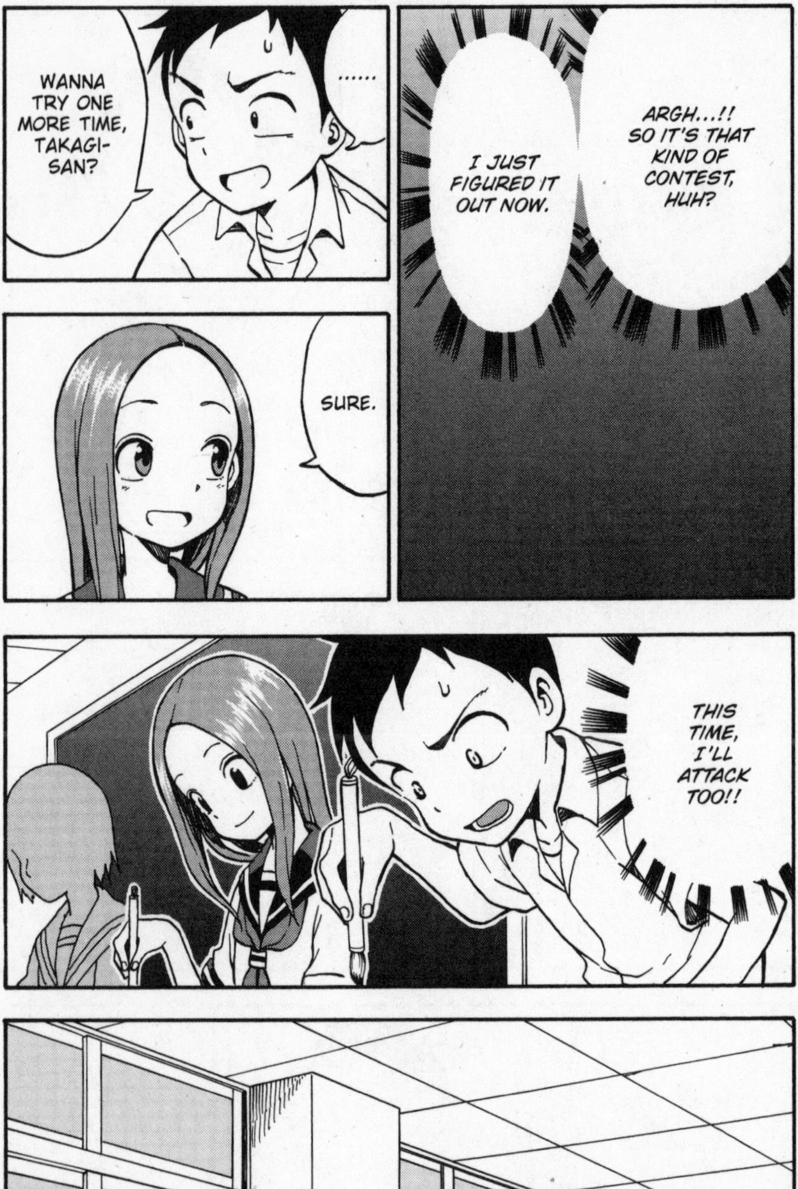
ARGH...!! SO IT'S THAT KIND OF CONTEST, HUH?
I JUST FIGURED IT OUT NOW.
......
WANNA TRY ONE MORE TIME, TAKAGI-SAN?
SURE.
THIS TIME, I'LL ATTACK TOO!!

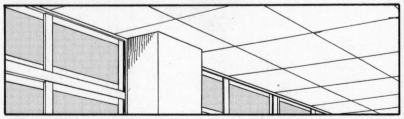

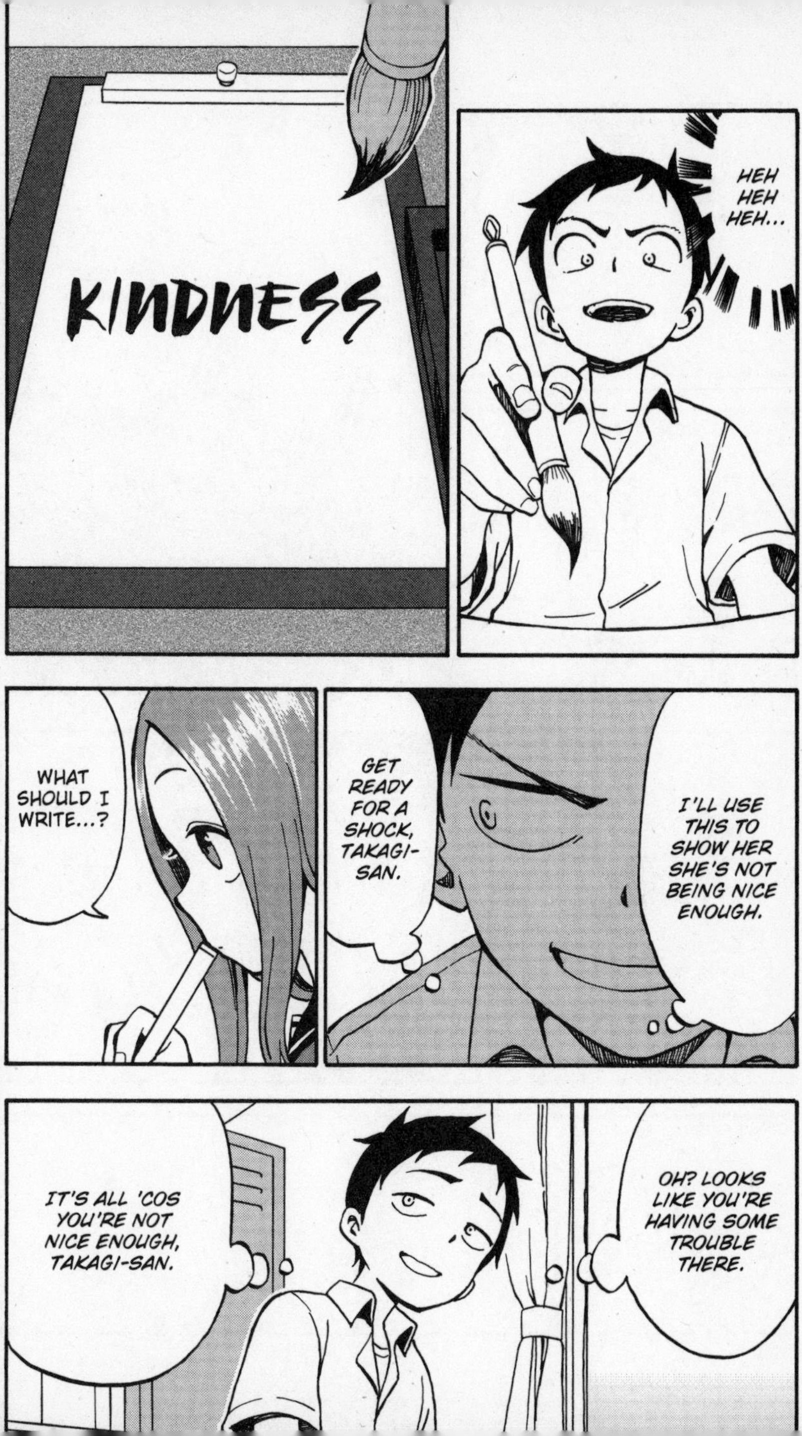
HEH HEH HEH...
KINDNESS
I'LL USE THIS TO SHOW HER SHE'S NOT BEING NICE ENOUGH.
GET READY FOR A SHOCK, TAKAGI-SAN.
WHAT SHOULD I WRITE...?
OH? LOOKS LIKE YOU'RE HAVING SOME TROUBLE THERE.
IT'S ALL 'COS YOU'RE NOT NICE ENOUGH, TAKAGI-SAN.

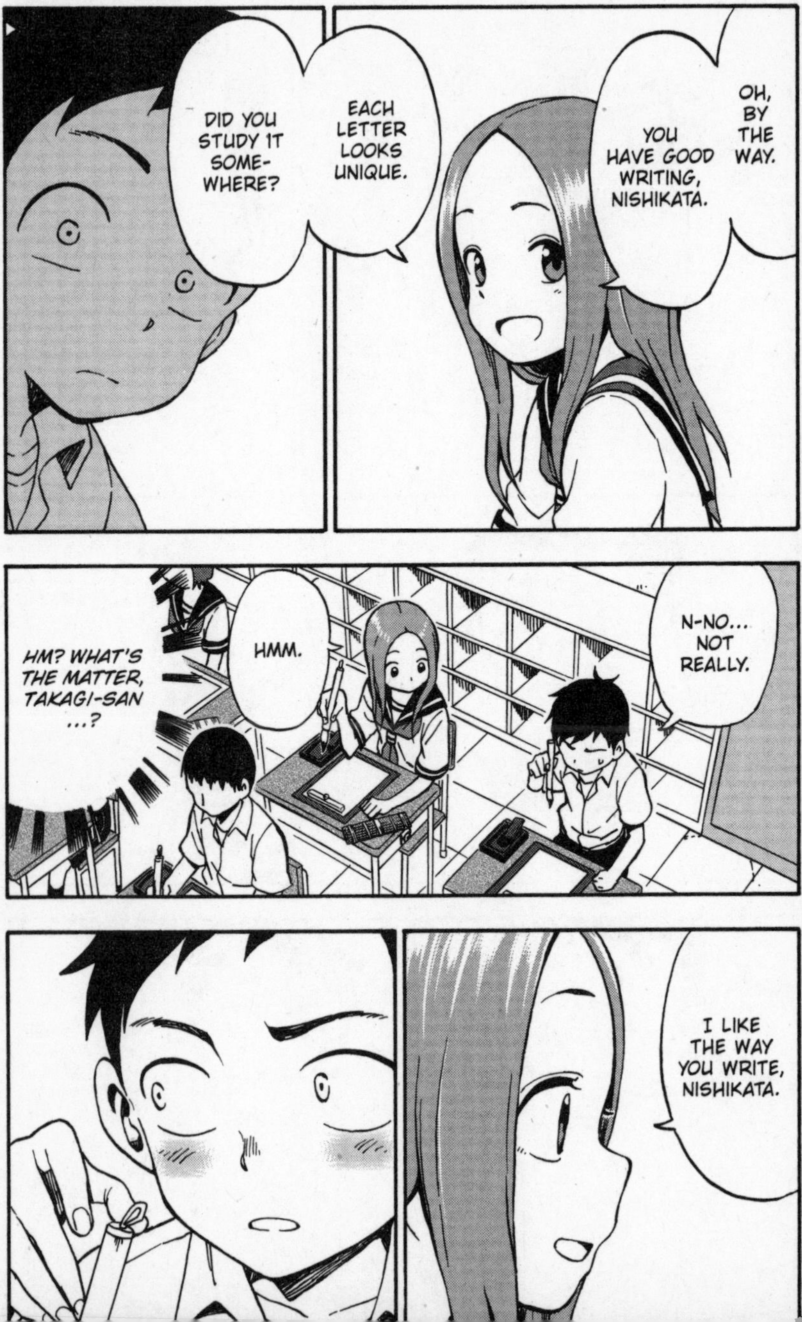
OH, BY THE WAY.
YOU HAVE GOOD WRITING, NISHIKATA.
EACH LETTER LOOKS UNIQUE.
DID YOU STUDY IT SOME-WHERE?
N-NO... NOT REALLY.
HMM.
HM? WHAT'S THE MATTER, TAKAGI-SAN ...?
I LIKE THE WAY YOU WRITE, NISHIKATA.

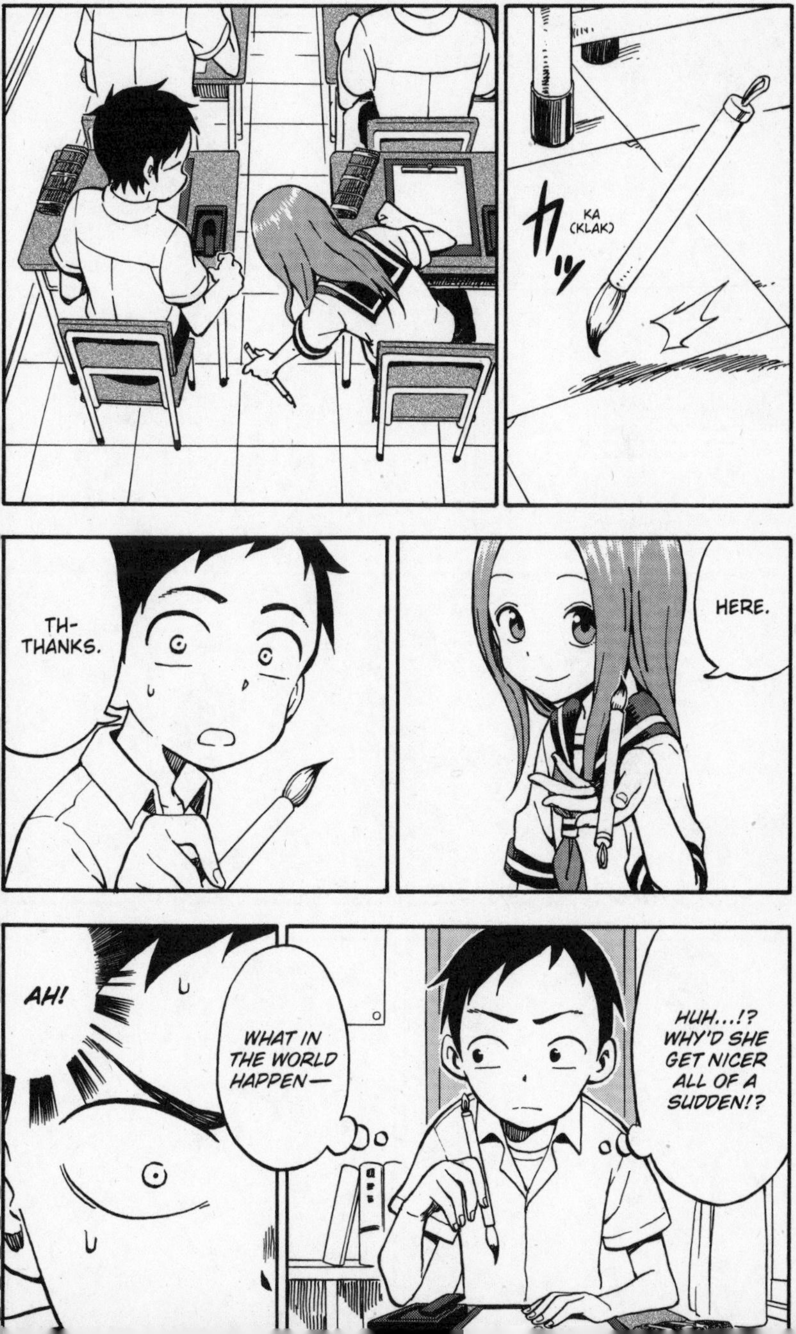

カッ
KA (KLAK)
HERE.
TH-THANKS.
HUH...!? WHY'D SHE GET NICER ALL OF A SUDDEN!?
WHAT IN THE WORLD HAPPEN—
AH!

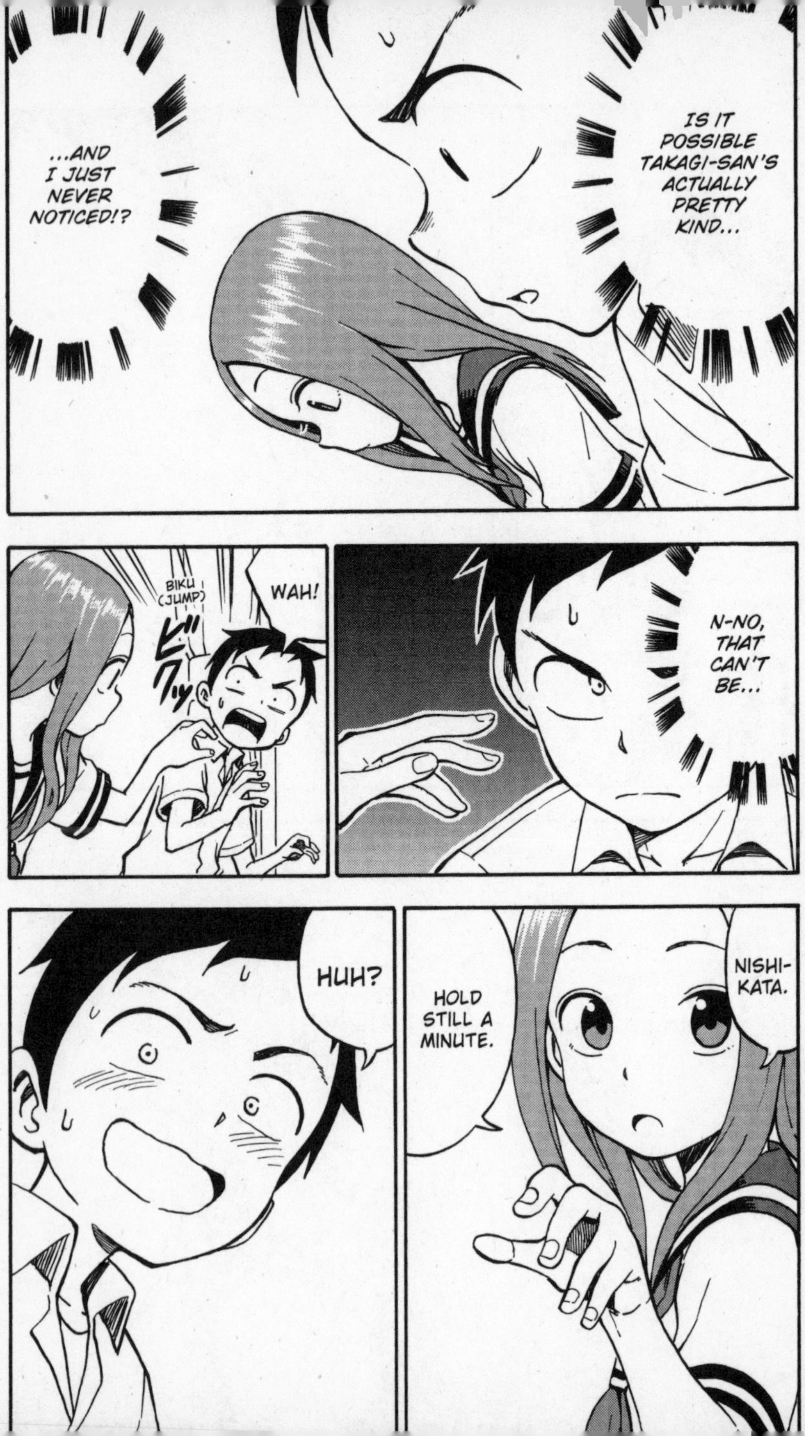
IS IT POSSIBLE TAKAGI-SAN'S ACTUALLY PRETTY KIND...
...AND I JUST NEVER NOTICED!?
N-NO, THAT CAN'T BE...
WAH!
BIKU (JUMP)
ビクッ
NISHI-KATA.
HOLD STILL A MINUTE.
HUH?

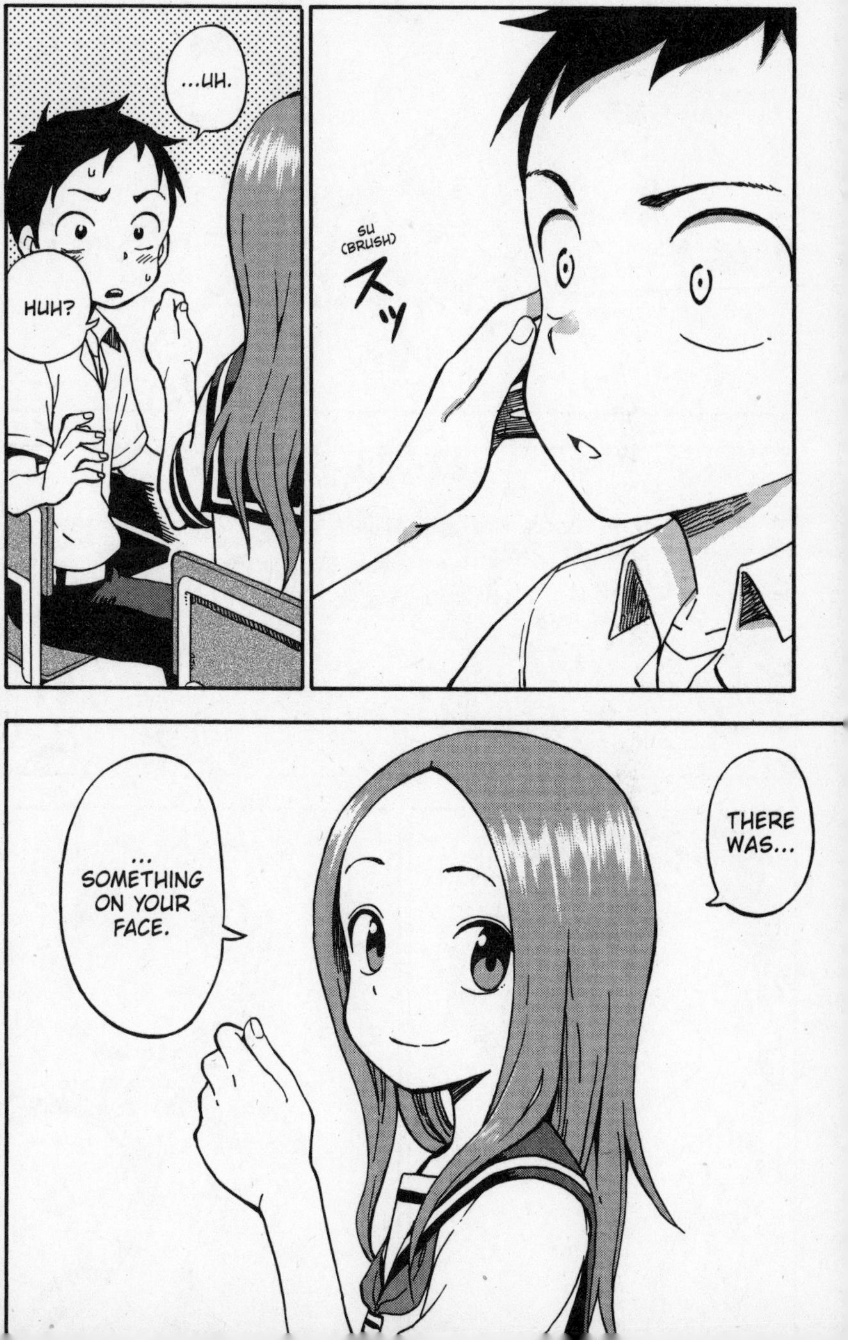
SU (BRUSH)
スッ
...UH.
HUH?
THERE WAS...
... SOMETHING ON YOUR FACE.

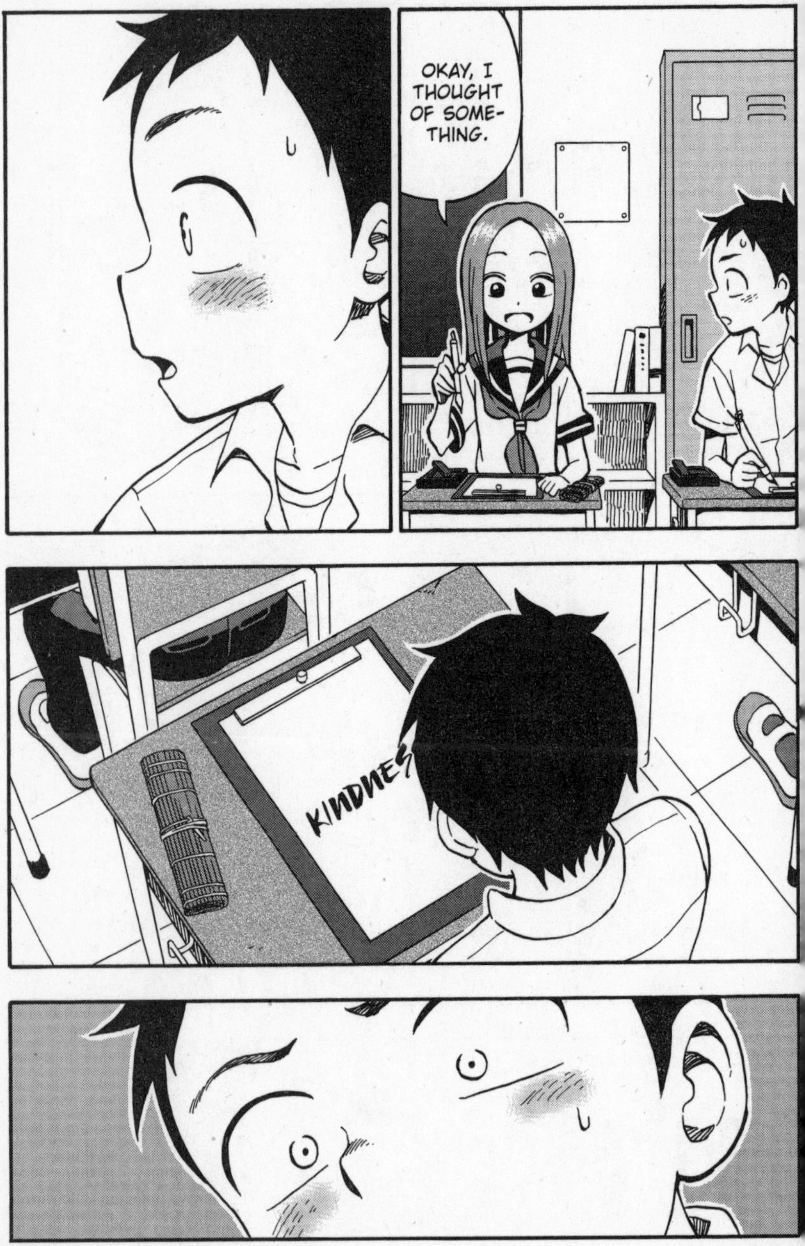
OKAY, I THOUGHT OF SOME-THING.
KINDNES

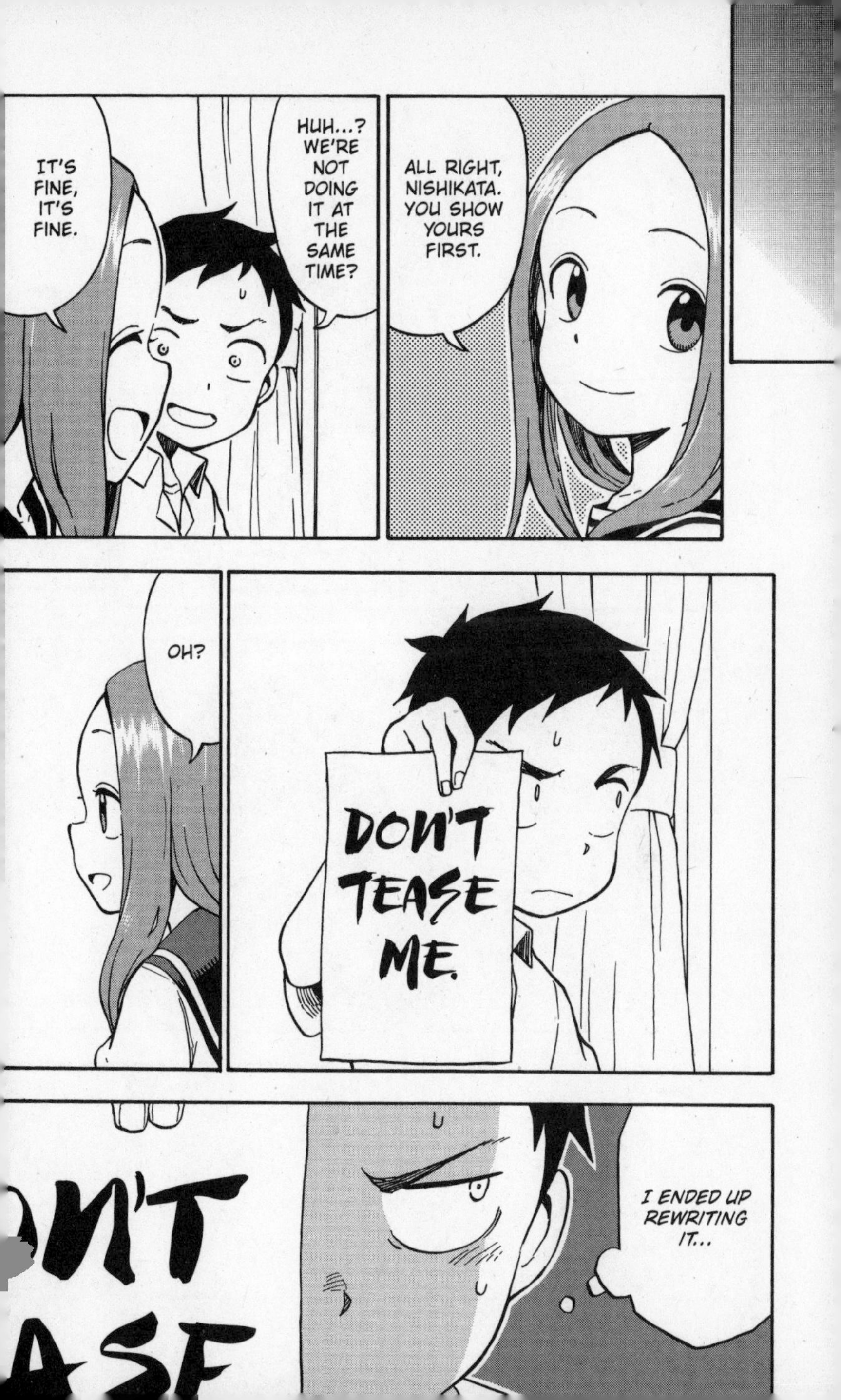
ALL RIGHT, NISHIKATA. YOU SHOW YOURS FIRST.
HUH...? WE'RE NOT DOING IT AT THE SAME TIME?
IT'S FINE, IT'S FINE.
DON'T TEASE ME.
OH?
I ENDED UP REWRITING IT...

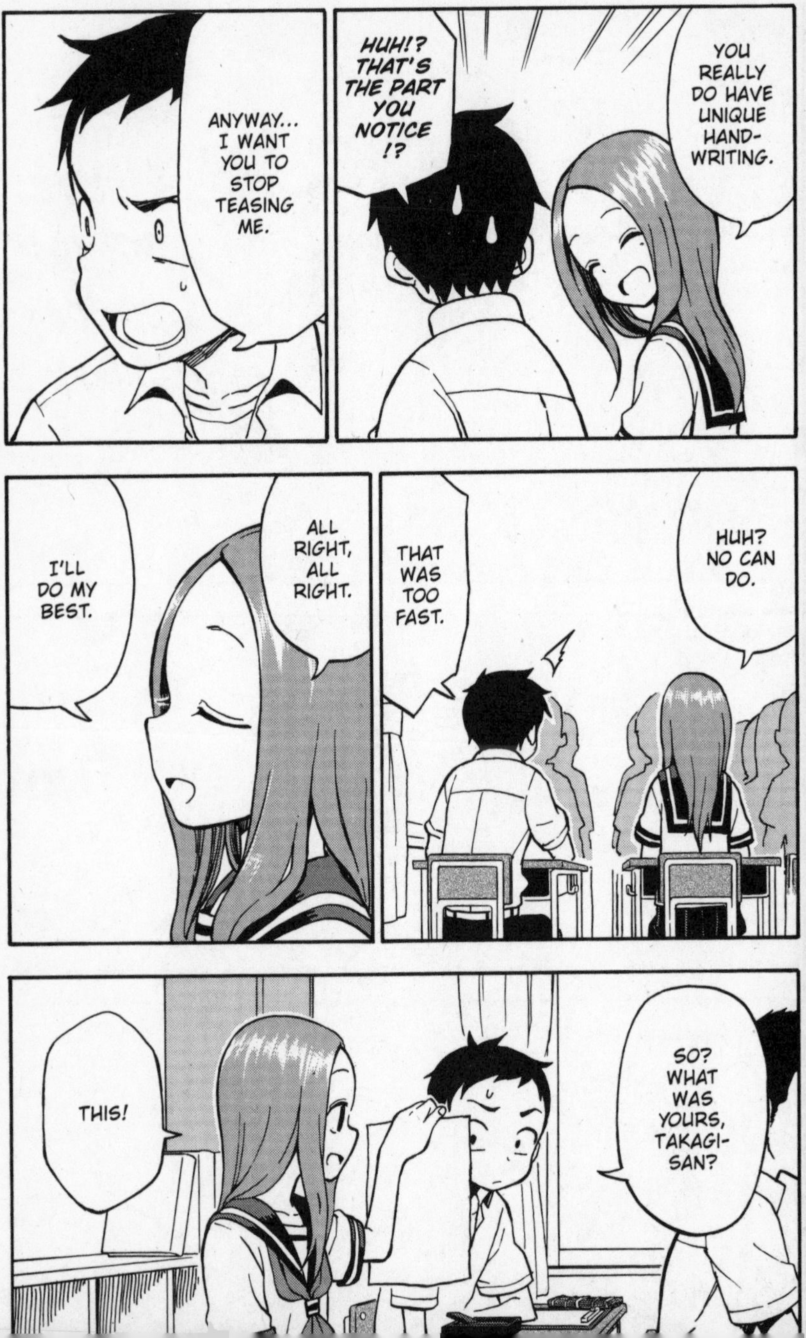
YOU REALLY DO HAVE UNIQUE HANDWRITING.
HUH!? THAT'S THE PART YOU NOTICE!?
ANYWAY... I WANT YOU TO STOP TEASING ME.
HUH? NO CAN DO.
THAT WAS TOO FAST.
ALL RIGHT, ALL RIGHT.
I'LL DO MY BEST.
SO? WHAT WAS YOURS, TAKAGI-SAN?
THIS!

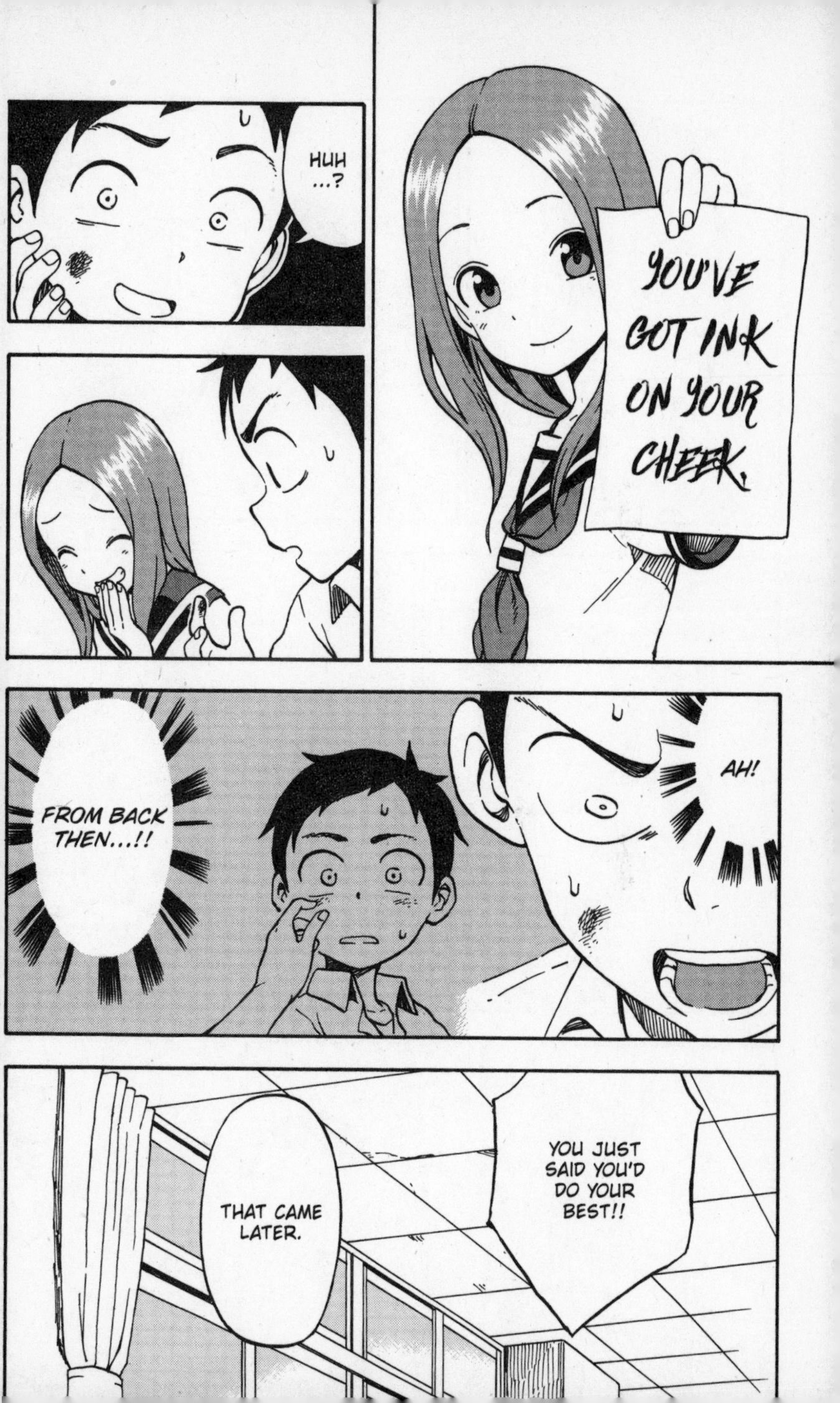
YOU'VE GOT INK ON YOUR CHEEK.
HUH ...?
AH!
FROM BACK THEN...!!
YOU JUST SAID YOU'D DO YOUR BEST!!
THAT CAME LATER.

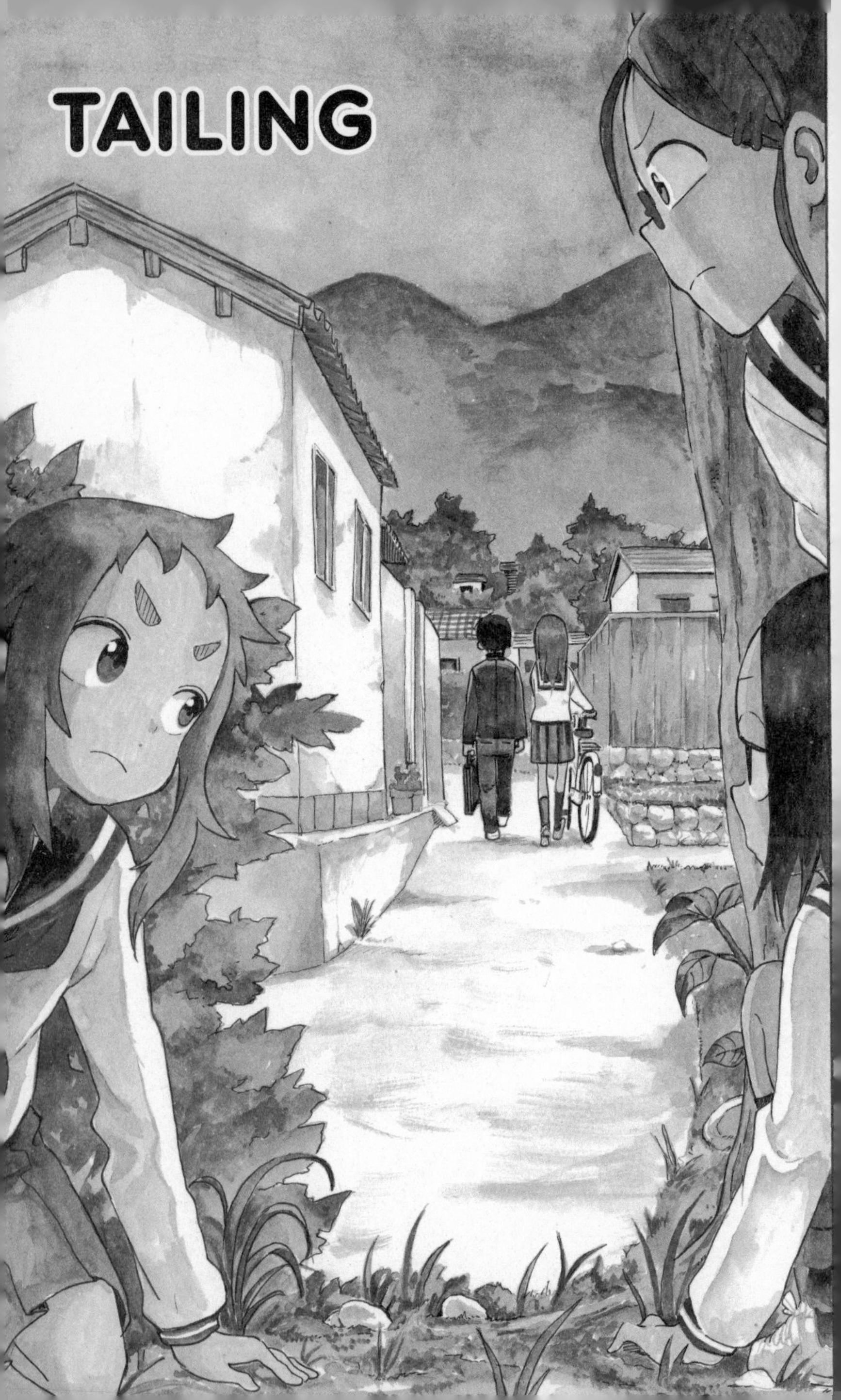
TAILING

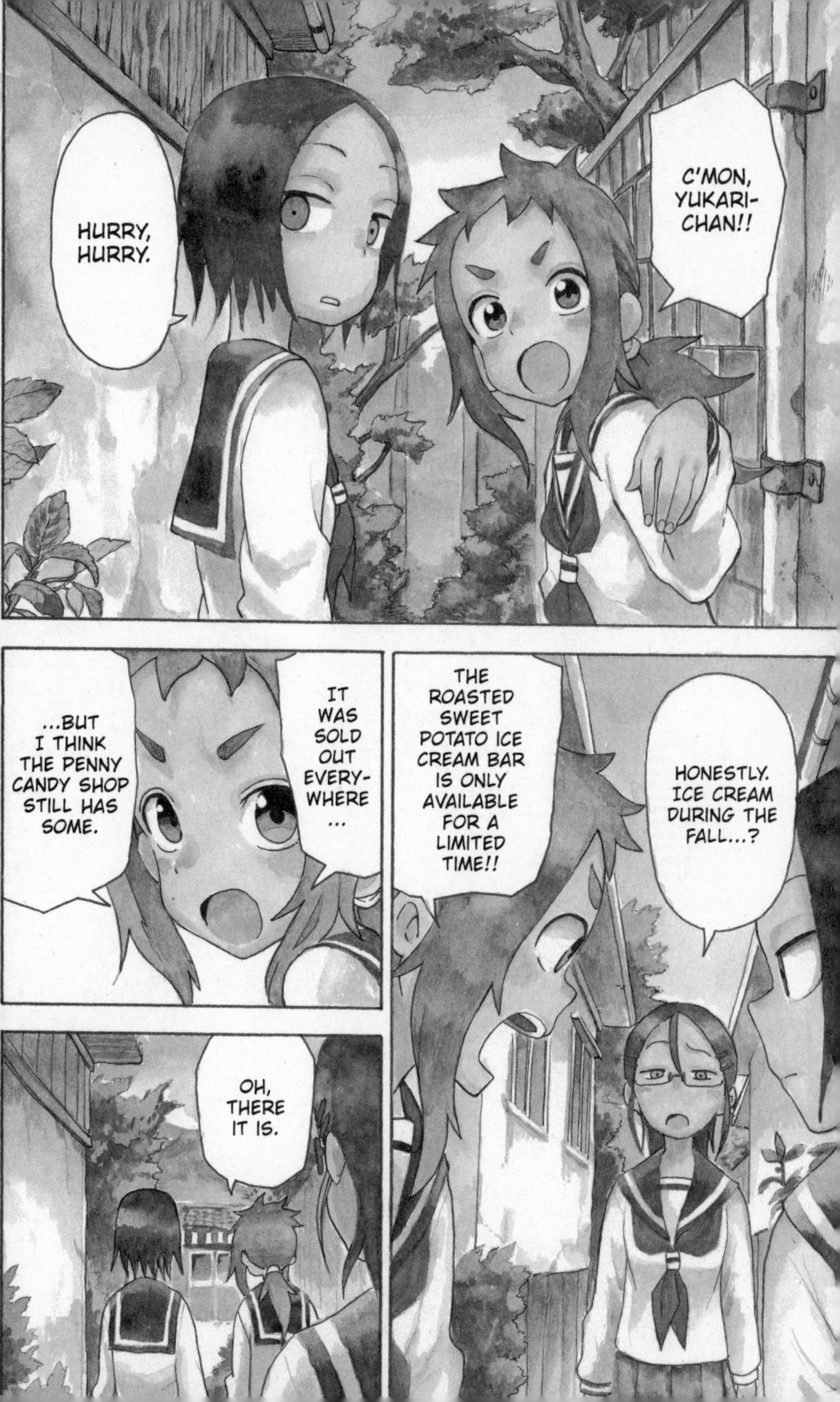
C'MON, YUKARI-CHAN!!
HURRY, HURRY.
HONESTLY. ICE CREAM DURING THE FALL...?
THE ROASTED SWEET POTATO ICE CREAM BAR IS ONLY AVAILABLE FOR A LIMITED TIME!!
IT WAS SOLD OUT EVERYWHERE...
...BUT I THINK THE PENNY CANDY SHOP STILL HAS SOME.
OH, THERE IT IS.

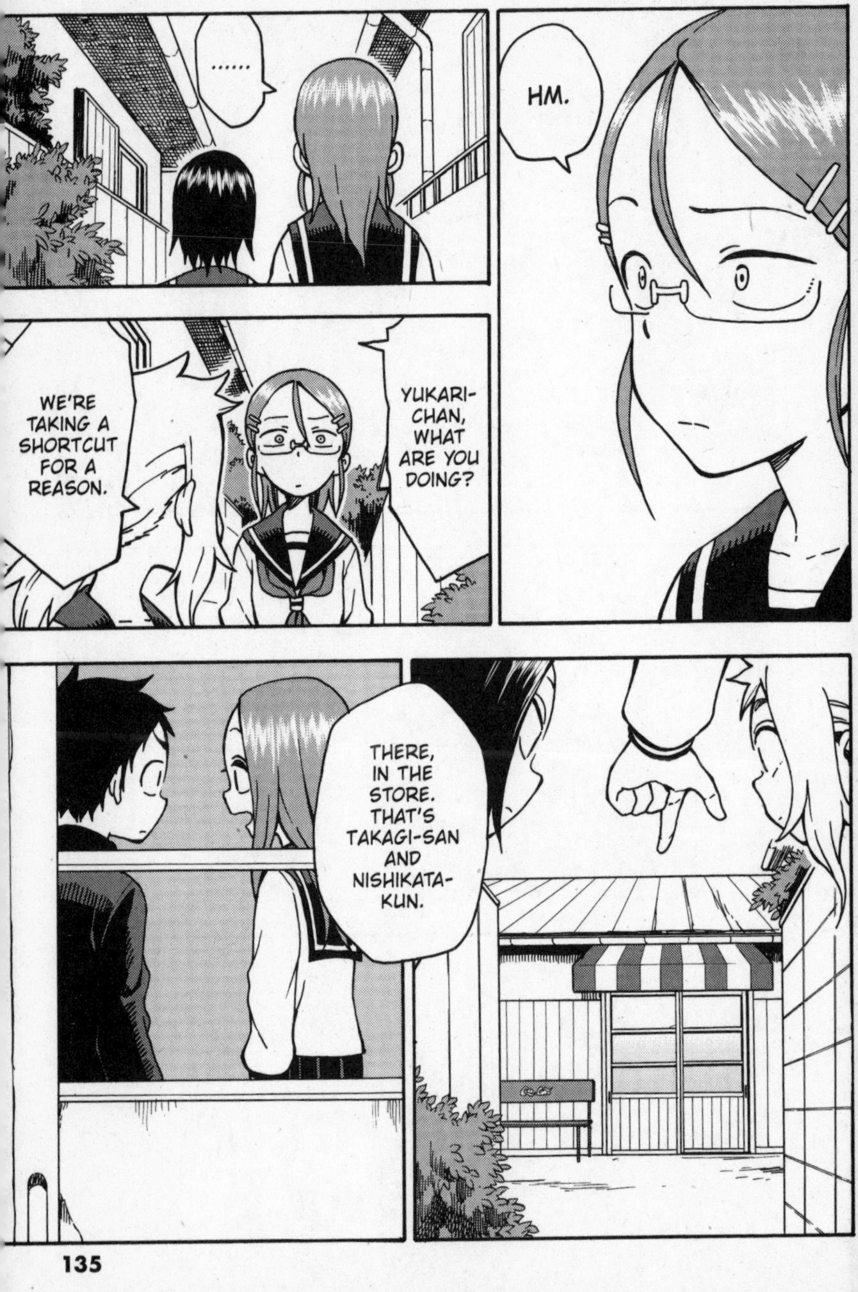
HM.
......
YUKARI-CHAN, WHAT ARE YOU DOING?
WE'RE TAKING A SHORTCUT FOR A REASON.
THERE, IN THE STORE. THAT'S TAKAGI-SAN AND NISHIKATA-KUN.

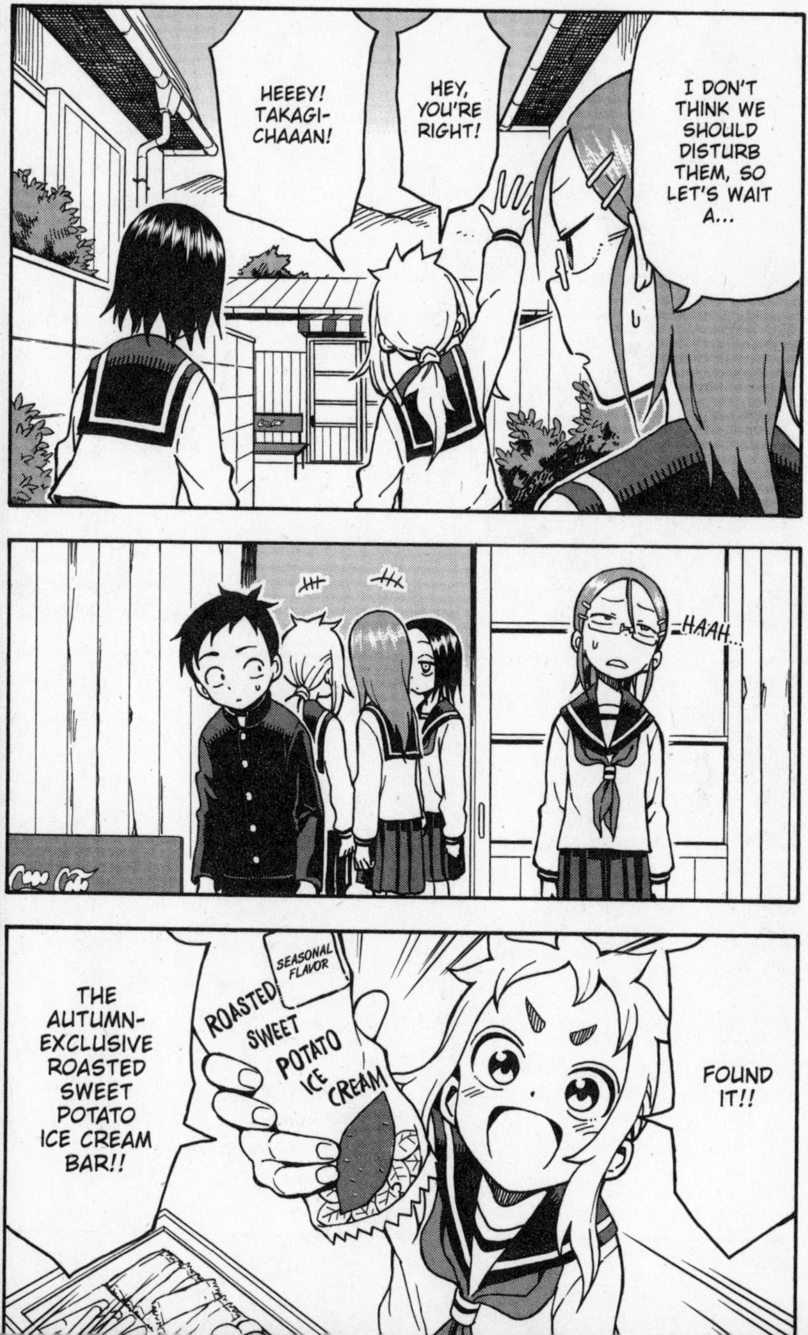
I DON'T THINK WE SHOULD DISTURB THEM, SO LET'S WAIT A...
HEY, YOU'RE RIGHT!
HEEEY! TAKAGI-CHAAAN!
HAAH...
FOUND IT!!
SEASONAL FLAVOR
ROASTED SWEET POTATO ICE CREAM
THE AUTUMN-EXCLUSIVE ROASTED SWEET POTATO ICE CREAM BAR!!

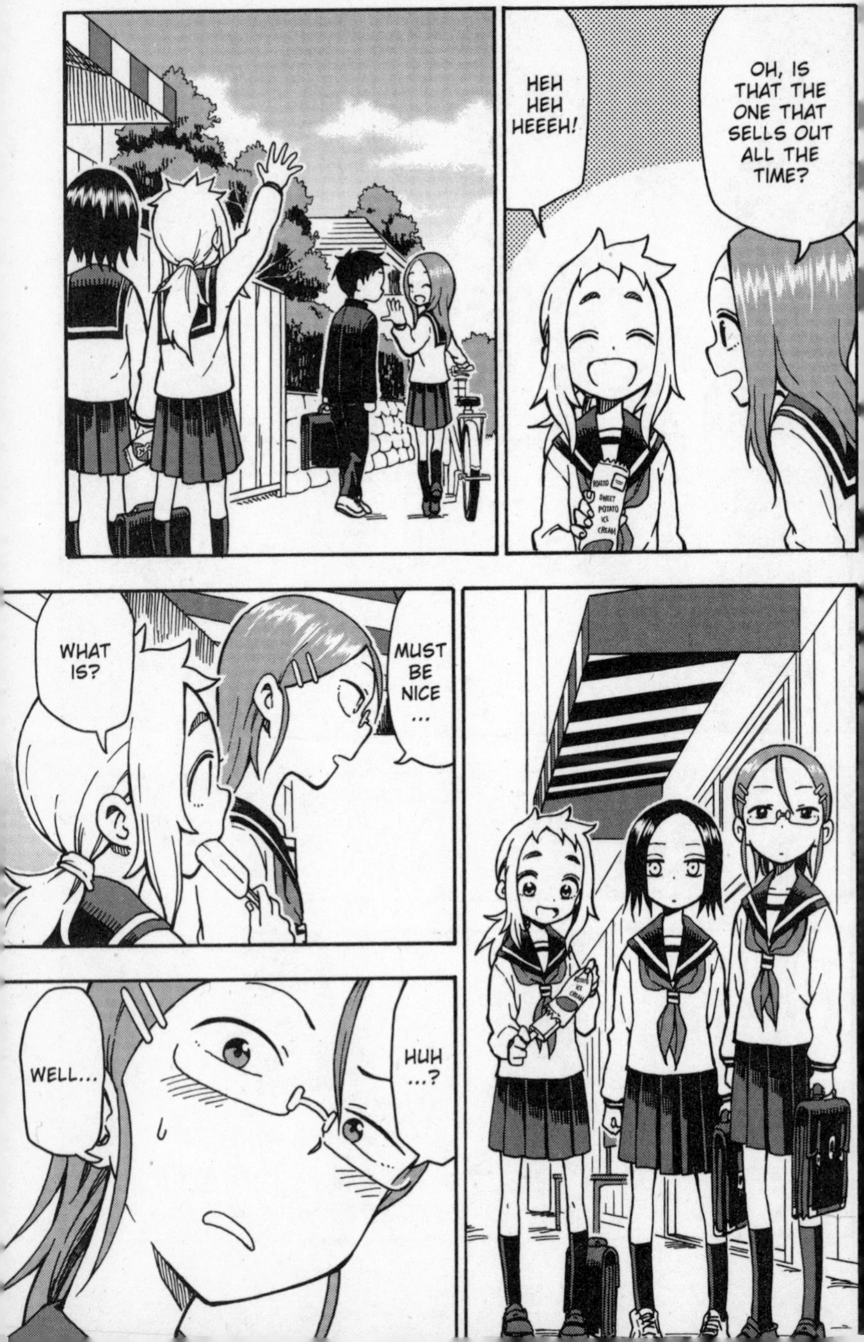
OH, IS THAT THE ONE THAT SELLS OUT ALL THE TIME?
HEH HEH HEEEH!
ROASTED SWEET POTATO ICE CREAM
MUST BE NICE...
WHAT IS?
HUH...?
WELL...

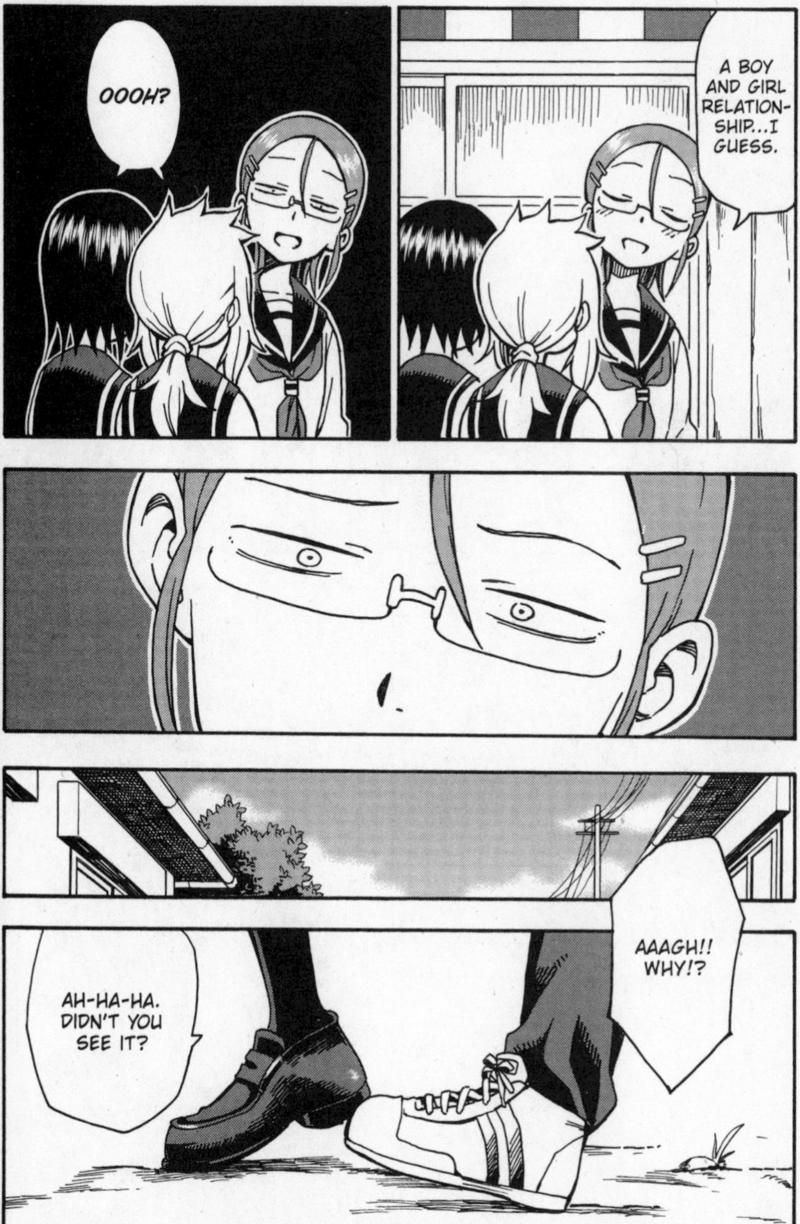

A BOY AND GIRL RELATION-SHIP...I GUESS.
OOOH?
AAAGH!! WHY!?
AH-HA-HA. DIDN'T YOU SEE IT?

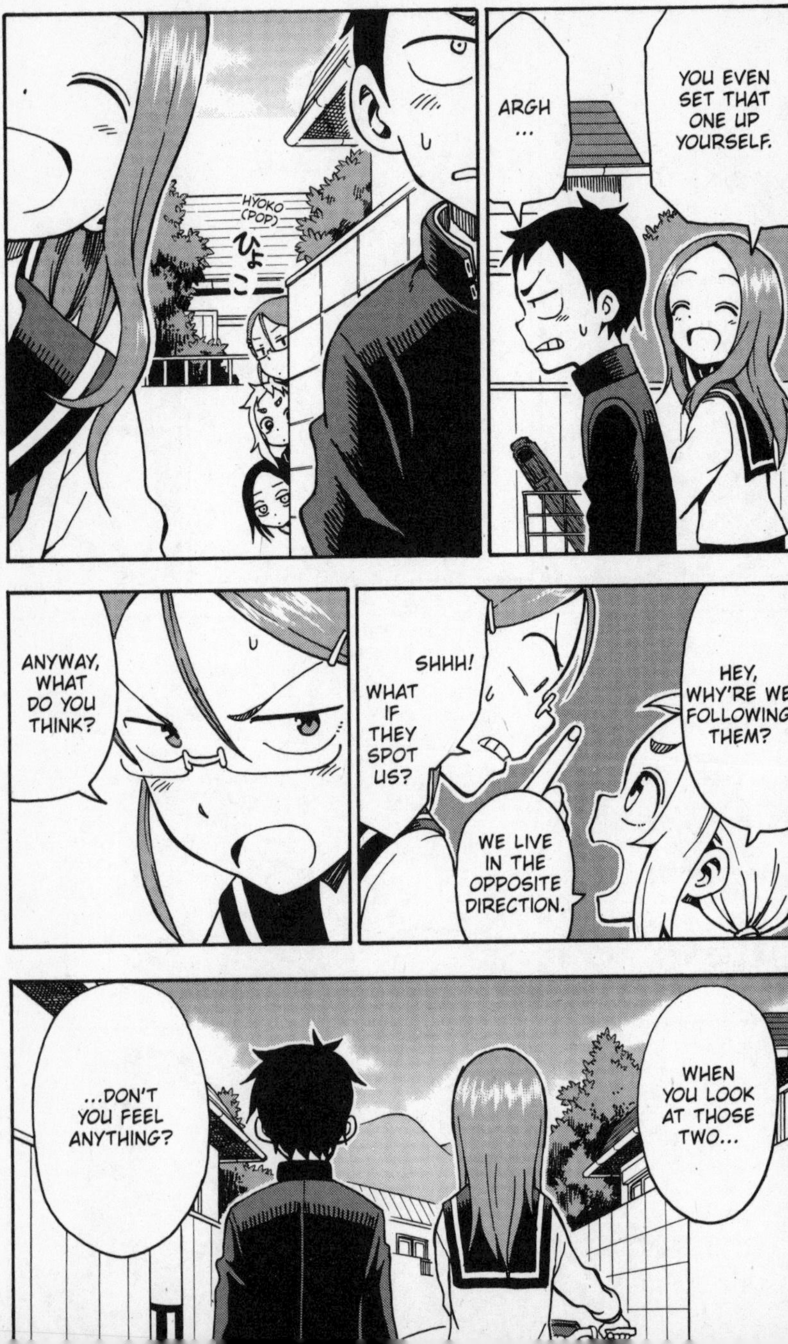
YOU EVEN SET THAT ONE UP YOURSELF.
ARGH ...
HYOKO (POP)
ひょこ
HEY, WHY'RE WE FOLLOWING THEM?
SHHH!
WHAT IF THEY SPOT US?
WE LIVE IN THE OPPOSITE DIRECTION.
ANYWAY, WHAT DO YOU THINK?
WHEN YOU LOOK AT THOSE TWO...
...DON'T YOU FEEL ANYTHING?

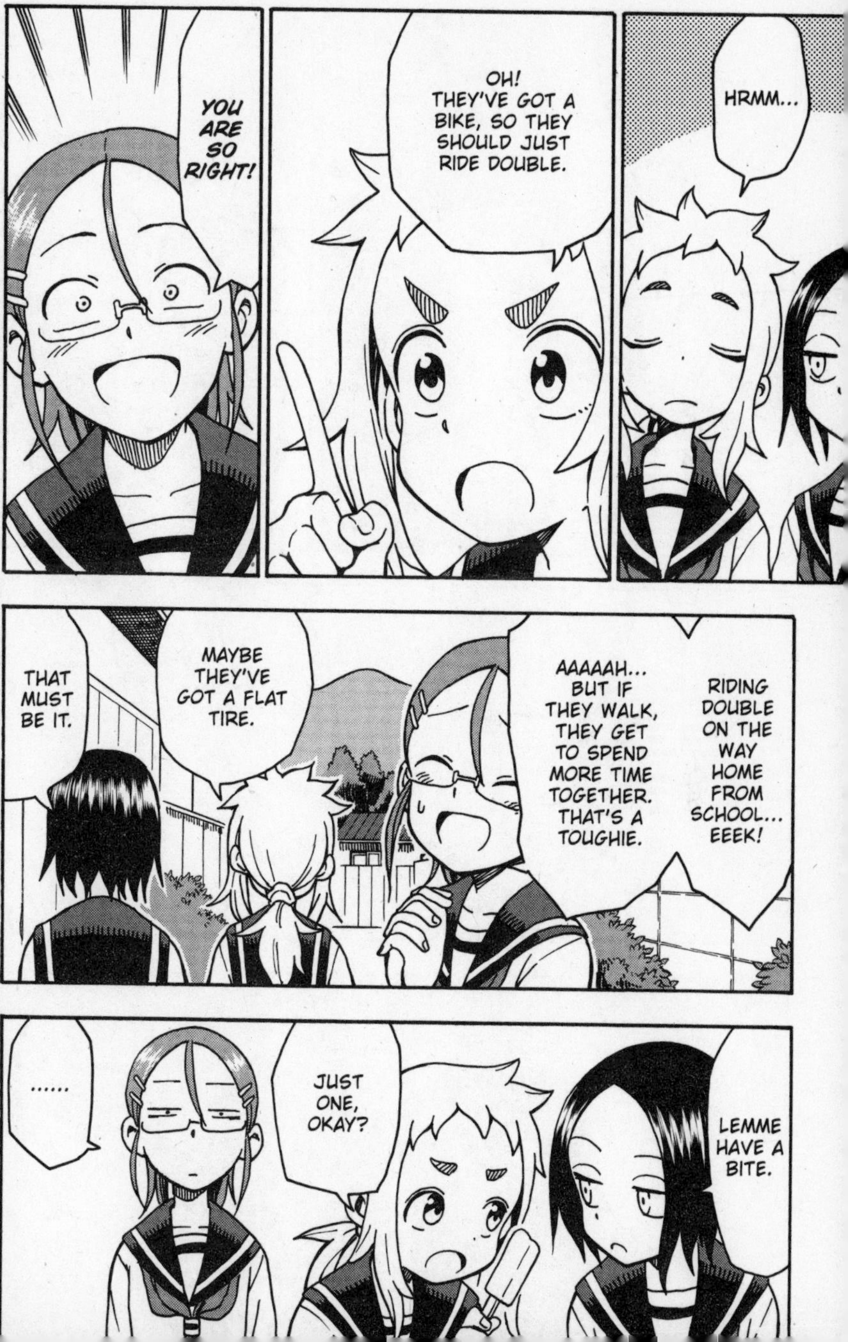
HRMM...
OH! THEY'VE GOT A BIKE, SO THEY SHOULD JUST RIDE DOUBLE.
YOU ARE SO RIGHT!
RIDING DOUBLE ON THE WAY HOME FROM SCHOOL... EEEK!
AAAAAH... BUT IF THEY WALK, THEY GET TO SPEND MORE TIME TOGETHER. THAT'S A TOUGHIE.
MAYBE THEY'VE GOT A FLAT TIRE.
THAT MUST BE IT.
LEMME HAVE A BITE.
JUST ONE, OKAY?
......

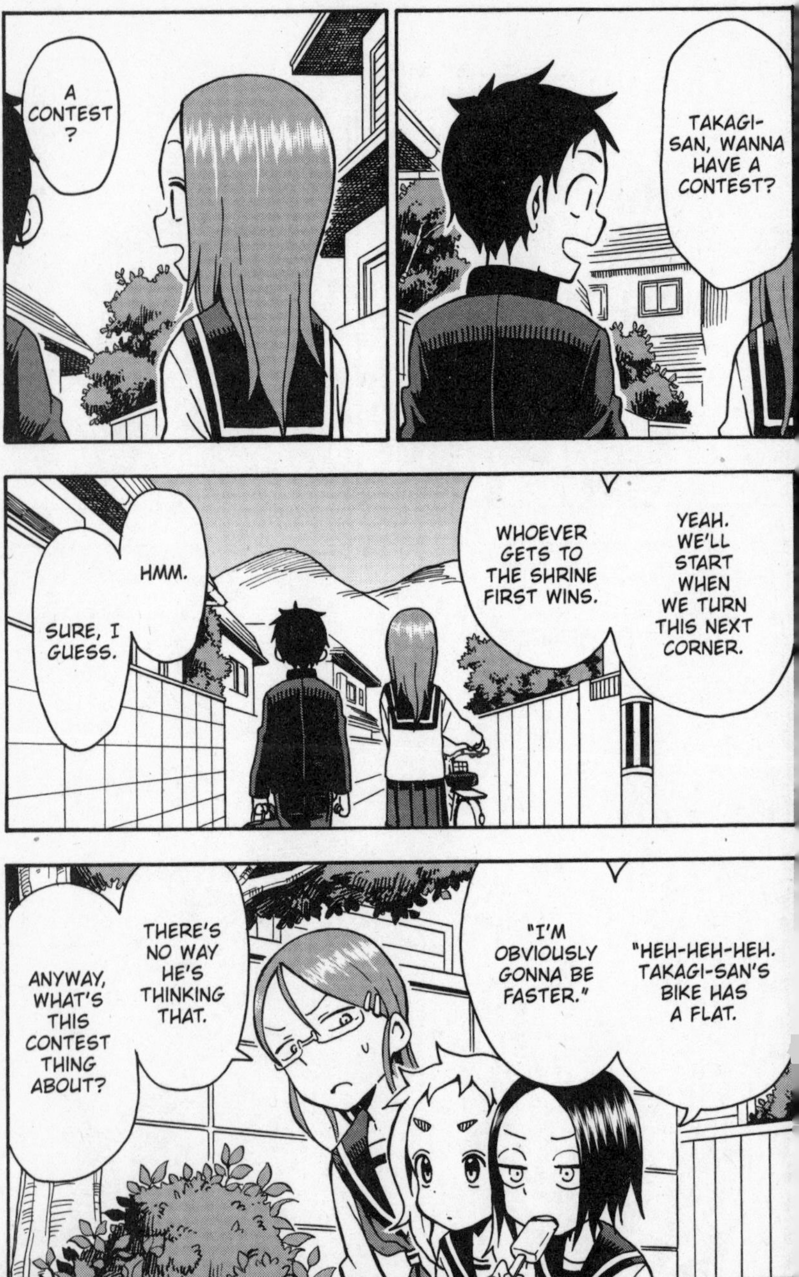
TAKAGI-SAN, WANNA HAVE A CONTEST?
A CONTEST?
YEAH. WE'LL START WHEN WE TURN THIS NEXT CORNER.
WHOEVER GETS TO THE SHRINE FIRST WINS.
HMM.
SURE, I GUESS.
"HEH-HEH-HEH. TAKAGI-SAN'S BIKE HAS A FLAT.
"I'M OBVIOUSLY GONNA BE FASTER."
THERE'S NO WAY HE'S THINKING THAT.
ANYWAY, WHAT'S THIS CONTEST THING ABOUT?

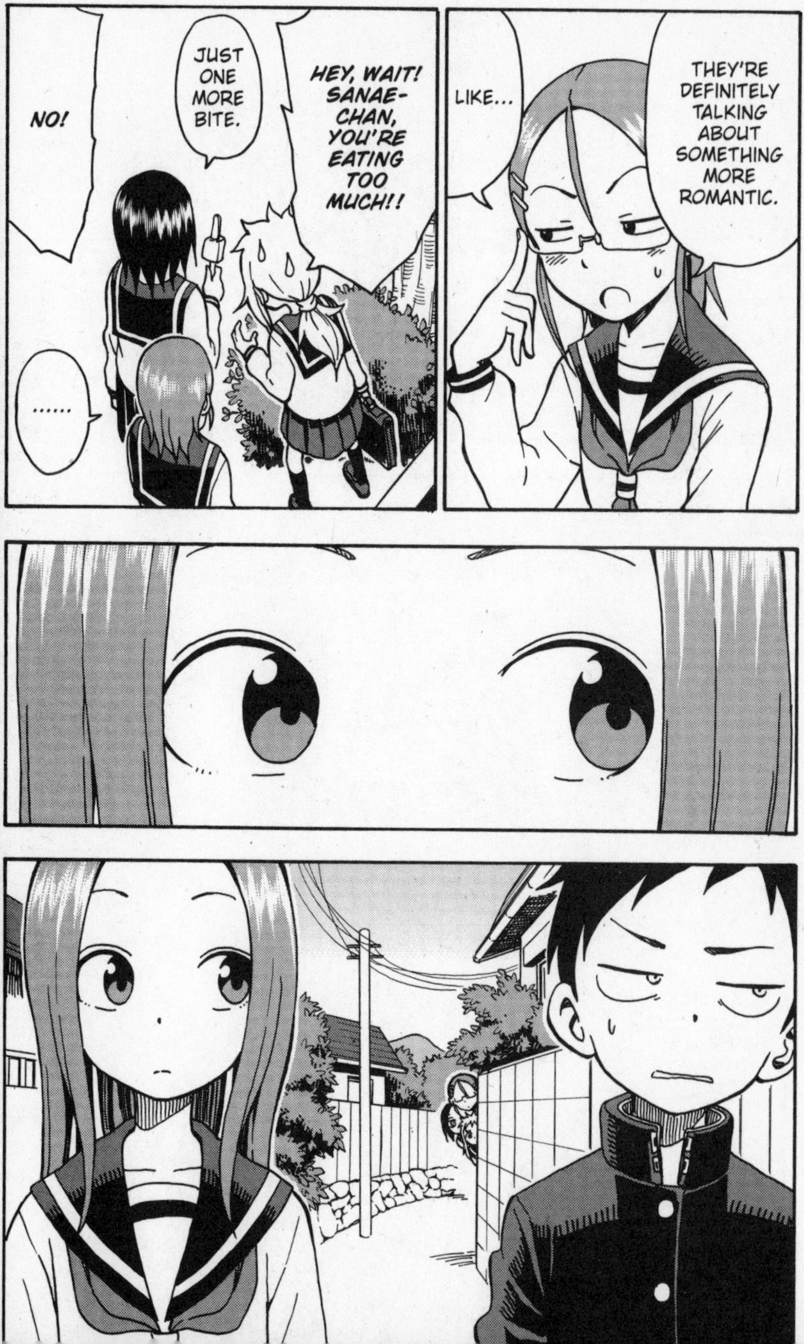
THEY'RE DEFINITELY TALKING ABOUT SOMETHING MORE ROMANTIC.
LIKE...
HEY, WAIT! SANAE-CHAN, YOU'RE EATING TOO MUCH!!
JUST ONE MORE BITE.
NO!
......

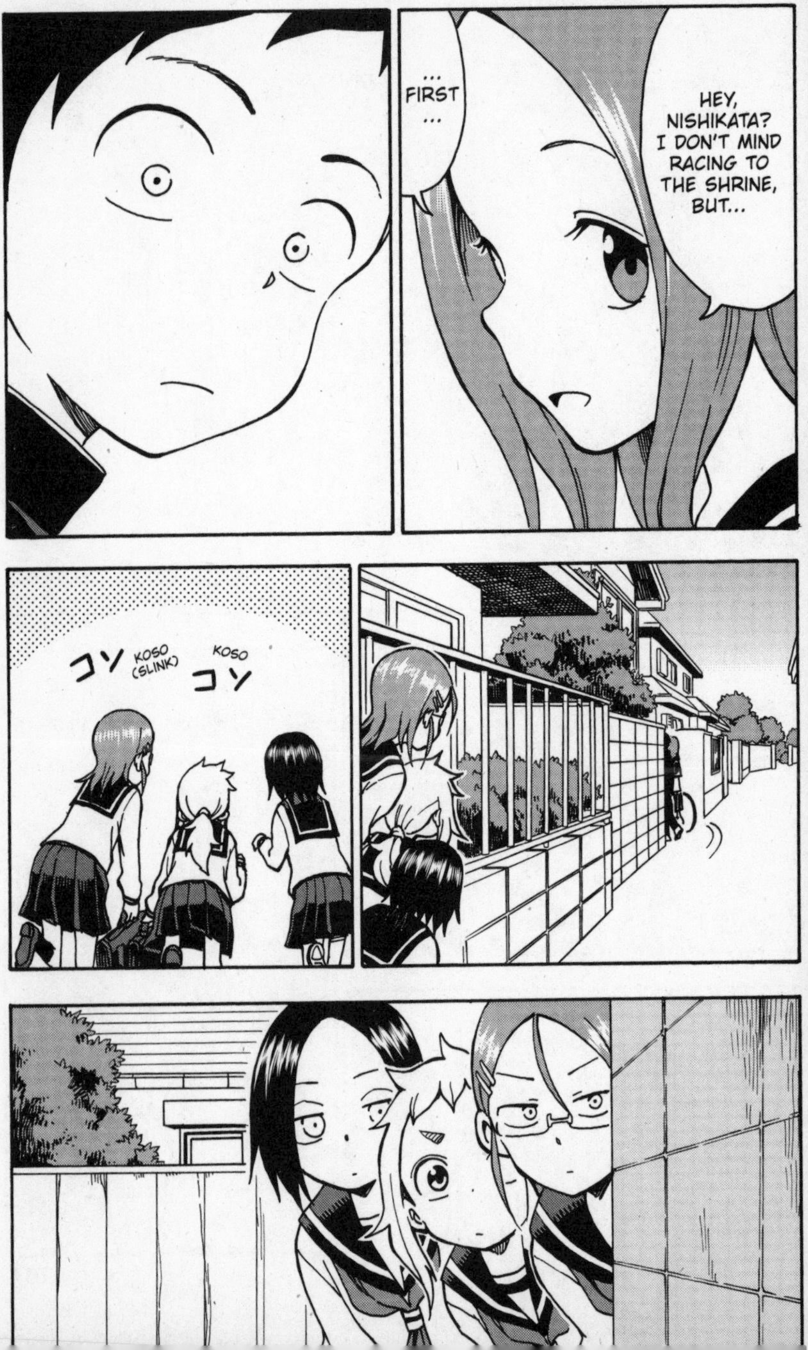
HEY, NISHIKATA? I DON'T MIND RACING TO THE SHRINE, BUT...
... FIRST ...
コソ
KOSO
コソ
KOSO (SLINK)

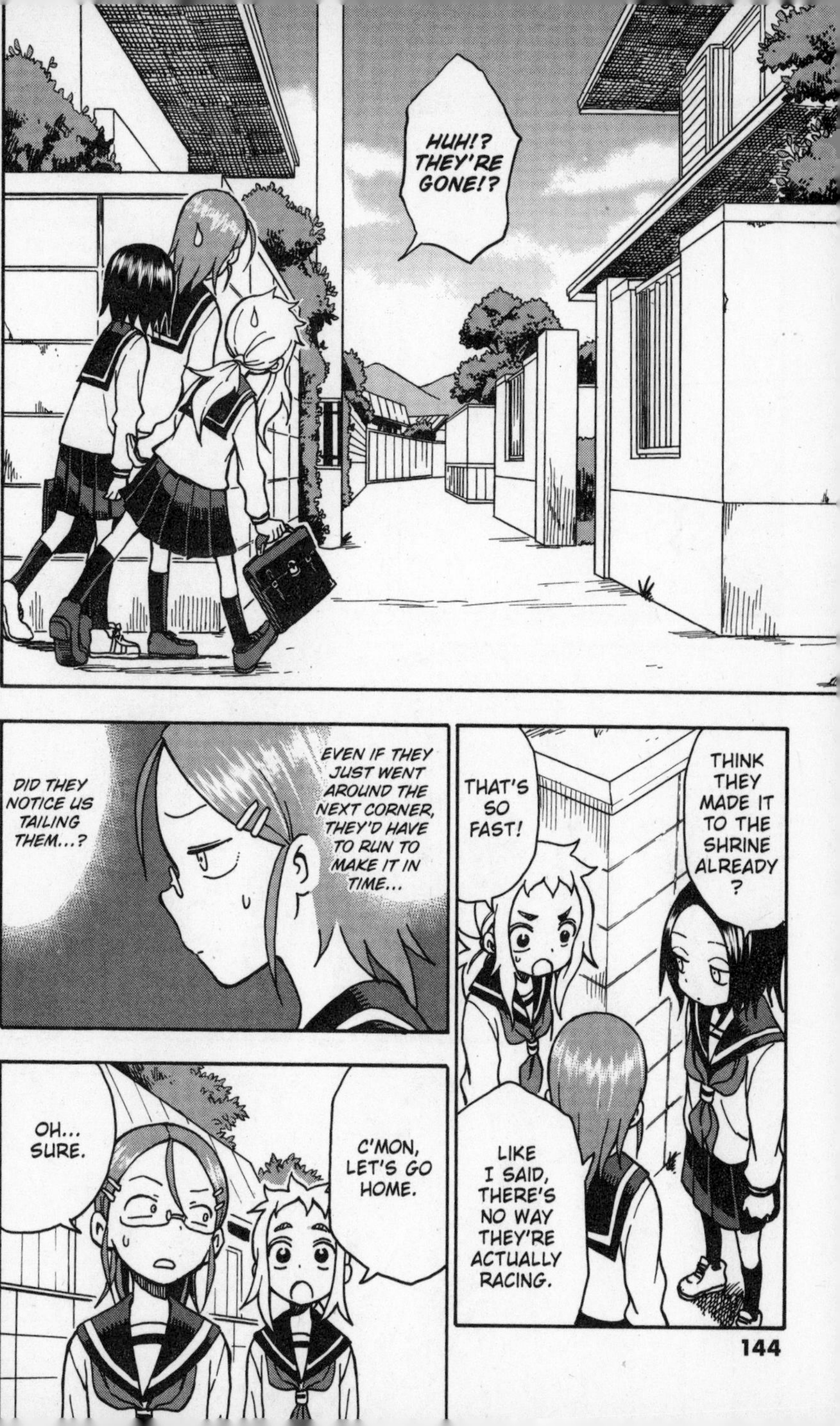
HUH!? THEY'RE GONE!?
THINK THEY MADE IT TO THE SHRINE ALREADY?
THAT'S SO FAST!
LIKE I SAID, THERE'S NO WAY THEY'RE ACTUALLY RACING.
EVEN IF THEY JUST WENT AROUND THE NEXT CORNER, THEY'D HAVE TO RUN TO MAKE IT IN TIME...
DID THEY NOTICE US TAILING THEM...?
C'MON, LET'S GO HOME.
OH... SURE.

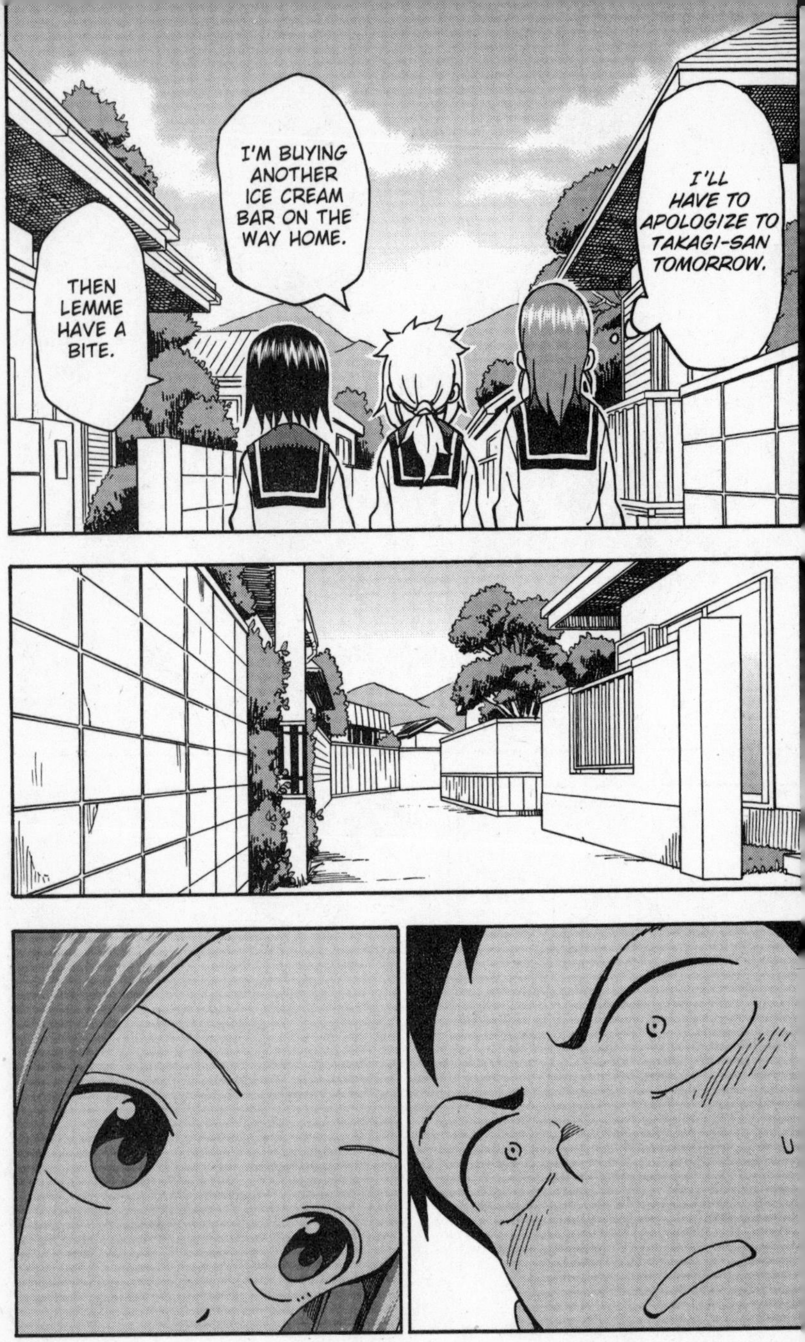
I'LL HAVE TO APOLOGIZE TO TAKAGI-SAN TOMORROW.
I'M BUYING ANOTHER ICE CREAM BAR ON THE WAY HOME.
THEN LEMME HAVE A BITE.

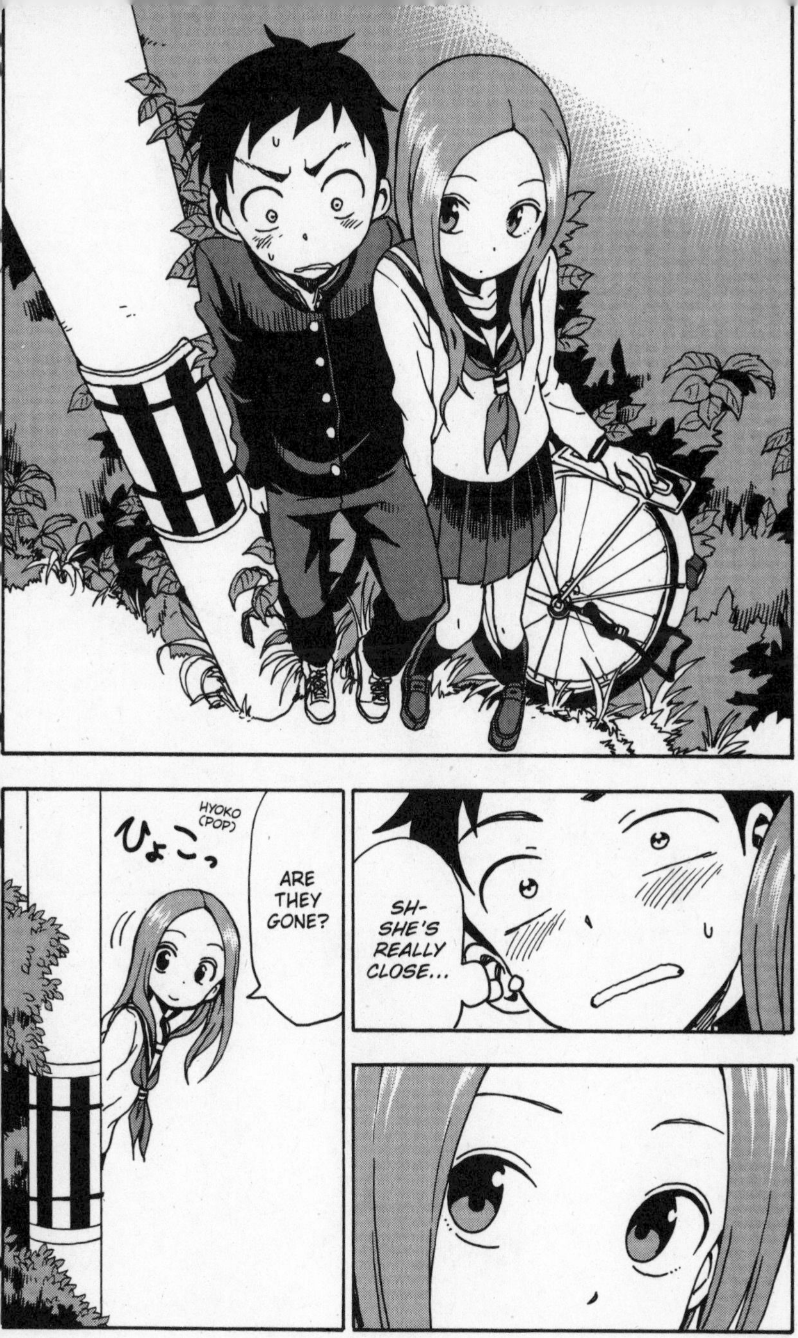
SH- SHE'S REALLY CLOSE...
ひょこっ
HYOKO (POP)
ARE THEY GONE?

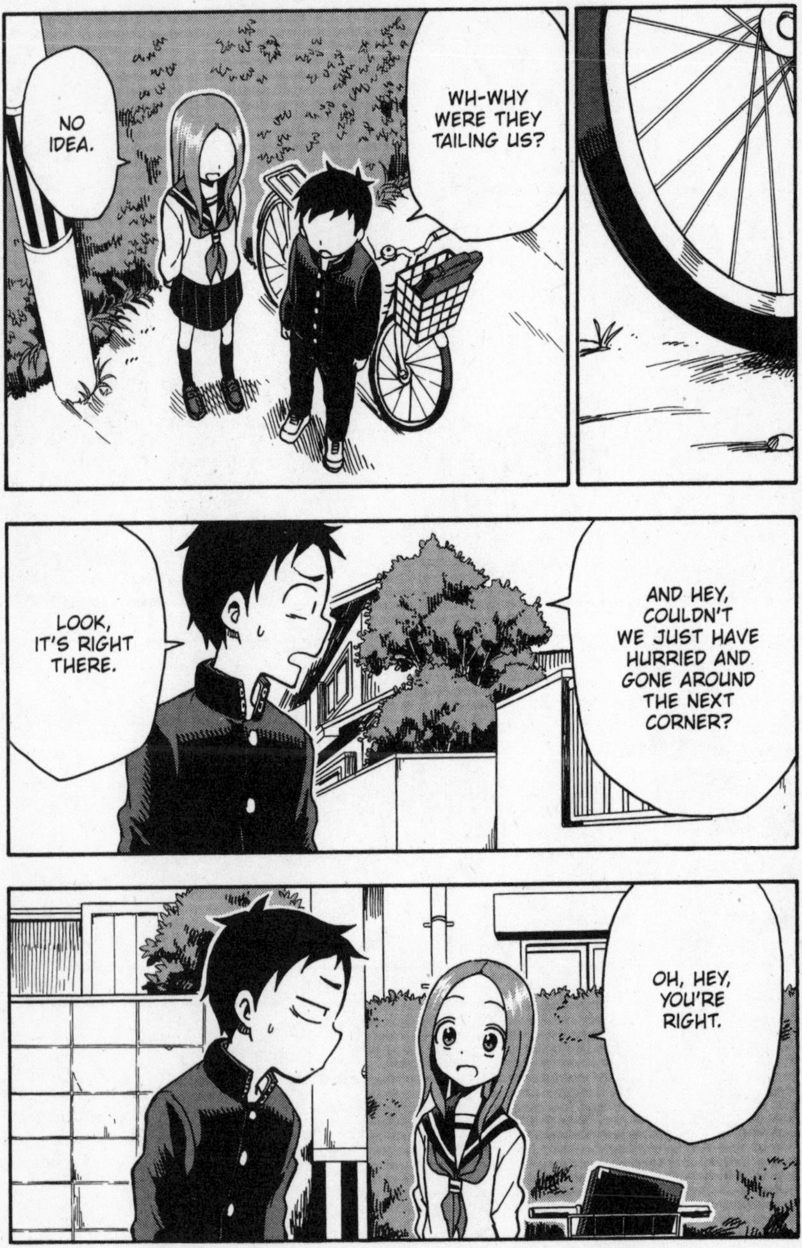
WH-WHY WERE THEY TAILING US?
NO IDEA.
AND HEY, COULDN'T WE JUST HAVE HURRIED AND GONE AROUND THE NEXT CORNER?
LOOK, IT'S RIGHT THERE.
OH, HEY, YOU'RE RIGHT.

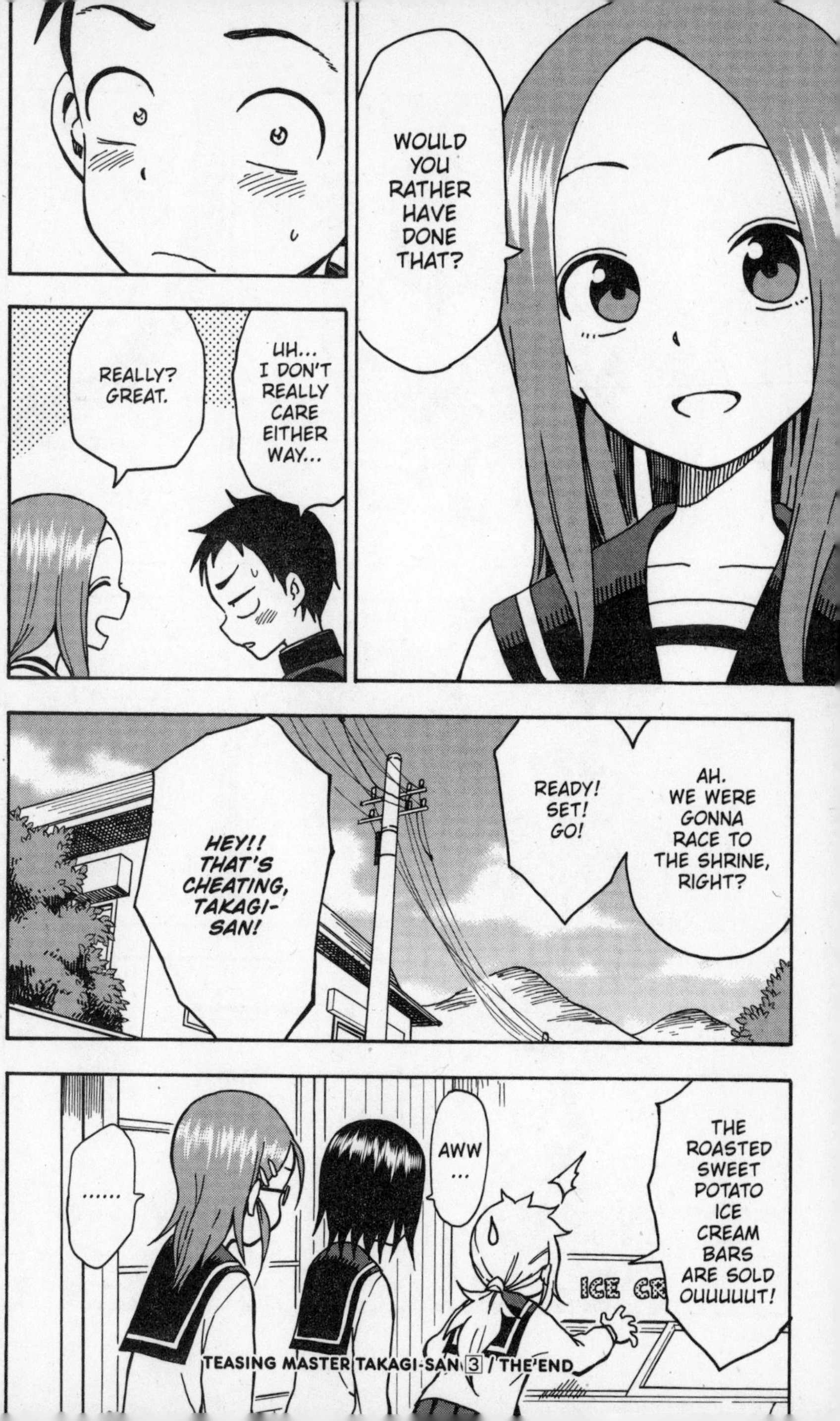
WOULD YOU RATHER HAVE DONE THAT?
UH... I DON'T REALLY CARE EITHER WAY...
REALLY? GREAT.
AH. WE WERE GONNA RACE TO THE SHRINE, RIGHT?
READY! SET! GO!
HEY!! THAT'S CHEATING, TAKAGI-SAN!
THE ROASTED SWEET POTATO ICE CREAM BARS ARE SOLD OUUUUUT!
ICE CR
AWW ...
......
TEASING MASTER TAKAGI-SAN 3 / THE END

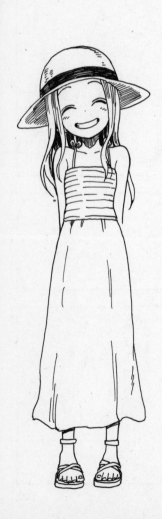

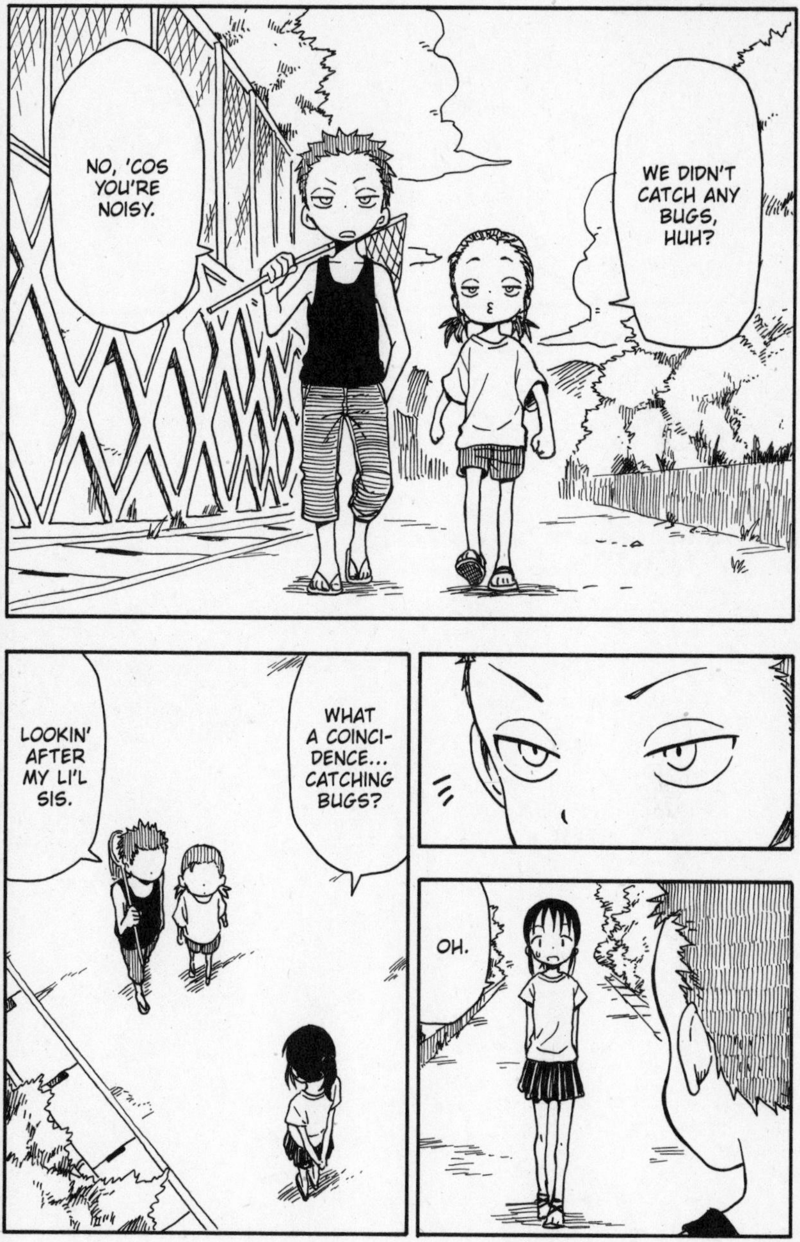
WE DIDN'T CATCH ANY BUGS, HUH?
NO, 'COS YOU'RE NOISY.
OH.
WHAT A COINCIDENCE... CATCHING BUGS?
LOOKIN' AFTER MY LI'L SIS.

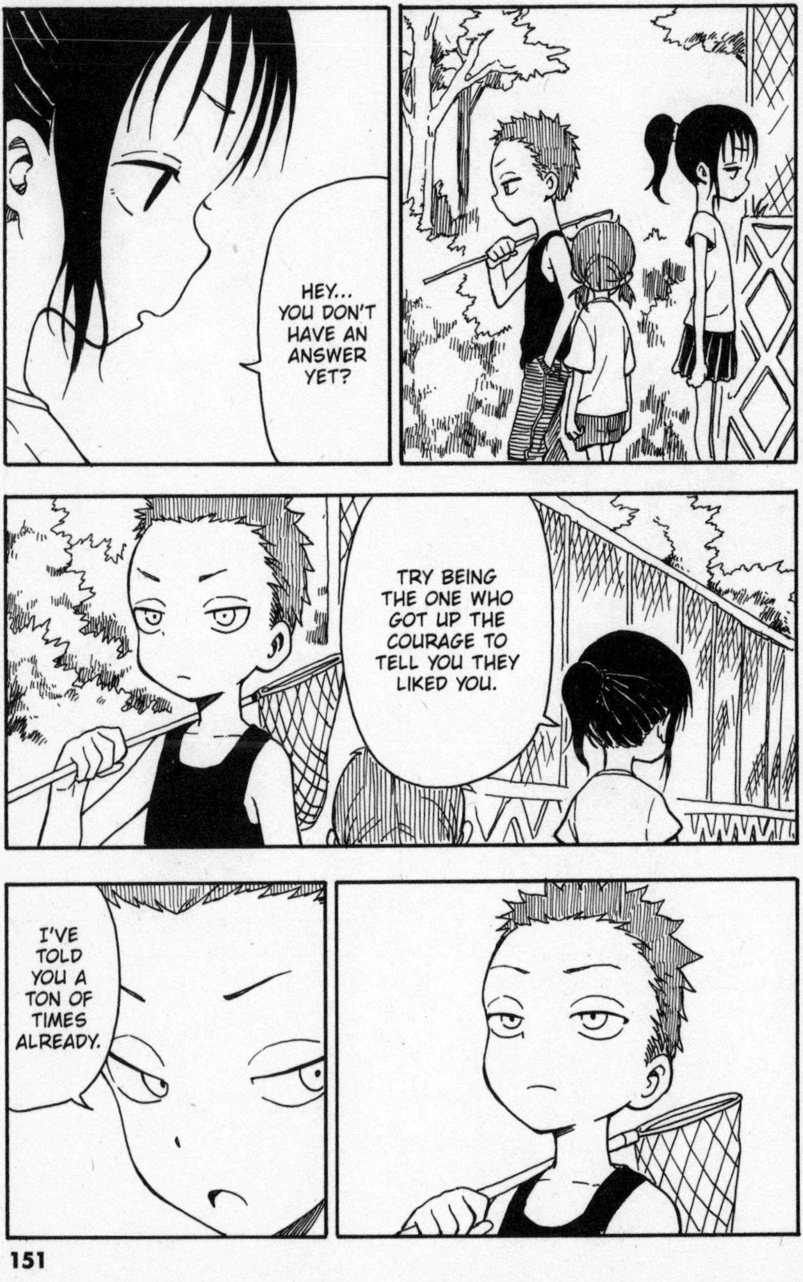
HEY... YOU DON'T HAVE AN ANSWER YET?
TRY BEING THE ONE WHO GOT UP THE COURAGE TO TELL YOU THEY LIKED YOU.
I'VE TOLD YOU A TON OF TIMES ALREADY.

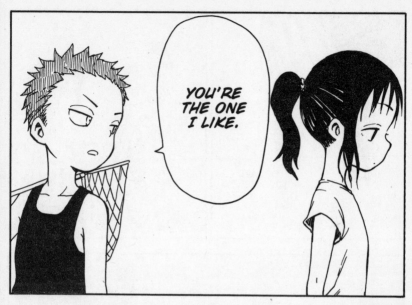

YOU'RE THE ONE I LIKE.

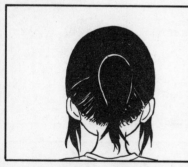

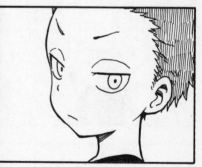

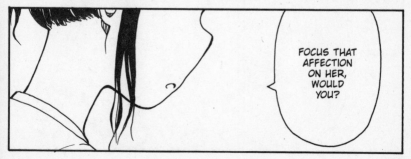

FOCUS THAT AFFECTION ON HER, WOULD YOU?

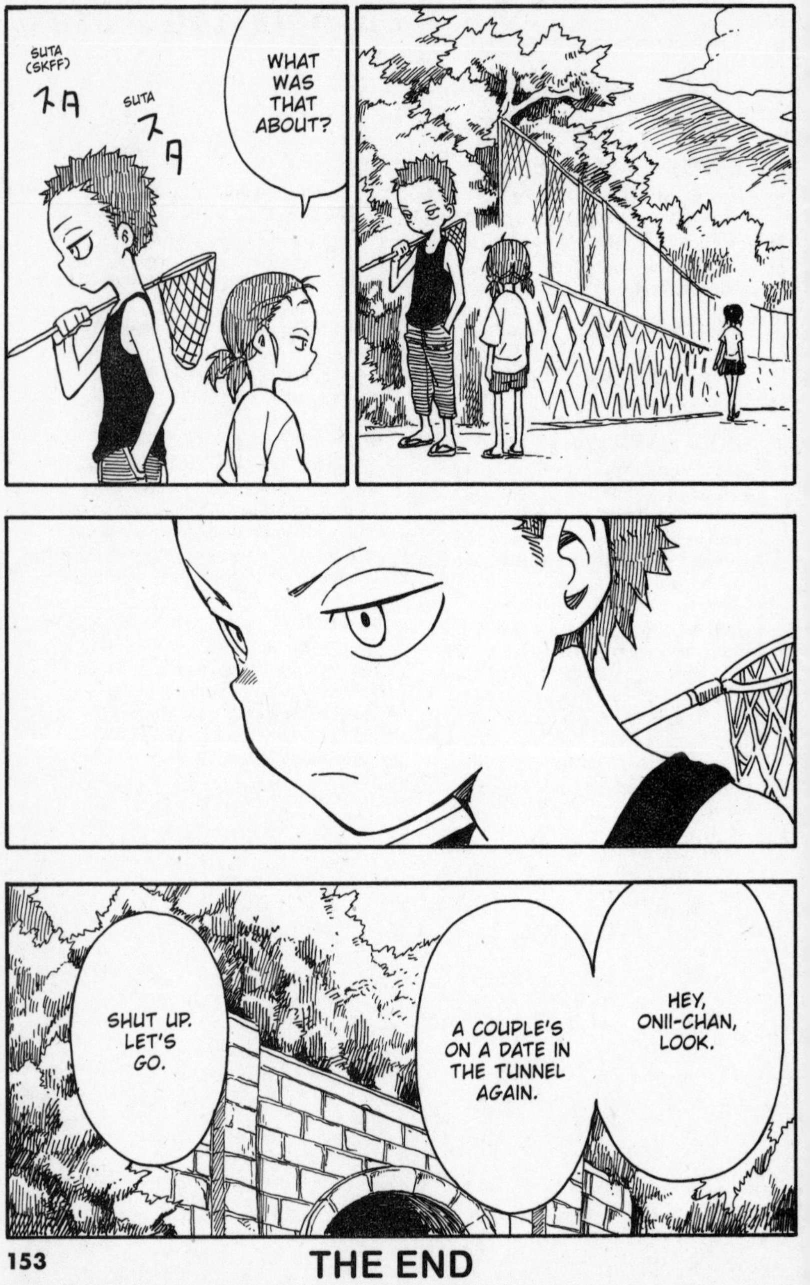
WHAT WAS THAT ABOUT?
SUTA (SKFF)
スタ
SUTA
スタ
HEY, ONII-CHAN, LOOK.
A COUPLE'S ON A DATE IN THE TUNNEL AGAIN.
SHUT UP. LET'S GO.

THE END

Translation Notes

COMMON HONORIFICS

no honorific: Indicates familiarity or closeness; if used without permission or reason, addressing someone in this manner would constitute an insult.

-san: The Japanese equivalent of Mr./Mrs./Miss. If a situation calls for politeness, this is the fail-safe honorific.

-kun: Used most often when referring to boys, this indicates affection or familiarity. Occasionally used by older men among their peers, but it may also be used by anyone referring to a person of lower standing.

-chan: An affectionate honorific indicating familiarity used mostly in reference to girls; also used in reference to cute persons or animals of either gender.

-senpai: A suffix used to address upperclassmen or more experienced coworkers.

-sensei: A respectful term for teachers, artists, or high-level professionals.

Page 8
In Japanese, test of courage, *kimodameshi*, literally translates to "testing one's liver." *Kimo* means "liver," and *dameshi* means "to test." Tests of courage are usually played during the summer in large groups as a part of school activities. These tests involve going through haunted houses, abandoned buildings, and scary locations at night.

Page 39
Japanese schools normally provide students with summer and winter uniforms. Students are expected to change into their summer uniforms in June and their winter uniforms in October.

Page 78
Mountain yam porridge over rice, or *yamaimo-gohan*, is a mixture of grated mountain yam, raw egg, and broth served over rice. Mountain yam is good for you, but it has a notoriously slimy texture.

Author's Note

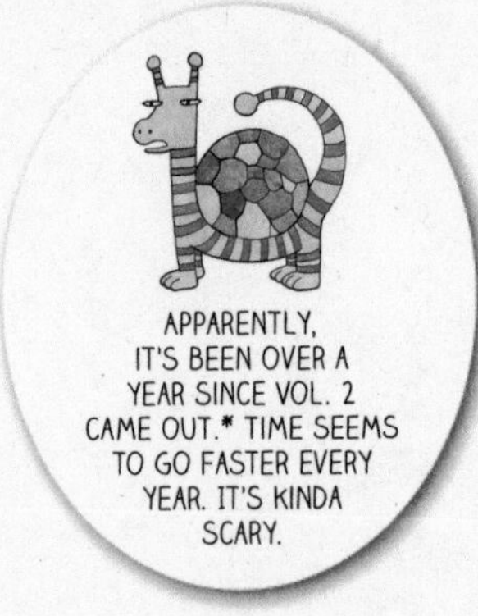
APPARENTLY, IT'S BEEN OVER A YEAR SINCE VOL. 2 CAME OUT.* TIME SEEMS TO GO FASTER EVERY YEAR. IT'S KINDA SCARY.

*IN JAPAN

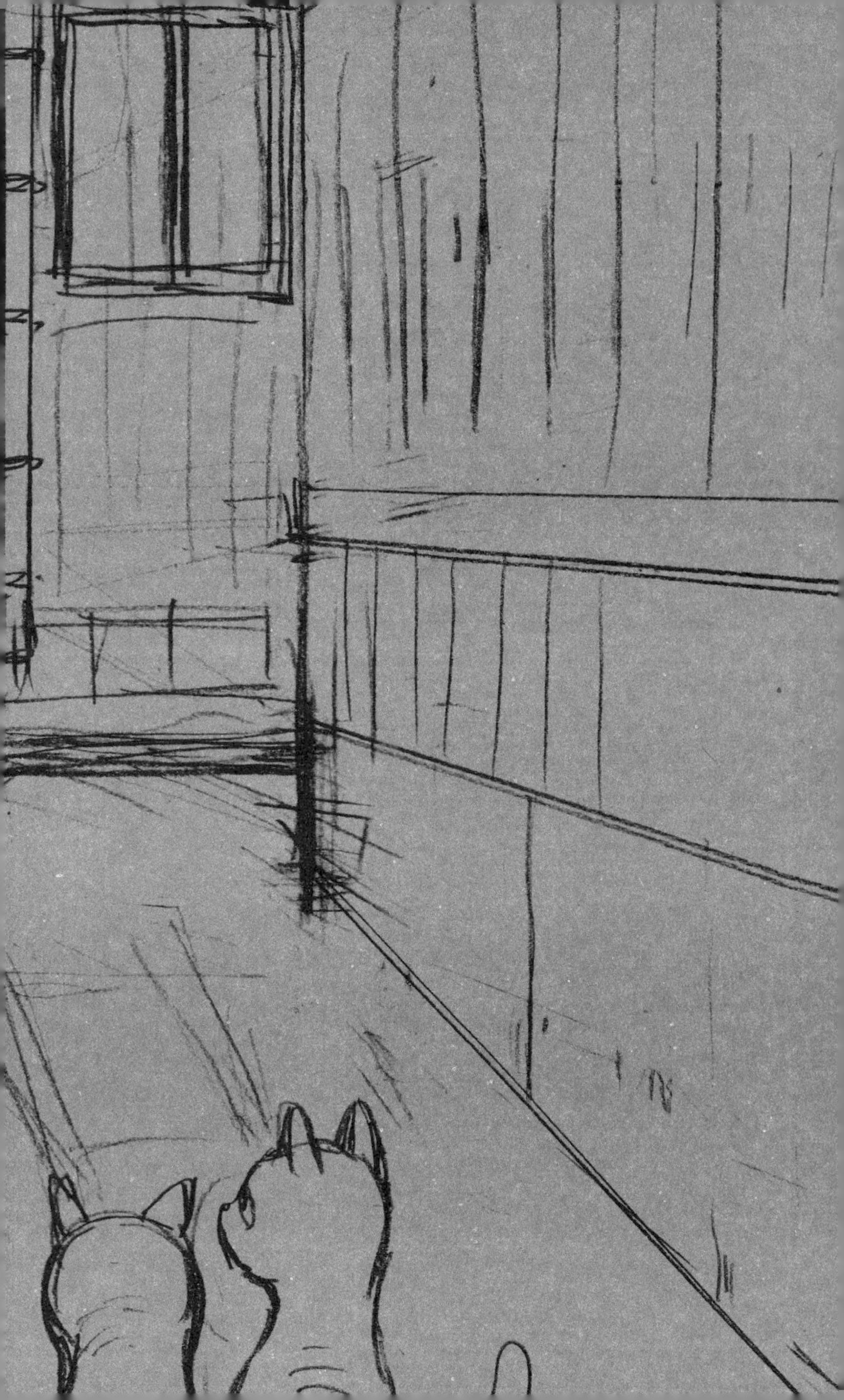

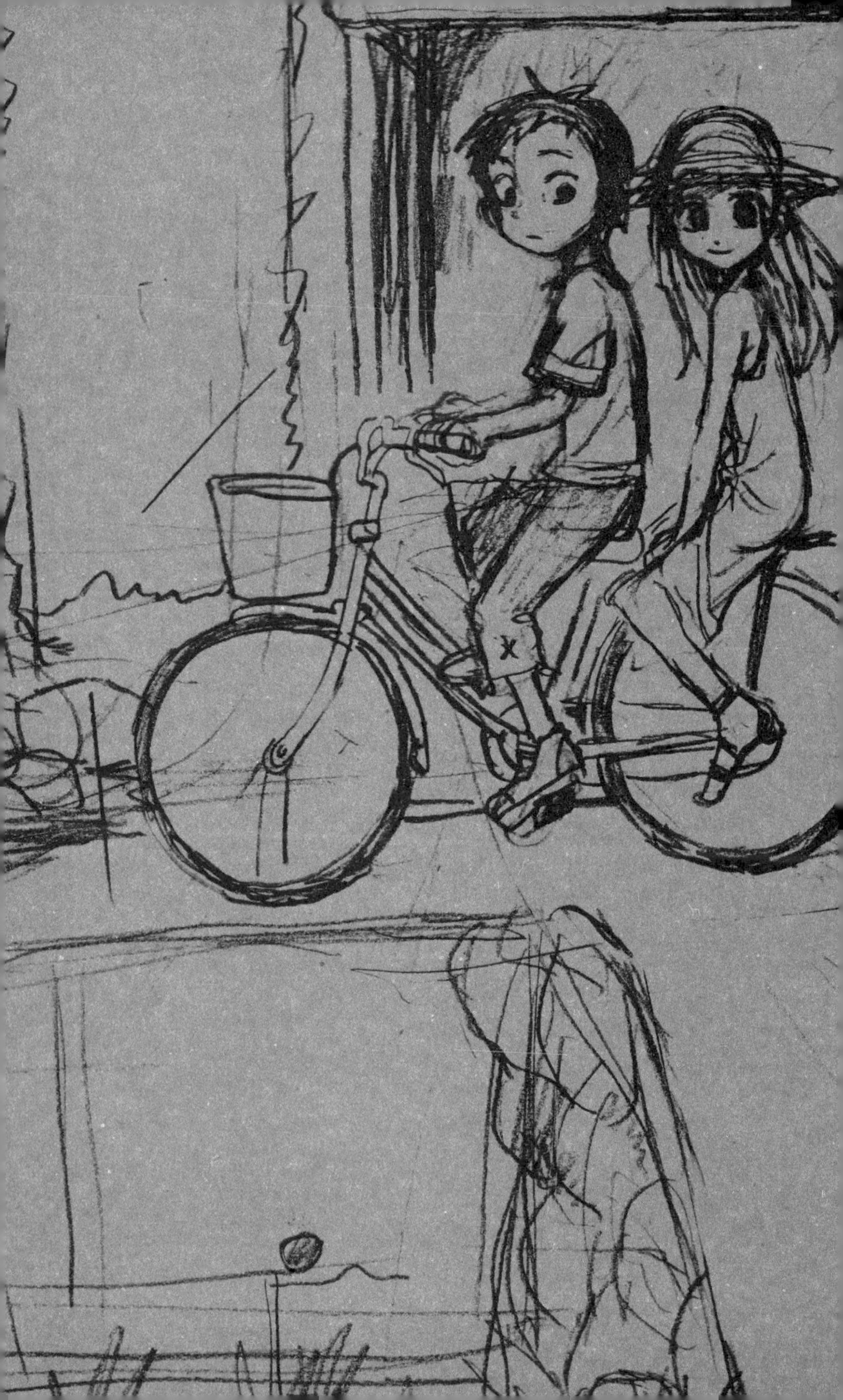

A Loner's Worst Nightmare: Human Interaction!

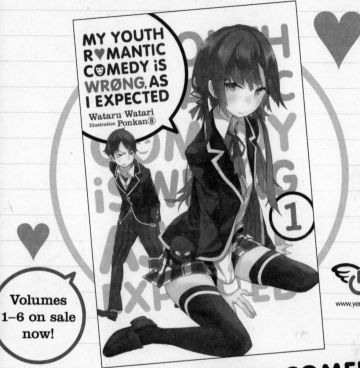

MY YOUTH R♥MANTIC COMEDY iS WRØNG, AS I EXPECTED

Wataru Watari
Illustration Ponkan⑧

Volumes 1–6 on sale now!

MY YOUTH R♥MANTIC COMEDY iS WRØNG, AS I EXPECTED

Hachiman Hikigaya is a cynic. He believes "youth" is a crock—a sucker's game, an illusion woven from failure and hypocrisy. But when he turns in an essay for a school assignment espousing this view, he's sentenced to work in the Service Club, an organization dedicated to helping students with problems! Worse, the only other member of the club is the haughty Yukino Yukinoshita, a girl with beauty, brains, and the personality of a garbage fire. How will Hachiman the Cynic cope with a job that requires—*gasp!*—social skills?

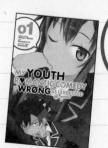

Check out the manga too!

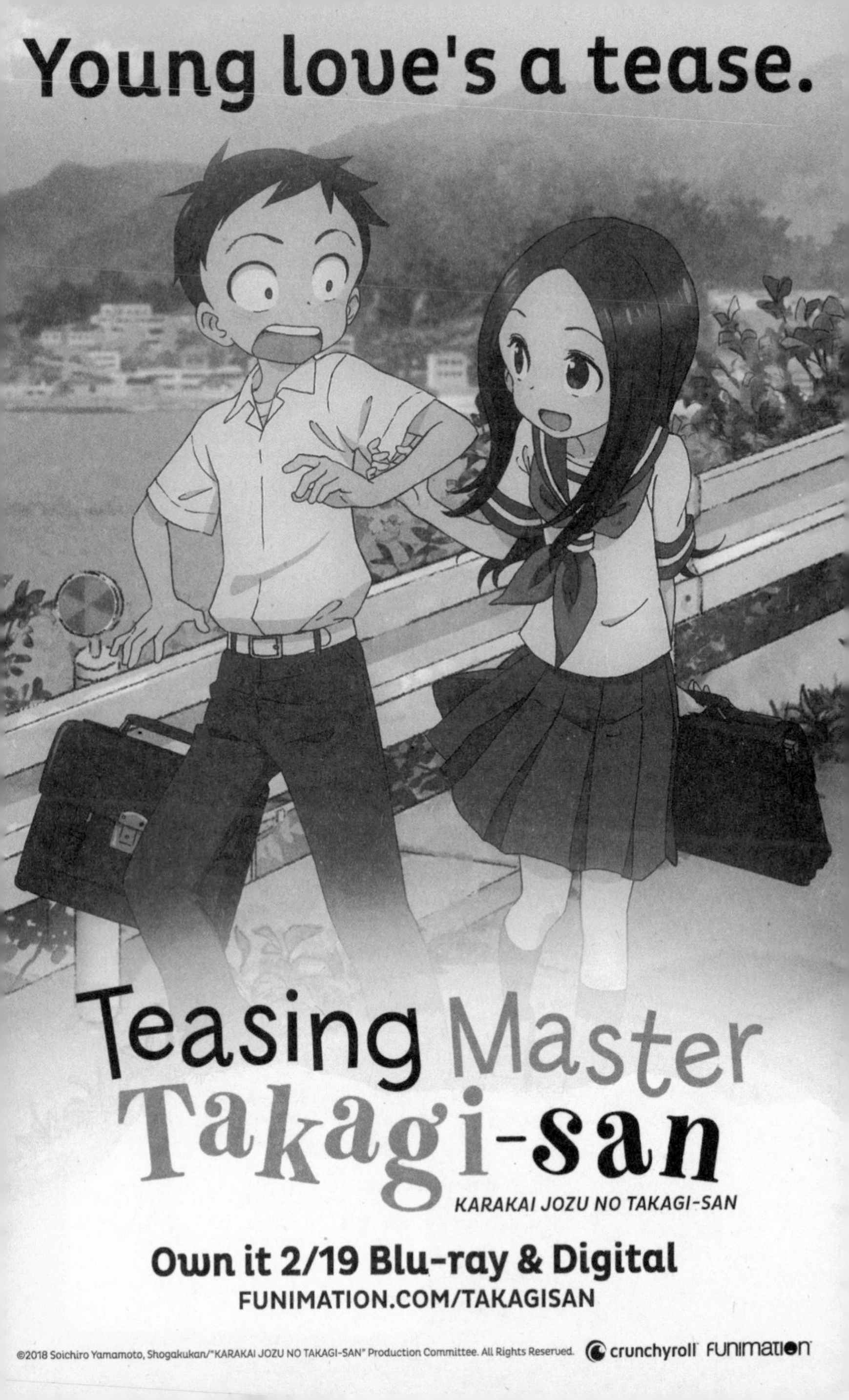
Young love's a tease.
Teasing Master
Takagi-san
KARAKAI JOZU NO TAKAGI-SAN
Own it 2/19 Blu-ray & Digital
FUNIMATION.COM/TAKAGISAN
©2018 Soichiro Yamamoto, Shogakukan/"KARAKAI JOZU NO TAKAGI-SAN" Production Committee. All Rights Reserved.
crunchyroll FUNimation

Teasing Master Takagi-san ③

Soichiro Yamamoto

TRANSLATION: Taylor Engel ♦ LETTERING: Takeshi Kamura

KARAKAI JOZU NO TAKAGI-SAN Vol. 3
by Soichiro YAMAMOTO
© 2014 Soichiro YAMAMOTO
All rights reserved.
Original Japanese edition published by SHOGAKUKAN.
English translation rights in the United States of America, Canada, the United Kingdom, Ireland, Australia and New Zealand arranged with SHOGAKUKAN through Tuttle-Mori Agency, Inc.

English translation © 2019 by Yen Press, LLC

Yen Press
1290 Avenue of the Americas
New York, NY 10104

Visit us at yenpress.com

facebook.com/yenpress
twitter.com/yenpress
yenpress.tumblr.com
instagram.com/yenpress

First Yen Press Edition: January 2019

Yen Press is an imprint of Yen Press, LLC.
The Yen Press name and logo are trademarks of Yen Press, LLC.

Library of Congress Control N

ISBN: 978-1-9

10 9 8 7 6 5

WOR

Printed in the United

D1091343